"SPOOKY, SURPRISING, AND UNSETTLING."
T. Jefferson Parker

"GRUESOMELY ENTERTAINING."
Washington Post Book World

"CONVINCING AND DISTURBING."
San Jose Mercury News

"GREGG HURWITZ KNOWS HOW TO WRITE A THRILLER!"
Michael Connelly

"A GREAT READ!"
Sue Grafton

Raves for GREGG HURWITZ's electrifying thriller DO NO HARM

"Gregg Hurwitz knows how to write a thriller! *Do No Harm* is a gripping page-turner packed with an insider's knowledge of the practice and politics of medicine. Hurwitz has put together a medical/psychological detective story that sticks in the mind long after the last page is turned."

Michael Connelly

"*Do No Harm* is the perfect blend of suspense, pacing, strong storyline, compelling characters, and a villain who will knock your socks off. Great combination and a great read!"

Sue Grafton

"The action comes fast and steady . . . In his most ambitious book to date, Hurwitz delves convincingly into the world of medicine, psychology, and investigative techniques . . . [An] adeptly researched, well-constructed tale about science gone awry."

Publishers Weekly

"Convincing and disturbing . . . Hurwitz's careful attention to . . . the very fine villain . . . sets up the most unusual aspect of *Do No Harm*: the author's and the protagonist's compassion for a perpetrator. This runs so contrary to the temper of our time that it shocks. I admire it."

San Jose Mercury News

"Hurwitz has done it again with this spooky, surprising, and unsettling thriller. Good characters, a suspenseful plot, and a shock of an ending. Hurwitz gets better with every book."

T. Jefferson Parker

"Hurwitz is a brilliant storyteller . . . He has written a fast-paced plot with nicely defined characters."

Library Journal

"Gleefully violent and compelling . . . *Do No Harm,* a big, fast-action thriller by the heir apparent to Michael Crichton and Robin Cook, is perfect beach reading."

Las Vegas Mercury

"Intriguing . . . believable . . . brisk entertainment . . . Hurwitz's hero is fully realized."

Washington Post Book World

"A smoothly written, gripping fabric of believable incidents, ethical questions, and changing relationships."

Booklist

"Great psychological suspense . . . A breakneck-paced novel whose twists and turns will chill you to the last page."

Bookshelf

And praise for his previous thriller MINUTES TO BURN

"Action-adventure and thriller fans, take note—if you want to read someone who writes with the intelligence of Crichton, the military tech know-how of Clancy, and the spine-tingling intensity of Koontz, allow me to introduce you to Gregg Hurwitz. You're going to love *MINUTES TO BURN*."

Jan Burke, Edgar Award-winning author of *Wine*

"The science is fascinating, the story is exciting, and the plot moves with the unstoppable precision of a SEAL team mounting an assault."

Robert Crais, author of *The Last Detective*

"Vivid . . . engrossing . . . A rousing actioner reminiscent of *Jurassic Park, The Dirty Dozen,* and *Lord of the Flies,* and maybe even *Beowolf* . . . Hurwitz demonstrates once again that he is a thriller writer to be reckoned with."

Kirkus Reviews

"Hurwitz's novel has a breakneck drive, chilling realism, and graveyard tension. Hang on to your hat."

James Thayer, author of *The Gold Swan*

Also by Gregg Hurwitz

THE TOWER
MINUTES TO BURN

Available in hardcover

THE KILL CLAUSE

GREGG HURWITZ

HarperTorch
An Imprint of HarperCollins*Publishers*

This is a work of fiction. Names, characters, places, and incidents are products of the author's imagination or are used fictitiously and are not to be construed as real. Any resemblance to actual events, locales, organizations, or persons, living or dead, is entirely coincidental.

HARPERTORCH
An Imprint of HarperCollins*Publishers*
10 East 53rd Street
New York, New York 10022-5299

ISBN: 0-06-000887-3

First HarperTorch paperback printing: August 2003
First William Morrow special printing: August 2002
First William Morrow hardcover printing: August 2002

Printed in the United States of America

Visit HarperTorch on the World Wide Web at www.harpercollins.com

10 9 8 7 6 5 4 3 2 1

For my father, Alfred L. Hurwitz, M.D.,
who taught me that ethics are never timid,
rarely convenient, and always vital

ACKNOWLEDGMENTS

Melissa Hurwitz, M.D.: My staunchest (and longest) supporter and one hell of a reader

The memory of my grandfather, David Hurwitz, M.D.

My mother: For everything

Matthew Guma: My indefatigable advocate and not-so-indefatigable bourbon cohort

Marc H. Glick and Stephen F. Breimer: Dedication personified

Jess Taylor: King of Commentary, Queen of Vitriol

Michael Morrison: My esteemed publisher

Lisa Gallagher and Libby Jordan: Marketing gurus

Dr. Jordan B. Peterson, Professor of Psychology, University of Toronto: Who continues to be a major influence on my life. Blame him.

G___M___: For his expertise on everything from digital transmitters to shoe profiling

Matthew Lissak, M.D., Neuropsychiatric Institute: For his insight

Marshall Morgan, M.D., Director, UCLA Medical Center Emergency Room: For allowing me to shadow his attendings and residents

Don Mebust, M.D.: For showing me the UCLA ER from abscess to zoster

Keith Lewis, Embalmer/Autopsy Tech, UCLA Med Center: Brilliant raconteur of the grisly

Peter Catalino: For the med student tour

Officer Marlin Hill: For helping me get down the attitude and the argot
The two John Does: For stuff
Professor Michael S. Berlin, M.D., Director, Glaucoma Institute/Beverly Hills: For his generous counsel on matters ocular
Mohammed M. Elahi, M.D., FRCSC–Plastic Surgery: For his guidance about burn treatment
Robert Andonian, M.D.: For input regarding Peter
Charlotte Brinsont-Brown, L.C.S.W.: For enlightening me on aspects of Children's Services
Bret Nelson, M.D.: The next generation
The booksellers: Thank you
My readers: Who make it all especially worthwhile

DO NO HARM

CHAPTER 1

FACE white and blistering, eyelids swollen nearly shut, hair falling from the front of her scalp in thin clusters, the nurse stumbled blindly through the UCLA Medical Center Emergency Room doors, both hands waving in front of her. Her cries came from deep in her chest, rapid animal sounds that twisted into raspy moans by the time they left her mouth. A half-moon darkened the V of her scrub-top collar, and the skin along her clavicle had whitened and softened.

She tried to say something, but it came out a guttural bark.

A Hispanic gardener leapt up from his seat before the lobby's check-in windows, cradling the bloody bandage wrapping his hand and knocking over his chair. He circled wide as the nurse advanced, as if afraid of attack or contamination. A mother holding her five-year-old stepped through a set of swinging doors, shrieked, and beelined to the safety of the waiting room. The guard at the security desk rose to a half crouch above his chair.

A blister burst near the woman's temple, sending a run of viscous fluid over the mottled landscape of her cheek. Open sores spotted her lips, and when she spread her mouth to scream, her Cupid's bow split, spilling blood down her chin. She groped her way along the wall, her shoulders racking with sobs, her mouth working on air.

An expression of horror frozen on her face, Pat Atkins

circled her desk in the small triage room, knocking over her first cup of morning coffee, and ran into the lobby toward the woman.

The woman retched, sending a thin spray of grayish vomit across the vivid white wall. She lunged forward, her shin striking the overturned chair, and tumbled over, breaking her fall with the heels of her hands.

Pat sprinted over, shouting at the security guard, "Tell them to get Trauma Twelve ready!"

She reached for a pulse as the nurse rolled onto her back, sputtering and gurgling, leaving a hank of hair on the clean tile floor. When Pat saw the nurse's ID badge, she inhaled sharply, running a hand over her bristling gray hair.

"Jesus God," she said. "Nancy, is that you?"

The swollen head nodded, the whitish raw skin glistening. "Dr. Spier," she rasped. "Get Dr. Spier."

Nearly knocking over a radiology resident with an armful of charts, David Spier sprinted into the Central Work Area bridging the two parallel hallways of exam rooms that composed his division. He pointed at an intern and snapped his fingers. "Carson's supposed to stitch up a leg in Seven. Go keep an eye so he doesn't duck out—you know how he is with sutures. And I need a urine on Mitchell in Eight."

He stepped across the CWA, patting his best resident on the shoulder. "Diane—let's move."

Diane handed off the phone to a nurse and pivoted, her shoulder-length straight blond hair whipping around so the nurse had to lean back out of its way. Grabbing the pen from behind her ear, Diane slid it into the pocket on her faded blue resident scrubs. David rested a hand on her shoulder blade, guiding her into Hallway One. They both shuffle-stepped back as the gurney swept past them and banked a hard left into the trauma room. They followed behind, David resting his hands on the back of the gurney. The nurses folded in on the patient's writhing body, a wave of dark blue scrubs. Pat leaned over, slid a pair of trauma shears up the moist scrub top, threw the material to the sides.

"What do we have?" David asked.

A nurse with shiny black hair glanced up. "Caucasian female, probably midtwenties, some vomiting, erythematous blisters on face and upper chest, eyes are opaque, moderate respiratory distress. Appears to be some kind of chemical burn." She reached down and untwisted the ID badge from the mound of fabric. Her face blanched. "It's Nancy Jenkins."

The news rippled visibly through the nurses and lab techs. Though they were accustomed to operating under duress, having a colleague and friend wheeled into the ER in this state was beyond even their experience.

David glanced at Nancy's blistering face, her pretty blond hair lying in loose strands on the gurney, and felt a chill wash down his chest to his gut. He recalled when they had wheeled his wife in here two years ago, the night of his forty-first birthday, but he caught himself quickly, checking his thoughts. Instinctively, his physician's calm spread through him, protective and impersonal.

He quick-stepped around the gurney so he could examine Nancy's face. Her eyelids and lips were badly burnt. If the caustic agent dripping from her had gotten into her eyes and down her throat, they were dealing with a whole new host of problems.

"Get me GI and ophtho consults," he said. "And someone contact the tox center. Let's get the offending agent ID'd."

Pat glanced up from her post behind Nancy's head. "Some nasal flaring here, and she's stridorous." She chewed her lip. "Hurry with that monitor."

"Find me some pH strips," Diane called out. "And let's get saline bottles in here stat."

A clerk ran from the room. Two nurses dashed in, pulling on latex gloves and snapping them at the wrists.

"Was it an explosion?" someone asked.

"Doubt it," Pat said. "Nancy walked in herself—it must've happened right outside. Security's already contacted the police."

"She's working hard," David said, glancing at the skin sucking tight against her ribs and around her neck. "Supraclavicular and substernal retractions. Let's get ready to tube her."

Nancy tried to sit up, but Pat restrained her. Nancy's breath came in great heaves. "Dr. Spier," she said. Her voice was thick and rough, tangling in the swell of her throat.

David leaned over Nancy's face. The skin around the blisters was whitening, contrasting sharply with the red bulges. She appeared to be trying to go on speaking.

His hands fluttered near her jaw, ready to check her airway. "I'm right here, Nancy. We're gonna get you taken care of. Can you tell us what substance we're dealing with?"

IVs being hung, pulse ox sliding on the finger, scrubs cut free from her legs and tossed into a trash bin. Cardiac leads plunking down across her chest like bullet holes.

Nancy coughed, contorting on the gurney.

"Heart rate's one forty," someone said. "O-two saturation's low nineties and dropping."

David leaned closer. "Nancy, can you tell us?"

The green line on the EKG monitor showed tachycardia, the peaks and valleys getting mashed closer and closer. Her arm rose, a hand pawing limply at air.

No more time. He pulled her jaw open and peered down her throat. Ulceration of the oropharynx, subacute airway compromise from edema. Whatever had gone down her throat had irritated the tissue, causing massive swelling. He needed to secure an airway quickly before her throat closed off.

David tilted her head back to give her throat maximum patency. "Push twenty mgs of etomidate and one hundred of rocuronium," he said, his voice ringing sharp and clear even to his own ears. The drugs would sedate and completely paralyze Nancy. She'd be unable even to breathe unless they could get a tube down in her to do it for her. "Laryngoscope," he said.

The L-shaped tool slapped the latex covering his palm. Positioning it in his left hand, he then slid the blade down along her tongue, using the small attached light to guide it past the epiglottis. The laryngeal swelling was bad, even worse than he'd noticed at first glance. He couldn't see the vocal cords between which to guide the endotracheal tube.

He glanced up at Diane, who was performing the Sellick maneuver, applying pressure to the cricoid membrane beneath Nancy's larynx, trying to bring the vocal cords into view for him. It wasn't working.

"Someone get on the horn to anesthesia and see how long it'll take to get a fiberoptic scope down here," David barked. If the swelling got too bad, he could look through the thinner scope and maneuver down the trachea.

He repositioned Nancy's head and tried again, but still couldn't make out the vocal cords behind the swelling.

"Crich her?" Diane asked.

David shook his head. "Not yet. Before we cut, I'll try to tube her blind and see if we get lucky." Though the swelling prevented him from eyeing the anatomical landmarks, he began pushing the endotracheal tube, tracing a path along the underside of the laryngoscope blade down Nancy's throat. He pulled the laryngoscope from Nancy's mouth. The clear ET tube remained, protruding a few inches from the line of her teeth. David removed the metal stylet that ran down its length and inflated the cuff at the other end, which was buried somewhere in Nancy's throat. He popped the end-tidal carbon dioxide monitor on the end of the tube, then attached the oxygen bag valve atop the monitor.

Diane pulled her stethoscope from across her shoulders, cleared her hair with a head jerk, and positioned the plugs in her ears. She listened over the lungs, then switched to the stomach, as David pumped the bag with his hand. "I'm getting a gurgle," she said.

The ET tube had wound up in the esophagus rather than the trachea, the usual result of tubing someone blind. Diane was picking up stomach noises rather than movement through the lungs. Nancy still wasn't breathing.

David pulled the endotracheal tube from Nancy's mouth; it swayed beneath his fist like a bloody snake.

"Her O-two sat's dropping. . . ." Pat said, a note of panic creeping into her voice.

Nancy's flesh was going from white to blue.

"Is the fiberoptic scope here?" David asked.

A clerk leaned into the room. "Not yet, but anesthesia said it's on the—"

David reached for a scalpel, fingering beneath Nancy's larynx for the cricothyroid membrane with his other hand. He cut lengthwise along the membrane, opening up a surgical airway in her throat. Diane had the three-pronged retractor in his hand immediately; he slid it into the cut and it opened like a tripod, spreading the hole. Feeding a 4.0 ET tube into the hole, David plugged the other end into a ventilator hose. The ventilator breathed for her, pushing air through the tube into her lungs.

Her chest started rising and falling, and her oxygen saturation climbed slowly back up past ninety. Airway secured. Now he'd have to identify the offending agent.

He glanced up at the nurses. They were moving a little slower than usual, still shell-shocked. A lot of looks to Nancy's face.

"I know this is hard," David said, gently yet firmly, "but right now we're just dealing with an injured body, like any other body. Have you drawn blood?"

Pat nodded.

"Send off a CBC, a chem panel, type and screen, and get a rectal. Does someone have my pH strips?"

The black-haired nurse slid a gloved hand between Nancy's limp legs.

Someone handed David a yellow pH strip and he laid it across Nancy's cheek. It dampened quickly, but did not change. He threw it aside. "Not an acid," he announced. Pat was ready with the red strips; he laid one on Nancy's forehead and one just beneath her eye. Almost immediately, they turned a glaring blue.

David cursed under his breath. A base. Probably Drano. Acids are nasty, but they attack tissue in such a way that the skin scars quickly, usually protecting healthy underlying tissue. Alkali, on the other hand, produces a liquefaction necrosis, saponifying fats, dissolving proteins, penetrating ever deeper into the tissues. Unlike acid, it keeps burning and burning, turning flesh to liquid. Same way it opens clogged drains.

Diane glanced at the blue pH strip and immediately began dousing Nancy's face with saline.

"Follow her lead," David said. "Irrigate the hell out of her." He raised one of Nancy's lids with a thumb and stared at the white cloudy eyeball. Corneal opacification. More bad news. He picked up a little 250-cc saline bottle and flushed the eye. "Someone find me some Morgan lenses." Each of the hard Morgan lens contacts connected to a tube that could continually flush the eyes with saline. As they were seldom needed, he hadn't used Morgan lenses for about ten years.

The blistering lips and swollen throat indicated that the alkali had gone down Nancy's throat. If it had burned through her esophagus, letting air escape into her chest cavity, he would have to get her to the OR immediately. If it hadn't fully penetrated, then the alkali remained on the esophageal walls, eating through additional tissue, and there was very little they could do about it.

He slid an X-ray cassette, encased in a dull silver case, beneath Nancy's body. "Everyone in leads!" Everyone present threw on lead aprons as Diane positioned the X-ray unit over Nancy's body and threw the switch. Quickly, they repeated the procedure until they'd completed serial chest and abdominal films. A lab tech slid the final cassettes out from beneath Nancy and handed them off to the radiology tech, who scurried from the room.

"Check for free subdiaphragmatic air, mediastinal emphysema, and examine lung parenchyma for signs of aspiration," David yelled after the tech. "Did he hear me? Someone make sure he heard."

Several nurses and lab techs were spraying down down Nancy's face with saline bottles. Water and runoff drenched the gurney sheets.

"Should I get ready to drop an NG tube to lavage the stomach?" Diane asked. "Dilute the alkali?"

"No, it's contraindicated," David said. "It can cause retching or vomiting, and the alkali could migrate back up the tube, reexposing tissue. Plus, you could drop the thing right through a weakened esophagus wall into the mediastinum. Getting her stomach pumped isn't worth the risk of boxing her."

A nurse's hand appeared seemingly out of thin air, handing Diane another saline bottle.

Carson Donalds ran in, breathing hard, and shot looks around the room with the mixture of anxiety and disorientation typical of a medical student. He ran a hand through his mop of curly blond hair, his eyebrows disappearing under the front line of his bangs. "I heard you have a pretty gnarly alkali burn." He saw Pat's face, then glanced at the body and took a step back. "Fuck. Is that Nancy?"

David's bottle spat air, so he tossed it into the bin, grabbed another, and continued irrigating the eyes. "Dr. Donalds," he said, taking a calm, didactic tone, "why don't we use emetics for alkali ingestions?"

"Because she's paralyzed and tubed and the last thing you want is her barfing up and asphyxiating," Carson said.

"How about if she wasn't tubed? Would we use an emetic then?"

"No. You don't want to reexpose the esophageal tissue to offending agents on the way back up."

"And?"

Carson shook his head.

"Dr. Trace?" David said. He didn't look up from the eye he was spraying, but he sensed Diane's head pivoting.

She switched the saline bottle to her other hand, squinting as a wayward squirt caught her across the brow. "Increasing intraluminal pressure generated by emesis is speculated to increase the risk of perforation when the tissue is markedly weakened. Carson, get your ass over here and give us a hand."

Carson lunged forward and grabbed a saline bottle. Diane nudged him with a shoulder. "What are the three reasons we don't use charcoal to soak up alkali in the stomach?" she asked.

"Four reasons," David said.

Diane grimaced at being corrected but didn't look up.

Pat switched IV bags, then checked Nancy's blood pressure cuff, her face stained with grief and shock. With twenty-three years as an RN under her belt, Pat was the den mother of the ER nurses; that's why she'd followed Nancy in here, probably sending one of the more junior nurses out front to triage. Her crew cut was shot through with sweat.

"I don't know any," Carson confessed.

David raised an eyebrow at Pat. "Pat?"

"Why are you pimping a nurse?" Carson asked, a competitive note finding its way into his voice. Most doctors only fired questions at med students, interns, or residents.

"Because, in general, they've been around longer and know more than arrogant med students."

Pat looked over quickly, her cheeks quivering. "I . . . what . . . ?"

"Would you like to tell Carson here, and Dr. Trace, the *four* reasons we don't use charcoal to soak up alkali in the stomach?"

Pat managed to regain her focus, which had been David's aim in questioning her. "One, activated charcoal doesn't absorb alkali. Two, it obscures the endoscopic visual field. Three, if the patient is perfed, it would leak right into the mediastinum, and four, it's a vomit risk, and Carson and Diane already pointed out those pitfalls."

"That's right." David glanced around the small room bustling with people. A few faces still looked upset, and a lab tech was holding one of Nancy's limp hands. "We have a damn sharp team here," he said. "Don't worry, and stay focused."

A clerk leaned through the door. "Dr. Jenner's ringing through."

"Aah," David said. "Our ophthalmologist."

The telephone behind David emitted only a half ring before he grabbed it, first handing off his saline bottle to a nurse and pointing. "Keep flushing," he mouthed, pivoting to miss an IV pole a lab tech pulled around.

"Dr. Jenner, just in time. We need you down here, got a bad alkali exposure to the eyes."

"Was the skin around the eyes burnt?" Dr. Jenner's deeply textured voice was low, rolling, authoritative.

"Everything's burnt. The cornea's cloudy white."

"So the endothelium's already not functioning. Are you irrigating?"

"Saline."

"Good. Osmosis advantage."

"I can't find the Morgan lenses."

"Don't worry about it. They're outdated and overrated. Just get the eyes open and keep irrigating copiously. Once the eyes are better cleared, give her a drop of Pred Forte to stop the inflammation and a drop of Cipro for infection. I'm on my way."

Diane glanced up at David as he hung up the phone. He chewed his lower lip. "Pat, can you call GI again, ask what's taking so goddamn long on our consult?"

The radiology tech poked his head into the room, fresh back from the X-ray suite in the rear. "No free air," he said.

That was good—at least the alkali hadn't eaten through the esophagus, allowing air to escape into the body. Yet.

Diane leaned forward over Nancy's body, and she and David brushed foreheads. Her eyes jerked quickly away. "Sorry."

"How are you doing on the eyes there, Carson?" David asked.

Carson nodded. "Okay. But I think she's gonna need a corneal transplant." He leaned over, examining the other eye. "Two."

"We're going to apply some Cipro and Pred Forte drops. Can you get them ready?"

A uniformed UCLA Police Department officer strolled in; David was immediately irritated by his casual gait. The cop cleared his throat. "I have some questions I need to—"

"This patient is unconscious and can't answer questions."

"Well, I'll need to take a—"

"Not right now," David said. "Out, please. *Out*."

The cop shot him a good glare before retreating.

The nurses and techs continued to irrigate Nancy's flesh, lined on both sides of her body like feeding pups.

"Good, good," David said. "We're gonna keep irrigating her for hours."

Pat looked up, a little moist-eyed, and nodded. "We'll be here."

The wall phone rang, and a tech grabbed it, then held it out to David. "Dr. Woods."

David shot a latex glove into the trash bin and fisted the phone. "What took you?"

"I was in on a—"

"We have an alkali burn, some ingestion. No free air on the film."

"Ulceration of oropharynx?"

"Yes. And acute laryngeal swelling. We had to crich her."

"We like to have them swallow a little water, push the alkali down the esophagus into the stomach. Greater area, protective acids." Dr. Woods's voice was slow and droning. It reflected his personality.

"The swelling was already acute, and I didn't want to run the risk of her vomiting it back up," David said, a note of impatience creeping into his voice.

"Smart . . . smart. Unfortunately, there's little you can

do to mitigate esophageal damage. Liquefaction necrosis happens almost instantaneously."

"Yes," David said. "I know."

"Fever? Whites are normal?"

"No. Yes."

"I'm going to need to get down there and take a look."

"In the meantime?" David waited through what seemed an eternity.

"One-fifty of Zantac IV stat to reduce the stomach acid. That should prevent stress bleeding and ulcerations as well."

"We'll see you shortly."

"Okay. Very we—"

David set the phone down on the cradle and relayed the order. He glanced at the monitor, admired the healthy baseline rhythm. Blood pressure 160 over 100. Respiratory rate at eighteen. Pulse 120. Oxygen saturation 99 percent.

He pulled a deep breath into his lungs and exhaled loudly. It took a conscious effort to relax his muscles and let his shoulders sink. Diane leaned forward over Nancy's face, continuing to irrigate her eyes. A wisp of hair arced across her cheek, finding the corner of her mouth.

An intern skidded on the floor, accidentally sliding past the door. She hooked the frame with a hand as she leaned in. "Golf cart versus Buick. Two forty-three-year-old males with penetrating head wounds. ETA two minutes. We're prepping Procedure Two."

David shot his other latex glove at the trash bin and headed for the door.

CHAPTER 2

"YOU let me the fuck back there or I'll mop the floor with that ratty head of yours."

The police officer's gloved hand was inches from Carson's nose, pointing, as David approached them. Carson stepped back and glanced at the floor. He did not look pleased at the prospect of his prize locks being used to clean the tile of Hallway Two.

"Excuse me, officer," David said, pulling Carson farther back with a hand on his shoulder. "I'm Dr. Spier, chief of the ER Division. What can we—"

"You'd better step back," the officer said, the words coming in a low hiss through his teeth. Though he was cleanly shaven, incipient stubble dotted his face. It was only a little after 10 A.M., David thought. That's a lot of testosterone.

The cop's shoulders were broad, made broader by the dark, dark blue LAPD uniform that stood out in the stark white hall like a stroke of paint. His hair was neatly groomed, flicked to one side in a clean part. Though he looked younger than thirty, the hard flat sheen of his eyes bore witness that they'd already seen much beyond the purview of civilian eyes. His eyebrows, sharp strokes above his supraorbital arch, lent his face a sharp, focused cast.

David glanced quickly behind him for a white security uniform, but saw only pink and blue scrubs. He wasn't sure how helpful a security officer would have been in the face of a belligerent cop anyway.

David spread his arms slightly, his hands splayed, palms out. "You seem agitated," he said. "I'm sorry."

The cop took a deep breath and David eyed the name tag above the pocket line on his right breast. *Jenkins*. Nancy's brother?

David looked up and caught Jenkins's hard stare. "I'm sorry," he repeated.

"Listen, Doctor, I need to know *right now* where my sister is."

Seventeen years in the ER had left David not unfamiliar with how to deal with hard-ass LAPD cops. He forced a curt smile. "Nancy's in Trauma Twelve. I'll be happy to take you back to see her once I check on her, make sure a visitor won't interfere with the doctors and nurses who are still treating her. I'm sure you don't want to do anything to endanger her."

Jenkins's nostrils flared slightly. David debated asking him to step out through the swinging doors to Admit but decided not to fight that battle.

David backed up and pointed Carson toward the Central Work Area, saying in a low voice, "Get a female nurse over to keep an eye on Mr. Jenkins, please, and ensure he stays put." Jenkins was aggressive and upset—a woman would more likely calm him down, and he probably wouldn't pick a fight with her. "And I heard we've had some press milling around triage. Have security clear them out."

David passed through the CWA, dodging nurses, and ducked into Trauma Room Twelve. Nancy's body lay bare on the gurney, pale except for the red blisters on her face and throat. She was still unconscious, the ventilator pushing air into her lungs. Two nurses continued to irrigate her face and eyes.

A young nurse sat on a chair in the corner, sobbing, her yellow hair falling over her face in thick, yarnlike clumps. She was new to the ER, but David recognized her: one of Nancy's college roommates whom she'd recruited to the Division. In fact, he recognized the faded Aztec-print scrub top that was shaking with her sobs as one of Nancy's.

Pat crouched in front of her, rubbing her upper arm in tight ovals. A lapse in her usual truck-driver toughness.

David pulled a sheet up over Nancy's body, to just below the wounds on her upper chest. Her arm rested atop the sheet, and David noticed the band of pale skin around her ring finger. She'd caused something of a paperwork mess a few months ago when she'd changed back to her maiden name on all employee files.

The younger nurse continued to cry. David crossed to her and leaned over so he could see her name tag. "Jill," he said softly. "I know this is very hard for you, but I'm going to have to ask you to head back to the doctors' lounge. We have some family coming in. Her brother."

Jill stood unsteadily, her thick locks damp and sticking to her wide freckled cheeks. David touched her arm reassuringly. Pat led her out, passing Diane as she entered.

"I see you got someone from head and neck to revise the crich to a formal tracheostomy," David said. "Nice call."

Diane nodded. "Monkey see, monkey do."

A grin touched David's lips. "How flattering."

"We're getting ready to move her to the ICU. Woods is eager to scope her."

"I'm bringing Nancy's brother back to take a look. He's LAPD." David stepped closer to Diane and lowered his voice. "A real hard-on. Brace yourself."

Diane sighed, blowing her bangs up in a puff. Her cheeks were flushed, accenting the icy tint of her green eyes. She beckoned with both hands. "Bring it on."

David went to find Jenkins. It wasn't hard. He hadn't budged. He stood dead center in the hallway, thick arms crossed over his chest, making patients and personnel swerve to go around him. With a small nod, David gestured for him to follow back to the room.

When Jenkins saw his sister's body lying supine on the gurney, some of the protective cruelty washed from his face, and David caught a glimpse of his features unflexed and more softly arrayed. It was easy to forget how young Jenkins was, but in the split second before his veteran's toughness snapped up the slack in his face, David saw the pain striking his youthful core.

Jenkins shuffled forward, lips trembling as he viewed his sister's face. David rested a hand on his shoulder. Jenkins's cheeks colored in twinning ovals, though the rest of his face drained of color. An eerie effect. He raised a fist and coughed into it. "What *is* this?"

"She sustained a bad alkali exposure to the face," Diane said. "But she will survive."

Nancy's head was still cocked back in the sniffing position, the clear plastic tube running into the hole in her neck. A milky white eye gazed out blankly from between swollen lids.

Jenkins's hands fisted, then relaxed. *"Sustained,"* he muttered. "Why are her . . . why are her eyes all screwed up? Is she blind?"

"I'm afraid she probably is," Diane said. "When she comes to, she'll be able to distinguish light from dark, but that's about it. She'll also have uveitis, which will cause extreme photophobia."

"She'll be sensitive to light," David said. "It'll hurt her eyes." He saw Diane's chin dip ever so slightly and knew she was scolding herself for not speaking to Jenkins in nonmedical terms.

"Once the inflammation stops," Diane said, "she

might be able to have a corneal transplant. If she does, her sight could recover up to ninety percent."

"How long does that take? For the inflammation to stop?"

"Could be weeks, could be months. But we have a top ophthalmologist, Dr. Jenn—"

"What do you do in the meantime?"

"Keep irrigating, for now. We want to minimize the chance of scar tissue causing adhesions between the eyeballs and the eyelids."

"The eyelids," Jenkins repeated dumbly. Some color was returning to his lips, but his eyes retained their glassy sheen.

He reached a hand toward Nancy's forehead; it hovered above the raw, weeping skin. He bit his lip hard, fighting a tremor into submission. "Why's she . . . ?" His finger traced a path around the tube running through her trachea.

"She ingested some alkali, which caused her throat to swell," Diane said. "That's why we had to intubate her. We've already had an excellent gastroenterologist down here—he's going to scope her right now so he can figure out how much damage her esophagus sustained. It may have been badly compromised."

"In which case . . . ?" Jenkins's face was hardening again, the skin drawing tight across his high cheekbones.

"In which case it'll have to be removed and replaced. But let's not get ahead of ourselves."

The two nurses worked industriously with their saline bottles. Nancy's limp body shone with moisture from her scalp to the line of her breasts.

"How about the scars? On her face?"

Diane took a deep breath. "We'll get her into plastics and see about—" The intensity in Jenkins's eyes stopped her midsentence. She looked down, studying the tip of her sneaker that protruded beneath the wide cuff of her scrub pants. "It'll scar," she finally said.

Rage erupted through Jenkins's entire body at once. He turned and backhanded a loose IV pole. The force of his swat sent it flying back into a supplies cabinet, where it cracked the thick glass. One of the nurses emitted a little yelp, and the other dropped her saline bottle, which rolled back and forth on the floor in an oscillating arc.

Just as quickly as it had come, Jenkins's rage dissipated. He stood slightly hunched, shoulders rolled forward, breath hammering through his nostrils.

Diane caught David's eye and mouthed, *Security?* He shook his head.

Jenkins's breathing evened out. "I'm sorry," he said, to no one in particular.

David calmly walked over, picked up the dropped saline bottle, and handed it back to the nurse with a reassuring nod. Cautiously, the nurses went back to work on Nancy.

"Alkali," Jenkins said. "That's the same as lye, isn't it?"

"Yes," David said.

"I don't understand. I've spilled that stuff on my hand before. Burns a little, but it doesn't . . ." His voice trailed off as he regarded his sister.

"If it's washed off quickly, the damage can be dramatically reduced. But if it's left on, it's terribly corrosive. It's especially harsh on the soft tissue of the throat and eyes." David stepped around into Jenkins's line of sight. "We'll continue to do all that we can."

"Thank you." Jenkins touched a fist to his mouth. "Who's working the case?"

"Two UCLA PD detectives," David said.

"We'll see about that," Jenkins muttered. Lips pursed, he looked down at his younger sister's face, blistered and swollen. A pulse beat in his temple. "Is the fucker in custody?"

"Have they confirmed it was an assault rather than an accident?"

Jenkins's laugh stabbed the air. "I don't think she tripped and fell face first into a vat of Drano." The skin under his eyes was puffy, as though he'd been crying. His hair was mussed up in one spot in the back; it looked all the more sloppy, given the neatness of the rest of his appearance. "Nancy wasn't the kind of girl to have enemies."

"Isn't," David said. "She *isn't* the kind of girl to have enemies."

"That's right," Jenkins said. "No enemies at all." He smoothed the front of his uniform shirt with his hands. "Just an ex-husband."

"Look," David said. "We don't know—"

"Guess what he does?" Jenkins said, with a crisp little smile.

Diane shook her head.

"A plumber. Fucker totes Drano for a living." He glanced back down at the gelatinous lesions pocking his sister's face, and his grin vanished. "Thank you for your help." He walked so briskly from the room that David felt the breeze across his cheeks.

He and Diane exhaled audibly. One of the nurses shook her head. "He can sure give off some heat," she said.

Diane glanced over at David. "Do *you* think it was an assault?" she asked.

"I know one thing," David said. He pulled his stethoscope from across his shoulders and repositioned it around his neck. "I'd hate to be her ex-husband right now."

CHAPTER 3

THE black-and-white idled up to the front of Tavin's Tavern, a shady bar off Pico in the West Side. Hugh Dalton, a gruff heavyset man with wrinkled, sallow skin that resembled a paper bag, hunched over the wheel, squeezing it with two thick hands. He stared at the cheap signage—backlit plastic letters mounted on the cracked stucco next to the door. The second *T* was flickering.

"Witty name," he grumbled.

"You call your guy at the *Times*?" Jenkins asked.

"Not yet." Dalton's eyes shifted along the dash. "UCLA's been pushing to keep this under wraps."

Jenkins glowered at him. "We both know that if we don't get a media storm going, this case'll get triaged in an evidence locker along with every other garden-variety assault."

"I doubt it. It's throwing heat on its own. Press is already running." He held up his hands in calming fashion. "Relax. I'll call the *Times* anyways. Stoke the fire."

Jenkins snapped the casing off his hefty Saber radio. Hair and clots of dried blood clogged the mouthpiece beneath. He rolled down his window and blew into the unit, clearing it, then clipped it back onto his belt. He pushed open the passenger door and started to step out of the vehicle, but Dalton grabbed his arm.

"You sure you want to do this?" Dalton asked.

Jenkins leaned back into his seat. Dalton kept his bulldog head steady, studying Jenkins's face. He was more than ten years Jenkins's senior; his experience and three years of partnership made him one of the few people who could question Jenkins directly.

"Her eyes were opaque," Jenkins said. "Looked like soggy hard-boiled eggs." He shook his head. "Opaque."

He got out of the car and, after a moment, Dalton followed suit, grunting as he shifted his weight. "If it's his regular hangout," Dalton said, "we'd better keep an eye out for buddies steeled with liquid courage."

Jenkins hit the thick wooden door with both palms. The bartender's hand made a nervous grab for under the counter before he saw the uniforms. Dalton wagged a finger at him as Jenkins surveyed the room, and the bartender showed off a grin resembling a piano keyboard.

Two older men nursed something on the rocks at the bar. The tables in back hosted a blue-collar crew, mostly construction guys and carpenters drinking the aches from their joints. A smattering of Bud Ices decorated the tables. Saloon-style doors guarded the bathrooms and the back door.

Nancy's ex-husband was not there.

"Help you boys with something?" the bartender asked.

Dalton turned him a wan grin that bunched the bags under his eyes. "We'll let you know."

Back stiff, Jenkins crossed to the first full table. "I'm looking for Jesse Ross."

A blond construction guy looked up, his bottle frozen midtoast. Bits of pink insulation clung to his mustache. "What's going on?"

Jenkins calmly reached over and plucked the bottle from his hand. He set it down firmly in front of the guy, a single knock on the table, then leaned forward until their noses almost touched. Dalton scanned the bar quickly, then took a step to the side so his view of the other workers was clear.

"I'll tell you what," Jenkins said, still inches from the man's face. "I'll ask the questions, you supply the answers." He stood back up, crossed his arms, and flashed a quick bullshit grin. "How's that sound?"

"Shit, man," one of the other workers mumbled. "Terry didn't mean no harm."

"Terry can answer my fucking questions," Jenkins said.

The saloon doors creaked open, and Jesse stepped forth, a short stump of a man whose small head was accented by wide, spoonlike ears.

"Watch out," Dalton said in a bored monotone. "I think he's holding a gun."

Jesse cocked his head slightly to one side, confusion melting into panic. His hands sank nervously into his pockets when Jenkins's head snapped around.

Jenkins crossed the bar toward Jesse at a near sprint, his body blocking the construction workers' view of him.

"Don't reach for the weapon!" Jenkins shouted. "I told you not to—"

He hit Jesse with the bar of his forearm, knocking him off his feet and through the saloon doors, one of which swung back and clipped him in the forehead, breaking the skin. He swore loudly and kicked one door free from the hinges, exposing Jesse's quivering body. Jesse had rolled onto all fours, his head bouncing as he tried to breathe. Jenkins hammered a black Rocky combat boot down into his ribs, knocking him flat to his belly. "Don't reach for the piece!"

Two of the construction guys rose to their feet and Dalton pivoted, snapping his fingers. He shook his head, the sagging skin of his jowls swaying with the gesture. They sat back down.

Jenkins grabbed Jesse by the collar of his flannel shirt and his belt and hurled him out the back door, out of sight. Pausing, Jenkins faced his partner through the broken saloon door, an anachronistic player in a bad Western. Blood ran down his forehead, forking over his right eye. He slapped his hands together twice, slowly, as if dusting them off, then turned and stepped through the back door.

The bar was deathly silent.

Dalton scratched his cheek, his knuckles pushing his rubbery skin to the side, then he unholstered his pistol and trudged slowly back through the broken saloon door and out into the alley behind the building. Jenkins had already worked Jesse over pretty well. His fist, which was hammering up and down on Jesse's face, was tightly wrapped in a terry cloth. The terry cloth, freshly borrowed from a car wash, looked nice and hard, crusted with dried soap and wax.

Jesse's nose bent hard to the left, and his teeth were black with blood. His cheeks were swollen and abraded; the terry cloth would obscure any fist marks, making his injuries look the result of a fall during pursuit. He'd pulled himself to his knees, arms curled protectively over his head, cringing and crying.

Jenkins spat out words as he battered Jesse. "How could you do that to her face? Her pretty fucking face? How could you?" His blows were mostly missing now, glancing off Jesse's arms and the top of his head. His voice was high and unusually emotional. "Maybe she wouldn't have left you if you saw to her fucking needs, you little monkey!"

The blood from Jenkins's cut had smeared, rouging his cheek. He stopped punching and turned to Dalton. "Gimme your throw-down."

Dalton raised his pant leg and eyed the dinged-up .25 auto nestled in his ankle holster.

Jenkins bent over, fisting Jesse's hair and yanking back his head. "You know what happened?" he hissed.

"You were packing. I came at you and you struck me. I retaliated with reasonable force."

Jesse shook his head. "No, I didn't. Jesus Christ, I wasn't. I'm not packing. I'm not. What are you doing?"

"And then you came out here, fell down during foot chase, we had a little standoff, and you gun-faced me."

"Get your confession," Dalton murmured to Jenkins. He tossed him the .25 and Jenkins crouched, holding the handle out to Jesse. A line of drool found its way down Jesse's throat, staining his white undershirt a dark red. His breath was coming in gasps. "I didn't . . . I didn't . . . What happened to Nance? What happened to her?"

He leaned forward, palms on the cracked asphalt, and bounced up and down like a Muslim praying. More blood leaked from his mouth.

Jenkins stood and unsnapped the button on his holster. "What happened to her? You threw lye in her face this morning, you motherfucker."

Jesse looked up, his broken face suddenly mournful. "Is she . . . will she be . . . ?"

Dalton turned to guard the back door, but Terry, the blond construction worker, had already stepped through, arms raised. Jenkins unholstered his gun, but Dalton stepped quickly between him and Terry.

"Yo," Dalton said. "Seems you walked into a bit of a situation here."

Terry's voice wavered slightly, but it drew some strength from an undercurrent of righteousness. "He couldn't have hurt Nance this morning," he said. He reached for his back pocket, and Jenkins shouldered Dalton aside, pistol aimed at Terry's head. Terry whipped his hands back up in the air, chest heaving beneath his denim jacket. Dalton reached around to Terry's back pocket and pulled out two Southwest Airlines ticket stubs.

"We just got back from Vegas a few hours ago," Terry

continued. His head was drawn back from the direction of Jenkins's Beretta, as if the pistol were emitting heat. "We stayed at the Hard Rock. A ton of people saw us there." He lowered his arms slowly. Jenkins kept his gun raised, both hands on the stock.

Jesse was rocking on his knees. "What happened to Nance?" he wailed. "Is she alive?"

Dalton crouched over Jesse and took him by the wrist. A stamp was smeared across the back of his hand. *Cheetah's*. A Vegas strip club.

Dalton stood and walked back inside the bar, his shoulder brushing Terry's. After a moment, Jenkins lowered his pistol. He reached out a hand and rested it on Jesse's matted hair. Jesse continued to rock and wail. "Is Nance all right?" he sobbed. "Did someone kill Nance?"

"No," Jenkins said quietly. "She's still alive."

Jesse collapsed, crying with relief. Jenkins holstered his weapon, touched Jesse gently on the head again, and left him crying on the asphalt.

CHAPTER 4

HUNCHED over the pocked wooden table so his broad shoulders arced into a hump, Clyde studied the plastic bottle of DrainEze with flat, unblinking eyes. A filthy window screen filtered the breeze into dusty gasps of air that swirled among the scattered papers on the floor before dying in the room's stench. Half-drunk cans of Yoo-Hoo dotted the countertop in the adjacent kitchen, amid pots filled with congealed macaroni and cheese, and pans caked with the burnt remains of refried beans.

Perched on his knees, his hands were oddly swollen, gathering thickness around his knuckles and hairy wrists. They raised to the tabletop and rested nervously at the edge, twitching. His pitted fingernails scraped along the wood. A twisted metal lamp cast a cone of light before him. He seized a syringe and turned it a half rotation before testing the needle with the tip of a finger. The bezel broke the puffy skin and he yelped, pulling the needle away. He closed his eyes reflexively, murmuring to himself. "Three, two, one. Stand back from the door. *Back from the door*." The mantra seemed to calm him. When he opened his eyes, the anxiety on his face had dissipated.

Working the meat of his injured fingertip between the thumb and forefinger of his other hand, Clyde produced a bead of blood, which he lapped up.

He wore faded blue hospital scrubs. Physician's scrubs. A beatup navy-blue corduroy baseball cap sat low across his wide crown, his balding scalp visible through the netting in the back. It bore no emblem. Both his cheeks were marred with acne scars, deep irregular indentations that held the shadows of the room. A high thin scar above his right ear notched his hair, which he kept short on the sides and back but long and stringy on top, perhaps to disguise his hair loss. Though he was not grossly obese, his extra weight hung on him loose and flaccid. A single key dangled from a thin ball-chain necklace, which disappeared into the folds of his neck.

His tongue darted from his mouth, tensed, the tip poking at his upper lip. Beneath the table, his feet seemed to move independently, pushing into each other, flopping and scratching like two dogs at play. His Adidas sneakers had yellowed with age and grown brittle along the soft middle soles.

He swallowed the orange tablet he'd been sucking on, then spooned another helping of instant coffee from the jar directly into his mouth. A grimace twisted his face momentarily, then faded. He chewed slowly, some of the grains gumming at the corners of his lips. His mouth pulsed a few times, then he swallowed hard, tilting back his head as though gulping down a vitamin.

A rat scurried unseen through the mound of unwashed clothes that curled around the base of his twin bed. The bedside lamp, a yellow porcelain number bearing a Motel 6 sticker, had been draped with a thin purple scarf. It provided meager, diffuse light.

His pupils twitched twice to the left. He grunted through his nose and turned back to the work at hand. Pushing the needle into the gray DrainEze bottle, he withdrew the plunger, filling the syringe with the vivid blue liquid. With a jerk of his thumb, he pushed the syringe down, sending a thin spurt of alkali across the tabletop. The liquid pooled in minuscule drops, eating slowly into the wood. His wide mouth split in a grin, the corners curving back toward his low-set ears.

Two other DrainEze bottles sat on the table, industrial-sized with juglike handles. Two glasses of cloudy water waited near his right hand, beside a small surgeon's tray that contained syringes, needles, and a scalpel. His right shin nudged an open metal footlocker holding a host of medical tools and devices.

Across the thigh of his scrub bottoms, a series of tiny holes in the fabric revealed glossy spots of scarred skin. Cautiously lowering the needle, Clyde positioned it just past the last hole in the scrubs. He sank the plunger slowly, allowing several drops of liquid to dribble from the needle. The liquid ate quickly through the thin scrubs, and he shrieked and jerked his leg as it began to attack his flesh.

Grabbing the glass of water, he poured it over the wound. The water darkened his scrubs in a flame pattern, with licks reaching down his calf. Holding his leg still with his other hand, he poured the second glass of water over his thigh. Then he placed both hands flat on the table and sat perfectly still, whimpering softly as the last drops of alkali continued to burn in his flesh. His face grew shiny with sweat.

After a while, Clyde stood and headed into the kitchen. He filled a glass with water from the tap and drank it, three times successively, before placing the glass back in the cluttered sink. Opening a can of wet cat food, he dumped the contents on top of the mound of cylinder-shaped servings already overflowing the small bowl. Twitching his fingers, he made a kissing noise, but no cat came.

The skull tattoo on the outside of his flabby biceps caught his attention, and he returned to the footlocker, produced a cotton ball, and doused it with rubbing alcohol. The skull lifted easily from his skin, blackening the moist side of the cotton. Continuing to rub at his biceps, he lumbered to the clothes mound at the base of his bed, unearthed a stained mirror, and propped it against a wall. With a raspy groan, he slid from his scrub bottoms, then stood and stared at his reflection. A series of alkali burns dotted his right thigh, like the marks of small, burrowing insects. Most of them were scarred over, gnarled knots of fire-red flesh. The freshest wound wept a clear, viscous fluid, which caked on the thick black hairs of his leg.

Cupping his limp penis in his hand, Clyde crossed to his bed and pulled the strewn sheets up into rough position. When he climbed in, his bulk took up most of the width of the bed, his shoulders pressing back into the child's headboard. He dug for a pack of cigarettes beneath the sheets and squeezed it until the top popped open. Only two cigarettes remained. Placing them in his mouth side by side, he lit them together and smoked them as one unit.

The blackness outside his window had lightened to a grayish cast. Smoking his cigarettes and plugging his leaking wound with a fat thumb, he waited for morning.

CHAPTER 5

THE modern Greek-style house peeked out from behind bunches of pampas grass and fan palms, the leaves throwing perfect shadows against the white stucco. Between the home's windows, vines of split-leaf philodendron snaked up the walls, the glossy dark-green leaves flapping in the breeze like atrophied wings. On the front lawn, two large palm trees crisscrossed like necking flamingos. Situated on Marlboro Street in Brentwood, David's house was a few blocks south of Sunset but still close enough that the occasional passing semi ever so slightly vibrated the paintings on the walls. The house seemed almost shy, set back a good twenty yards from the street.

A blaring car horn in the distance awoke David at 5:30. He turned beneath his comforter, removing his earplugs and placing them in a nightstand drawer. He heard the traffic immediately, and wondered if there was a more effective brand of earplug that might rescue him from the all-hour sounds of Sunset Boulevard.

His king-sized bed sat centered beneath a window that

overlooked the thin side yard. No blinds or drapes dressed the window; he liked to awaken with the gathering sunlight. Aside from a solitary padded chair in the corner on which David hung his white coat, the room was entirely bare. He still slept on the right side of the bed—he'd never felt comfortable making the migration to the middle. The sheets on the left side remained almost perfectly smoothed. He found something immensely depressing about the blank strip of still-made bed beside which he slept every night.

David reached for the phone immediately and dialed the ICU.

"Yes, hello, Sheila. Dr. Spier here. We sent a woman upstairs yesterday, and I wanted to check in on her. Nancy Jenkins."

"Oh." Sheila exhaled loudly. "What a thing. Such a sweet woman." The tone of her voice was not heartening. "She was doing better in the late evening," she continued. "She even regained consciousness and spoke briefly with some detectives, but then things went to hell in the middle of the night. Her temp shot up; we took a portable upright chest, saw she'd developed free air, and rushed her to the OR."

Despite David's efforts, the alkali had won out. Dr. Woods's endoscopy yesterday evening had revealed that Nancy had sustained 3a grade esophageal injury. It had been a mess down in her throat. Exudates gooping the membranes, deep focal and circumferential ulcers, and black blisters of necrotic tissue, waiting to slough, heal over, or simply give way. One of the focal necrotic patches in her esophagus had finally blown out in the night, allowing air and infection to escape into her body.

David swung his legs out of bed and rested his feet on the thin beige carpet, careful not to disturb the perfect pattern the cleaning lady's vacuum had left last Wednesday.

"Unfortunately, Dr. Freedman had to do a subtotal resection of the esophagus," Sheila continued. "I believe he pulled up a segment of small bowel to replace it." She paused, and David heard a sheet rustling. "Small bowel?" she said. "Why not colon?"

"The small bowel has more active peristalsis," David said.

"Oh." He could hear the nurse breathing during the long pause. "We did everything we could," she said, more sadly than defensively. "As you know, everyone's really following her closely. I've had more phone calls checking up on her. Nurses, lab techs, docs, reporters calling every five minutes . . ." When she spoke again, the sharp anger in her voice startled David. "What kind of a bastard does a thing like this?"

"Well," David said, letting the hypothetical question hang and fade, "I'm glad she's in your hands now."

"Yeah . . ." Sheila sighed again, and David heard the phone rustling against her cheek. "To tell you the truth, Doctor, I'm getting tired of giving out bad news on this one. Dispensing misery is a tough way to make a living."

He rubbed one eye with the heel of a hand. "Pretend you're an IRS agent."

Her laugh was soft, but genuine. He said good-bye and hung up the phone, then stared at it for a moment. Three minutes into Monday, and he already felt like shit.

By now, with all he'd seen, perhaps he should have grown desensitized to medical emergencies. Suicide attempts where the bullet blows out the cheekbone but leaves the brain intact; motorcycle wrecks ending in near-decapitation-by-stop-sign; children beaten so frequently about the mouth that their frenula are torn, the stringy halters no longer connecting the upper lips to the gums. But every time he thought he'd seen it all, something found its way through the swinging ER doors to push the limits of his experience a few inches further. His experience was his strongest ally and darkest companion, a pupil ever dilating. Yesterday morning had once again proven that the world had an inexhaustible hoard of surprises. What kind of sickness had to fester in the coralline whorls of a human's brain to cause him to direct a viciously corrosive substance into another human being's face?

Heading into the shower, David scrubbed methodically from his forehead to his toes, washed his hair, and let the hot water steam him for a few minutes before getting out. His feet perfectly centered on the white bath mat, he stared at his reflection in the mirror. By most estimations, he was a handsome man—the kind of handsome that comes not from distinctive or striking looks, but from features that are even and predictable, and therefore pleasing. A square, masculine jaw, light brown hair cropped short and worn slightly mussed, not-too-thin lips with a pronounced Cupid's bow, and two eyes that were a light shade of blue, just short of interesting. His crow's-feet were not quite visible from this distance unless he squinted. His neck seemed less firm and muscular than it had been five years ago, but he wasn't sure if that was based on a glorified remembrance. He decided he was holding up okay. Still attractive, if a little ordinary.

Drying his back, he headed into his bedroom and placed his pajamas neatly in their drawer before dressing in his scrubs. He lifted his white coat off the chair in the corner and pulled it on, then removed his stethoscope from the inside pocket, and laid it across his shoulders. Until he felt the weight of the stethoscope around his neck each morning, he felt partially unclothed.

Walking into the study, he admired the perfectly even shelves, the rows of books organized by size and genre. Diplomas lined the far wall, framed in a cherry wood.

Harvard undergrad and medical school, equally pompous with their scrolled Latin, started the row, followed by his UCSF residency certificate and board certification for Emergency Medicine. One of his Outstanding Clinical Instructor plaques hung slightly crooked. He straightened it with the edge of his thumb.

Turning to the large brass birdcage in one corner, he sighed before removing the drape. The Moluccan cockatoo awakened instantly on its perch, shifting from one black claw to the other. A bright salmon-pink crest protruded from behind its head, a flair of color on its otherwise cream body.

"Hello, Stanley," David said flatly.

"Elisabeth?" it squawked. "Where's Elisabeth?" David's wife had spent three painstaking weeks one summer training the cockatoo to ask for her when it wanted to be fed. Stanley's repertoire of comments had not since been expanded.

"On vacation in the south of France," David said.

It nodded its head to gnaw at something in its breast feathers, the long erectile crest spreading behind its head like an exotic fan.

David sprinkled some birdseed into the small cup secured to the cage bars, grimacing when some fell to the hardwood floor.

"M&M's," the cockatoo squawked. "Where's Elisabeth?"

"Took off for Mexico with embezzled funds."

The cockatoo regarded him suspiciously with a glassy black eye. "Where's Elisabeth?"

"Training Lipizzans in Vienna," David said.

His mother, were she still alive, would not have been pleased with the fact that David drove a Mercedes. Along with Doberman pinschers and von Karajan, they were, in his mother's mind, forever associated with the Third Reich. And though David would never admit it, the cast of the back-tilted headlights of his E320 sometimes reminded him of the requisite round spectacles perched on every Nazi nose in bad '50s films.

He passed the imperious Federal Building on Wilshire, the perpetual protesters outside imploring commuters to honk to free Tibet, and drove into the heart of Westwood. Turning onto Le Conte, he steered wide to avoid the grime kicking up from the jackhammers at the site across from the hospital. For two months, construction crews had been working day and night converting the building next to the Geffen Playhouse into a large retail store. A burly worker swung a sledgehammer at a 4-by-4 supporting a section of defunct scaffolding, and the section keeled over slowly, sending a burst of dust across the road. The olive hood of David's car dulled with the pollution. He made a note to schedule a trip to the car wash on his next free afternoon.

A thought seized him, and he pulled over and approached the crew of construction workers. The muscular worker stood in the midst of the fallen scaffolding, a sledgehammer angled back over one shoulder. He wore a goatee that tapered to a point. His white undershirt was soaked with sweat, permitting an enormous swastika tattoo to show through. Covering his torso from his clavicle to the top of his belly button, the tattoo had been poorly inked. A black box of a probation-and-parole monitor was strapped to his ankle on a thick metal band.

David's immediate thought was that this man could be the alkali thrower. He worked in the vicinity—he would have had easy access to the ambulance bay. David immediately reproached himself for having such a severe and unfounded first impression. The man turned a hard gaze in David's direction as David approached, and he noticed a slight facial asymmetry. The other men continued to work.

"Hello, I'm Dr. David Spier. I work in the Emergency Room at UCLA."

"Zeke Crowley."

David watched Zeke's large, callused hand envelop his own. David pointed to the monitor on Zeke's ankle. "I had to cut one of those off once."

"Not your own, I'd guess." Zeke's voice, gruff and forceful, fit his appearance.

David smiled. "No, for a procedure on a patient, back when I was a resident. It kept getting in my way. I called the number on the tag. The operator was a bit of a pain."

"They tend to be." Zeke coughed into a fist. "Spier. That Jewish?"

"Sometimes. I'm sure you heard about the alkali attack that took place here yesterday. I was wondering . . . well, I just thought given your location here, you might have seen something."

"*Sometimes,*" Zeke repeated. "How about in your case?"

"Yes. It is. Anyone here see anything?"

Zeke ran his fingers down his goatee and twisted the end. "Nope."

Zeke seemed to have too much confidence to have committed the attack on Nancy. His aggression, David guessed, would be more direct and muscular. Fists and kicks. If he assaulted someone, Zeke would want them to know it was he who was punishing them. From what David knew of the alkali throwing, it was pathetic and cowardly. Repressed, somehow.

David studied Zeke closer. His right eyelid drooped, and the pupil was constricted. There was a decided lack of sweat on the right side of his face. Ptosis, miosis, and anhidrosis. The probable diagnosis came to David, quick and gratifying. He pushed his medical thoughts aside. "What time do you guys start?" he asked.

Zeke crossed his arms, his thick forearms flexing. He studied David for a moment. "A lot of you guys are doctors, huh? Doctors and bankers. Crafty bunch."

"Did you not hear my question?"

"Cops already came through here, stirred the shit, asked for alibis. The way I see it, I don't have to answer to a smart-ass doctor."

David felt suddenly foolish about his hunch. Of course the police would have thought to interrogate the construction workers to find out if they saw anything. He was glad they were covering their bases; it wasn't his place to be out here beating the bushes.

"You're right." David turned to go, then stopped. "You've had a recent trauma to your neck."

Zeke rocked the sledgehammer on his shoulder. "How the hell do you know that?"

"What's occurring in your face, I'd bet, is Horner's syndrome. It's a result of disruption of the sympathetic nerves in the cervical neck."

Zeke studied David long and hard, then broke eye contact. "I got whacked by a falling 2-by-4. About two weeks back. My face has been kinda messed up since."

"It might resolve on its own, but why don't you come into the ER so we can take a look. You'll probably need a referral to see a neurologist, just to be safe." David reached in his coat pocket for a business card. "Don't worry—if you're uptight about it, we'll be happy to find you a doctor of whatever ethnicity you prefer."

Zeke's smile was surprisingly soft, despite the sharp edges of his facial hair. The card looked minuscule in his palm. Zeke folded it and shoved it in his back pocket.

David headed back to his idling car.

He zipped around the kiosk and into the parking lot for the Center for Health Sciences, a tiered outdoor structure that stepped its way down from the medical plaza to Le Conte Avenue. Walking through the concrete maze of stairwells and levels, he emerged from the lot and headed along the sidewalk that curved down into the underground ambulance bay and ER entrance. Checking his watch, he saw he was five minutes late to be twenty minutes early.

Halfway down, he paused and regarded the small strip of grass and plants to his left. A waist-high light stuck out from a row of bushes. He realized he was standing in precisely the same spot that Nancy Jenkins had been when assailed with the alkali. What had she seen? A movement in the bushes, a flash of a face? And then a sudden, blinding pain.

A hand clutched David's arm, and he jerked violently around. Ralph took a quick step back, his bleached-white security shirt pulling free from his pants on one side. He wore a polished pin on his shirt—an eagle clutching the American flag in its talons. A former marine who'd done two tours of duty in Vietnam, Ralph had come back to the States and found himself, like so many other veterans, with few options. He'd spent several years living between the streets and the VA on Wilshire before taking control of his life again. After slipping and breaking a finger at a UCLA football game, he'd come into the ER, where he'd impressed David with his gruff, determined nature and no-bullshit honesty. David had put out feelers for jobs throughout the hospital. A trainee security position had quickly led to a full-time job, and now Ralph was one of two chief security officers.

"Whoa!" He smiled. "Shit, Doc. Didn't mean to scare you."

David placed a hand on his stomach. "I think I'm just

a little on edge, with all the . . ." He gestured to the bushes.

"We amped up our patrols," Ralph said. "Eight security officers instead of five."

"That's good to know. Do you think this person is planning another assault?"

"Looks more like a personal vendetta thing to me." Ralph thumbed his belt and leaned forward, his voice lowered. "The word is, Nancy told the detectives she saw a tattoo on the guy's arm. Didn't see his face. Just an arm with a tattoo and then the stuff all in her eyes." He shook his head, blank-gazing at the bushes, as if the assailant were suddenly going to reappear. "I can't imagine Nancy had any enemies, but who the hell knows. I seen stranger things, that's for sure."

David fingered his stethoscope absentmindedly. "Did the person shout anything at her? Interact with her in any way?"

"Not from what I heard." Ralph's eyebrow dipped in a curious squint. "Why?"

"That just seems odd. If it is personal, I mean. I'd think the attacker would want to express his anger, make Nancy aware of why she was being victimized. The attack seems so impersonal." David shook his head. "Not that this is my field."

"Well, until there's another attack, it's an isolated incident," Ralph said.

David's lips pursed in a slight smile at Ralph's unintentional syllogism. "Yes," he said. "That's true."

"But we're keeping a few more sets of eyes around the area, just in case. To keep things safe and to ward off the media vultures." As if on cue, a news van pulled up just past the kiosk. A reporter hopped out and began rolling footage against the backdrop of the hospital. Ralph shook his head wearily. "All morning long."

A security guard appeared swiftly, disrupting the reporter's shot, and immediately began arguing with the cameraman.

"I guess the higher-ups don't dig the press. They have us on the reporters like brown on shit." Ralph placed his hands on his hips and grimaced, showing off a crooked front tooth. "I never knew Nancy's brother was a cop. You met him, right?"

David nodded. "I had the pleasure, yes."

"Well, our guy pulled two no-nos: attacking a hospital and an officer's relative." Ralph whistled. "I hope he likes attention, 'cause he's got a lotta people gunning for him now."

"The detectives seemed as . . . intense as Nancy's brother?"

Ralph raised his eyebrows, his face taking on a you'd-better-believe-it cast. "If you pardon my language, Doc, someone fucked with the wrong girl."

CHAPTER 6

HUGH Dalton turned a half rotation, spilling coffee over the side of his mug as he showed off his rumpled slacks and JCPenney pinstripe shirt. His solid brown tie stuck in his shoulder holster. Jenkins pulled it free for him.

"Whaddaya think?" Dalton said. "From two-striper to D-one in the blink of an eye." He grimaced. "Three year blink of an eye, but who's checking."

"I'm surprised you finally passed the exam," Jenkins said. "Let alone the oral."

Dalton emptied a carton of orange juice into a glass jug and set it on the table next to a plate stacked high with Eggos. "I appreciate your vote of confidence."

"I'm losing a good partner. Don't expect me to turn cartwheels."

"At least you're losing me to a promotion, not a coffin." Dalton shouted down the hall, "Breakfast's on the table. Get out here or I'll eat it myself." He turned back to Jenkins. "You know I will."

Jenkins eyed his significant gut. "No argument here."

"Well? How do I look?"

"Like my high school geography teacher," Jenkins said. "Mr. Perkins packing heat." He smoothed the front of his own freshly ironed uniform, then polished his badge with a cuff. "Tell me you're not gonna miss the monkey suit."

"I'm not gonna miss the monkey suit." Dalton drained his coffee and thunked the chipped cup on the table. "No more uniform for this dick." He leaned back in the direction of the hall. "If I have to come get you . . . !"

Jenkins cleared his throat. "Tell me you're gonna be able to get the case from the jackass campus cops."

Dalton raised an eyebrow. "Believe you me. The Captain's already hot for it. ACID THROWER TAKES AIM AT WESTWOOD. Where there's press, there's *juris*."

"Lye. It was lye."

"You think the *LA Times* knows that?" Dalton grunted. "Besides, it'll help ID the false confessions." He poured himself a glass of orange juice, smelled it, then poured it out in the sink. "I want you to finish checking Nancy's papers and files for any services she's recently paid for. Workers in the house or yard. Look through her credit card bills for anything she might've ordered that would've been delivered. She wore her scrubs around the house sometimes, right?"

Jenkins's nod was barely discernable.

"Well, they have UCLA MEDICAL CENTER printed right on 'em. Who knows, our sicko delivers a package, she answers the door in her scrubs—" He stopped when he saw the expression on Jenkins's face. "You get the picture." He smoothed the skin of his jowls with an open hand. "How's she doing? Nance?"

The points of Jenkins's jaw flexed out, then disappeared. "I'm gonna break somebody's face over this," he said.

"I'm gonna help you."

Two girls, ages nine and twelve, scampered down the hall into the kitchen, dumping their backpacks near the door. The twelve-year-old set a purple sequined purse on the tabletop and stared at the Eggos with displeasure.

"Eat," Dalton said. "No purses at school. Drink your juice."

The younger girl pointed at the stack of waffles. "You forgot to toast that one." Dalton removed the frozen Eggo from the stack and tossed it in the sink. The twelve-year-old took a sip of orange juice and spit it back into her cup.

Jenkins glanced at his watch. "I gotta head," he said.

Dalton nodded with mock formality. "Patrolman."

Jenkins eyed Dalton's cheap dress clothes, and his hard features loosened for a moment. He nodded back. "Detective," he said.

The yellow Buick ran the red light at Broxton and Weyburn and pulled up to Jerry's Deli in downtown Westwood. Ted Yale, a tall, even-featured detective with a clean yacht-club look, stepped out from behind the wheel, snapped his gum, and readjusted the knot on his designer tie. When Dalton got out from the car, a cluster of Chee•tos fell from the folds of his pants to the sidewalk.

Yale entered the deli briskly, and Dalton followed,

squinting at the bright lights, the flashy Broadway posters, and the neon signs. Yale's head pivoted like a periscope, locking on two men reclining in a corner booth. One of them, a handsome black man with a broad mustache, was evidently telling a joke. His hands traced gestures in the air.

"Over there," Yale said, gesturing with his chin. "You can always tell 'em by the cheap shoes." He glanced down at Dalton's shoes, then back up at his face. "Sorry."

They crossed the deli and slid into the booth, taking the two outside seats. The men looked up. "What the fuck?" the black detective said.

"You Gaines?" Yale asked. "And Blake? UCLA PD?"

Blake, an older man with a blond mustache and deeply textured face, ignored the two newcomers; his eyes fixed on Gaines. "What's the punch line?" he asked.

Gaines looked nervously from Yale back to his partner. "Hanukah Lewinsky." Blake laughed, slapping the table with the palm of his hand and making his water dance in the glass.

"Hey," Dalton said. "I got a joke for you. What's the only thing more boring than a UCLA cop?" He looked from Gaines to Blake. "A *retired* UCLA cop."

Blake pinched a lemon between his fingers and let it drain into his water glass. "Let me guess. Judging by the demeanor and the sense of general entitlement . . . LAPD."

"Demeanor," Yale said. "Good word."

"To what do we owe?" Gaines asked.

"We're taking over one of your cases," Yale said. "Sister of someone on the job. The captain-three feels quite strongly, as does our department."

"The Acid Thrower?" Gaines shook his head. "Uh-uh."

"Lye," Dalton said. "It was lye."

"I know the drill," Blake said. "High-profile case.

Everyone's gonna try 'n' squirm in and get some, like pups at a tit. No way."

Yale smiled curtly. "Let me remind you—"

" 'UCLA Police will handle all crimes that occur on UCLA property, including nonacademic facilities, and incidents involving UCLA personnel within a mile from campus if they are connected to the victim's association with UCLA.' " Blake wrinkled up his textured face and cocked his head at Gaines. "What's the name of that big hospital again?"

"The UCLA Medical Center," Gaines said. "I believe."

"*UCLA* Medical Center," Blake said. "That's right." He touched his forehead with his fingertips.

"With the exception of . . . ?" Yale asked.

No one answered.

"With the exception of homicide and rape, which are investigated only by the Los Angeles Police Department." Yale smiled, pleased with himself.

Blake said, "Last I checked, no one got raped or murdered."

"Attempted homicide. Mayhem. Assault with a deadly weapon."

"Attempted homicide is a stretch," Gaines said. "More like attempted plastic surgery."

Dalton came up from his seat hard, his thighs knocking the table. "Don't you fucking joke about this," he hissed through clenched teeth. "Don't you dare."

Blake mopped up his spilled water with a napkin. With a flick of his eyes, Yale signaled Dalton to sit. Though younger, Yale, a detective-second, outranked him.

"She was a good friend of the department," Yale said calmly. "In addition to being his ex-partner's sister."

Gaines raised his hands in an apologetic gesture. The

waitress approached the table and Yale shooed her with a flick of the wrist.

"Veterans services, counseling, fund-raisers for families of men downed in the line of duty," Dalton said, anger still coloring his voice. "She was a good kid." He leveled his eyes on Gaines. "When's the last time you worked a mayhem?"

"Plus it's state property," Blake continued, as if there had been no interruption in his conversation with Yale.

"However," Yale said, "there's a five-hundred-yard jurisdiction overlay. Not to mention the fact that the suspect schemed to commit the crime in the city. Though the actual execution of the crime occurred on state property, in all likelihood, he had to go to and from the city to arrive at the crime scene."

"In all likelihood," Blake repeated. A red bloom appeared beneath the rugged skin of his face, either anger or frustration.

"Did you tighten down the hospital?" Yale asked. "On the off chance it was random?"

Blake nodded. "Warned personnel."

"Your report appeared to be devoid of leads," Yale said.

"We have leads," Gaines said. "We're looking into an ex-husband."

Dalton's elbow flared as he scratched the side of his head. "I think it's fairly safe to say he didn't do it."

"Well," Yale said. "Now that we've run through all your leads . . . "

Gaines fingered the edge of his plate. "She said the guy had a tattoo. Shape of a skull, but she wasn't sure. We're running it."

"This case'll exhaust your resources," Yale said.

"Bullshit," Blake said. "It's an isolated incident, and we have it under control."

"Did you hold the crime scene?" Dalton asked.

"We got there late." Gaines looked down at his toast, yellowed with yolk.

"You found a jar with alkali residue thirty yards from the ER entrance, and you didn't hold the scene?"

"We preserved the evidence," Blake said. "And combed the area for more. We found two cigarette butts nearby—lab pegged 'em as Marlboros—but they'd been ground to nothing."

"No prints on the jar?" Yale asked.

Blake shook his head. "Smooth gloves. Probably latex."

"According to your report, the cigarette butts were found near a waist-high footlight off the sidewalk that curves down to the ER entrance. If he was smoking, that meant he was waiting there for some time. He might not have been wearing gloves while he waited, not wanting to look suspicious. The top of the light is aluminum. Given it's waist high, he very well could have leaned on it as he waited. Did you print it?"

Blake ran his tongue along the inside of his bottom lip. "No."

"So let's go print it now," Gaines said. "It's off the sidewalk in the shrubs, not like people go back there and handle it all the time."

Yale's face stretched tight in a flash of a smile. "The sprinklers at Zone Six of the Medical Center run at five-fifteen in the morning, something I would have assumed you'd know, given your tremendous UCLA expertise. Unfortunately, I didn't read your report until eight-thirty." He tapped the table with a forefinger. "*That's* why you hold a crime scene." He leaned back and crossed his arms, raising wrinkles in the shoulders of his blazer. "Sorry, boys. This one comes down from the Captain. We're taking it over."

"Don't worry," Dalton said. "I'm sure there's some interesting campus cases you can work on. Harassing e-mails, late library books, a good date rape or two."

"Have the evidence sent to our labs," Yale said. He threw a crumpled twenty on the table and rose. "Breakfast's on the West LA Detective Bureau this morning."

CHAPTER 7

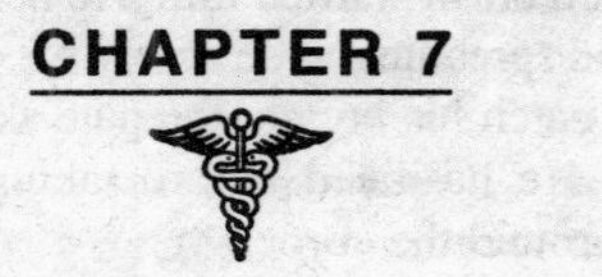

THE iridescent fish caught the glimmer of the sun even through the store window. Separated in bowls sitting side by side on a table in a window display, the two Siamese fighting fish swam tight, excited circles. Every few seconds, they darted back to face each other through the glass, like compass needles pulled north.

Clyde pressed his face against the outside of the window. The fish were all the more ferocious for their elegance. Long, flowing fins, scales shimmering red and blue, they drifted, tensed, drifted, Samurai warriors fighting in loose robes.

The cheap cardboard sign folded name tag–style on the table beside them read *BETTA SPLENDENS.* KEEP SEPARATED.

The bells on the door jangled as a gaunt man with wispy hair and round spectacles exited. He pulled a full ring of keys from his pocket and locked the dead bolt.

"What're you doing?" Keeping his forehead pressed to the glass, Clyde rolled his head so he could see the store owner.

"Closing up for lunch."

"I want those fish." His puffy finger pressed into the glass, pointing.

"Be back in twenty minutes."

"I want them *now*."

The store owner smiled curtly, pushing his glasses back up the bridge of his nose with a knuckle. "I'll be back in twenty minutes. I'll be happy to help you then."

The store owner was a few steps around the corner when the loud crash startled him. He nearly lost his footing, one hand spreading wide across his chest. It took him a minute to catch his breath, the pale skin beating above his temple. He hesitated before taking small tentative steps back around the corner.

He gasped. The store window had been smashed, and bits of glass were scattered through the display area. The man who'd stood out front was gone. A few curious pedestrians threw the store owner glances from across the street as he neared the window fearfully.

A brick, pulled from the loose walkway of the arts and crafts shop next door, had been hurled through the window, smashing one of the fish bowls. The other lay on its side, water dripping off the table.

The two magnificent fish flopped among the shards of wet glass on the tabletop. The blood leaking from the blue one's gills rouged its scales. It paused between movements, gills fluttering.

The vermilion betta flipped itself off the table's edge, landing in an open bag of teal aquarium rocks. It wiggled a few times more, then lay still, its streamers limp like wet toilet paper.

CHAPTER 8

SANDRA Yee, the most animated of the ER residents, flashed David dueling thumbs-up as he walked down Hallway Two to the Central Work Area. She was literally bouncing in her white Reeboks. The fact that she was only 5'2" made her excitement all the more endearing.

"I caught a big-ass *triple a* on a fifty-five-year-old. Surgery just swept him upstairs." She bent gracefully in an operatic bow.

"Abdominal aortic aneurysm? Good catch. Probably saved his life." David squeezed her shoulder, and she put her arm across his lower back.

"Thank you, thank you." Sandra turned, heading down the hall, whistling her theme song, "Look at me, I'm Sandra Dee" from *Grease*.

An elderly radiologist snapped his fingers after her. "Excuse me! You wanted the read on the broken arm?"

"I'm sorry," Sandra called over her shoulder. "You must have me confused with some other short Asian." She jogged off, sneakers squeaking on the tile.

David turned away to hide his smile. He entered the CWA, where a potpourri of scrub tops gathered around the main desktop, heads riveted on the portable TV the clerks kept on a cabinet near the board. "Any update on the alkali thrower?"

A clerk glanced up from the phones, shaking his head. "Only good scoop was some guy stopped a robbery at the

Kinko's on Wilshire. Scared off the robbers, took a bullet in the ass, then split before the cops showed. But no new word on the fuckhead who attacked Nancy."

David felt his good mood instantly dissipate.

One of the nurses shook her head. "I hope they nail the bastard soon."

Two interns crashed through the door and jockeyed for position around David.

"Fifty-two-year-old female presents with—"

"Nineteen-year-old comes in with a nickel lodged in his—"

David held up his hand, fighting his way to the board. "One at a time." A prescription order appeared in front of his face and he glanced at it, then signed it. Somewhere down the hall, someone moaned, a loud sound that grew to a scream.

David slowed to accommodate the throng around him. "Who's screaming and why?"

"Homeless Harry," a nurse said. "We've had to keep him in four-point restraints ever since Diane did a rectal on him."

"You'd have to keep *me* in four-point restraints if Diane did a rectal on me," one of the medicine interns joked.

David said, "She'll be flattered to hear that."

"I need sign-offs in Six, Nine, and Fifteen-One," a resident said.

David checked the board to see what patients they had where. "Why are we so far behind? Where's Don?"

"Our other attending is, as usual, missing in action."

Sandra swung her head around the corner. "I take odds on the lounge."

"I'll take the cafeteria," someone else shouted out.

David fought to keep his anger at Don from showing. "Excuse me for a minute." He walked down the hall to the doctors' lounge, but there was no sign of Don Lambert, the missing attending. As David left the lounge, Don nearly collided with him, cradling a banana, two bags of chips, a can of Coke, and an El Pollo Loco burrito in his arms. The banana slapped to the floor, and Don crouched to pick it up.

"Goddamn it! Watch where you're—" Don stood up and looked at David's face for the first time. "Oh, Dave. I'm sorry. I didn't realize it was you."

"You were in the cafeteria?"

He nodded. "I haven't taken a break since—"

"Dr. Lambert, we always have two attendings from three to eight because these are generally the busiest hours. No one—not even those of us who have been on since eight—have taken a break yet. Just because we aren't completely slammed today does not give you an excuse to go AWOL for half an hour at a time. Plus, you know the staff's been upset about Nancy's attack. You should be keeping a closer eye on them."

Don set down his food on a nearby chair and skimmed a hand across the top of his perfect ledge of blond hair, a red stone glinting from his gold chunk of an alma mater ring. His piercing blue eyes and relaxed, apathetic air made him irresistible to the women on staff. He rarely walked through the hospital corridors without being accosted by female patients and visitors. "I was gone for fifteen minutes," Don said, doing little to hide his irritation.

"Fifteen minutes is enough for two traumas to roll in here and put me on overload," David said. "Surely you've paid enough attention during your shifts to notice that things heat up rather quickly when they heat up."

"Don't treat me like an imbecile."

"Then don't give me reason to treat you like one." David sighed, then took a calmer tone. "Look, Dr. Lambert, I'm a relatively flexible guy—"

At this, Don snickered.

"—but there is one thing for which I will not stand and that is compromising the care in this facility. You've been irresponsible on more than a few occasions, and I'm reaching the end of my rope. As an attending, you should be setting an example."

"Name one time I've put a patient at risk." Don picked up his banana and peeled it. "Well?"

David could feel his face growing red, but he fought down his anger. "Think of it as taking preventative measures." He was walking away when he heard Don call his name. He took a moment before turning around.

"When your wife came in here," Don said, "didn't I take excellent care of her? I mean, didn't I do everything that any excellent doctor would have thought to do? That *you* would have thought to do?"

It took David a moment to find his voice. His right hand instinctively went to his wedding band, which he still wore. "Yes," he finally said. "You did."

Don took a bite of banana and David felt his impatience growing as he waited for him to chew and swallow. Don gestured with his hand, the banana peel flopping over his thumb. "Let's just give the devil his due, all right?"

Too disgusted to respond, David walked back toward the CWA. In the hall, Diane was talking Carson through the process of putting a shoulder back in joint, letting him use her arm to practice the motion. David passed the nearest doorway and saw a young man in a UCLA tank top on the gurney inside, cradling his right arm, the shoulder clearly out of joint. If the kid knew the medical student resetting his arm was practicing the gesture for the first time two feet from his line of sight, he probably would've gotten up and walked out of the building.

"I hear you ducked out of tying sutures again this morning, Dr. Donalds," David said.

Carson looked up sheepishly. "The kid was a little uneasy. I didn't want to cart out a big needle or anything and freak him out."

"Oh. So you used Dermabond for *his* benefit."

"Exactly."

David pointed at him, mock authoritatively. "You're going to be my first professional embarrassment if you don't learn to stitch by the end of this rotation. Next windshield job we get in here, you're tying every last suture."

Carson gloomily returned to practicing on Diane's arm. David saw her cringe when he rotated it too briskly, and felt a fresh wave of sympathy for the injured kid. Hands-on training. Despite its drawbacks, the only way to train doctors.

When David swung into the CWA, Don was fielding questions and folders from a flurry of clerks and nurses. Pat was holding Don's arm a little too firmly, her face drawn tight. "I *really* think you should give Lembeck in Three something for the pain."

Don tapped Pat's shoulder with the chart and gave her a brief smile. "If you want to fly the plane, you really oughta be a pilot." Using the chart, he pushed her gently toward the door. "We need a vaginitis whiff test in Exam Eight."

"Carson told the wrong Martinez she was pregnant," one of the clerks said.

"I did not," Carson yelled from the hall.

"Poor girl was only fifteen." The clerk imitated a girl's crying voice: "But I only kissed him," he wailed.

"Jesus," Don said. "Always double-check the Martinezes and the Ramirezes. They all lo—" He caught David's glare and cut off his sentence midthought.

Jill appeared before David out of nowhere. "Houston, we have a problem. Gunshot wound in Four. He claims he has no insurance and would like to pay in cash."

"A GSW?" She nodded, and David quickened his pace to keep up with her. "Location of the wound?"

She swung open the door, revealing a man with a clean-shaven head, lying facedown in a gown on the gurney. He did not look up.

"Rear end," Jill said.

CHAPTER 9

WHEN David closed the door, the man rolled onto his side and regarded him with red, mouselike eyes. Though his scalp was shaven clean, David could see from his eyebrows and the tint of the stubble that he was a redhead. The Kinko's hero.

"What's your position here?" he asked.

"Why?" David said. "Am I in trouble?"

"Are you the attending?"

"I am." David picked up the chart, noticing much of it was blank. "And you are . . . ?"

The man glanced nervously at the closed door. "Ed Pinkerton."

"Ed Pinkerton," David said, writing it down. "That'll do."

"Look, I had an accident cleaning my gun and shot myself."

"In the ass?"

"Yes. In the ass. I would prefer that we handle this quickly, and with as few people as possible. Getting through the press outside made me nervous enough."

"Depending on how deeply that bullet is lodged, I may have to call surgery."

Ed swung his legs down, leaning heavily on his hands to keep the weight off his rear end, and found his feet. "I'm sorry," he said. "Maybe this wasn't such a good idea."

He grabbed his shirt from the chair and started putting it on. The shirt had been covering a red book. The title caught David's eye—*Wiretapping and Electronic Surveillance*. A bookmark with a logo that appeared to be a brain protruded from between the pages. Ed quickly draped his pants over the book, hiding it again.

David went to rest a hand on Ed's shoulder, then thought better of it. "Listen," he said, "let me take a look. Maybe I can handle it down here."

Ed held his eyes for a moment, as if deciding whether he could trust him. "You won't call PD?"

"I'm vaguely familiar with your history," David said. "This was a gruesome copy accident, correct?"

Ed grimaced. "A day at Kinko's gone terribly awry." His skin was almost impossibly pale; the blue cubital veins forked through the soft underside of his forearm like roads on a map. Ed studied the ceiling for a moment. "I won't bullshit you," he finally said. "I'm on parole, and I've been making good for me and my little girl. I shouldn't have gotten involved the way I did, breaking up that robbery. I wanted to protect the workers in there, but I don't know how this'll play to my PO. It'll probably be fine, given the eyewitnesses and all, but I'm not eager to find out. I'd appreciate your help here."

David studied his face, searching for signs of dishonesty. He decided he liked what he saw. "If I report the gunshot wound, you're going to limp out of here before the cops show up. Given that your injury was sustained on the right side of the law, I'd rather have you walk out upright." He nodded once, slowly. "Deal?"

Ed ran a hand over his bald scalp. "Deal."

He lay back down and David parted the gown in the

back and examined the wound. "Someone's been prying at this," David said.

"My buddy got the slug out with a pair of snub-nosed pliers."

"A .38?"

"Yeah. But it wasn't a full slug."

"How can you tell?"

Ed looked up at him, blank-faced.

"Okay," David said. "Stupid question. So we're dealing with fragments."

David spread the wound slightly to examine it, and Ed didn't so much as flinch. David removed a blanket from a cupboard and tossed it to Ed. "I'm going to have to get you down to fluoroscopy."

"Is it on this floor?"

"Yes." David kicked the foot paddle on the gurney to the right, releasing the brake, and slowly backed the gurney out the door. Lying on his side, Ed pulled the blanket up tight to his chin so it blocked most of his face, and turned his head into the pillow.

David signaled Diane to follow him when he wheeled Ed past the CWA, and she came quickly, tapping a chart against her thigh. He immediately noted the firm set of her mouth. "What's the problem?"

"Fifty-five-year-old Greek woman came in with some acute anxiety. I'd like to hold her until she settles but her insurance won't cover it." Diane looked down at the gurney as it rolled along, noticing Ed for the first time. "Hello."

Ed nodded, a brief movement of his half-buried head.

David took the chart from Diane and glanced it over. He pulled a pen from behind his ear, crossed out *acute anxiety*, and wrote *acute shortness of breath with a secondary diagnosis of anxiety*. He handed the chart back to Diane and winked at her. "Problem solved."

They banged through some double doors and weaved their way through the labyrinthine corridors of Level B.

"One of the great advantages of ER medicine is our freedom to exercise our own discretion." David glanced down at Ed. "Isn't that right, Mr. Pinkerton?"

Ed's beady eyes watched him with amusement from the Ewok swathing of the sheets.

"Not always," Diane said. "The Director of Health Sciences Communications just issued a memo to all employees reminding us of the 'long-standing policy that all media interaction is to be conducted through the HSC office.' "

David whistled. "The board must be leaning pretty hard."

"Having lye flying around probably provides a good pucker factor," Ed said.

David banked the gurney right into the fluoroscopy suite, and he and Diane donned leads to protect themselves from the radiation. He positioned Ed on his back, swung the X-ray arm over his right buttock, and stared at the small screen of the monitor. The two bullet fragments stood out white against the gray bones, just medial to the head of the femur.

"You were right," David said. "Two frags."

From the look on Diane's face, she had put together the patient with the news story. She took a moment to grab the silver forceps David was offering her.

"The wound is superficial enough that I think we can handle it here," David said. "A lot of tissue protecting the bone back there. Does it hurt?"

"It's not pleasant." Though beads of sweat dotted Ed's bare scalp, his face showed no sign of pain. When Diane inserted the metal forceps into the wound and angled down toward the first bullet fragment, they too showed up white on the monitor.

David directed Diane with a gesture, then indicated

how she could hold the forceps for better control. She followed his instructions perfectly, her tongue poking out her cheek in a point.

"How old are you, Mr. Pinkerton?" David asked.

"Thirty-nine."

"Have you been screened for prostate cancer?"

"If this is an excuse for giving me a rectal, I don't date doctors." Ed's first grimace lit his face as Diane dug deeper with the forceps. "No," he said. "I haven't."

Diane glanced up at David, one eyebrow raised in an unasked question. Probably wondering why he was raising the issue when prostate screening usually didn't start until age fifty. "Any family history?" David asked.

"No."

"Well, sometime in the next few years, you might want to get checked out. Think of it as the fifty-thousand-mile tune-up on your car."

The first bloody bullet fragment plunked down on the metal tray. Biting her lip, Diane eased the forceps back in the wound.

Ed's hand clenched into a fist, then released. "I'll bear that in mind," he said.

The curtains separating the five exam areas in Exam Fifteen rippled each time a gurney zipped by. After wheeling Ed behind the fourth curtain to get bandaged, his chart balanced across the bumps of his feet, David had been pulled into the next section, Fifteen-Three, by an imploring Persian mother to examine her little girl.

With a broad, smiling face and brown, almost liquid eyes, the girl ran circles in the small space between the curtains, singing, her jarring footsteps causing her voice to vacillate as if she were yodeling. She stopped, swaying on her feet, and laughed. Her mother drew her back against her legs, ruffling her hair, then wet a finger and wiped a smudge off the girl's cheek.

David removed his white coat so as not to intimidate the girl, and crouched so he was eye level. Meeting her on her own terms.

Following his cue, the little girl squatted also. David laughed. "No, hon, you don't have to crouch. I'm just trying to get a better look at you."

After an openmouthed burst of laughter, the little girl fell down and sat Indian-style. With one hand on the floor, David eased himself down so he too was sitting, his legs kicked awkwardly to the sides. The girl's mother covered her mouth to hide her smile. The girl laughed again and grabbed his hand with both of hers.

David slid the stethoscope from his shoulders and around his neck with a single practiced movement, spreading the branch with one hand and wiggling his head until the earplugs settled correctly. There was always some comfort in feeling the heavy instrument fall into place, like a well-worn wallet sliding into a back pocket. "I'm just going to—"

"Dr. Spier?"

David turned to see Officer Jenkins and another, older officer standing behind him. "This is a private exam area," David said, scrambling to his feet and feeling more than a little foolish. "Your sister has been moved to—"

"We received a call about a gunshot wound," Jenkins said.

"You did?" Beneath the curtain beside them, David saw Ed Pinkerton's feet hit the floor. "I don't recall calling one in."

"You didn't. We were contacted by triage. You know, you're required by law to—"

"I know, I know. Do you handle all calls involving the hospital?"

"You might say I've taken a particular interest."

"I can understand that."

The older officer, Jenkins's partner, stepped forward, and David noticed two stripes and a star on his sleeve. His name tag read: BRONNER. "We need to question the patient," Bronner said gruffly. "The one who sustained the GSW."

Ed's foot disappeared and came back down ensconced in an untied shoe.

"Why don't you follow me out to the CWA?" David said. "We'll check the board and see where he is." David crouched near the girl, and she followed his lead again, laughing. He smiled. "I'll be right back."

The officers followed him silently down Hallway One into the Central Work Area. David perused the board, finding Ed Pinkerton's name. "Fifteen-Four," he said. "Looks like he was one curtain over from us."

The cops exchanged a look, which David pretended not to notice. Another silent walk back to Exam Fifteen. David pointed to the curtain to the fourth exam area. "Behind there."

The curtain rattled on its pegs as Jenkins swiped it aside. An empty gurney. A single spot of blood stood out on the sheets. David feigned exasperation. "I don't know . . . I never discharged him. He must've snuck out on us." He turned to the officers, letting his hands slap to his sides. "I don't know what to tell you."

Jenkins clenched his jaw, speaking through his teeth. "This patient was one curtain over and you didn't know it?"

"There are a lot of patients here under my care. It's sometimes difficult to keep track of them all."

Jenkins held David's gaze. "Right."

"Sorry about that."

"Word around the station is you're not always the biggest team player."

"I guess that depends what team."

Bronner tapped Jenkins on the back. "This is a jerk-off," he said. "Let's go."

Jenkins didn't seem ready to leave.

"You know we don't give a shit about the GSW," Bronner said. "C'mon."

Jenkins took a step back. "I'll see you around, Doctor."

David nodded, and Jenkins followed his senior partner out. David realized he'd been holding his breath, and he exhaled deeply.

A slip of paper beneath the empty gurney caught David's attention, and he bent to pick it up. It was the bookmark he'd noticed earlier marking Ed's place in the small red book. A sketch of a brain, evidently a logo, decorated the top, the cerebral hemispheres slightly misshapen. AMOK BOOKSTORE was written beneath it in an odd Aztec print. David's eyes traced down the length of the bookmark, finding the strange motto at the bottom. THE EXTREMES OF INFORMATION.

He knew before he glanced beneath the turned-back sheets that Ed's chart was missing.

CHAPTER 10

THE men with their tattoos and glistening muscles worked among the weight machines, pretending not to notice the onlookers, who clustered with their Muscle Beach T-shirts, shooting pictures and herding children. The first weight of dusk had settled through the air, but storefront lights illuminated the men through the chain-link fences that set the weight area apart from the Venice Boardwalk and the beach beyond.

Clyde watched from the anonymity of the crowd, a face among other faces, another body sweating in the August night. He had only recently begun to emerge from his apartment again, and he still found the brief stirrings of breeze to be invasive. Inside the pen, a bald man with a pointed goatee and two hoop earrings broke protocol, turning to the onlookers and spreading his massive arms wide. The prongs of his triceps gripped the undersides of his arms like claws. The crowd erupted with noise; cameras flashed.

Clyde looked down at his own arms. White and fleshy. In front of him, an overweight little boy with a cardboard-stiff baseball cap pushed up on tiptoes. Kobe Bryant slam-dunked in faded purple and yellow on the back of his T-shirt. The boy's hands, red and sticky with the remnants of some summertime snack, pushed and clutched at the shirts in front of him, leaving colored smudges.

An enormous black man lined large metal disks on each side of a weight bar until it bowed under the weight. He sat on the edge of the bench press, crossing his arms in front of him. The crack of his shoulders was audible even over the noise of the crowd. He leaned back, taking the bar from the cradle, bringing it to his chest, and hammering it back up in the air with triumphant grunts.

Standing in the crowd, a face among faces, Clyde watched the man labor and imitated his grunts, softly at first, then growing louder. He didn't realize he could be overheard until a blonde in front of him turned, eyes aglitter with sparkling makeup, and stifled a giggle with a hand. He looked quickly away from her eyes, staring silently at the gum-dotted pavement, and she whispered something to a friend before turning her attention back to the muscular men. Clyde's hand found the key around his neck, his thumb working it over like a rabbit's foot.

Gradually, his eyes lifted from the pavement, studying first the blonde's straw-bottomed clog that raised her foot so her ankle flexed, then the split sheath of her capri pant leg, which embraced the pink cylinder of her calf. Her bottom, firm and rounded, protruded abruptly from beneath her blouse. He leaned forward until he could smell her hair spray. He leaned forward until he was pushing up against her full behind, a face among faces in the press of a crowd.

Her thin shoulder blade pushed back ever so slightly into his soft chest as she jockeyed for space, not yet aware that his jostling was directed. Ahead, the weights clinked against each other; the men strained and flexed. His breathing quickened, taking on a faint groaning. Her neck firmed with realization. Her head started to pivot, slowed with shock.

Before the eyes could reach him, Clyde turned and pushed through the crowd, head lowering on the wide stalk of his neck, hands sinking into his pockets. People spread and closed behind him.

"Fucking pervert!" she yelled from somewhere in the crowd. She yelped, a short hiccup of disgust and fear. "You fucking sicko! God*dam*n it!"

Clyde left the lights of the boardwalk behind and threaded through the darkening streets and alleys. The ocean breeze had left a staleness on everything—cardboard boxes slumping curbside, rusting hoods of abandoned cars, the soft, rotting wood around doorjambs. He slid his thumb across his filmy fingertips, the motion growing quicker and quicker until his hand was a blur.

He stepped onto Main Street and joined a current of people at a crosswalk. An old blue Civic had pulled too far into the intersection, blocking the crosswalk, and the woman sat foolishly at the wheel as the stream of pedestrians split around her car. His footsteps grew firmer as he approached, the bustle of people flowing all around him. With a grimace, he altered his step when he reached the car.

His hand flew forward, smashing palm down on the blue hood. The woman jerked back in her seat. He stood perfectly still, leaning toward the windshield, glowering, the front license plate hitting him midshin. Fear replaced shock in the woman's face, and she opened her mouth, but then caught a closer look at his red-rimmed eyes, the angry heaving of his chest. Her mouth dangled open, like that of a broken doll's.

The crowd continued to move around the car, people glancing and then moving on or not even noticing him at all. And suddenly he was gone, a dying whisk of movement, the sweaty imprint of his hand slowly evanescing from the metal of the hood.

CHAPTER 11

SHIFTING the stack of files in his lap, David lay back on the exam table he'd adjusted like a chaise longue, propping his feet on one of the gynecologic stirrups. He continued with his paperwork, enjoying the quiet serenity of Exam One.

Diane barged in, startling him. "Oh sorry. Didn't realize you were . . . What are you still doing here?"

David checked his watch: 21:25. He hadn't realized he'd been there for an hour and a half after his shift ended. He was accustomed to working late, preferring the excitement of the ER to the solitude of his too-large house, but it alarmed him how quickly the habit had grown. Arriving a few hours early, leaving later and later, shouldering extra days on call—anything to avoid reconstructing a personal life without Elisabeth. His house was quickly becoming a million-dollar stopping place between shifts.

He looked at the paperwork before him. Nothing important, nothing pressing. Exhaustion pooled through him all at once, jumbling his thoughts. He squeezed the bridge of his nose. When he released it, he was touched by the concern in Diane's eyes.

"I don't know," he said. His stomach grumbled so loudly both he and Diane glanced at it.

"Come on," Diane said. "Let me buy you dinner."

A hospital cafeteria is a depressing place at night. Spouses with vacant, grief-haunted eyes, children pulling IV poles, parents slurping inconsolably on tepid coffee, the sleepless hours gathering in half-moons beneath their eyes. Their lethargy draws a sharp contrast with the bustle of the interns and nurses in scrubs. But even the grieving and the dying have to eat.

David stared at the food on his tray—a Milky Way, a half-eaten chicken sandwich, a small container of apple juice. Diane bit into an apple and shrugged. "What did you expect on a resident's salary?"

"This is perfect," David said. "I wouldn't have made it any farther afield without falling on my face." He studied his reflection in the back of a spoon. "Jesus, maybe I should check myself in."

"You don't look *that* bad. Mrs. Peters still swooned when you checked her eyes this afternoon."

"She's ninety years old. With glaucoma."

"She told me she thinks you look like George Clooney."

David pursed his lips to keep from smiling. "And what did you say?"

Diane twirled her straw in her Coke. "I told her no one looks like George Clooney."

"True," David said. "True."

Diane cocked her head slightly, amused. "I'd bet you were a great womanizer before you got married."

He shook his head.

"No? Why not?"

He shrugged. "I guess I liked women too much." He fished a crumb of some sort from his apple juice and wiped it on the tray. "And I married young."

"What did your wife look like?"

A web of images entangled him. A white snowball smudge on her winter sweater. The first movement of her face in the morning, sleep-heavy and gentle. His hands lifting her wedding veil. He imagined her the night of their fifteenth anniversary. The twin strokes of her hips beneath a sleek black dress. They'd gone to a gallery opening in Venice where Elisabeth, as the *LA Times* art critic, had been fawned over by dealers and struggling artists alike. After a few hours, David had snuck her off to Shutters in Santa Monica, where they'd sat out on the balcony of their hotel room, holding hands, listening to the waves rush the shore in the darkness.

"Her smile made me weak," he said.

"David . . ."—Diane looked away— ". . . am I delusional in thinking there's something going on between us?"

"Positively schizophrenic. It must be your Yale education."

"It's a tough question to ask. Why don't you answer it seriously?"

"You're right," he said. "I'm sorry." He pried at the hard bun of his chicken sandwich as if he'd developed a sudden intense interest in baked goods.

"The few times we've been out . . ." Diane squeezed one hand with the other. "For the life of me, I can't figure out if they're dates or just an attending and a resident talking shop outside work. I mean, we're alone . . . we're at dinner . . . but we're talking about lesions and contusion fractures."

"An attending and a resident," he repeated.

"Well?"

"We've worked side by side, hands in the mud, for—what?"

"Almost three years."

"Three years now. You're one of the best residents I've ever had the pleasure to train. I consider you a colleague. Not a resident."

The glimmer of a smile cut through the discomfort on Diane's face, just for a moment. "I didn't know that," she said. "But it still doesn't answer my question."

"Look . . ." David realized his voice was shaking ever so slightly. "I've definitely thought about . . . but we can't. . . . I can't. . . ."

"Why not?"

He leaned back in his chair, trying to find what he wanted to say. "Diane, I'm almost twice your age."

"I'm thirty-one and you're forty-three. That's nothing. Elizabeth Taylor has married men twenty years younger."

"She doesn't have the same performance anxieties, I'd imagine."

Diane played with her straw some more, poking at ice cubes. "All right," she finally said, with a slight hint of humor. "Why don't we make a deal? I won't call you on your lame-ass excuses, but when we do overlap socially, no more talk of lesions and contusion fractures."

She extended her hand across the table and he shook it, mock formally, before settling back in his chair. He crossed his arms and fought off a grin. "So what's your middle name?" he asked.

"Allison."

"You like dogs or cats?"

"Dogs."

"What's your favorite kind of lesion?" She scowled at him, and he held up his hands defensively. "Just kidding. What do your folks do? Are they doctors?"

"We don't *all* come from high-powered medical families. Not all our fathers have grand rounds auditoriums named after them."

"It was named for my mother, actually," David said.

Diane whistled. "What was it like growing up in *that* house?"

"A lot of pimping at the dinner table. Name the eight bones of the wrist. The twelve cranial nerves. The five components of the Apgar score." He tilted his head. "My mother was chief of staff here at the NPI from '60 to '71, and she recruited a lot of the world's preeminent physicians—in all fields—to come lecture and teach at the Med Center. It wasn't uncommon for a few Nobel Prize–winning physicians to show up for dinner. The instructors and department heads that came through . . . it was truly amazing."

"Who was the better doctor, your mother or your father?"

"It's tough to say. They were in pretty divergent fields. My mother was a psychiatrist, my father a neurologist. My father passed away when I was young. Prostate cancer."

"That's why you asked Pinkerton about a prostate checkup today even though he was only thirty-nine?"

"We all have our pet illnesses, I suppose." David's

mind followed some flight of reason, and he found himself saying, "My mother just went in '99."

Diane nodded, and he was grateful she didn't offer any platitudes. He'd wanted to share the information with her, not elicit sympathy.

A man in a wheelchair rolled slowly past, tray cradled on his atrophied knees.

"My mother was a tough woman. All fire and ambition. I never saw her crack. Not once." David drew his hand down across his face, like a window blind. "When she was in her late sixties, she headed up the Disciplinary Review Board here. She had to call a young male nephrologist into her office to confront him about a claim made against him by a young woman. When she reprimanded him, he rose, locked the door, and beat the shit out of her. Broke two ribs." He watched Diane's slender eyebrows rise and spread. "The only thing my mother was upset about afterward was her lack of medical judgment in not being able to predict she was dealing with an unstable man." He set both hands on his tray and pushed it slightly away. "*That* was my mother."

"A lot to live up to?"

"A lot of people spend their lives trying to overcome their upbringing. I spent mine trying to fulfill it."

"And have you?"

"My mother was pretty disappointed when I decided to enter Emergency Medicine."

"Why's that?"

"If a surgeon is a glorified carpenter, an ER doc is a glorified carpenter with an inferiority complex." He laughed. "As you know, it's generally not considered the most cerebral field."

"Your mother might have thought different if she'd seen you in action," she said. Her eyes quickly lowered. "Pardon my schoolgirlish fervor."

"Medicine was a different thing back then. As has often been said—doctors of my parents' generation were the first for whom medicine was a science and the last for whom it was an art." Pulling a napkin from the dispenser, he wiped all the crumbs on the table into a neat line. "My mother never really forgave me for entering ER. As if it were a slight against her. My father wouldn't have minded, I don't think—he and I were always quite close. He was a charming, handsome man. Tall and broad. When I was a kid, he used to tell me I was the kind of person he wanted to be when he grew up." David smiled at the memory. Suddenly self-conscious, he looked up at Diane. Her blond hair was down across her eyes in front, and she brushed it aside.

"Jesus, I'm sorry," he said. "Talking about myself all night. I guess it's been awhile since I've talked. Openly."

His hands were folding the napkin in neat squares, and she reached out and stilled them.

Leaving the cafeteria, David averted his eyes from the large bas-relief letters over the double doors to the right, as was his habit. He did not have to look to know what they read: SPIER AUDITORIUM. The name hovered overhead, as it did everywhere throughout the hospital.

Speaking into a walkie-talkie, one of the new security guards breezed by with a female nurse, presumably escorting her to her car. David was glad to see that more precautions were indeed being taken after the assault on Nancy.

A Mexican woman quietly worked a mop across the lobby floor, bringing the tile to a polished shine. Behind her, a chemotherapy-bald boy ran out of the hospital gift shop, stuffing a stolen Snickers in his pocket. The hefty register lady thundered after him, all but shaking her fist.

Good for you, kid, David thought. Run, Forrest, run.

He trudged down to his car, passing a few security guards on the way, and headed lethargically for home. He was glad to see the news vans had finally cleared out. On to the next tragedy, the next big story. Just past San Vicente, David pulled into a corner Shell station, swiped his credit card through the slot, and started to fill up his tank.

While the gas pumped, he sat in the car, his mind playing through the cases of the day, picking at them from all angles to see if he'd made any mistakes. His mind kept returning to Diane, and from there, to Elisabeth.

There is no way to predict an embolus. A perfectly healthy thirty-five-year-old, not even into middle age, no family history of disease, no hypertension, no diabetes, no vascular disease. One day she throws a clot, it lodges in her basilar artery, and for seventeen crucial minutes the brain is denied blood. Seventeen crucial minutes are enough to suck a loving, intelligent woman dry of thought and emotion, to leave her a living husk. Sometimes it takes less time than that.

David had been the chief attending the night Elisabeth had been wheeled in—sick call on his birthday—so, knowing his medical judgment would be impaired, he'd let Don Lambert take lead. Of the first few hours in the ER, he remembered only scurrying bodies and the thick numbness of his tongue. Awhile later, his wife had lain in a limp recline upstairs in the MICU, the sheets humped over her inert body.

The pattern of her gown had been repetitious and infantile, pale blue snowflakes on a white background. David recalled certain images vividly—the drops of urine inching dumbly along her Foley catheter like items on an assembly line; the hum of the ventilator pushing air down the endotracheal tube and through the snarl of plastic into her throat; her thin gown wrinkling slightly as her chest rose and fell, rose and fell.

They'd EEG'd her promptly at David's request, his legs trembling beneath his scrubs. It had shown no activity at all, no wave forms. A still sea.

She'd been tracheotomied and G-tubed, the monitor showing sound vitals. Her body was stable. A perfect life-support system for a dead brain.

Elisabeth had signed a living will. David had maintained his composure, perhaps due to the fact that he was a physician practiced in high-intensity, emotional decision-making, but more likely because he'd seen too many times the other roads that lay ahead. They'd given him some time alone with her body before removing her from life support.

He'd sat in a typical bedside post—leaning forward in the padded chair, chin resting on the union of his fists. He remembered being struck anew by how different the MICU was from the sunken B Level of the ER, in which nurses and doctors scurried among the wounded like industrious ants. The unit exuded a calm, almost peaceful air. Here it was easy to forget that one moved among the sick and dying. The scents were better contained, the nurses more personable, the floors and walls better scrubbed.

Elisabeth's skin had been pale and smooth, like porcelain. Her arm had protruded from the papery cuff of her gown, her skin gray against the white sheets. Her simple wedding band provided the only stroke of color against her flesh.

David had flattened his hand across her forehead and studied her eyes, but he'd seen nothing in them but the faintest flicker of his own reflection. It had taken him only a few moments to determine that Elisabeth's presence did not reside in her body any more than it did in the hospital room.

He had not been moved to tears. He had not been sure

what he'd been expecting, but it hadn't been the cold nothingness in his wife's eyes.

The neurologist had been waiting outside the door. He'd rested a hand on David's shoulder. "Are you ready?" he'd asked.

"I'm not going to stay," David had said.

The nurses and doctors on the floor had seemed surprised by how briskly he'd left.

As David had driven home, the first edge of morning had leaked over the horizon, imbuing the air with a dreamlike quality. He'd pulled into the garage, removed his shoes, and stood motionless in the foyer for a full minute.

It hadn't been until he'd walked down the long hallway and sat on their large empty bed that he'd broken down. His hands had started shaking first, then his arms, and then he'd wept softly and erratically, his wife's pillow pressed between his hands.

A blaring horn on Wilshire brought David back from his thoughts. He put the car in drive and pulled away, but slammed on the brakes when he heard an awful metallic clunk. He got back out and picked up the broken gas handle from the ground; he'd pulled away with the handle still in the tank and torn it cleanly off.

He walked slowly back to the well-lit booth.

"I'll bill the usual account," the attendant said.

David managed a weak nod. "That'll be fine."

CHAPTER 12

CLYDE woke up a few minutes past three, though he'd been squirming in the sheets since two, his scrub bottoms twisting around his legs. The pillow, smudged with sweat, had claimed a few more strands of his hair. His wide feet pattered across the dirty floor to the bathroom. He pissed heavily for nearly a full minute, splattering the toilet seat, which he'd neglected to raise.

A rind of soap clogged the sink drain. He picked up a plastic McDonald's cup from the floor—filled and drank, filled and drank, filled and drank. He avoided his reflection in the medicine cabinet mirror when he swung it open. A box of orange lozenges remained half-full. He popped two from the foil sheet and sucked them hungrily, working up saliva to swish around in his mouth.

Opening another can of cat food, Clyde added it to the slop overflowing the bowl, scaring up a swirl of flies. Pacing around the small apartment, bits of cheese and crumbs sticking to the bottoms of his feet, he smoked two cigarettes simultaneously, which seemed to quicken his step. He covered his eyes with the heels of his hands, his breathing intensifying until his chest heaved up and down. Climbing into bed, he pulled the dirty sheets up to his chin. He ground the orange lozenges into a paste and swallowed it.

He lowered the sheets and sat up, staring at the footlocker at the base of the table. It lay open, rolls of gauze visible among the glistening medical equipment. A container of DrainEze sat out, casting a solitary shadow on the scarred tabletop. He struck his head with the flats of his hands. A few more strands of hair came out, stuck to his sweaty palms.

A frightened whine started in the back of his throat and rose to a deep bellow. He stood up and shuffled through the mound of dirty clothes to the far wall. He'd stolen a snapdragon from the retarded home, potted it badly in a soggy ice-cream carton, and set it in the corner. Now, he pushed the plant to one side, revealing a disused heating vent. He fumbled in his pockets and removed a money clip. A cheap Mexican design with two fake-turquoise horses rearing on a hammered brass nub, the money clip hid a thin penknife in its side. He dug the knife open with a dirty nail, then slid the blade behind the edge of the vent for leverage.

The surrounding wall crumbled a bit when he pulled the vent out, and Clyde stared reverently at the solitary bottle of pills before touching it. The bottle was unmarked, the pharmacist's label removed and the underlying gum scraped off with a fingernail. He tapped three pale yellow capsules into his palm and took them there on his knees, swallowing them without water. Before returning to bed, he replaced the vent and the plant.

Lying back, he closed his eyes. "Three, two, one," he murmured. "Step back from the door. Three, two, one, step back from the door back from the door back from the—"

Tears pushed their way out under his eyelids, streaking down his temples to the pillow. His hands pushed and clawed at the sheets, fisted and loosened. Finally, he sat up, the key swaying from his ball-chain necklace like a pendant.

Throwing the sheets aside, he crossed quickly to the table, seized the container of DrainEze, and hurled it into the footlocker with such force it nearly bounced out. Slamming the lid shut, he fisted the key and yanked, his necklace breaking easily. His hands were shaking so severely, it took him several tries to slide the key into each of the smooth circular locks, but finally he had the footlocker secured.

Storming across the musty room, he slid the window open with a grunt, tore the screen from its pegs, and hurled the key outside. It bounced once on concrete and lost itself in the strip of thick weedy grass beside the sidewalk.

The beads of sweat that had formed on his forehead were starting to run, stinging his eyes. He dashed to the heat vent again, skinning his bare knees as he slid, and pulled aside the snapdragon, his fat fingers digging into the soft plaster around the vent. He dug two more capsules from the translucent orange bottle and swallowed them. He had the bottle back in its hiding place and the vent pushed into the wall when he tore it aside again, unscrewed the bottle, and swallowed two more pills.

He went to the bathroom and urinated again, then drank three more glasses of water and got back into bed. His fingers tapped his chest several times, lightly, where the key usually rested. His breathing quickened into an animal's whine. He got back up and stood at the window, forehead and hands pressed to the pane, eyes searching the weedy strip below.

Within the hour, he was out hunting on his hands and knees, the beam of his flashlight playing like a small beacon through the tall blades of grass.

CHAPTER 13

CLYDE parked at a metered spot on Le Conte and walked up toward the Medical Plaza, turning so the construction workers across the street couldn't make out his face. He wore scrubs and a loose gray sweatshirt. His scrub bottoms, like most, had a hidden pocket inside the waist on the left side, a simple stitched flap of fabric designed to keep credit cards or prescription pads safe from grabbing hands and aortal spurts. Clyde had wedged his money clip inside.

One of his hands was hidden beneath the sweatshirt, causing it to bulge. He tugged on the bill of his blank navy-blue corduroy hat, pulling it low so it shadowed his features. The early-morning air was crisp, though there was little breeze.

Ducking behind some foliage near the PCHS lot, he watched the attendants in the kiosks about thirty yards away. For the most part, they kept their eyes on the cash registers and the incoming cars, paying little attention to the walkway that sloped down to the ambulance bay. Located at the rear of the small underground parking area, the actual entrance to the ER was not visible from street level.

A security guard emerged and headed up the walkway, whistling, his eyes on the bushes to his right. He reached the top of the slope and turned into the covered section of the PCHS lot, the section that led back into the hospital. There were no news vans in sight.

Clyde's latex-gloved hand emerged from beneath his sweatshirt, holding a Pyrex beaker, its gradations marked in white. It held a blue viscid liquid. Breathing heavily, he removed the foil covering, balled it up, and tossed it into the gutter. It rolled a few feet before falling down a sewer grate. Clyde withdrew back into the bushes, hidden by a cluster of palm fronds, and used his cheap digital watch to time the security guard's patrol.

It took the guard five minutes and twenty-four seconds to walk a full loop through the hospital and reappear. The guard emerged from the ambulance bay again, heading up the walkway, head swiveling like a dog tracking prey.

Pressing the beaker of alkali to his stomach, Clyde crouched in the bushes, waiting for the security guard to disappear once again into the larger lot. Then, mopping his forehead with the sleeve of his sweatshirt, he stepped from the bushes. The rise and fall of his chest quickened.

He walked casually past the kiosk, keeping his eyes on the ground. A harried woman was loudly voicing her objections to the parking rates, pulled up so the black-and-white striped arm nearly rested across the hood of her Taurus. Neither of the parking attendants noticed Clyde.

One hand staying beneath his sweatshirt, Clyde shuffle-stepped down the walkway into the subterranean ambulance bay, careful not to sway too much. Three rivulets of sweat arced down his left cheek. At the bottom of the ramp, two ambulances had been left deserted along the curb. He slid between them and the wall.

A couple lingered by their car in the parking slots across the ambulance bay, and Clyde pressed his cheek against the cold metal side of the ambulance until their engine turned over. His breath came quick and pressured, like a sprinter's. The car chugged up the ramp toward the open sky and disappeared from sight.

The ambulance bay was silent.

The automatic glass doors to the ER stood about fifteen yards to his left. He watched the doors and waited, trying to get his breathing under control. He had about three more minutes before the security guard would reappear. He held the Pyrex beaker with both hands, gripping it so tightly his knuckles whitened. The blue liquid lapped up the sides as his hands trembled.

A sudden noise as the ER doors pushed open. He ducked, peering through the ambulance windows. The driver-side window was down, and the ambulance interior smelled of pine disinfectant.

An Asian woman emerged from the doors, her clogs echoing off the enclosed walls. She wore blue scrubs.

Clyde's nostrils flared as he drew breath. His eyes were dark and flat, stones smoothed in a river's bed. He did not blink.

Pulling a cigarette from a pack she kept hidden in the inside breast pocket of her scrub top, she lit it and inhaled deeply, throwing her head back. An indulgent moan accompanied her exhalation.

His pounding footsteps alarmed her. The lighter dropped on the asphalt and bounced up, almost knee-high. Her face spread in a scream and both arms went up, intercepting most of the blue liquid. A spurt found its way through, dousing the left side of her face as she turned. She yelped and fell over, her palms slapping the asphalt.

Clyde pulled to a stop right above her and watched, head cocked. Gasping, she kept her eyes squeezed shut, evidently unaware that the alkali had struck only the side of her head. Her arms and legs scrabbled on the ground. She found a knee, then her feet, and then she ran back toward the ER doors, arms flailing blindly in front of her.

Clyde tossed the Pyrex beaker aside. It bounced twice but remained stubbornly intact. Walking briskly back to the ambulance, he removed his sweatshirt, revealing a worn scrub top. He threw the sweatshirt through the open ambulance window, aiming for the back, then pulled off his corduroy hat and tucked it in the band of his scrub bottoms so his top hung down over it. His pallid face tingled with a blend of horror and perverse gratification.

The woman ran into the wall a few feet to the left of the ER entrance and toppled over. She rose again, mouth down-twisted, chin slick with drool, and felt her way along the wall toward the doors, sobbing louder now. She kept her lips pressed tightly together, so her crying sounded muffled and throaty. Oddly, she still did not scream.

The doors swung open automatically before her hands could find them, and she stumbled through. Clyde followed her in silently as she navigated the small, deserted hall, so close behind her he could have stroked the soft fabric of her scrub top. She missed the turn and banged against one of the pay phones, knocking the receiver from its perch. She felt her way back to the open air as the dangling phone began to bleat.

He tried the stairwell door to the side of the pay phones. It was locked and did not budge. He returned to his position behind her, a running back floating behind a blocker. She fumbled forward, her breathing harsh and rasping, that of a dying animal's. Her hand went to her face and came away with a clump of hair. Her shoulder struck the wall and she half turned, enough for him to see the white blisters rising in patches on the soft skin around her ear.

She stumbled through both sets of glass doors and collapsed on the lobby floor, wheezing. He stepped past her quickly before anyone noticed her. Someone screamed, and all at once the room was a whirlwind of scrubs, ringing phones, running patients. Putting his head down, he turned through the swinging doors into the ER proper and strode purposefully through the hallway.

Two nurses blew by, wheeling a gurney, then the security guard he'd observed outside ran past, shouting into his radio, "Call for all officers! Zones Two and Six! Call for all officers!"

A doctor dashed from an exam room, barely clipping his shoulder. Clyde glanced down just in time to notice his ID badge: DR. DAVID SPIER. Without so much as a backward glance, the doctor ran toward triage.

Keeping his eyes on the cheap tile, Clyde turned right at the radiology suite and threaded back into the huge maze of hospital corridors, leaving the commotion behind.

CHAPTER 14

DETECTIVE Yale signaled the ambulance to stop as it came down the ramp. The driver hit the brake, nonplussed. A criminologist snapped photographs by the curb and Dalton stepped around him and picked up the Pyrex beaker with his pen. It slid easily into the plastic bag another officer held open for him.

The paramedics struggled to offload the patient but were having difficulty yanking the gurney out uphill. A security guard appeared at the top of the ramp and gave them a hand. Yale pulled his arm away when David grabbed it. "You should've learned by now not to handle a police officer like that," Yale said.

David was impressed by the coolness of his eyes. "Sorry. I'm a little tense."

Another cop approached David immediately and thrust a clipboard at him. It carried a Crime Scene Attendance Log, and David signed it as he continued to address Yale. "You can't shut down this ambulance bay. It's an emergency entrance—it's imperative that we get patients down here and through those doors in a hurry."

The paramedics wheeled the gurney down the ramp, leaning back to slow it. An old woman wearing an oxygen mask sat up, gripping the metal rails, her eyes bulging almost comically. They passed Yale and David and were slowed by Dalton, who steered them wide of the scene, then through the doors, ensuring they didn't touch anything.

"I haven't shut anything down," Yale said. "But I can't have people contaminating the area. We need to preserve the integrity of the scene. Surely I don't have to explain to you that this is a serious matter we're dealing with."

"No more serious than having patients with acute conditions delayed en route to the ER."

"We'll see that the patients make it inside in timely fashion." Yale snapped his fingers at Dalton and pointed to the side of the parked ambulance. "Logical hiding place. Have Latent check the side of the vehicle for prints." He glanced at David's ID tag. "You be sure to inform me of any potentially violent patients who come in."

"I'll help as much as I can, but there are patient confidentiality issues," David said.

"There are people getting their faces burnt off." Yale turned away, raising a knuckle to his nose. His Rolex slid out from beneath his cuff; the smooth rotation of the second hand showed that it was real. Family money, no doubt. He couldn't afford that watch on a police detective's salary.

David stepped around Yale so he was facing him again. "Please get this ramp clear as soon as you can. We can't have patients going critical out here because you're putting a crime scene ahead of a medical emergency."

Yale sighed, putting on a weary expression. "Dr. Spier, we're just doing our best to cut down the number of patients you *do* get."

The morphine had mellowed Sandra out substantially, constricting her pupils and giving her limbs a lax, almost fluid flexibility when they moved. Diane clutched Sandra's soft unscarred hand as she poured water down over her blistering left forearm.

David crouched on the far side of Sandra's bed as Pat worked the left half of her face with a saline bottle. From his vantage, her profile was lovely. The smooth brown skin of her cheek, the soft line of her sternocleidomastoid, the arch of a penciled eyebrow. The contrast between the halves of her face was brutal. He did not want to rise from his crouch.

". . . couldn't see anything," Sandra continued, her voice a drone. "When I looked up, I just saw the stuff coming at me." She seemed oblivious to the people working industriously to repair her face. "But I knew it was him. I fell down, and I knew to make sure I kept my eyes squeezed shut."

Pat ducked her face behind a hand as a sniffle escaped her. Diane looked over, resting a hand on Pat's wrist. "We got it from here," she said softly. "Don't worry."

Pat turned, averting her face, and headed out of the exam room. She hurled the saline bottle as she exited, and it popped open when it struck the floor.

It was the first time David had seen her lose her temper.

". . . didn't want to scream," Sandra said. "Didn't want

to open my mouth so he could throw the stuff down my throat." A halting breath. "I don't want to be like Nancy." Her voice went high, and broke, so her next words were almost soundless. "Oh God. Oh God."

"You're all right." David wanted to stroke the unmarred side of her face, feel it soft beneath his fingers, but he did not. "Nothing went in your eyes or down your throat. You just sustained burns on one side of your face, which we have under control."

"It stung," Sandra said. "It stung so bad but I couldn't scream. I couldn't open my eyes." A single tear beaded at the pointed corner of her eye and streaked down her perfect cheek. David wiped its trail away with his thumb, wanting to keep the cheek pristine.

"Why did someone do this to me?" Her head rolled loosely to the right so she was facing him. The blistering had blown her cheek out of shape—a weeping, pitted bulge of ruby and white. Much of the hair had fallen from the side of her head. The flesh at the base of her ear had been eaten away, the divots pooling with serous fluid and saline. Her tragus was burnt down to a small nub.

David felt himself shot through with a burst of anger so sudden and intense it left him nauseous. He shook his head and laid the backs of his fingers across the unscathed skin of her forehead. "I don't know."

His legs were shaking when he rose from his crouch.

Dalton tossed the In-N-Out bag in Yale's lap. Yale quickly picked it up, trying to work a spot of grease out of his pants with a fingernail.

"Sorry," Dalton mumbled. He raised the remaining crescent of double cheeseburger to his mouth and angled it in.

Yale glanced inside the bag, closed it, and set it aside

on the bench. He stretched his legs, running his eyes around the grassy quad of the Medical Plaza.

A burly male patient in a hospital gown flirted with a nurse near the wide steps of the hospital entrance. He leaned in to whisper something to her, and she drew back slightly.

Dalton wiped his nose with his sleeve. "I took another look at the construction guys on Le Conte. Two of them have arm tattoos, but neither one resembles a skull. One of the guys is a parolee, got popped for a B and E in '96, but he's alibied three times over. Other guy's tat looked like jailhouse ink. I'm gonna run him, but he's also got a solid alibi."

"We're looking for a disorganized offender," Yale said. "He's smart enough to wear latex gloves, but discards evidence at the scene. I think he gets close to the victims by necessity—he's not sophisticated enough to figure out how to do dirty work from afar."

"I don't know about that. There's a hundred easier ways to fuck someone up." Dalton sighed. "It's just too bad neither vic got a good look."

Yale signaled to Dalton that he had a crumb on his cheek. "That could be something psychological, not just strategic." He pressed his fists together, lining up the knuckles. "Maybe there's another motivation to his not wanting to be seen. Maybe he's got some physical impairment he's ashamed of."

"Limp or something?"

Yale shook his head. "Probably not. Too memorable. Someone would've noticed—and remember, he's vanished into thin air twice. I'm thinking something less immediately visual. Something you only notice if you talk or interact with him. Glass eye. A lisp. Bad acne. Something. I think he doesn't want to be seen. I think he's *afraid* to be seen. Self-conscious. Avoids eye contact. As soon as the victims are aware of him, they have Drāno flying in their eyes."

"Not a single fucking eyewitness. The goddamn ER doesn't post guards at the doors. Everyone comes in in their vehicles, so the guys in the parking kiosks are the gatekeepers. No one walks to the ER."

"God bless LA," Yale said.

Dalton scratched his head. "Well, now that we have two vics, at least we can rule out a personal attack on Nance."

"I don't know," Yale said. "We gotta cross-check records, see if there's any patients both Nancy and Sandra Yee treated. Could make sense. Nurse and doctor. Maybe they fucked someone up, pissed him off."

"They're reading like crimes of opportunity to me. We've found no evidence to show he stalked either of the victims. And believe me, me and Jenkins dug hard for any unusual shit in Nance's life." Dalton picked a loose string off his shirt. "I think anyone who stepped through the ER doors into the ambulance bay at that moment was gonna catch the faceful of lye. Yee just got unlucky."

"Smoking kills," Yale said.

"I think he would've hit anyone."

"Male *or* female?"

"Crimes like this, I'd guess he's at least sex-specific."

"Yeah." Yale nodded. "Yeah."

Dalton pushed a hand through his hair, leaving his bangs sticking up on one side. "Maybe he's got a vendetta against the hospital."

"Or nurses, or doctors. Or professionals, for all we know. Like you said, he's not picky with who he's hit so far. Tall Caucasian nurse and a short Asian doctor. Sounds like a porn." Yale popped a smile, then lost it at Dalton's glare. "Gallows humor. The one saving grace of the job. Lighten up. I want to bust the piece of shit as much as you do."

"You may want to bust the POS," Dalton said, "but I got three years in uniform with her brother, and I've eaten food off her table after more than one graveyard shift. I'm looking forward to losing a few bullets in this guy's skull."

"I understand," Yale said. "But that's of little utility."

Dalton glanced down at the ground, his neck wrinkling into another chin, and scratched his forehead. Then he nodded.

"Both assaults occurred during conventional work hours," Yale said. "Maybe our boy's unemployed."

"That would fit the low sophistication level of the crimes."

"The fact that we're dealing with an insecure, disorganized offender tells us something about the victims he chooses. And the locale. They'd both be within his comfort zone. This isn't the kind of guy to stray to new territory to hit his marks." Yale took in the breadth of the plaza. "I think he knows his way around here, maybe even works nearby, and he's familiar with doctors and nurses." He tapped his chin with a knuckle, a rare inexpedient gesture. "We should check records for plaintiffs in malpractice suits against the hospital."

"Though pursuing legal avenues would imply resources and wherewithal not necessarily in keeping with our profile," Dalton added.

"True." Yale snapped his gum. "I'm thinking he's too old to be a student at UCLA, but we probably can't rule it out given we're right on campus. You talk to CAD?"

"They're running a PACMIS and a CCAB, seeing if anything rings the cherries," Dalton said. "Should hear back tomorrow." When the Crime Analysis Detail officer put the alkali assaults through the Police Arrest Crime Management Information System and the Consolidated Crime Analysis Database, similar crimes in the area would show up immediately. The list would include anything in Westwood, on campus or off.

Dalton sat on the bench beside Yale, and they watched the burly patient near the hospital steps try to embroil a passing woman in conversation. She smiled curtly and kept walking. "Could be anyone," Dalton said. "Could be that fucker right there."

Yale shook his head. "No sir. Our guy fears women. That guy . . ." He stabbed a finger in the man's direction. "That guy's got confidence." A note of admiration found its way into his voice. "He'd be a keeper and a player, not a hit-and-runner. He'd be a Bundy. Our guy's a welfare Berkowitz."

Dalton stared hungrily at Yale's unopened In-N-Out bag. "The alkali came back from lab. Danny said they're all pretty much sodium hydroxide and sodium hyposomething, but the surfactants are different. Our boy's using DrainEze. Ever hear of it?"

"No."

"Exactly. Aside from being sold in a few drugstores, it's mostly used institutionally. Schools, factories, warehouses . . ."

"And hospitals."

"Bingo. They don't use it here, though. I'm giving a look at other places in the area, see who stocks it. It's a long shot."

"They're all long shots," Yale said. "But we do have one thing going for us."

"Two cases, same MO."

"That's right. We have the victims tied through the hospital, and we know where he likes to commit his assaults."

Dalton's smile was crooked. "That means we know where to wait."

Yale tapped his temple with a finger.

David and Jenkins appeared at opposite sides of the

plaza at about the same time. They both made their way toward Yale and Dalton, neither noticing the other. Yale watched the impending collision with dismay. Dalton picked up on his tense posture and followed his gaze. "Oh. Shit."

David reached them first and squatted before the bench, white coat spreading behind him like a cape. "I was told you were up here. I was wondering if you had any strong leads I could bring back to the ER."

"Well," Jenkins called out as he approached. "If it isn't the good doctor. What brings you off your turf?"

David rose quickly, so as to face Jenkins on his feet. "I just wanted an update. To see when you think you'll have this guy safely in custody."

Jenkins laughed a hard laugh. David waited patiently through the performance. "Safely in custody," Jenkins repeated. "That's a good one."

"Why," David asked, "is that a good one?"

Dalton stood. "Jenkins," he said, his voice low and soothing.

"No," David said. "I want to know."

A pulse was beating in Jenkins's temple when he looked back over at David, and David realized for the first time just how dangerous a man he was.

Yale remained sitting through the ensuing silence, arms spread across the top of the bench. "There are certain rules, Dr. Spier," he said, speaking as if to a child. "One does not attack schools, hospitals, police stations, or the people who work there. These are direct attacks on the institutions and people that keep our cities functioning. The breaking of such rules does not—*cannot*—go unpunished."

It took David a moment to find his voice. "I agree."

"Such attacks are unacceptable."

"I agree," David said again, in a measured tone. "But

punishment doesn't really fall under either of our job descriptions, does it?"

"I'll tell you what falls under—"

"Jenkins!" Yale snapped, sharply but without anger. Jenkins closed his mouth. It seemed to take considerable effort. Dalton put his arm around Jenkins's shoulders and walked him a few paces away. Jenkins shrugged off the arm but followed.

Yale adjusted the knot of his tie, though it was already perfectly straight. He exuded a calmness lacking in the other two officers. The only thing unreasonable about him was his Joseph Abboud four-button bird's-eye suit. "No, Dr. Spier," he answered. "It doesn't."

David lowered his voice so Dalton and Jenkins couldn't overhear. "These are my staff members getting hurt. I just want to assure them they're being protected. I'd like to bring something back to settle them. Whatever you can disclose."

"I'll be happy to direct you to our PIO."

"PIO?"

"Public Information Officer."

"Oh," David said. "I see." He heard the hard fricatives of Jenkins cursing behind him. Dalton had a hand hooked around his neck in a half hold, half embrace. "I think it's important that we all keep our heads in the middle of this," David added.

The evenness of Yale's stare was unsettling. "Jenkins is just a patrolman," he said. "Dalton and I are detectives. It's under control."

"I'd just . . . the mood in the ER . . ." David drew a deep breath, trying to figure out what he wanted to say. "I don't think any of us want things to turn ugly."

"I believe they already have, Dr. Spier."

"In our professions, it doesn't do us any good to give in to hatred."

"You don't know anything about my job. I'd suggest you refrain from proffering advice about it." Yale's upper lip curled slightly. The first sign of anger. Fair enough—David hadn't realized how condescending his words were until they were out of his mouth.

He tried to proceed more cautiously. "I know this is the kind of liberal bullshit you hate to hear, but the man we're dealing with may even be aware of the fact he needs help. Have you considered that? You could use that information somehow to catch him. He's targeting people right outside the ER, feet away from the treatment and care they need. Subconsciously, maybe he doesn't want them to get hurt."

Yale tossed the unopened In-N-Out bag at a trash can a good five yards away and hit it dead center. "If he didn't want people to get hurt," he said, "he wouldn't throw Drāno in their faces."

CHAPTER 15

PETER Alexander's balance was not aided by the aquarium walkway that ran from the reservation desk to the restaurant proper, but David knew better than to offer his assistance. The hostess watched as Peter lurched and waddled, arms spread wide as though he were anticipating a hug. A fat-eyed parrotfish darted quickly underfoot and Peter swayed, one of his leg braces clinking against the back of a chair. The hostess slowed her pace and caught David's eye, but David kept his hands in his pockets and shook his head.

The crowd at Crustacean evinced Beverly Hills's notion of upscale—cell phones and silk shirts, movie moguls, and the occasional high-priced call girl. Peter's unusual gait caught a few glances, but most people had directed their attention elsewhere by the time he passed.

They reached the base of the stairs and the hostess turned, flustered. "I'm sorry, but the table is upstairs. I can see how long the wait is down here. I didn't know . . . when you made the reservation no one told us that . . ."

"Actually," Peter said, with a smile and an aristocratic tip of his head, "I prefer upstairs."

He gripped the banister, but seemed displeased with its height. He beckoned David with a hand and David turned around, making his shoulder available. Peter's oversized hands were unnaturally strong, and David was grateful for his blazer's shoulder padding. Leaning over, Peter readjusted his loafer around the curved base of his leg brace. The metal had stretched and distorted the mouth of the shoe, lining the oxblood leather with tan wrinkles.

Turning sideways, both hands on the curved banister, he swung one stiff leg out behind him, hooked it on the first step, then pivoted his hips so his other leg followed. He slid his hands about a foot up and repeated the motion. Step number two.

The hostess glanced nervously up the curved length of the staircase. There were over thirty steps to the top. David took the menus from her with a smile.

"It's the table for two in the back corner," she said.

David kept a few steps behind Peter as he worked his way up. Peter was winded when he reached the top, and he mopped his brow with a floppy white handkerchief.

A paddle fan turned slowly above their table. An effeminate waiter took their order with his hands clasped together, leaning forward as if into a strong gust of wind.

Peter pulled off his coat and hung it over the back of

his chair. His black hair, shot through with gray, was unruly and animated—the hair of a composer. David knew Peter was at least twenty years his senior, though they'd never arrived at his age conversationally. Along with Peter's disability, which he never expounded upon, his age was simply off-limits.

"Your mother would have captured the bastard herself," Peter said. "Bound him with her stethoscope and dragged him kicking and screaming to a seclusion room in the NPI."

The Neuropsychiatric Institute's nascence had occurred under David's mother's tenure. She'd been actively broadening psychiatry's horizons, back when most practitioners of the field were busy merely scrubbing off the stains of witchcraft and mysticism. Peter had known her since his young days as a fledgling urologist.

"Dr. Evans called me this morning," David said.

"How is our vibrant chief of staff?"

"Charming but hard-assed, as usual. Wanted to ensure I was keeping on top of the ER, leaving no loose ends for the press to grab hold of."

"Our alkali thrower has captured LA's imagination. The media loves gory details."

"Fuel for a city characterized by ADD. But I suppose it beats hearing about Jennifer Aniston's hair." David set down his menu and aligned it neatly with the edge of the table. "We just can't let all this slow the hospital down."

"It's a nightmare," Peter said. "Last night, I had a nine-hour standing surgery that got out after one in the morning. They made me wait nearly forty minutes so a security guard could walk me to my car. Forty minutes."

The smell of garlic heralded dinner's arrival. Two steaming plates of king prawns resting on beds of swirled linguini. Peter reached to center his plate before him but withdrew his hand quickly, a flash of panic lighting his eyes. He spilled some ice water on his hand where it had touched the plate, though there was clearly no sign of redness or swelling.

David continued the conversation as the waiter served—a rudeness in which he did not usually indulge, but the waiter had annoyed him earlier by asking twice if he was sure he didn't want wine.

"It has been wretched," David said, realizing with some amusement that he'd inadvertently mirrored Peter's tone of faux-English prissiness. "Now that it's confirmed that the attack on Nancy wasn't an isolated incident, I've been assured that the hospital's security level will go through the roof." He shook his head. "One of my medical students almost maced a homeless man in the ambulance bay. She was wearing scrubs—he was approaching her for help."

"One can hardly blame her," Peter said. He manipulated his knife and fork gracefully, hands turning in deft, fluid motions. It was a pleasure to watch him dine.

"The last thing we need is a war mentality on the floor," David said. "Especially with the demographic moving through there. And people are angry." Absent-mindedly, he tapped the tines of his fork against the plate. "God, are they angry."

"And why shouldn't they be? Two lovely young practitioners mauled and mutilated. At the place where they *render medical care*."

"Yes, thank goodness they weren't homely sewer workers."

Peter regarded David humorlessly. "You understand what I'm saying," he said. "This business is vile. Simply vile."

"I'm taking that as a given," David said. "And believe me, I knew both these women, and treated them when they came in. What I'm saying is, we need to look closer. Violence should not attenuate our medical empathy."

"Bah!" Peter said. Peter was the only person David knew who said "Bah." "A little anger is a good thing." Peter fiddled with his wire-rim glasses, cleaning the circular lenses with a corner of his napkin. The clipped, meticulous movements of his hands betrayed his irritation. "This man—he's the result of what? A bad tour of duty? Castration threats from an unloving mother? It's not an excuse. None of the hands we are dealt contain a Get-Out-of-Morality card. We grow and we fight and we cope." His finger, pointing down into the tablecloth, grew white around the knuckle. "This man is deserving of our anger."

"He has my anger," David said. He set down his fork, resting the neck on the lip of the plate. Peter watched him closely, intelligently. "I'm sorry," David said.

Peter nodded, his mouth drawing down in a thoughtful frown. "As physicians, when confronted with someone like this assailant, we're instinctively drawn to explanations involving psychopathology or mental illness. But we shouldn't fool ourselves." He raised his fork, coiled with linguini, and pointed it at David. Something in the gesture gave it monumental weight. "Odds are, he's a malicious, sadistic bastard, whether he's sick or not."

"I know that," David said.

Peter twirled his fork, capturing more linguini. "Do you?"

They ate in silence for a while. David stifled a yawn with his napkin.

"You look like hell," Peter said. "Burning it at both ends?"

David nodded wearily. "I can't work the way I used to."

"You're getting old." Peter's eyes twinkled when he

laughed. "When I used to work the Air Force base down in Riverside, I'd get these young macho pilots in for vasectomies. Married a few years, knocked out a few kids, didn't want to worry about impregnating their wife or anyone else with whom they happened to be sleeping. I'd get them done, and afterward I'd tell them to be careful and use protection because they were still shooting live rounds for another thirty ejaculations. And they'd just smile and say, 'Thirty squirts? I'll get that taken care of this weekend, Doc.' "

David laughed.

"Do you know what the moral of that story is?" Peter asked. He drew out the pause dramatically. "You can't go like you used to."

An attractive middle-aged woman walked past their table, adjusting a satin spaghetti strap on her dress. David felt a rush of melancholy. There was no wine to blame it on. "If I ever lost this, my work, I'd . . . I don't know."

"Lose your work? You're at the height of your career."

"I can't work ninety-hour weeks anymore."

"I never could."

"But I could. *I could.*"

Peter leaned back in his chair, as if that provided a better vantage from which to regard him. "You inherited your mother's vanity."

David rubbed the bridge of his nose with a knuckle. "I inherited the runoff."

"She was a great woman, your mother, but she was cruel in the way great people are cruel. You have none of that." Peter picked at a prawn with his fork, but did not spear it. "Do you know why great people are cruel? They have so much of themselves to protect." He reached down and adjusted one of his leg braces. David caught a flicker of a grimace before Peter replaced it with a smile. "We all have our limitations," Peter said.

Peter insisted, despite David's protestations, on picking up the check—a habit he'd developed when David had been a penniless intern and persisted in, David believed, to perpetuate an air of affectionate condescension.

David folded Peter's jacket over his arm and waited patiently for him to rise. It took them nearly five minutes to make it down the stairs and to the lobby.

CHAPTER 16

BRONNER scooped the wedge of tobacco dip from his lower lip with a curled finger and flicked it out the window. Jenkins sat rigidly in the passenger seat, watching the sun dip to the horizon. They headed up Veteran, the rolling hills of the cemetery sprawling to their left. The white posts of the soldiers' graves rose like glowing pickets into the dusk.

They turned on Weyburn, heading into Westwood Village, the large tower of the hospital looming to the east. Students clustered around the outdoor tables at the Coffee Bean on the corner. UCLA blue and gold was everywhere—backpacks, sweatshirts, hats, jerseys. Apparently unable to find a chair, a girl with exceedingly long legs bent over a fluorescent blueberry laptop. A pair of jean cutoffs were stretched tight over her rear end, the bottom curves of her buttocks just in view beneath.

Bronner cleared his throat and got a good phlegm rattle. "I remember when computers were new. I remember when they were tan or white. Now they got all these damn colors. Don't know whether to boot 'em up or hang 'em on a Christmas tree."

Jenkins looked from the girl's high hard ass to Bronner's face. "And *that's* what you find worthy of comment?"

"Easy there, young Jedi. I so much as double-take, my old lady'll fly over here on her broomstick and staple my eyelids shut." Bronner turned the plain gold band on his ring finger. "Twenty-three years of wear and tear, and the fucker still fits snug as a hair in an ass crack. It's on till the finger falls off."

"You never cheated on her? Even when you were younger?"

Bronner shrugged. "I didn't inhale."

The light changed and they pulled forward. A UCPD car passed them, and the driver and Bronner exchanged nods.

"Jesus Christ," Jenkins said. "How many do they have running?"

"Called additional units down from UCSB and Irvine. A little extra backup."

"As long as Dalton and Yale have lead on the case, they can call in the Police Explorers for all I give a shit."

"You want to go visit Nancy?"

Jenkins glanced in the direction of the Medical Plaza. Night had fallen quickly, and the windows of the hospital shone as floating squares in the distance. "No," he said.

They patrolled the campus perimeter twice in silence before coming up behind a beat-up van with tinted back windows on Sunset. "That's a DLR," Bronner said.

Jenkins pushed himself erect in his seat. "You're right," he said. "That fucker Don't Look Right at all."

Based on the open layout of the streets surrounding the hospital and the speed of the suspect's departure, Yale had laid down the hypothesis that the suspect had used a vehicle to get to and from the crime scene. Jenkins and Bronner had spent the last twelve hours looking for DLRs.

Bronner steered into the other lane and pulled up to the van's blind spot. FREDDY'S INDUSTRIAL CLEANING was written on the side in chipped white paint.

Jenkins's jaw tightened. "Let's jack him up."

"Probable cause?"

"Rear license light?"

Bronner leaned his head to the window, checking. "Yup. Rearview mirror?"

"Yup. Pull forward." Bronner did, but the van sat too high for them to see the driver through the passenger window. "Front plate?" Jenkins asked hopefully.

"Yup." Bronner's eye picked over the car exterior. "Bingo. Cracked windshield." He fisted the radio and it chimed its distinctive LAPD chime, prompting him to speak. "LA, Eight Adam Thirty-two, traffic."

The van turned down Hilgard, and they followed a half block before Jenkins switched on the lights. Sorority row flew by as the radio crackled its response: "Eight Adam Thirty-two, LA. Advised traffic."

The van pulled to a halt in front of two enormous garbage cans at the curb.

"Eight Adam Thirty-two, traffic," Bronner said. "Eight hundred block south Hilgard on a black Chevy van, possibly mideighties. Twenty-eight, twenty-nine, please. License plate two Nora six eight one four two. Code four at this time."

He angled one spotlight into the driver's side mirror. Because the van's back window was tinted, he couldn't get the second one on the rearview mirror, but he put it through the back window anyway. They sat in the car for a moment, gathering themselves. Jenkins unsnapped his holster, then snapped it shut again. "A fucking industrial cleaner's truck. Isn't that perfect?"

They stared straight ahead, letting the suspect get nervous, waiting for traffic to clear.

Jenkins pulled out a small tape recorder, hit RECORD, and quickly rattled off the Miranda rights. He clicked the tape recorder off and turned a quick grin to Bronner. "Glad we got that out of the way."

Bronner cleared his throat, then took on a newscaster's intonation. "Why did you shoot the suspect, Officer Jenkins?"

"I feared for my life and the life of my fellow officer. Why did you shoot the suspect, Officer Bronner?"

Bronner cracked a grin. "I was concerned for my safety and the safety of others."

"Ready?" Both doors opened simultaneously, and the officers came up on the van on each side. They did not cross their paths.

The driver squinted into the flashlight, which Bronner held about two feet away from his face. Bronner's radio cord ran from his hip up his back, away from grabbing hands, the unit hooked over his shoulder. On the other side of the van, Jenkins shined his light through the tinted back windows, trying to get a look at the dark interior.

"What'd I do, man?" The driver, a heavyset man with wide, doughy cheeks and heavily gelled curls of hair, raised an arm to the flashlight's glare.

"License, registration, proof of insurance," Bronner said. Behind him, a broken sprinkler spurted a thick two-inch fountain that turned the lawn sleek like pelt. The runoff had left the sidewalk wet and spotted with snails. "Keep your left hand on the dash or steering wheel and reach with your right hand to your glove box."

"What are you—?"

"Don't make me ask again."

The driver leaned toward the glove compartment, his thin polyester snap-up pulling up out of his jeans. He did not seem to be concealing any weapons on his body. His sleeve rode up on his right shoulder, revealing a tattoo of Mickey Mouse. Perhaps through her panic haze, Nancy had mistaken Mickey Mouse for a skull. "Slowly," Bronner added.

The driver handed him the documents, then dug in his pocket for his wallet. Bronner held the flashlight to the registration but kept his eyes on the driver's hand until it emerged from his pocket. He glanced at the license. Frederick Russay.

Bronner clipped the license and registration to his shirt pocket, sliding it beneath the protruding pen cap.

"Is there some problem, officer?" A little more polite this time.

"Are you aware that you have a cracked windshield?" Bronner asked.

"Yeah, I guess. Is that like some big deal or something?"

"Would you mind stepping out of the vehicle please?"

"Why?"

"For our safety."

When Russay hunched forward, his shirt was stuck to his back with sweat.

"Get out of the vehicle," Bronner said, a bit more firmly.

"For a cracked—?"

"Get out of the vehicle immediately."

Russay scrambled quickly out onto the curb, leaving his door open. "Look, man, I don't know what's going on here, but I didn't—"

Bronner spun him and pushed him forcefully up against the side of the van. He patted him down, even checking his crotch for a piece dangling from a belly band. He found nothing. "Is there anyone else in the vehicle?"

"No."

"Mind if we take a look?" Bronner kept his forearm across Russay's back, pressing him forward into the side of the van.

"No. I guess not."

Bronner caught Jenkins's eye through the open passenger window and signaled him with a jerk of his head. Jenkins walked back to the rear of the van, snapping and unsnapping his holster. The street grew suddenly quiet. He threw open one door, and light fell into the van's dark interior from a nearby streetlight. The van smelled of Clorox, coffee, and wet rags. The flashlight's beam picked over the mounds of gear. Mops in dirty buckets, several coiled drain snakes, piles of dirty overalls. In the back, half hidden by an open toolbox, was a container of Red Devil Drain Cleaner.

The muscles stood out on Jenkins's jaw like walnuts.

He walked around and stood beside Bronner. "He's got lye back there."

"Could be legit if he is a cleaning guy," Bronner muttered.

"Could be," Jenkins said. "If."

Bronner nodded. "We'll know soon enough."

Russay moved his head, trying to turn around. "What are you guys—?"

A burst of static came through Bronner's portable, then it squawked, "Eight Adam Fourteen Los Angeles." Bronner walked a few yards up the curb. Jenkins kept Russay up against the side of the van, hands and legs spread.

"Eight Adam Thirty-two, LA," Bronner said. "Go ahead."

"Vehicle has no wants, no warrants. Vehicle comes back to Frederick Russay's Industrial Cleaning Corporation, one-two-two-five Armacost number two-ten, LA."

"Roger that. Can I get a twenty-eight also on a Frederick Russay?" Bronner unclipped the license from his shirt pocket and alternated his eyes between it and Russay as he read off Russay's social security number, date of birth, and license number.

Forearm resting lightly across Russay's shoulders, Jenkins waited for Bronner to give him a sign one way or the other. A Cabriolet with three brunettes slowed as it passed. Laughter and pop music. One girl waved, her arm undulating in the darkness like a snake in water. Russay's breathing was harshly audible.

Bronner tilted his head back and exhaled hard. "Be advised," his portable finally said. "There are no wants, no warrants. Subject has a total of six points. Two previous excess of speed, one in '94, one in '97. Everything else clear."

"Roger that." He released the portable button with a flare of his thumb.

Jenkins watched the slight slump of Bronner's shoulders and stepped away from Russay. Russay remained leaning forward against the van. "Get up," Jenkins said.

Russay stood up and tucked in his shirt as Bronner walked over and offered him back his documents. His hand closed over them brusquely, and his driver's license fluttered to the ground. He kept his eyes on Jenkins as he crouched to pick it up.

"That's all, Mr. Russay," Bronner said.

"So the crack in my windshield's okay?" Russay rested his hands on his hips. Warring emotions flickered through his face; he seemed unsure whether to be grateful or angry. Bronner gestured him to head back to the van, and he went, shaking his head in exasperation, the curls of his hair barely swaying under the weight of the gel.

Jenkins followed him, catching up as he slammed the door. "Mr. Russay?" he said, through the open window. The spotlight still shone on Russay's face, reflected off the side mirror. Russay raised his eyebrows. "We have your name and address."

"What does that mean?" Russay called after him. His voice rose a half octave into a nervous whine. "What the hell is that supposed to mean?"

Jenkins walked back to his vehicle, boots crunching snails underfoot.

CHAPTER 17

CLYDE walked with his head set low on his neck, as though he could retract it within his body. Corduroy hat blocking his eyes, hands shoved into his pockets, loose shoelaces trailing from his dirty white Adidas sneakers, he wandered the streets of Venice aimlessly. A clown with a large red banana of a smile walked past, trailing a beer cooler with MR. FUNFACE lettered on the side in bottlecaps. He looked pissed off.

Two young girls walked by, shuffling and dancing to Walkmans, metal protruding from their pierced brown bellies like the tips of fish hooks. They were quickly gone, the tinny blare of their muffled music floating away with them. The wheels of the clown's cooler hiccuped across sidewalk cracks, a dissonant night song.

Fluttering window curtains, sleeping drunks, cars with steaming windows—the streets were empty but alive, their inhabitants withdrawn like creatures of the woods. Clyde walked alone, casting a broad shadow, the asphalt slick with ocean film underfoot. A smell came off his warm flesh—not a typical body odor, but something unpleasant and stagnant, something backed up in his pores.

A car drove by and Clyde caught his reflection in the flash of reflected light from an apartment window—a wide man with red cheeks and a bowling ball of a head. He stiffened. The night drew itself around his shoulders like an icy shawl. He walked for a few blocks, the muscles of his face relaxing by degrees, and then he sat on an empty porch and wept. His weeping was vehement and prolonged. He pushed his balled hands hard into his eyes until his knuckles ground the bone of the sockets.

The breeze cooled his cheeks quickly. Removing his hat, he worked the bill until it was curved in a loose U. It fit more snugly, protecting the sides of his eyes.

A pair of red pumps appeared on the sidewalk in front of him. The toenails, painted pink, struck an unpleasing contrast. "Hey, honey-honey. You look lonely."

"Not lonely." His voice was still thick with mucus from crying.

"What, baby? Don't you be all mumbling at me."

"I'm not lonely."

"Why don't you look on up here at me? See what I can lay on that big strong body of yours. I said look on up here. Ain't nothin' down there on the sidewalk."

She crouched, legs bending wide, the two wings of a butterfly. She was not wearing panties. Natural, sagging breasts hoisted up in a pink tube top. "See anything you like?"

"Not lonely."

"Let's go for a walk. Last chance for the Tuesday night special."

He ducked his head down into his arms, hiding.

The legs straightened. "Shit, fool." She knocked his hat off and he raised his arm quickly, like a celebrity ducking photographers. His thick fingers scrabbled over the pavement for his hat. She threw her head back when she laughed, one leg locked, one swaying at the knee, her fists resting on cocked hips.

Clyde grabbed the hat and pulled it on roughly, not bothering to straighten it. Her laughter followed him up the street like a cluster of winged insects. He walked with his shoulders hunched, his head lowered. His mouth was twisted up as if his self-loathing had a taste. The fingers and thumb of his left hand slid against each other, rubbing and flicking, as though something were coating them that he needed to rub off. As he put a few blocks between himself and the woman, his posture grew more erect, his stride more emboldened. His feet carried him toward home.

A building had been torn down on his block, the scorched skeleton of a Chevy sitting up on blocks in the weed and rubble. Clyde removed a hidden pack of Marlboros from beneath the hood and lit two cigarettes, which he smoked at the same time. Someone had placed a stack of weekly newspapers over the springs where the driver's seat used to be, and he sat on them, placing his hands on the broken wheel. Smoke wreathed his head, catching on the pockmarks of his cheeks. His pupils jerked a few times, horizontally.

The run-down two-story house visible through the cracked windshield was now a home for retarded adults. A measly row of browning snapdragons lined one side of the sagging porch. He waited and watched the large upstairs windows, most of them illuminated with night lights, for signs of life. Last week, he had seen two of the residents grappling on a bed in what he had first mistaken for a bout of violence. Over the months, he had seen many strange things in the house for retarded adults. His insomnia had left him with so many more hours to fill, each day a long, rambling journey to the next.

He pulled his second-rate money clip from his pocket

and set it on the dash so he could admire it. The wad consisted mostly of wrinkled singles. He smoked the cigarettes down until they burned his fingers, then stubbed them out in the glove box. Closing his eyes, he murmured to himself, "Three, two, one. Three, two, one."

When he opened his eyes, a light was on in one of the upstairs rooms. A moment later, a back door opened and a heavy woman in her thirties walked out into the side yard. She wore a pink jumpsuit with a puffy bunny sewn on the front, and open-backed slippers. She tried to whistle but could not. Red cheeks, half-mast eyes, and a messy fountain of hair protruding from a flower-emblazoned scrunchy gave her the appearance of an overgrown child. When she stepped off the porch, a motion-sensor lamp cast a small cone of light on the ground. Elbows locked, she clapped her hands softly, still trying to whistle, though only a wet rushing noise issued from her lips.

A scraggly dog, ribs showing through a coarse gray coat, poked his nose around the far corner of the building. She waved to him and clapped again, stiff-armed. The dog moved toward her in a limping trot.

The dog drew nearer, sat, and growled, showing off a surprisingly healthy collection of teeth. The woman dug in her pocket, the cotton fabric of her pants pushing out in the imprint of her hand, and pulled out a fistful of moist tuna. A dollop fell from one of the spaces between her fingers, and the dog slurped it off the ground, tongue moving like a pink slug across the ground.

The woman crouched and the dog scurried back, teeth bared again.

"Um on," she said. "Um naw gonna urt you."

She spread her hand wide, revealing a mashed lump of tuna, and the dog tentatively approached, body coiled to spring back. He took the remaining tuna off the ground first, then moved cautiously to her hand, nose twitching. Then something in the dog gave way, and he docilely lowered the pointed tip of his snout into her hand. She giggled as his tongue played across her hand, almost squealing as he licked it clean.

The dog tensed and flashed back around the building when the car door slammed. She looked up at Clyde's approach. "Uht are you doing?" He drew nearer, and the dim porch light fell across his face. "Oh. It's you."

Her almost perfectly round eyes seemed pushed into the soft flesh of her face like buttons. Her cheeks, a raw red, crowded her mouth with folds. Another bunny decorated her thigh, smiling with white sequined teeth.

"Hey, honey-honey," he said. He pulled the thin blade from the side of his money clip, then flicked it shut with a deliberately casual gesture.

"Ello." She glanced nervously in the direction the dog had disappeared. "Uhr not onna ell em about my dog, are you?"

Four metal numbers nailed into the wall announced the house's address: 1711. He pried off one of the 1s with his blade, pocketed it, and turned back to the woman. "You look lonely," he said.

"You never um up ere. You ormaly ust sit in your ar."

"Not tonight." He crouched, found a stick, and dug its pointed tip into the dirt. "I want to go for a walk."

"I an't. I'm not suppose ta be out ere." The stars flickered overhead like winking diamonds. "I unt ant to miss orning bed check. Rhonda ill et angry."

"Don't worry," he said. "I'll have you back by then."

Her voice came high and pleading. "Uhr not onna ell em about my dog?"

He scratched his cheek, his uncut nails drawing blood from one of his zits. "Not if you come with me."

⊕

"Ee-yeew," she said, waving an arm in windshield-wiper sweeps in front of her nose. Clyde closed the door behind her and locked it.

"It doesn't smell," he said.

"It ure does."

He grabbed her and pinned her against the door. His fingers dug into her soft shoulders. "On't," she said. She stared at him. He blinked twice and looked away.

He walked a slow, sweeping circle around his apartment, stepping over the trash and clothes, then charged her and pressed his open mouth violently against hers. Her mouth was warm and dry, and surprisingly not sour from sleep. His eyes were squeezed shut, a defensive move for when she clawed at his face.

Instead, she kissed him back, her thick tongue making deep spirals in his mouth.

He pushed off her and wiped his mouth. "What're you doing?"

"Issing you. Unt you ant to iss me?"

Clyde's eyes went to the floor, his lips moving in a murmur. She stepped forward and put a hand under his chin, raising his head. He spun her and seized her around the waist from behind, shuffle-walking her to the bed. He bent her over, and she grunted when her elbows jarred against the mattress. Her jumpsuit bottoms came down easily, the elastic stretching to accommodate her wide rear end. He pulled them off roughly, and her slippers came with them. He fought her huge beige panties down to the crooks of her knees. She gave surprisingly little resistance.

He mounted her from behind, pushing and laboring through a panic sweat as the sequined bunny looked on from the pink puddle of cotton on the floor. After a few strokes, she responded with guttural noises, and he was alarmed and dismayed to realize they were colored with pleasure. He imitated them, drowning them out, pretending they were grunts of fear. His imagination could only stretch so far.

Limp and defeated, he climbed off her. They were both slick with sweat and unsatisfied. She sank down, flat on her stomach. She did not look at him. "Are you onna ell em about my dog?" she asked.

"Yes," he said.

She cried softly into a stained pillow. He sat and stared at the floor. Her quiet weeping went on steadily.

He reached under his bed and pulled out an old shoebox. The rubber bands around it had grown brittle, and one snapped as he pulled it off. He nudged her. She did not look up. He nudged her again, and she rolled to her side, face swollen and ugly.

He handed her the shoebox. Sniffling, she slid to the edge of the bed and sat with the box across her lap, staring down at it.

He studied the half-moon of grit rimming his overgrown thumbnail. "Open it."

She removed the lid, her head jerking back slightly at the odor. "Wow," she said. Reaching in, she removed a white seagull's wing, balancing it on her open palms like a crystal plate. It had been severed at the shoulder, and the scapular feathers were stained black with blood.

Clyde took it from her gently and spread it, the primary feathers fanning wide. She reached over and felt the longest feather, her thumb tracing its lines. She tugged on the wing, and he relinquished it to her. Her tears dried as she spread the wing, then contracted it, spread and contracted.

She did not seem to notice when he rose from the bed. He opened the footlocker and removed a container of DrainEze and a Pyrex beaker. Alkali filled the beaker quickly when he poured, the white gradation numerals outlined clearly against the blue liquid.

He put the DrainEze container back in the footlocker and closed it. The full beaker sat alone on the table. He stood beside it like a stern patriarch in a family portrait, knuckles pressed to the scarred wood. She did not look up from the wing. "It's eautiful," she said.

Clyde picked up the beaker and set it back down with a small thump. Still, she did not look up. She was playing with the wing and smiling.

The mattress bounced her up a bit when he sat beside her. "You need to go," he said.

Fingers working through the soft feathers. "Huh?"

"You need to go. If you go now, I won't tell anyone about your dog."

Her eyes narrowed—she had forgotten about the dog. She set the wing gently back in the shoebox and rose, her long jumpsuit top dangling over her thighs like a dress. She pulled up her panties, then yanked on her pants, forcing her legs through without pointing her toes.

Clyde held his sweating head in his hands. "Go," he said. "Go."

She paused beside the table, rising up on her tiptoes to peer into the Pyrex beaker, though it was clear. "Uht is this?" she asked. "It's pretty. Pretty blue."

He rubbed his temples, rubbed them hard. "Taste it," he said.

Tentatively, she dipped a fingertip into the liquid. It colored the tip of her print like a blue condom. She stared at it for a moment. "Ow," she said, shaking her hand. "Ow." When she twirled her finger in the fabric of her top, it left a blue stain on the bunny's cheek. "Ow," she said. She stuck her finger in her mouth, made a face, and spit onto the floor. She gagged and drooled a little.

"Go," he said. His fingers dug through his tufts of hair, gathering them.

"I on't like that," she said. She spit again.

He did not look up at the sound of the closing door, though his fists tightened around handfuls of hair.

"Go," he said.

CHAPTER 18

THE scream reverberated through the ER. Adrenaline pumping, images of flying alkali and blistering faces racing through his mind, David sprinted through the CWA to Hallway Two.

A disheveled man was shaking Pat against the wall, banging her head while two nurses and a lab tech looked on, stunned. "You stole my fucking tote bag," he yelled. "Where is it?" He wore a baseball cap, though the back of his head was sticky with blood.

Ralph was running down the hall, his full set of security keys jingling against his thigh, but David reached the attacker first and dug a thumb into the spinal accessory nerve at the base of his neck. The man yelped and dropped away from the pressure, as David hoped he would. As he fell, he swung his elbow and caught David in the temple. David reeled back, his free hand striking a stray crash cart, but he didn't release his grip. He caught the man's loose hand and found a pressure point, digging his nail into the fat part of his thumb. The man cried out and his body went slack again, this time long enough for David to get him on the ground. Ralph dove on top of him, then another security officer slid into the mix. The man spread himself flat and stopped resisting. He reeked of booze.

David emerged from the pile, a hand pressed to his temple. A flap of skin had lifted on the back of his knuckle where it had struck the cabinet. The white of his UCLA security shirt stained with blood from the back of the guy's head, Ralph hauled him to his feet.

"I didn't mean no trouble, man," the guy whined. "I just wanted my tote bag back."

Pat was bent over, hands on her knees, gasping. "He came in with a head lac. I was trying to get him into an exam room."

"Someone call LAPD, West LA station," David said. "Ask for Detective Yale."

As Ralph and another guard moved the man briskly toward the lobby, David turned to the staff who'd gathered around. "All right. Everyone who's not with a critical patient, into the CWA. Where's Dr. Lambert?"

A radiology resident breezed by. "MIA as usual."

David headed back first and waited patiently for the others to congregate, pressing some gauze to the back of his knuckle. "A few new considerations," he said. "Until the assailant is apprehended, we're going to have to be on heightened alert. The easiest way for the assailant to escalate his ER attacks would be to come in here posing as a patient. So grab a partner before going into a room alone with a male patient. And if you find yourself with someone who appears to be aggressive, get out of the room and find security. These are shitty conditions to work under, I understand, but for now they're a necessity."

An intern piped up from the back. "That guy they just hauled off. You think he's the guy?"

David raised the gauze from his hand and saw it was spotted with blood. "We can always hope."

⊕

David sat on the examination table, suturing his own knuckle. His first quiet five minutes of the day. Diane stood near enough that her thigh brushed his knee. She kept it there.

Yale had informed David within a few hours that they'd been unable to establish a connection between the man who'd attacked Pat and the alkali thrower. David had been surprised at the sharpness of his disappointment. The cops had found the tote bag that the man had been so desperate to protect in the waiting room under a chair. It hadn't contained lye after all. The cops were holding the man for assault, but Yale said he didn't fit the profile they'd been working up for the alkali thrower; he was too socially integrated.

David pulled the suture high, using his teeth to keep one side taut, and guided the needle through the loop with his thumb. "One-handed sutures. Reminds me of internship." He yanked the top of the string so the knot slid down and nestled near his flesh. "You should see Peter tie these. He's like a magician with his hands."

Diane rolled her eyes. "Maybe you should have been a surgeon."

"Cut this." She leaned over with the scissors, and he felt the softness of her hair on his forehead. He hoped his triceps didn't look too soft beneath the cut sleeves of his scrub top, and he laughed silently at himself for having such juvenile thoughts.

He rose briskly and opened the door. A group had gathered outside. Carson stood in the front. "Uh, Dr. Spier, we decided in light of your courageous escapades today, and your fighting spirit, we should present you with this prize." Pat handed him a box with a ribbon on it, and several lab techs giggled.

David opened it to reveal a pair of bright red boxing gloves. The group exploded in laughter. At Carson's prompting, David slid the gloves on, careful not to lift the suture, and raised his fists as Pat snapped a Polaroid.

They laughed and joked for a few minutes, and then David headed to the doctors' lounge to put away the gloves. When he opened the door, he recognized Sandra's mother sitting on one of the chairs, facing an open locker. A diminutive Asian woman with a sad, thoughtful countenance, she'd evidently come to retrieve her daughter's things. She held Sandra's white coat in her hands, her shoulders trembling. David realized she was crying.

Feeling foolish, he lowered his hands, red puffy globes in the boxing gloves. Lost in grief, Sandra's mother did not take note of his presence. He wanted to move forward to comfort her, to rest an arm across her shoulders, but found he was paralyzed.

After a moment, he pulled off his gloves, walked back to the CWA, and located Diane. "Sandra's mother is in the lounge," he said. "I think you might want to . . ."

Diane nodded and handed off the chart she'd been scribbling on. He watched her head back to the doctors' lounge without hesitation.

He felt suddenly ineffective.

CHAPTER 19

DALTON slouched down in the backseat of the LA Express Airport Shuttle van, and Yale looked over at him with a grin. "The windows are full tint," he said. "We're covered."

Dalton pulled himself up in his seat with a groan. "That's just how I sit," he said. Like Yale, Dalton wore a surveillance piece, the clear plastic tube hooking around his ear, the spring coils hidden beneath his hair. The tube connected to a wire that disappeared beneath his back collar, and hooked into a Motorola Saber radio strapped over one of his love handles.

"Our boys have been bedded down since five this morning," Yale said. He leaned forward and tapped the driver. "Jerry, bring it around through the parking kiosks and into the ER lot. We're gonna do a drive-through and see how it looks."

Because of the high-profile nature of the case, it had taken less lobbying to get approved for the overtime necessary to do a stakeout. In the end, the Captain had personally called the Mayor; he'd managed to pull six undercovers, whom Yale had briefed at the West LA station. Yale had asked Dalton not to attend the briefing, so he could assess the stakeout with fresh eyes.

Dalton leaned forward, focusing as they turned left off Le Conte and approached the parking kiosks. Blake, the older UCPD cop from whom they'd acquired the case, leaned out the window. He wore a baseball cap and a University of California Parking T-shirt. "That'll be five dollars please." He did not so much as glance at the two officers in the back of the van, maintaining their cover.

"Actually, sir," Jerry said, "we're just pulling down to the ER. I believe there's no charge for ER short-term parking."

"All right." Blake waved them forward.

"What the fuck?" Dalton muttered as they pulled away.

Yale shrugged. "UCPD wanted in, and, to be fair, they have a better idea how parking works here."

"Why not someone younger? For parking, you

should've pulled a twenty-two-year-old out of the academy or something."

"Politics," Yale said. "They're still chafing we yanked him and Gaines from the case, so we cut Blake in on the loop. Besides, given the second attack, we don't mind sharing juris as much. It's more than a glam case now. It's a fucking plague."

"If our guy's familiar with this area of the hospital, new faces might throw him."

"The parking workers switch all the time, from complexes all over campus. There are new faces every week."

Dalton made a noise of resignation and turned in the seat, taking in the surroundings as the van veered right and headed toward the ambulance bay. An old man sat on the bus stop bench, a girl with pigtails sitting on his lap and trying to untangle a yo-yo from her legs. An overweight woman assisted her elderly mother up the walkway from the ambulance bay into the PCHS lot. A homeless man padded by on Reeboks, pushing a shopping cart filled with cardboard boxes and plastic bags, and two Mexican gardeners worked on their hands and knees on the stretch of ground ivy to the right of the ambulance bay. A trench they'd dug left some piping exposed, and one leaned over with a wrench, pushing his fanny pack to the side. A scattering of tall trees, mostly pines, framed the edges of the buildings and the parking structure.

The van drove down the ramp into the subterranean ambulance bay and idled alongside an ambulance double-parked at the left curb. UCLA CRITICAL CARE TRANSPORT was block-lettered on the side; the back windows were blacked out. Yale slid the van door open and stepped out and immediately through the back doors of the ambulance. Dalton followed suit, slamming the ambulance door behind him. The two officers sat on small stools, peering out the one-way rear windows. The shuttle van U-turned in the narrow space and passed them, heading up out of the ambulance bay. Concrete pillars, painted blue at the bases, set off the parking strip to their left. Beyond that, near the entrance, a chain-link fence enclosed a utilities storage area. Plenty of natural light spilled down the ramp, and the rows of fluorescent lights overhead colored the far reaches of the ambulance bay a tired yellow.

From their seats, Dalton and Yale had a clear view up the ramp; any incoming traffic or pedestrians would have to pass right by them. Beyond the ramp, a patch of grass was visible, as well as the parking turnaround and the edge of a kiosk.

"Well?" Yale asked.

"Nice touch, finding Mexicans for the gardeners. You pull them from Southeast or 77th?"

"From 77th. How'd you make 'em?"

"For starters, there's an LA sun overhead and no sweat stains on their shirts. The fanny pack couldn't be more obvious—what the fuck, are they European gardeners? Plus, their hair's a bit high and tight, but not much we can do about that."

"What else?"

Dalton tilted his head back and closed his eyes. "Oh yeah," he said. "I went through the academy with Garcia."

Yale pressed his lips together to keep from smiling. "And here I thought it was your keen detective skills." His fingers found the microphone beneath his shirt and pushed the button. Since they were on TAC12, there was no need to speak in code. "Garcia, Garcia, Yale."

Outside, Garcia faked scratching an itch beneath his shirt and activated his mike. "Yale, Yale, Garcia. Go ahead." Since he barely moved his lips, his vowels were better enunciated than his consonants.

"You got a friend who wants to say hello."

Dalton smiled as he spoke. "Garcia, you lazy spic, if you're not gonna work out there, at least fake it well. Splash some water on your shirt in the front, and a bit beneath your arms. Tell your buddy too."

"Hugh Dalton, you motherfucker. I was sure you'd never get promoted."

"Every mutt has his day. Did you check the sprinkler timers? We can't have you getting doused out there and looking like a rookie."

"Already taken care of. Hey, I was sorry to hear about Kathy."

Dalton's face shifted, the folds and wrinkles rearranging themselves but staying the same. "Thank you," he said.

"She was a good cop."

Dalton nodded, as though Garcia could see him. His voice was a bit raspy when he spoke again. "Also, you gotta lose the fanny pack up front. Too obvious, especially with the drawstring."

"I already got my portable beneath my shirt. If I move the gun to my waistband, I'll bulk up even more."

"It'll still be less conspicuous than a big black brick strapped to your dick."

"All right. Over."

Dalton sat staring through the tinted windows of the ambulance, not looking over at Yale. "You gonna ask me what happened to my wife?"

"No."

"She was killed on a routine traffic stop last year. Pulled someone over and was approaching the car when a semi swerved and clipped her. Guy wasn't drinking or anything. He just leaned over, reached for the radio." His hand flared, then clapped to his knee. "She was a good cop. Great lady. Twice my IQ and four times my looks." He smiled faintly. "Not that that's saying much."

Yale pulled his Revos down over his eyes, despite the fact they were in an underground garage. "Kids?"

"Two girls. Nine and twelve." Dalton reached for the picture in his wallet but stopped himself. "Forget it."

Yale didn't insist.

Dalton cleared his throat, a little too loud. "Tell your homeless guy to wear shittier shoes tomorrow. The spanking-white Reeboks are a no-brainer. The overhang to this entrance is a parking area. Have him patrol up there from time to time in case our psycho decides to drop an alkali balloon down on a pedestrian. And have a UCLA PD car come by and roust him every now and then to make him look legit. That's all I got. I hope you didn't put anyone up a tree—they might be stealing our guy's hideout."

"No trees. We got a black female working reception inside, and a white male orderly standing by near the other entry control point."

"Just one other ECP?"

"Yeah, there's one hall into the ER from the hospital proper, but I'm pretty sure our guy's looking to hit here again. More open, closer to the streets, easier."

"So he thinks."

Yale nodded. "So he thinks."

"Getting bolder, isn't he, the fucker? He hit Nance up on the sidewalk. Took the second girl just about where we're sitting." Dalton looked down, as though he could see through the ambulance floor. "Came down here, right near the ER doors." His head snapped up. "What do we got east of the hospital? Anyone in the Botanical Gardens?"

Yale shook his head. "There are a lot of good hiding places down there, but we figured someone coming in from the east would've been picked up by the CCTV on the kiosk." The only closed circuit television camera near the ambulance bay entrance was mounted on the front parking kiosk, angled down and eastward, catching cars as they pulled through and paid. It recorded a wide scope and would have caught any pedestrian traffic looping around into the ambulance bay entrance from that direction. Yale had spent more time than he cared to recall watching the footage. Aside from the occasional woman in a low-cut dress, he'd found very little of interest. "We couldn't pull more than six undercovers," he continued. "I figured they were best used elsewhere."

Yale and Dalton had decided on a stakeout after several other angles had led to dead ends. Though the consistency of the assault location pointed to the hospital as the primary connection between Nancy Jenkins and Sandra Yee, Dalton had also been investigating the possibility of it being secondary. If both victims stayed in the same hotel attending a medical conference, for instance, they might have been selected by the suspect off the hotel guest list. Unfortunately, they'd taken no trips at the same time and had not attended any similar conferences. According to the women's credit card bills and records, there had been no overlap between workers and servicemen they'd had through the house in the last six months. Dalton had been briefly excited when he'd discovered they'd both received FedExes on the same day, but a few phone calls had confirmed that the packages had been delivered on different routes. The hospital files had been difficult to get hold of, but conversations with other physicians and nurses revealed little regarding patients Nancy and Sandra had treated together. It was looking more and more as though they'd been targeted merely because of their association with the hospital.

Yale had been slogging through pending lawsuits against the hospital and had yet to uncover any solid suspects. No reports on disgruntled ex-employees. No alkali- or even acid-throwing incidents had come back from PACMIS or CCAB. A car accident victim who felt he had received poor ER treatment last year had sent hostile letters to the hospital board, but he now lived in Massachusetts. Yale had run him through the Automatic Wants and Warrants System anyway and had found no red flags.

When Yale stretched, his hands touched both sides of the ambulance interior. Dalton shifted on the small stool and groaned, then checked his watch. The first two assaults had occurred in the early morning, two days apart. The last attack had been Tuesday, and it was now Thursday morning.

Someone was due to be attacked.

The stools inside the ambulance became increasingly uncomfortable as morning dragged into afternoon. Yale and Dalton received the occasional alert from Garcia and gave a few heads-ups to the officer working reception inside, but the majority of the patients and workers coming in were not suspicious. Blake had an argument with a news van that tried to pull past the parking kiosk down toward the ambulance bay and succeeded in fending it off without blowing his cover.

Despite the fact that Yale kept the front windows cracked, the ambulance remained stuffy; they couldn't run the air-conditioning without starting the vehicle and giving away their location. They ate lunch around one—sandwiches from Jerry's—then sat some more.

The officer disguised as an orderly called in laughing when a woman dressed as Barbie was admitted to the ER with bad flu symptoms. Evidently, the same Mattel executives who had purchased the UCLA Children's Hospital had hired and costumed a Barbie to tour the pediatrics ward, bringing good cheer and product placement to the sick children.

With the exception of Explosive Diarrhea Barbie, the rest of the afternoon passed without incident.

Nancy barely stirred when David stepped through the curtains surrounding her bed, though he made an effort to rattle them to alert her of his arrival. Her torso was slightly elevated, and she'd pulled her hospital gown up high to hide the scarring from her esophageal resection, a small act of modesty that David found at once pathetic and moving given the massive distortion of her face. A bandage pushed out her gown where they'd lifted skin for grafting from above her clavicle.

The ICU stood mostly empty—just an elderly man intubated across the way on a monitored bed, multiple IVs stringing around his arms. The sunset, diffused through the LA smog, glowed orange through the venetian blinds, lighting the room in bands of color.

David became aware of the intensity of his heartbeat and realized it was probably due to the ICU's similitude to the MICU, where Elisabeth had been removed from life support. He closed his eyes for a moment, clearing the thought.

"Nancy," he said softly. "It's me. David."

Her head rolled slowly to face him. Her response was relaxed and listless, as though she were moving underwater. "Dr. Spier." Speaking around a tongue sluggish with morphine.

He took in the shock of her face. Her eyes, milky white, shrunken and sightless, were those of a *Macbeth* witch. Bolsters covered her face from forehead to chin. Xeroform—yellow antibiotic-impregnated sheets—had been sutured into her face over the skin grafts and packed with cotton soaked in mineral water. Then the Xeroform's edges had been folded back over and tied like a package, molding the new skin into the wound so it would take. If the grafts hadn't been laid, the wounds would have contracted as they closed over, pulling her features out of proportion. Disfiguring contractions came in all shapes and sizes—smeared nostrils, drooping eyes, lips stretched wide and thin. Polysporin antibiotic ointment stood out in globs over the bolsters. Infection—the next fight.

David found he was talking. "—in four to five days, we'll get those bolsters off and see if the grafts took. The sutures are sheep gut, so they'll dissolve. I insisted the plastics guys get in right away. They found a pretty good color match with the skin from your supraclavicular and postauricular areas, and they pulled a bit more from your lateral thigh—"

She was shaking her head back and forth. "No more," she said thickly. "No more." Her voice was hoarse—when she was in the ER, he should've seen about revising her crich to a trach earlier.

David crouched, resting his forearms flat on her bed. "I'm sorry," he said. "Just know you're being taken care of."

"Scary," she said. "So scary. A man coming at me . . ." She made a noise like a sigh. "Did they catch him?"

The thought of the assailant free, plotting and moving among others, made David's mouth tighten. "Not yet."

"I heard he got Sandra too. Is she okay?" Nancy's voice was flat and droning, the words all blending together.

"She'll have some scarring, but she should be all right."

"Did she swallow any?"

He shook his head, then remembered Nancy couldn't see him. "No," he said.

"Where is she?"

"Her mother took her up north. She's being treated at Stanford, closer to home. I'm not sure if she's coming back."

They sat in silence. The overhead lights were giving him a headache.

"I don't want to work anymore," Nancy said. "Don't want to be around people." A bit of drool ran from the corner of her mouth down her cheek, tracing the edge of a bolster.

"You can see about that later. Work can help pull you through a tough time." He sounded platitudinous and foolish, even to himself.

Her head looked like that of a mutant insect in a '50s fear film. "I don't want to help others," she said. "Not anymore."

"Okay," David said. "Okay."

"They said I can't have a corneal transplant."

"No," David said. "I'm so sorry."

"Why"—she paused, sucking air—"why not? Why won't they let me?"

"You lost over half of your cornea. I'm afraid there's not enough to sew into."

"Either eye?"

"I'm afraid not." *I'm afraid, I'm afraid*—he thought about the construct and how little it conveyed, how clinical it sounded. This woman was blind and terribly scarred. When she could finally eat solid foods again, she'd experience pain swallowing and she'd probably regurgitate her food with some regularity. Her esophagus would scar and tighten, causing strictures. *I'm afraid* didn't quite cover the bases.

She was crying softly, her head weakly shaking. Her eyes could no longer produce tears. "I don't want to be blind," she sobbed. "I want to see things. Grass, people, movies. What did I do? What did I do?"

He stood dumbly over her, both of them painted with lines of exquisite sunset. "Nothing. You did nothing to deserve this."

"Is Sandra blind?"

"No, she was fortunate. The alkali didn't go in her eyes." *Fortunate*. Another doctor's crutch.

Hoarse, rasping sobs. "Why me and not her?"

David took her hand quietly and sat with her as she drifted back into a drugged sleep. He did not have an answer.

The Nintendo Gameboy made a woeful noise in Dalton's hands, and he cursed and banged it on his knee. "Game over," he said. "Wanna play?" He offered the unit to Yale, who regarded it disdainfully for a moment before snapping to attention at movement by the ER doors.

An elderly woman emerged, limped across the ambulance bay, and climbed into a blue Volvo. Yale grimaced and settled back on his stool within the cramped confines of the ambulance.

As the Volvo sputtered up the ramp and out of sight, Dalton strained to make out the license plate through the night air. "One Ocean Sam Charles three four seven," he recited.

Yale remained statue-still, his eyes fixed on the ER doors.

"Let's see," Dalton continued. "I'll take the four, which gives me three of a kind because of the red 'Vette and the Dodge Ram. What do you want? Hey—what do you want?"

Yale's eyes flickered over to Dalton. "Whatever."

"Not whatever. You have to pick something. Why don't you take the seven, which'll give you two pairs."

"Fine," Yale said. "I'll take the seven."

"Or you could take the four and go for a straight."

"The four," Yale said. "Great."

"Well, which one?"

Yale studied Dalton for what seemed a very long time. "The four will be fine."

Dalton started up on the Gameboy again. "These goddamn stakeouts can really try your patience."

"Indeed," Yale said.

CHAPTER 20

A black-and-white slowed as it passed Clyde, and he propped his cheek casually on his fist to block his face. His hands, slick with sweat, slid on the steering wheel until he tightened them. He drove up and down Le Conte under the glare of the morning sun, but there were no parking spaces open, so he pulled into the lot by the deserted Macy's building and parked in the far corner behind a Dumpster. He sat, his mouth pressed against the plush top of the steering wheel, one hand hanging limply over the gearshift that protruded from the steering column.

His car, a '92 Ford Crown Victoria, was brown, though the paint had chipped on the hood and trunk, revealing the dull, oxidizing metal beneath. Rust had eaten through the wheel wells, and the tires were worn nearly smooth in the middles. Carl's Jr. Superstar wrappers, Barq's root beer cans, and other pieces of trash littered the backseat and rear shelf. The beige upholstered interior reeked of smoke and ketchup. Cigarette burns had left holes in the seat cushions, the fringes black and hard.

Clyde pulled a packet of Noblemen's Zinc Lozenges from the glove box. The orange suckers were individually sealed into a foil sheet in rows of three. He dug with his nail a few times to catch and lift the corner of the foil backside from the thin plastic covering, then peeled back the foil and popped a lozenge in his mouth. Then he tore free a square containing another lozenge, careful to bend the sheet first along the perforations, and held it in a sweaty hand.

He pulled his navy corduroy hat low over his eyes, then removed a pair of latex gloves from his pocket and put them on. Beneath his sweatshirt, his scrub top, moist with sweat, clung to his body. He hid his ball-chain necklace with its dangling key in the dirty ashtray on the passenger door.

After a moment, he pulled the gearshift down into DRIVE and sat perfectly still, his foot on the brake. His lips, fleshy and moist, moved slightly. He murmured to himself as if debating whether he should drive away.

He shoved the shift lever back up to P and got out. Leaving his keys hidden atop the left rear tire, he headed for the hospital.

The second morning of the stakeout had been nearly as uneventful as the first. Dalton leaned against the tint-windowed doors of the ambulance, gazing longingly up the ramp to the rectangle of blue sky. About every twenty minutes, Yale flicked a bit of lint from his pants or shirt; aside from that, he was still.

Garcia and the other gardener had been back on their shift since five in the morning. Dalton and Yale had remained holed up in the ambulance overnight. Neither noticed the medicinal scent of the vehicle's interior anymore. It smelled of sweat, a browning apple core from Yale's lunch the previous day, mothballs from Dalton's shirt.

"If nothing happens by noon, I'm gonna take a break," Dalton said. "Go home and check up on the kids and the sitter."

"If nothing happens by noon, we're up a creek," Yale said.

Day Three since the last attack. Assuming their guy, like most violent offenders who select random victims, was working on some kind of internal clock, their window was closing. There had only been a two-day gap between the first victims.

"Maybe he retired," Dalton joked.

Yale had a habit of sitting still when he spoke, keeping his hands at rest on his knees or the seat. "He's got a taste of it now. The power, the control." He moistened his lips with his tongue. "I'm worried he wised up and moved on. Switched locations on us. Two attacks establishes a pattern, maybe he knows we're waiting."

"We can't wait much longer," Dalton said. "Only have overtime clearance for the weekend." He muttered something under his breath. "I wish we had the manpower to stake out the other ERs in the area."

"They're on alert. That'll have to be good enough."

Dalton gripped the stool and leaned back. "It's never good enough. Every one of these attacks we miss, it's a lifetime of—"

Yale held up his hand and reached for his portable. "Yale, Yale, Garcia," crackled through. "Eyes up. Eyes up. Suspicious guy on the PCHS lot periphery, southeast corner. Keeping one hand under his sweatshirt. Looks like he's wearing scrub bottoms."

"What's going on?"

There was a full minute of silence, which neither Yale nor Dalton interrupted.

Blake finally cut in, announcing himself over the radio. "He's sort of lurking in the bushes over there. Got one eye on Garcia."

"Did he make him?"

"Don't think so, but I'm not sure he's gonna risk an assault with two gardeners right there. Guy looks fifty-one, fifty. Eyes all bugged out, talking to himself. If he *is* our guy, we got a real Kooky Lucy on our hands."

Dalton had one hand on the door handle, but Yale tapped it and waved a slender finger. "Don't jump him. Could be a diversionary tactic. Grover, are you there?"

They heard the rattle of the shopping cart when Grover broke in. "In the lot right above your heads. I'm on my way. Hard to move fast in these old motherfucking shoes."

"Don't move *too* fast," Dalton growled.

"Suspect is moving in, taking a closer look," Blake said.

A vein throbbed in Yale's temple when he spoke. "Can you see what he has beneath his sweatshirt?"

Dalton turned to Yale with pleading eyes. "Let's go, let's go," he hissed.

"Blake, call Jenkins and Bronner, tell them to move into position behind him on Le Conte in case he bolts," Yale said into the radio. He swung open the back door and stepped out into the fresh air, inhaling deeply. "Let's go take a look."

The two gardeners continued to work the ditch, removing a pipe of some kind, and Clyde waited in the shade of the trees, his cheeks puckering as he sucked on a lozenge. One of them glanced up briefly in his direction, then bent back down and adjusted something with a wrench.

Clyde gazed back toward Le Conte and took a few steps in that direction before a woman pushing a stroller came into view on the sidewalk ahead. Backing up until his shoulders pressed against the concrete wall of the PCHS structure, he watched her. His gloved hand fondled the Pyrex beaker, making masturbatory bulges beneath his sweatshirt, until she disappeared from view. He turned back to the hospital, his wide jaw set, and took a few tentative steps toward the ambulance bay, his hands shaking.

When he stepped from the cover of the bushes, he froze, his eyes tracking the homeless man pushing a shopping cart along the far edge of the drive-through. The man crossed behind the kiosks, heading his way. One of the gardeners spoke down into his chest, and then two men in shirts and ties broke from the shadows of the ambulance bay, one of them wearing dark sunglasses.

Emitting a stifled yelp, Clyde scurried back toward Le Conte just as a patrol car pulled up to the curb. A tall, lean officer jumped out, one hand reaching for his pistol.

When Clyde turned back to the hospital, the men in ties and the homeless man were heading for him in a dead sprint, and he shrieked and stumbled through the bushes along the side of the parking structure, losing his hat.

Shouts filled the air and a police badge caught the sun and gleamed, and he ran, leaves whipping against his face, heading for the car ramp that led up onto one of the exposed lots. His jarring footsteps caused the alkali to lap up the sides of the Pyrex beaker, and then his sweatshirt spotted in the front and he screamed, his foot catching a tree root. He pitched forward and couldn't get his hand untangled from his sweatshirt to break his fall, so he struck the ground forcefully with his chest and cheek, the Pyrex beaker shattering beneath him.

Wailing, hands scrabbling over his sweatshirt, he curled and writhed on the dirt at the base of a pine tree, and then they were there, tall discordant figures blocking out the sun and pointing guns—men in suits, a parking attendant, police officers, a homeless man. The sweatshirt pulled tight across his fat stomach, and every time it shifted, shards of Pyrex dug into his flesh, the alkali eating into healthy skin and open wounds alike.

Hands reached out at him, but he fought them, clawing, and then a policeman's boot came hard in his side and he was screaming and jerking on the ground, yanking in vain at the sweatshirt.

Loud, stabbing voices.

"Don't touch him!"

"He's got lye all over himself!"

"Gloves! Gloves!"

"Frisk him."

"Grab that arm. Somebody grab that arm!"

"I don't want to get the shit on me."

"Call HazMat. Call Animal Control."

He was flipped over onto his stomach and he bellowed, his mouth bent wide, dry lips cracking. A thread of saliva connected the corner of his mouth to a pine cone near his cheek. Cuffs clamped down hard around his wrists. A knee pinned his shoulder to the ground on either side and hands fluttered all around him—up the lengths of his legs, under his arms, in his crotch. Glass crunched beneath him, against his gut and chest.

A cluster of onlookers gathered on the sidewalk at Le Conte.

"Check the scrub top—there's a hidden pocket inside the breast."

A hand scrabbling over his breast, darting into his inside pocket. Empty. "Ow, shit!" The man jumped back, wiping blue liquid off his hand.

"Stand back! Stand back! Grab his arms. Stay clear of the sweatshirt. It's doused."

One of the uniformed cops pressed a pistol to the back of Clyde's head and Clyde closed his eyes, but someone grabbed the barrel, pulling it away. "Are you fucking crazy? You can't do that."

"Watch me."

A scuffle. Someone fell. Searing pain.

"You can't do it. It's too obvious."

"There's press around."

"Do we haul him in?"

"There are civilians watching."

The air smelled of rankled flesh. Clyde screamed as loud as he could, a high-pitched, girllike warble, his open mouth pressing into dirt and pine needles. The spasms in his throat distorted his words. "It hurts oh God it hurts."

"I hope so, you motherfucker."

"Now you know. Now you know."

They stood back, framing his writhing body like trees fringing a pond. Faces smug with satisfaction. One of them crossed his arms.

Clyde rocked and lurched like a trussed calf, his entire body shuddering, his arms pinned behind him. His sobs came as pained wet grunts. "Oh God it hurts. It hurts so bad. Three, two, one, stand back from back from oh my God no."

"Should we bring him into the ER? We're gonna have to bring him in."

"Fuck that." A wad of spit landed on his cheek. "Let him burn."

CHAPTER 21

DAVID heard them coming before he saw them—the loud bellow of a wounded animal and a crescendo of shuffling boots. The doors slammed open as the officers shoved the man through, and David lowered his chart and closed the door to the exam room he'd just left.

Jenkins held an animal control come-along pole, the

wire noose at the end of the shaft cinched around the wailing man's neck.

"Oh God. Help me. Make it stop help me make it—" Another loud, wavering cry.

Jenkins released the spring catch and pulled the noose free. The man instantly collapsed. He lay facedown on the floor, his arms bent back behind him, wrists cuffed. Still gloved in white latex, his hands stuck up like some sort of plume.

The officers stood in a half circle behind him.

Jenkins flashed a cold grin at David. David looked from the gardeners to the homeless man to Yale and Dalton, realization dawning.

David ran forward and crouched over the man. "What happened? What happened to him?"

"Alkali," Yale said. "During our pursuit, he tripped and spilled on himself."

"His sweatshirt is soaked. Bring me trauma shears. Someone bring trauma shears! How long ago did this happen?" David pulled a pair of gloves from a box on a nearby cart and pulled them on. "Get a stretcher!"

Patients and staff had spilled out of the exam rooms and the Central Work Area into Hallway One, gawking. Leaving her post at the triage desk, Pat strode through the swinging doors behind the officers. Don stood in the middle of the hall behind David, hands stuffed into his physician's coat.

"Clear the hall of patients," Dalton barked. "Now!" Doors slammed shut and patients scurried.

The man's cheek pressed flat against the floor. Saliva sprayed the tile when he whimpered. David checked his pulse, which was racing. At first, he thought the man's face had been burnt, but then he realized the redness was severe acne. Wisps of hair wreathed his scalp, which was shiny with sweat.

David would need to get the patient out of the cuffs to treat him. Right now, the man seemed more scared than dangerous. Posture limp and slumped. In case he became agitated, someone should be standing by with a high-potency neuroleptic for IM rapid tranquilization. However, the sight of someone waiting with a needle might alarm and anger him. If it came down to it, David would try to talk the patient into taking sedatives orally—it would be less violating and would make the man feel as though he were an active participant in his treatment. For now, he needed to be calmed and reassured.

"You're in a safe place," David told him. "I'm here to take care of you. I need to ask you some questions. Are you taking any drugs?"

A long drawn-out groan. Could mean yes, no, or nothing.

"Is this alkali? I need to know if this is alkali."

The man's head rocked up and down against the floor in a nod.

David looked up at the officers. "How long ago did this happen?"

"I don't know," Yale said. "Five minutes maybe."

"Uncuff him. We have to get him out of this sweatshirt."

Dalton shook his head. "No way, Doc. Ain't gonna happen."

"Saline bottles!" David tried tearing the moist sweatshirt with his hands, but it didn't give. His gloves came away blue and he shot them off onto the floor and pulled on another pair. "Trauma shears—where are the trauma shears? And someone call psych—preferably Dr. Nwankwa. Give him a heads-up."

The staff members stood still. Their stares, hardened with hatred for Clyde, were nearly tangible. The hall took on an eerie dream silence.

David turned the man on his side; he rolled willingly. The entire front of his sweatshirt was doused in alkali. A few jagged edges of Pyrex protruded. The fabric smelled heavily of cigarette smoke. "They walked so slow," the man sputtered.

"We'll give you something for the pain," David said. "Some morphine."

The man shrieked and bucked. "No shots," he cried. "No needles."

"Okay, okay. How about pills?"

"I don't take pills," the man moaned. "Pills are for faggots."

Leaning in the doorway of Exam Fourteen, Jill slid her pen into her scrub top. The material above the front pocket was lined with ink from near-misses. "I hope it hurts," she muttered.

"Jill," David snapped. "The patient can hear you."

"I hope so."

David found himself looking for Diane, though he knew it wasn't her shift. He'd have to find support elsewhere.

The man was sobbing. "They made me walk slow and burn."

David tried to quell his rising anger at his staff. Still, no one was moving to help him. "Where the hell are those trauma shears!"

Pat stood behind Jenkins, the overhead lights catching the black hairs peppered through her gray buzz cut. The skin around her eyes was drawn taut, sending a network of wrinkles through her cheeks. Her expression was one David had never seen.

The man flopped and screeched.

"Can someone move? Will someone get to work here?" David's voice was high and thin. Nobody responded.

One of the undercover cops, dressed as a parking attendant, stepped forward. "Let's go, guys," he said. "Do your jobs."

"Pat," David said. "Bring trauma shears."

Pat glared down at the man. She did not move. An instantaneous sweat covered David's back, and he felt a tingle roll across it. "This is not a choice for us to make." He spoke slowly, his voice shaking. "There is no decision here."

Slowly, Pat crossed her arms.

Choking on rage, he rose and shoved past Jill into Exam Fourteen. Carson watched him from the far side of the hall, shocked. David grabbed some trauma shears from a tray, and holding his stethoscope so it wouldn't slide off his shoulders, half jogged back to the patient. Aside from the crusted red acne, the man's face was corpse-white.

"I have to flip him over. Take off the cuffs."

"No way," Jenkins said. "No fuckin' way."

The cop dressed as a parking attendant stepped forward, but Jenkins placed a hand on his chest. "Don't even think about it, Blake."

The man's shoulders hit the floor with a slap when David rolled him onto his back. His arms were twisted beneath him, and he shrieked.

"I know," David said. "It hurts, but we're doing this to help you."

Don watched, feet planted, hands in his pockets.

"I'm going to cut your sweatshirt off, because it's burning you," David said, fighting to keep his voice level. "I'm going to cut it using these scissors." He slid the open trauma shears up the front of the fabric. "What's your name?"

"Not telling."

"Hey, hey." David leaned over, close to the man's face. It smelled sticky and sweet, like orange-flavored candy.

"It's okay. I'm here to help you. What's your name?" The man's eye beat a few times as it pulled over to look at David. David looked away quickly, wanting to avoid eye contact that could be interpreted as confrontational. A shiny puddle of drool had collected on the tile where the man's mouth had been.

"Clyde."

David threw the halved sweatshirt open like a blazer. A few pieces of glass and the broad lip of a Pyrex beaker tinkled to the floor. Luckily for Clyde, the beaker had shattered between his sweatshirt and his scrub top. The stencil on the scrub top featured a seal, below which UNIVERSITY OF CALIFORNIA MEDICAL CENTER: UCLA, UCI, UCSD was written in a jailhouse blue. It could have been stolen from this very hospital. The top yielded easily to the blade, and David saw that the thin layer of material had helped to lessen the damage. The alkali had soaked through, leaving the skin red. In a few spots, white blisters were beginning to rise. Minor cuts covered his chest and lower neck, but little glass had made it all the way through the scrub top into the wounds.

"Try to slow your breathing, Clyde," David said. "We don't want you to hyperventilate." His voice betrayed his anger and exasperation. "We need to irrigate!"

Finally, a hand holding a saline bottle extended toward David, a woven leather bracelet around the wrist. David took the bottle from Carson and began spraying. Carson crouched on Clyde's other side and joined him.

"Missed a spot," Jenkins said sardonically, pointing at a large blister under Clyde's nipple.

David ignored Jenkins, leaning forward so his face was near Clyde's. "We're spraying you off with water now. We're doing this to wash off the alkali that is burning you."

Clyde shifted on his bound hands, squealing with pain. No one else came near them; the staff and officers standing back in their muted ring. "I didn't want to," Clyde whimpered. "I was going to, like before, but I didn't want to do it."

"Let's get him to an exam room. Dr. Lambert, get me a stretcher. A stretcher." David glanced up, his mouth pursed with anger. *"Get me a stretcher now!"*

Don returned David's gaze for what seemed an eternity, the only sound in the hall that of Clyde's whimpering. Finally, he turned and walked leisurely to retrieve a stretcher. It took him ten seconds to turn the corner, his slow pace mocking David.

Sweat dripped from David's forehead onto Clyde's face, and he leaned back and wiped his brow with an arm. "We have to get him on a bed. We don't have time to wait while Dr. Lambert plays games. Carson, keep irrigating." David turned to the cop Jenkins had referred to as Blake. "And you. Will you give me a hand?"

Clyde was heavy and limp, and David and Blake had to struggle to get him to his feet. He was taller and wider than either of them, and they staggered under his weight. The other officers watched closely.

David looked over Jenkins's shoulder at Pat. She held her head high on her slender neck, stately and pitiless. Disdain and hatred twisted her face into an ugly mask. "Get the hell out of my ER," David said. Her face crumpled, and he felt a flash of satisfaction move through the molten haze of his anger.

He and Blake pivoted and began to drag Clyde toward Exam Fourteen, Carson continuing to douse him with saline, Yale and Dalton walking on either side. Clyde was unsteady on his feet. Jenkins followed closely behind, palm resting on the butt of his pistol, and the other officers dissipated slowly, heading back out through the doors. By flanking David and Clyde, Yale, Dalton, and Jenkins created the illusion they were assisting.

"We're going to help you," David said. "Do you understand that I'm here to help you?"

Tear tracks streaked Clyde's cheeks like clown paint. He nodded, his chest heaving.

"What else can we get you, Doctor?" Jenkins asked quietly. "A plumber's snake to clear out his throat? A bag for his head, maybe?"

"Should we give him five, one, and one?" Carson asked.

Five milligrams of Haldol, one of Cogentin, and one of Ativan. He'd be out in ten minutes and stay that way for hours. "I don't want to go there yet," David said. "I'd like him lucid. He's been fine so far."

"That's because he's in handcuffs," Jenkins interjected.

David turned to Clyde. "You won't give us any trouble?"

Headshake.

"You promise?"

"Promise," Clyde cried. "I promise." He closed his eyes, muttering, "Three, two, one."

David felt a burning sensation along the tender skin inside his biceps. Alkali. He wiped it off hastily on his scrub top. "Watch your arms," he warned Blake.

Clyde finally found his feet and helped them the last few steps into the room, snuffling and yelping, and then they had him seated at the edge of the gurney. Carson continued spraying Clyde down, the saline pooling in his lap. His scrub bottoms turned dark with the liquid, clinging to his thighs and crotch.

David grabbed two saline bottles and stepped into the hall. Many of the staff members were standing around, rubberneckers milling in the wake of an accident. Don had just returned with the stretcher David had requested. He tossed it on the floor. David took in each face, the cold, peering eyes.

He and Carson would need help. Given the patient's

history of violence against women, selecting male staff seemed clearly the right course. "You two." David snapped his fingers and pointed to a male nurse and a male lab tech, neither of whom he recognized. "In here and help Carson. Move it. *Now!*"

The nurse took a step forward, then the lab tech followed. David handed them each a saline bottle as they shuffled past.

David regarded the others for a moment. "In my seventeen years practicing medicine, *this* is the most horrifying thing I've seen." His voice sounded foreign to him. "On top of which you've allowed the floor to come to a standstill. Get back to work immediately."

He stepped back in the room and faced Yale. Jenkins's hand hovered over his Beretta, making David intensely nervous. Blake stood to the side, clearly uneasy. "Uncuff him," David said. "You've had your fun, now we need to get at him to treat him."

"No, sir," Jenkins said. "You're dealing with a dangerous man."

"We're dealing with a patient injured with alkali under suspicious circumstances who hasn't even been booked, let alone convicted of anything."

"The guy got caught stuffing alkali under his shirt. I think we both know—"

"Uncuff my patient!" David stepped forward, eye to eye with Jenkins.

Yale pressed a hand against David's chest, which David knocked aside. "The best we can do is put him in four-point restraints," Yale said. "Would that be better?"

"We handle a lot of potentially violent patients."

"Would it be better if we got the suspect in four-points?" Yale repeated calmly.

David took a deep breath. "Yes."

"*Hard* restraints."

"Fine. The security guard up front can get them for you. Please hurry."

Dalton strolled out to fetch the restraints, as David scribbled the order. The nurse and lab tech were standing a few feet back from Clyde as they sprayed him down.

"What do you mean, restraints?" Jenkins asked. "Throw some water on him and let's haul his ass to Harbor."

"Back off, let us do our job. You can do yours later." Seeing his words were having little impact, David tried a more pragmatic approach. "You want him to stand trial wrapped in bandages?" he asked. "What do you think that'll do for jury sympathy?"

He turned around and examined the patient. The fact that the scrub top had remained between the alkali spill and Clyde's flesh had really limited the damage. The irrigation was coming along nicely—there would be some painful blistering and a few cuts, but nothing too serious. Morphine would have helped Clyde's pain, but he'd reacted violently earlier when David had mentioned giving him a shot, and David didn't want to risk agitating him again now that he'd calmed down.

David stepped forward, again careful to avoid Clyde's eyes. Clyde's lips were moving slightly, and David realized he was counting backward from three, over and over.

"We're just spraying the alkali off you," David said. "We're trying to make the burning stop."

Clyde's lips stopped their quiet chant for a moment. "Thank you," he said.

"We have some questions for him," Yale said.

"Uncuff him and let us treat him," David said over his shoulder. "You can question him in an hour."

Jenkins grabbed David's shoulder from behind. "This guy fucked up two of your nurses—"

"A nurse and a doctor, and we don't know the patient is responsible."

"Why don't you stop worrying about him so much and let us get what we need. *We* brought him in here."

David stared down at Jenkins's hand until he removed it from his shoulder. He looked around for Blake, his sole ally among the cops, but he'd left the room. "That was your legal responsibility," David said. "Not a favor."

"*He* is not the victim here," Jenkins shouted through clenched teeth, jerking a finger violently in Clyde's direction.

"We need you out," David said. He turned to Yale. "I need him out. He's agitating the patient."

"We'll get the *suspect* secured, then give you a little space," Yale said.

Dalton returned with the leather restraints. He walked behind Clyde's back, circling the gurney, and Clyde grunted and whipped his head around, trying to keep him in view. Carson and the nurse and lab tech were startled back a few steps. Jenkins grabbed Clyde's legs roughly, and Clyde thrashed as Dalton undid the handcuffs. The two quickly had Clyde flat on his back, strong leather restraints binding his ankles and wrists to the metal rails of the gurney. David directed them to bind one of Clyde's hands up and the other to the railing down by his waist so if something went wrong, they could turn him on his side to minimize the risk of aspiration.

The skin on Clyde's chest was raw and shiny where it wasn't raised in blisters, but it looked as though most of the alkali had been flushed off. He was in a much better position for Carson to access the burns on his chest, and the four leather cuffs held his limbs tight enough that the others weren't afraid to work more closely on him.

"All right," David said. "That's enough. He's not going anywhere. I can take it from here."

"We'll be outside," Yale said.

"Have fun," Dalton added. He had to grip Jenkins's forearm to move him from the room.

The room hadn't been prepped for a potentially violent patient, so David removed both IV poles, sliding them out into the hall and leaving the door slightly ajar. He found some scissors near a bag of O-negative blood that had been left on the counter from the previous trauma, and slid them into his pocket. The lab tech wore a shirt and tie, having not yet changed into scrubs for the day, and David pulled him aside and whispered to him to take off his tie before going near the patient. He caught Carson's eye and gestured for him to remove his yin and yang earring.

"Stand back from the door," Clyde was muttering when David turned his attention back to him. "Stand back from the door." He kept his eyes closed, as though he were praying. His hands were puffy, perhaps swollen from the cuffs.

He repeated certain phrases like mantras, David realized. The recitations seemed to have an obsessive-compulsive element to them; maybe they were uttered for the same reason some people with OCD wash their hands forty times a day—to reduce anxiety.

David crouched so he wouldn't have to lean over Clyde in threatening fashion. "We're going to remove your gloves now—"

Clyde screamed, balling up his hands into fists behind his back.

"Okay, okay," David said. "We'll wait till later. We'll take the gloves off later. How's the pain? Is it better?"

Clyde nodded. "Still burns but it's done eating its way through me. I know. I can tell when it's done."

"Do you want some pills for the pain?"

"I told you, *I don't take pills*." His crying and screaming had finally stopped, though he was still breathing hard. A small wedge of Pyrex glimmered in a cut near his left armpit.

"I'm going to reach across you," David said. "And I'm going to use these forceps to remove a sliver of glass from one of your cuts."

"Okay," Clyde said.

David leaned over, but Clyde's left arm was locked down by his waist, blocking the cut. He turned to Clyde, again doing his best to avoid what could be perceived as threatening eye contact. "I'm going to untie one of your arms to get at the cut. I'm doing this so I can help you. Remember, you promised not to give me any trouble."

Carson took a half step forward. "Look, I don't know—"

Clyde's sweaty head moved up and down in a nod.

David untied the restraint and raised Clyde's arm, the thick leather band remaining around Clyde's wrist. He bent down, navigated the forceps carefully into the wound, and removed the piece of Pyrex. He lowered Clyde's arm back to the metal rail and secured it again, threading the leather strip through the hasp.

Carson let his breath out in a rush.

Clyde raised his head weakly and stared at David as the others continued to flush his wounds with saline. His voice hitched in his chest. "Thank . . . thank you," he said.

David thought of the Xeroform bolsters stitched into Nancy's face and strongly resisted the urge to tell him to go fuck himself.

CHAPTER 22

"TO say I'm pissed off would be an understatement." By the time David entered the doctors' lounge his rage had turned to disgust. He had pulled most of the staff who had been on the floor during the incident into an impromptu meeting, leaving Carson and a few nurses to oversee the floor. Pat had apparently followed his orders and left. Nurses and interns crammed onto the cheap vinyl couch, leaned against the coffee-stained sink, and sat cross-legged on the floor.

He looked blankly from face to face. Almost all of them lowered their eyes from his stare. "A patient comes into our division in acute pain, requiring emergency treatment, and we withhold care. A top-notch medical facility *withholds care*. I can't . . ." The words were jumbling in his mouth, so he paused and took a breath. "I'm meeting with Dr. Evans today, but I can't even begin to figure out how I'm going to present this."

A few of the interns stiffened at the mention of the hard-nosed chief of staff.

He couldn't recall ever seeing the staff so uncomfortable. Nervous shuffling, regretful expressions. One of the nurses looked up to stop her moist eyes from leaking. A medicine intern raised a fist to stifle a cough.

"Outside these doors, the world can be as vicious and cold as it wants. People don't help each other. People don't have to help each other. In here, we take care of them, trite as that may sound."

"That man is a vicious mutilator of women who got a taste of his own medicine." The anger in Don's voice surprised him.

"That man is a *suspect*"—David emphasized the nouns with jabs of his open hand—"but that's the cops' concern. To us, he's a person with a serious injury, like any other."

"Just doing our job, huh? That's the philosophy you want to rely on?"

David's stomach was awash with acid and rage. "The Hippocratic Oath, Dr. Lambert, is the philosophy I rely on. We took an oath, every one of us, that we would work by our medical ethics and hold them above everything else. What does it mean if that oath ends beyond the point that someone is appealing, or mentally sound? Or likable?"

"It's not that black and white."

"It is precisely that black and white. If we can reduce the pain of another human being, we do it."

"How can you want to show that man compassion?"

"Compassion? It has nothing to do with compassion. *This is our job.* If you don't like it, go be a goddamn accountant. But you can't stay here and think you can call your own shots."

The others watched the exchange with stunned expressions.

David took another moment to gather his composure. "It is not our place to question our patients' morality. Do you really think you can keep your footing on that slippery slope? What next? We stop treating criminals? How about people who cheat on their income taxes? Do we let them lie in pain? The mentally ill? Do we deny them medical care? Do we?" David's arms were tensed before him. "That man in Fourteen could very well be mentally incapacitated. Leave judgment to the courts, and do the jobs you swore under oath to do."

"I never abandon my own instincts," Don said. "Not for any code of ethics."

"Fine," David snapped. "If that code of ethics doesn't work, try this one. I'm the division chief, and you will listen to me. So do your *fucking* job. All of you. *Now*."

He walked out and left the door standing open, the murmurs following him a few yards up the hall. Whether the confrontation had done any good or not, he felt considerably better.

He returned to the CWA and checked in with Carson, noting the emptiness of the ER's main axis. Aware that he had just acted like the kind of manager he'd sworn he would never be, he focused on the board as the other staff members trickled back to work.

Preoccupation stayed with him for the next few hours. His concentration wandered; his movements were mechanical. He forgot a patient's name during an examination for the first time since June of 1987.

The rest of the staff gleaned the fact that he didn't want to interact with them. Except for essential exchanges, the nurses left him alone. The interns went to Don to present cases and have their orders signed. Don spent his time alternating between gloating over his newfound popularity and sulking like a scorned girl.

When David stopped by the CWA later, the room quieted as he entered. He glanced at the board. Aside from an MI and a severed finger, things appeared to be quiet, so most of the staff were hanging out on the stools or leaning on the counters, catching up on paperwork.

Don's hand rasped over the stubble he kept *Miami Vice* length. His eyes, beneath his perfect brow, were intensely angry. Jill touched David's arm, a gesture he thought was apologetic. The others ignored him.

He nodded at Jill, a bit awkwardly, and walked from the room. Before heading to his lunch meeting, he went to check on Clyde. He was just about to turn the corner when he overheard Jenkins talking to the two LAPD cops stationed outside the closed door to Clyde's room. They looked tall and hard in their uniforms, their black belts laden with tools and weapons. Yale stood by also, silent and seemingly uninvolved in the conversation.

"—business end of my nine-millimeter," Jenkins was saying. David peered around the corner and saw him remove his pistol and aim it at an imaginary victim, execution-style. The hall was momentarily deserted; David had decided to direct new patients to the rooms off Hallway Two until Clyde was moved.

One of the uniformed cops muttered something, though David picked up only snatches. ". . . doc releases him . . . get your hands on . . ."

"That's right," Jenkins said. "We'll file it under DSAF: Did Society a Favor."

David was unsure how to gauge the severity of Jenkins's grandstanding, but he felt his face tingling with the panic mixture of anger and sudden dread. Yale leaned against the door but didn't comment. Was he complicit in Jenkins's scheming, or did he believe Jenkins was simply venting?

David pulled silently back from the corner and headed to his meeting. It took him nearly ten minutes to negotiate the cafeteria lines and locate two opposing seats at a table, and he found himself fondly recalling the days of the separate physicians' dining room. He had already finished eating when he spotted Sandy Evans crossing the cafeteria toward him, juggling a soft leather briefcase and a forest-green tray covered with a mound of food. She wore a well-tailored charcoal suit, and wore it well for a sixty-five-year-old. Her hair, chestnut with auburn highlights, was shag-styled down around her neck.

He was glad to have pinned her down for lunch; the last time he'd needed to speak to her on short notice, he'd had to scrub in and catch up to her in the OR. Speaking through surgical masks tended to blur the words, and though surgeons never seemed to mind, David had always found a certain stark irreverence in discussing unrelated issues over an opened patient. To accent her points, Sandy had pointed at him with a Kelly-clamped segment of resected bowel.

David rose slightly in the black cafeteria chair, and he and Sandy touched cheeks in a semblance of a kiss. Aside from her husband, David was the only person she permitted closer than a handshake, an indulgence granted him only because she'd had an exceedingly close relationship with his mother. She was much like David's mother in many regards—the stern attractive looks, the insatiable ambition, the aggressive set of the shoulders. Even their faces sometimes blended in David's memory; both had a hard-shelled, resilient cast, the result of weathering myriad broadsides early in their careers from male colleagues and superiors. But David felt Sandy's similarity to his mother most keenly in something unexpected and unsettling—his desire to please her.

Sandy dropped her briefcase on an empty chair and lowered the tray to the table, a bottle of Gatorade rolling toward the edge until David grabbed it. Her voice was deep and throaty, a smoker's voice, though she'd never smoked a single cigarette. "The Board of Directors wants a complete media blackout, and rightly so. One suture untied, and we'll have a scandal on our hands. ABC, CNN, MSNBC, and Fox News are all pressing my office for comment, and they're expecting me to roll over. Little do they know." Her vivid green eyes gleamed. "They'd better gear up for one hell of a dogfight, 'cause this old bitch don't roll over unless she's in the mood." Her eyebrows, lightly penciled, rose beneath her bangs. "Oh, it's true. You can ask Stephen."

David absentmindedly bent a plastic fork in half. "I'll take your word."

Sandy opened two containers of yogurt, unwrapped a burrito, and lifted the lid of a cardboard box from the grill. Sandy still jogged five miles every morning, and ate like an NFL linebacker. "Sounds like you've had your hands full today," she said around a mouthful of chickwich.

"More than you know," he muttered.

"What?"

"Nothing." David shook his head. "What happened this morning—the *entire division* not stepping in to provide care—I've never seen anything like it."

"People react violently when friends and colleagues have been injured."

David looked up, shocked. "You're condoning this?"

"Hey!" She pointed at him with the end of a banana. "Direct that righteous Spier anger elsewhere, David. I'm on your side here. If I condoned your staff's behavior this morning, I'd be perfectly capable of expressing that sentiment, so don't get pissy with me over implications."

"All right. I'm sorry. I apologize."

"If you'll pardon the equestrian metaphor, David, you're one of my Thoroughbreds. You were the youngest division chief in the history of this hospital, and I leaned like hell to get you that post, not because your mother was my mentor and dear friend but because you are that good. You're one of maybe three department heads here whom I trust implicitly, across the board, without question." Her voice was hard and driving, as if she were still being challenged.

"Would you like me to apologize again?"

Her lips pursed and pulled to one side in her distinctive smile. "No. Once was sufficient. Now, I agree that your staff's behavior was egregious. I'm merely pointing out that, however misguided and asinine, there are extenuating circumstances here. Now let's talk about this. First of all, what's this man's name? The patient."

"Clyde."

"Clyde? Who the hell's named *Clyde*?" She looked at David, miffed, as if he were somehow responsible for naming him.

"That's all he'll give up," David said. "No last name either."

"All right. How many staff members refused to help you?"

"Everyone."

"David, if the radiology tech or a desk clerk didn't pitch in, that's not relevant to this discussion. I'm interested in how many members of ER staff who receive and treat new patients refused to help you."

David thought for a moment. "Seven. Four nurses, two interns, and Don Lambert."

"All right. So legally, we're concerned with seven people here."

"My concerns are ethical, Sandy. Not legal."

She finished chewing a bite of burrito. "Hurrah, David. However, what *I'm* concerned with, in running this facility, is the area where your ethical concerns cross the boundary into legal concerns."

"Or PR concerns."

Her penciled eyebrows pulled up as she appraised him. "You inherited your mother's moral sense, but it's a shame you didn't inherit her overriding grasp of politics. It's the only thing that stands between you and a future post as chief of staff."

David ignored the dig. "How do you intend to handle this issue, Sandy?"

"Well, we've long known that Dr. Lambert is a lazy SOB, but when he's focused he's actually quite competent, and he is very popular among the staff. Do you really want to push this? It'll be a big stink. Do you feel your patient's care was compromised?"

"Well, I couldn't get to him as quickly—"

"*Truly* compromised?"

He bit his lower lip. "Probably not."

"All right. Now let's bear in mind that we are dealing with a very specific situation. This man was attacking ER workers. While the behavior of your staff is inexcusable, I'm not concerned that they'd withhold care from other patients. And the likelihood of someone *else* attacking ER workers and then needing medical care at the hands of that same staff . . . well, we know how remote a possibility that is. You have to pick your battles. Now let me ask you again. Do you really want to push this?"

David suddenly felt quite nauseous. "I want them to be formally reprimanded, yes."

A woman trudging slowly past glanced over at him, and he realized the intensity in his voice was making it carry.

"Don't get me wrong, David. I'm as pissed about this as you are. In fact, I'm planning on personally meeting with all seven employees and tearing them each a new orifice. What I'm asking is, do you want to involve the Ethics Committee? Risk Management? The California Medical Board?"

He rolled the soft lining skin of his bottom lip between his teeth. "No."

"All right." She smiled curtly. "I'm quite good at being furious. By the time I'm through with those seven, they'll have the Hippocratic Oath tattooed on their foreheads."

He nodded, somewhat formally, and she returned the gesture, amused.

"Now I've got another tangentially related headache," Sandy said. "As I mentioned before, the media's been crawling all over the hospital, jamming the phone lines. It's not the kind of press we like, but, even worse, it's interfering with the hospital's effectiveness. When can you get this . . . *Clyde* on his way to the Sheriff's station?"

"It's complicated."

"No, David, it's not. Get him stable and get him moved."

Sandy leaned back and crossed her arms, an amused, attractive little smile playing across her face. "One of the rules when dealing with Thoroughbreds is that you don't rein them in too much. They lose some of their fire, their passion. So I'm making a suggestion, not a directive, and you can throw it out if you'd like."

He knew what was coming, and he knew he deserved it.

"More people look up to you here than you're aware," Sandy said. "You're part of the bedrock of this hospital. I heard you lost your cool pretty badly this morning. That unsettles people. Whether we like it or not, your division is under intense scrutiny because of this case—both internal and external scrutiny."

David took this in, trying to strip away his anger and defensiveness, and find some utility in the information. "Your suggestion?" he asked.

Sandy rose, picked up her tray, which was littered with gutted food containers and fruit rinds, and winked at him. "Keep your clay feet covered."

CHAPTER 23

YALE emerged from Exam Room Fourteen, jotting something in a worn black leather notepad. A rubber band held several yellow sheets to the top cover, marking his place. As David approached from the cafeteria, Yale flipped the pad shut and slid it into his sport-coat pocket. The two LAPD officers had been replaced by UCLA PD cops, who now stood guard at the door.

"Dr. Spier," Yale said. He took a few steps toward David, perhaps so the officers wouldn't overhear the conversation to come. "We'd like to get the suspect moved to the jail ward at Harbor. As I'm sure you're aware, the ward there is a high-security treatment zone, and we think it will be safer for everyone involved when we get him moved there. Is he stable?"

"I'd like to continue irrigation for a few hours. Alkali continues to burn deep within the skin, even when it looks like it's been cleaned off."

"Yes," Yale said. "We've learned that the hard way."

"I also need to get him stitched up."

"Can't that wait and be handled at Harbor?"

The last time David had checked, Clyde was still reporting pain. David had his hesitations about releasing a patient in a fragile state into the hands of officers who were less than concerned about his health and safety. He thought about how slowly they'd sauntered into the ER with Clyde screaming and burning in their hands. Jenkins's execution pose with his pistol. "I need to keep an eye on him for a few more hours, see how things settle. I don't want him moved in this condition."

"I'd really prefer—"

"Maybe tonight."

"What time?"

"We'll see how he's doing at eight, nine o'clock."

That would give David more time to observe the burn's course and make sure the gashes were stitched and cleaned up. Plus, Jenkins's shift should be over by then. David would be less concerned about turning Clyde over to a more impartial officer.

Yale glanced over his shoulder, and the two officers at the door looked away quickly, pretending they hadn't been eavesdropping. "I'm gonna be honest with you," Yale said. "It's not going well in there. He won't talk to me."

"Maybe you alienated him too much during the arrest."

"Perhaps."

"What took you so long getting him to the ER?"

"We were busy subduing and frisking him. Minor considerations like that." Yale tapped his pen, a cheap Bic ballpoint, against his lips. "I'm thinking maybe you could try to loosen him up for me."

"That's really not my job, Detective Yale. The psych consult will be along shortly, and I'm sure—"

"Dr. Nwankwa. I'm familiar with him and not optimistic he'll be looking to advance our cause."

"Advancing your cause is not his job. Or mine. Our job is to treat patients."

"In any event, I'm not permitting Dr. Nwankwa to see the suspect. This is not the time for a psychiatric assessment."

"Fine. I need Dr. Nwankwa to assess the patient's

need for antipsychotic medication. If we can keep Clyde calmed down, that benefits both our agendas." David crossed his arms. "My treatment of this patient will be unimpeded."

Yale studied David with clever, shiny eyes. "You know, Dr. Spier, our jobs share certain similarities. We're both exposed to elements of society few people deal with. We both see people at their worst—in pain, terrified, furious, suicidal, dead. Just like you think I don't know my ass from . . . Just like you think I don't know much about what goes on in the ER, I can tell you, you don't know much about how things work on the street. Your code of ethics holds up just fine in here, between the scrubbed white walls, but there are different kinds of choices, different kinds of pressures and stresses and concerns out there. This man is a predator—"

"A *suspected* predator."

"Please keep your voice down, Dr. Spier. I'm saying that this man is a suspected predator, and when you deal with predators at large, free from restraints and backup, you might find your politics sliding slowly to the right."

"My politics are irrelevant to my ethics. I'm sorry you don't understand that."

"I learned my ethics wading through dismembered bodies, drug labs, and homemade torture chambers."

"So tell me, then," David said. "How do you think a suspect *should* be treated?"

"Is this the issue at stake? You wouldn't be holding this patient for reasons other than to provide critical medical care? As you're well aware, that would be overstepping your bounds, Dr. Spier."

"The patient is still in need of critical treatment."

"I see." Yale took a step back.

David cleared his throat. "Will Jenkins be involved in the transfer?"

Yale studied him closely. His pupils were dark and smooth; in the sterile overhead light, they resembled obsidian. "Jenkins will be involved as long as he wants to be involved." His little smile was cold and efficient. "He's got a first-class crush on the suspect. Won't leave him alone, even for a minute. He's sitting out in his patrol car on Le Conte right now, just in case we need him for anything."

"In medicine, physicians don't treat their family members." He did his best not to picture Elisabeth's face. "There's too much emotion there. Might make a bad decision."

"Dalton and I are running the show, not Jenkins. But I'm not going to take away his involvement. This is his way of dealing. So we let him drive behind the transport vehicle, let him twirl his lights and run his siren. He needs this."

"He's under a great deal of stress, and he's highly unstable. What are you going to do if he comes undone? Acts rashly?"

"There are any number of things about me that are questionable, Dr. Spier. My competence is not one of them."

David pointed to the closed door of Exam Fourteen. "That is a sick individual in there. Sick and violent, but also confused and scared. He needs your protection."

"And why do you trust me and not the others?" Yale said. Through all David's dealings with Yale, this was the first hint of anger he'd heard in his voice. "Because I can afford the same suits as you?"

"You wear *better* suits than I do, and no. I trust you more because you're the only one not acting like you want to treat my patient like Rodney King."

"Let me tell you something," Yale said, stabbing a finger at David. "You can take your classist disdain and shove it. You think you understand what goes on in our lives? Do you think you even understand what went down in the Rodney King fiasco? There were twelve officers on the scene for a reason. Why don't you look into it?"

The two officers by the door listened intently, leaning to make out more of the conversation.

A sharp noise of disdain escaped from the back of Yale's throat. "Patrol officers can get killed any minute of any day. Especially in this city. Why do they do it? What's your knee-jerk answer to that? They're all just power-hungry pigs, right? Bullshit." His hand rested lightly over the badge clipped to his belt. "They do it to protect and serve civilians. Even arrogant bastards like you."

His usually stoic face lined with emotion, and in that instant David saw right through him. The defensiveness, the pressured speech, the hint of hurt that found its way into his voice—it all reeked of regurgitated argument. Anger ossified by rejection. His wealthy background was betrayed by the split-toe stitching of his Cole Haan loafers, his family's reception of his choice of vocation by the contentious set of his mouth. His affluence came at a cost; it was thorny-stemmed. Yale seemed to sense he had given too much up, for he looked away and took a step back, his lips twitching like a boxer's.

"I don't want to argue about Rodney King," David said.

"Then don't bring him up."

"I'd just like your reassurance that there won't be any vigilante retribution against my patient."

The two men studied each other, still-faced and tense. "A suspect has never come to harm under my command," Yale finally said. "*Never.*"

David extended his hand. "Is that a guarantee?"

Yale regarded David with contempt. "I don't give guarantees." He walked away, leaving David and his proffered handshake behind.

When David stepped out of the ambulance bay, a man with slicked-back hair and a florid madras shirt confronted him, readying a notebook and sliding a pen from behind his ear. "Hear you're having some problems with your staff."

"Who are—? No. Everything's fine."

David kept walking, but the reporter followed him, hovering off his elbow. He held up his notebook and declaimed, "Sources inside the hospital indicate that there are growing tensions between Division Chief David Spier, members of his own staff, and the police."

"Please," David said. "Not now."

"I can make you look better if you talk."

"You can make yourself look better if you change your shirt."

The man pulled to a halt, grinning. David was happy to leave him behind. He paused on the dirt path near the PCHS structure. A small blue puddle continued seeping into the ground near one of the trees, and David recognized the few surrounding shards as Pyrex. The kicked-up dirt betrayed the recent struggle between Clyde and the officers. The area was partitioned off with yellow police tape.

Just ahead, a police car idled at the curb on Le Conte. As David drew near, Bronner exited the passenger side, heading across the street toward a coffee shop, picking up his feet in a heavy jog. Jenkins sat behind the wheel, flipping through some fliers with grainy black-and-white photos.

David leaned toward the open passenger window,

hands on the sill, his position and the painted Ford LTD making him feel, ridiculously, like a prostitute. "Excuse me."

Jenkins did not look up. "Dr. Spier," he said.

"Mind if I . . . ?" David gestured to the passenger seat.

Still no eye contact. Jenkins jotted something in his pad. "You can sit in the back."

After a moment's hesitation, David opened the rear door and climbed in. The backseat was composed of a solid plastic mold, with no cracks into which suspects could stuff drugs or weapons. A crime alert flier sat on one side, a displeased African American male with FUCK LAPD tattooed across his forehead peering out from the fuzzy photo. David scooted across to the middle and viewed the back of Jenkins's head through the protective Plexiglas shield that separated the front and back seats.

Jenkins had been kind enough to leave the small window open in the Plexiglas shield. A strip of his face peered at David from the rearview mirror, but David could not make out his eyes through his Oakley blades.

"The ICU nurse told me you've had a rough time going in to see your sister, so I wanted to let you know she's making good progress. The skin grafts are taking so far, and plastics is feeling quite confident. She fought off an internal infection pretty well, and—"

"Something tells me you didn't come all the way out here to talk about my sister." Jenkins's voice, deep and resonant, betrayed little emotion.

David realized just how claustrophobic the backseat of a cop car was. The strip of Jenkins's face remained perfectly centered in the rearview mirror. He had mastered silence as a weapon, and David found it a powerful one.

He wasn't sure how to find the balance between condescension and communication. "What happened to your sister was horrible. And I know . . . and if there's anything I can ever do . . . But the patient is a—"

"Patient," Jenkins sneered.

"The suspect is a very sick man. Disturbed."

"Sick enough to wear a fake tattoo to throw off our investigation? Sick enough to use surgical gloves because they leave a less distinctive print than leather gloves? Don't buy the dummy routine, Doctor. Our boy's pretty clever for someone sick in the head."

"People can be smart and still be unbalanced. Imagine how ill you'd have to be to do the kinds of things he's done."

"That doesn't interest me."

"Even if this guy is guilty, he's still got rights. You don't want to give his future attorney any ammunition against the DA, do you?"

Jenkins shifted in his seat and then finally turned his head. David stared back at his own distorted reflection in the broad band of Jenkins's sunglasses. "My sister is blind. She has to barf up into napkins for the rest of her life. Dead skin falls off her face in gray patches. And you're more concerned about the guy who did it."

Across the street, Bronner emerged from the shop, holding two cups of steaming coffee.

"I'm extremely concerned about Nancy. But she isn't my patient anymore. The suspect is."

"Then go back to the hospital and take care of him so we can take him off your hands."

David slid toward the door on the hard plastic seat. "I can't," he said sheepishly.

"Why not?"

"The door handle won't work."

CHAPTER 24

HER careful arrangement of designer-styled, blond-highlighted hair bounced as she leaned back on the gurney. Her hand, set aglitter by deep maroon fingernails, clutched a cell phone to her ear. Her lips stretched full and amorphous, blown out of proportion by collagen injections. Dark eye shadow filled the hollows beneath her eyes, where long-vanished tears had deposited it.

"Oh yes," she said into the phone, in a socialite's singsong cadence, "it's been awful. I tried to kill myself this morning. . . . Um-hmm. Prozac, codeine, and a bad Bordeaux. Threw it all up by the time the paramedics arrived. You'll never believe where they brought me. The UCLA emergency room. I was *terrified*. Thought I'd get doused with alkali on my way through the doors." She picked at a cuticle. "What's that, darling?" She glanced up at the resident at the bed beside hers, drawing blood from another woman. "One of them is, I suppose, in a Billy Baldwin sort of way."

Carson looked up from his chart and nudged David. "Welcome to West LA."

"Think compassion, Dr. Donalds. Where else do you think a lonely, depressed woman could get this much attention?"

"On *Jerry Springer*."

David coughed to cover his smile.

Dashiell Nwankwa suddenly filled the wide doorway

to Exam Ten. "You rang?" he asked, his booming voice causing Carson to drop the chart he was holding. David walked over to greet Dash as Carson crouched to gather the scattered papers.

Dash had to duck slightly to get through the doorway. At 6'8", 280 pounds, Dash's was an imposing presence. His face, so dark it diffusely reflected the lights of the room, was partly blocked by an overflow of thick-braided dreadlocks. Like most psychiatrists, he wore a dress shirt and tie, but during medical school he'd had to slit the already-wide sleeves of his scrub tops a good two inches to get his arms through.

Dash's appearance was so remarkable that several psychiatry programs had rejected him on that basis, claiming it would compromise his ability to interact with patients and put them at ease. After he failed to match in a fellowship program, Dash sued each of them in a widely publicized series of cases, winning admission to each department. The cases were decided in large part by his near-perfect grades through Columbia Medical School, and his excellent recommendations. The chair of UCLA's psych department had stepped in early in the proceedings and offered him a spot, and though he had not originally applied to UCLA, he'd elected to sign on. His performance through the four-year program had been so impressive that he'd been offered a teaching position immediately afterward, and he'd quickly become a prominent member of the department.

He was also a favored expert witness for the defense. He looked tough but spoke convincingly about mental illness—a good combination for winning the jury's trust. Most expert psych witnesses, thin-necked and bespectacled, were quickly painted as wimps soft on crime. Because of Dash's experience with violent patients and criminals, he'd been David's first choice to assess Clyde.

"What do we have here?" Dash's voice, so deep it found resonance in David's bones, was mitigated with a musical lilt—the faintest whisper of a Nigerian accent. He glanced over at the woman on the bed behind David and Carson, who continued to chat on the cell phone. "Suicide attempt?"

"How'd you guess?" Carson said.

"Carson, why don't you take over," David said. "Dash, our guy is in Fourteen."

As they moved toward the door, the woman's purse, just beyond her reach on a metal tray, began to vibrate.

"Is that your pager?" Carson asked, reaching into the purse. The woman froze, silent for the first time, her mouth a lipsticked O near the phone's receiver.

Carson withdrew an eight-inch vibrator and stared at it, mortified. Dash's laughter, even choked down, made the light casings rattle overhead.

As they reached the end of Hallway One, David shot a nervous glance at the two officers guarding the door to Clyde's room. He turned to Dash, lowering his voice. "It was all I could do to slide you past the cops. Everyone's on edge. Anyone asks, you're assessing his need for antipsychotic meds."

"Got it."

"And keep tight-lipped. Some tabloid schmuck faked a concussion this afternoon just to get in here and poke around."

David breathed evenly and deeply as he approached the room, gathering himself. His stomach churned, a morass of yet-unidentified emotions—fear, anxiety, duty of some ill-defined sort. Anger was in there as well, he realized, in no small amount.

He nodded to the officers and paused for a moment,

hand on the doorknob, searching for compassion. He fought past Nancy's face, and Sandra's, past the blue liquid that burned and ate flesh, past the disgust that caked the edges of his perception—the disgust that sprang, innate and full-formed, when he pictured Clyde's acne-scarred face. When he turned the doorknob, he felt calmer, more detached.

He was ready to see his patient.

He swung the door open quietly, and he and Dash entered. Clyde lay on the gurney, bound, eyes closed, drawing deep breaths. David and Dash approached him and stood a few feet back from the gurney rail. "Hello, Clyde. It's Dr. Spier again."

"Spier," Clyde murmured. "Like the building."

"Yes, but spelled differently. I'm here with Dr. Nwankwa from the Neuropsychiatric Insti—"

Clyde's eyes opened, a ripple of terror transforming his features from placid to violently agitated. He screamed, straining with his limbs against the restraints, bucking and thrashing. Dash calmly took a step back and signaled David to do the same.

"You said!" Clyde bellowed. "You said you'd help me!"

"I'm trying to," David said.

Clyde's frantic eyes flickered to Dash. "Get him *away*."

"Dr. Nwankwa is here to help y—"

"Get him away!"

Dash took another calm step back and sat down in a chair against the far wall. Clyde stopped thrashing and lay flat on the gurney, his chest heaving.

"Don't let him near me," Clyde said. He tucked his chin to his chest, hunching his shoulders, his eyes turned to the wall.

"I won't come near you," Dash said softly. "I'm just going to sit right here."

Clyde flopped over, his eyes darting to David and then quickly away. "Where were you? You went away. You said you would help me, but you didn't. Why is he still here? Have him go away. You said he would—"

"Dr. Nwankwa is here to try to help you. There are just a few—"

With renewed strength, Clyde thrust his torso at the ceiling, his arms bent back like wings. *"Don't let him near me!"* Veins stood out on his neck as he let forth a forceful, lengthy scream. His entire body strained. David waited for him to stop to catch his breath, but he only sucked in air and screamed again. His eyes were scrunched shut; his face was turning red.

Dash rose and stepped forward, touching David on the shoulder. He had to put his mouth to David's ear for David to hear him over Clyde's continuous, wavering scream. "I don't think we'll make much headway now." He tilted his head, indicating the door, and David followed him out. The officers outside regarded them with raised eyebrows.

Dash and David walked silently down the hall and into the empty doctors' lounge. David closed the door behind them. Dash sat heavily on one of the couches, resting his hands on his knees, and David took a seat opposite him.

David said, "Maybe he's got an aversion to psychiatrists."

"Or to black people," Dash said. "I got that reaction in a Denny's once."

David laughed. "Maybe it is race-based. But if we assume he's venting some hostility toward the hospital or its employees with his attacks, it's also relevant to see which staff members agitate him the most. He was largely cooperative with the ER staff—the first real fear and anger I've seen from him was directed toward you."

Dash pushed his fingertips together, musing. "He's too

agitated right now for me to push him. It's unfortunate we don't have the luxury—or the opportunity—to wait for him to settle a bit so I can attempt a prolonged interview or formal assessment."

"Any guesses?"

"Obviously, I can't glean much from that little exchange, on top of which the environment is less than conducive to interpreting his behavior, but I'll throw around a few hypotheses if you promise not to quote me." Dash settled back on the couch. "Deterioration of hygiene could indicate depression or schizophrenia, and means he's probably not well assimilated into a peer environment. Low-set ears might be a red flag for developmental problems or might not—at some point, one might check for spacing between his first and second toes. He seems to be fixated on you."

"Why do you think that is?"

"Maybe in light of what happened this morning, he views you as a savior."

"I barely interacted with him."

"Yes, but for all we know, you're the first person in his life to show him kindness in the face of opposition." Dash swept a stray dreadlock off his forehead. "He appears to be terrified of eye contact—he looks away almost constantly. That could be linked to insecurity resulting from his general unattractiveness—that he's afraid to be seen—but I think it's a bit more complex. I'm thinking his fear is linked to the nature of the crimes."

"How so?"

"He attacks women's faces. Their eyes." Dash smiled. "What do staring eyes represent?"

Despite the fact that Dash was nearly ten years David's junior, David didn't mind being treated like a resident. "Intense intimacy, usually hostility," David answered.

"Why hostility?"

"Because staring eyes presage an attack?"

Dash shook his head, dreadlocks swaying. "No. Because for those with low self-esteem, for those who are painfully insecure, staring eyes are the wellspring of shame. Think about it—Delilah blinding Samson, Oedipus putting out his eyes, Adam and Eve hiding themselves beneath fig leaves—all these acts took place after the *real harm* had already occurred. They are a *reaction* to the awful act, not the awful act itself. When we dream of shame, we're naked before others, caught with our pants down. A person who feels shame wants to turn away the eyes of the world, so they can't see his exposure, his vulnerability."

"Magical thinking. If you can destroy the eyes of those who look upon you, you can destroy shame. And your feelings of vulnerability and exposure."

"An oversimplification, of course, but yes." Dash shifted, and the couch creaked and groaned. "Clyde throws alkali in women's faces. It destroys their eyes so they can't shame him, destroys their beauty so they can't appear superior to him, destroys their mouths so they can't say bad things about him or laugh at him. The most efficacious way to keep someone from laughing at you is to make her weep."

"Well, he's certainly succeeded at that," David said.

"Yes. I'd guess that inflicting fear is one of his primary motivations. Replacing his own fear with that of someone else."

"I suppose it explains what seem to be motiveless crimes."

The first notes of Dash's laugh startled David in his seat.

"I've been on the stand enough to know there's no such thing as a motiveless crime," Dash said. "All violence is an attempt to achieve justice. All violence stems from perceived self-defense. Most crimes are an attempt to replace shame with pride." His smile gleamed white in his dark face. "Violent crime and state-condoned punishment are remarkably similar when you think of it. They both aim to avenge injustices."

"In Clyde's case, he must be avenging some injustice that has to do with the hospital. Or psychiatrists."

Dash shrugged, dreadlocks swaying. "Or nurses. His victims were two women in scrubs. He probably believes he attacked two nurses."

"Do you think he's a psychopath?"

"I don't. Psychopaths are glib and superficial. He seems to have deeply felt emotions. Rapidly fluctuating emotions. He went from cooperative to scared to angry like a Porsche going zero to sixty. I wouldn't be surprised to find some guilty rumination, depression, internal conflict, chronic feelings of emptiness—you know the symptom cluster."

David nodded. "Differential diagnosis. Not Otherwise Specified."

"NOS. The psychiatrist's crutch. Until I can get more out of him."

"I'd like to turn him over to LAPD a bit more sorted out. He certainly won't be in the most sympathetic hands."

"He seems to have some sort of bond with you. Maybe you should see if you can get him to open up. If you lead him to talk about the fear behind his crimes, rather than the crimes themselves, he might be more likely to talk. Zero in on his sense of injustice."

David stood, squeezing his fist so his knuckles cracked. "Well, I need to check in on him anyway. See if he's ready to ship out." He rested a hand on Dash's massive shoulder on the way to the door. "Thanks for the input."

Dash drew himself to his feet and glanced down. "Hey, David?"

One hand on the doorknob, David turned, an eyebrow raised quizzically. Looking at Dash's face, he could not locate the affability to which he had grown accustomed.

"Be careful."

CHAPTER 25

A burst of noise sped David around the corner, where he saw the UCPD officers standing in the open doorway, one of them shouting for help. David saw Jenkins explode through the swinging doors of the lobby. Jenkins sprinted for Clyde's room, boots hammering, and swept inside.

David was already running down the hall, past the startled faces and the UCPD cops. He entered the room just after Jenkins. Clyde was thrashing violently on the bed in a seizure, limbs rattling the gurney rails to which he was bound. His eyes were rolled back, showing strips of white, and a line of drool ran down his cheek.

Pistol gripped tight in one hand, Jenkins charged the bed. David caught up to him a few steps from Clyde's gurney and placed a hand on his chest, which Jenkins quickly knocked away.

"It's under control," David said. "He's having a seizure."

Jenkins's eyes were still trained on Clyde. He swung his head slowly to face David, his pupils hard, black pinpoints, and in that instant, David had no doubt that he would have killed Clyde. David's adrenaline rush made his pulse beat at his temples. He met Jenkins's hard stare, the words coming like bullets from his mouth. "*Step back from my patient.*"

Two nurses and one of the UCPD cops poured into the room, and Jenkins's eyes suddenly loosened. He took a step back, holstering his weapon. "Just making sure the suspect was secure," he said.

David turned back to the bed and grabbed one of Clyde's arms, which went limp in his grip, even as the rest of his body continued to seize.

"Back up!" David dropped Clyde's arm and took a step back himself. He turned to the others, registering a quick relief that Jenkins had left the room. "Stand back."

Clyde moaned, spittle flecking his lips, his head bouncing from side to side on the pillow.

"Nice try, Clyde," David said. "You can stop now."

Clyde seized for another moment, then stopped. His tufts of hair had been swirled upright, and when he raised his head, chin shiny with saliva, eyes dark and unblinking, he looked demonic. His grin was sharp and slick, a curved blade. He looked nothing like the frightened, cooperative man David had treated earlier.

David had known Clyde was faking as soon as his arm had gone limp in his grasp. Generalized seizures occur in all limbs, and sections of the body don't relax under pressure.

Clyde said, "Can't blame me for trying."

"Would you mind leaving us alone?" David said to the nurses and the UCPD officer. They complied, the officer shutting the door behind them.

David was alone in the room with the bound man. He stared at him from about three feet, breathing heavily, trying to process all that had just nearly occurred. Shirtless, Clyde lay on his back, restraints tying his ankles to either side of the gurney, spreading his legs. His white-gloved hands looked odd protruding from the restraints.

Despite Dash's claims, Clyde was having no trouble making eye contact at the moment. A small line of blood curved from the slit beneath his armpit.

David waited until he could speak calmly. "That didn't do much good. You opened up that cut under your arm with all your thrashing. Why are you faking a seizure? Did you want to harm someone when they came to help? We're trying to take care of you here."

"Bullshit," Clyde hissed. His breath was paradoxically rank and sweet—there was an almost medicinal scent to it. His right foot waved back and forth, a pendulum ticking off seconds. "You left me. You left me and didn't come back."

David pulled over a chair and sat, to put his head lower than Clyde's. Maybe Clyde would be more comfortable talking if David assumed a submissive posture. "I have other patients I need to see. Other patients who need help the way you needed help."

"I don't need you."

David drew closer. The blisters on Clyde's chest were resolving. Though still raw, they had either popped or ceased swelling. Again, David was amazed at how well Clyde's scrub top had protected his flesh from the alkali.

"I'm not here to harm you, Clyde. I'm here to see that you get the medical attention you need. That's why I brought in the other doctor. Why didn't you like him?"

The room had not been prepared for Clyde—David and Carson had dragged him in because it was the nearest unoccupied exam room, and David had given it only a cursory once-over. Now he stood and searched the room more extensively for unsafe objects, just in case Clyde managed to work an arm free. A lumbar puncture kit, stained amber by Betadine, leaned from the trash can.

That meant there were needles, probably down in the trash liner. The unit of blood he'd spotted earlier remained on the counter nearby, among several packages of gauze. Clearly, it had been out of refrigeration for more than the admissible thirty minutes. He'd already removed the scissors; now he glanced in the drawers beneath the counter for scalpels but found none. An oxygen source box protruded from the wall. The flow meter was made of glass, but it was hard and small, like a test tube buried in the unit. It would be difficult to break.

"I hate you," Clyde said. "I fucking hate you." His lips quivered slightly. "The nurses came in here, told me you would leave me. They said you were saying bad things about me."

"I didn't say anything bad about you."

Relief washed across Clyde's face. "That's what I told them. I told them you were a great person, a great man, and you would never do that. I defended you."

David carried the trash can outside and set it by the door. "This has needles in it," he told one of the cops. "And could you please tell a clerk to call the blood bank, have them send someone down. We have a stray unit of O-negative that needs to be spoiled."

The officer nodded, and David returned to the room, sat, and faced Clyde. "I don't believe the nurses said those things about me. Do you think you're imagining some of the things they said?"

"No. No way." His breath whistled and wheezed. "If they take me away, will you come with me? You said you'd stay with me."

"I'll make sure you get the help you need," David replied evenly.

"*You*. I want *you*. You helped me. You helped cure me when no one else wanted to." Clyde's right foot continued its restless motion back and forth.

"I'm an ER doctor. I have to stay here."

Clyde strained against the restraints, and David noticed again the swelling of his hands. His wrists were chafed, one hand up over his head, one down by his side, like a playground monkey. David noticed an old stain on the cuff on Clyde's lower wrist. Probably semen. Sometimes they had to put guys on amphetamines in restraints, but they'd be hypersexual from the drug, so they'd turn on their sides to get at their penises and masturbate themselves bloody.

"Do you know why you're here?" David asked.

"Because I'm tied down. Where else am I gonna be?"

Concrete thinking. Pulling on a pair of gloves, David pressed forward into the Brief Mental Status Examination. "Clyde, do you know what month it is?"

His eyes beaded until they looked like small spots of oil. "Of course I do. You think I'm fucking stupid?"

David began applying Silvadene to the blisters on Clyde's chest, spreading the antibiotic cream with a fingertip. Clyde winced at his touch. David took care to lean back out of Clyde's space so he wouldn't feel crowded.

"No," David said. "I think you're sick. I want to help you."

Clyde laughed, a low snort. "They're running around the hospital scared of *me*. They have guards here because of *me*. I'm not sick. I know what I'm doing."

His vacillation between swaggering self-righteous criminal and emotional catastrophe was staggering in its range and rapidity. "What *are* you doing?" David asked.

"Making them sorry."

"Sorry for what?"

"For locking me up in the darkness. Not letting me out."

"Were you locked up? As a child? Were you kept locked up by your parents?"

"Noises and lights and snakes. They put the lights out on me. They put me alone. I just want . . . I just want them to be sorry. For the flashes and the noise."

Locked in the dark with snakes—it seemed too stereotypical to be real, like a serial killer's childhood case study. Perhaps the fantastic stories were an indication of delusions or hallucinations caused by LSD, PCP, or speed. Maybe even schizophrenia.

"Do other people think you have crazy ideas?" David asked. If the question was worded subjectively, Clyde would be more likely to answer it honestly.

"I don't . . . I don't know. I don't stay around people anymore." Clyde's speech was slightly slurred, as if he were speaking around a thick tongue. "Not people that can look at me back."

"You said you weren't taking any drugs. Are you sure about that?"

"I don't take any pills." The same defensive note David had encountered from him previously on the topic. David noted that he had changed *drugs* to *pills*. He seemed to be concerned with the issue of taking medicine, not illicit drugs.

"Did someone do something wrong to you?"

Clyde breathed hard for a moment, catching his breath. "I don't like the way they look at me. They always look at me like that here."

"Here? As in here at this hospital?"

"Yeah," Clyde said. "Yeah. But not anymore. Now *they're* afraid. You shoulda seen their faces after they got the stuff on them." His fingers, swollen knuckle-wide down their lengths, quivered as his hands twisted in the restraints. His fingernails were yellow and pitted. "I have plans. I'm smarter than you think. I can do things too. I know they're wrong, but I can do them and not get caught."

"What plans? What are your plans?"

"Maybe you can stop me. I couldn't. I couldn't stop me."

A slightly obese female tech stuck her head in the door. Clyde's head snapped up, the loose flesh of his cheeks and jowls taking a moment to still.

"I'm here from the blood bank to pick up—"

"Please, not right now," David said.

"Look, I came down here all the way from—"

"Not *now*."

With a scowl, she withdrew.

"See?" Clyde said. "Like that. Did you see how she looked at me?" He drew a ragged breath. "I just marked her. Marked her face, her eyes. She's there now, in my mind. Green dangling earrings. Freckles across her nose. Birthmark on her right cheek." David couldn't even recall the woman's hair color, but Clyde, in the four seconds she'd been in view, had drunk her in.

Clyde raised his head, examining the thick leather cuff that bound his wrist to the railing. "Now I see how you guys are clever, trying to catch me. I can be clever too. I have ways, I have better ways to get at people." Clyde began sobbing quietly. "I don't mean to. I don't like it. It's awful but I have to." He winced suddenly, squinting.

"Are you all right?" David asked. "Does your chest hurt?"

"God. Oh God. Dim the lights. Can you dim the lights?"

David crossed to the light switch and turned off the bank of lights directly over the gurney. The room glowed with light from the X-ray box, which someone had left on.

The only sound in the room was that of Clyde's labored breathing. David watched him in the soft-lit darkness. Clyde's request stemmed from either a headache or a sudden phobia, he wasn't sure which.

"When I go out," Clyde said, "the mask goes on. It protects me."

"Why do you need a mask?"

A single tear rolled down Clyde's red and swollen cheek. "I want their faces to be gone. I want them to be destroyed and ruined and no more."

Clear homicidal ideation, available means and well-formulated plans for continued attacks, lack of compassion, self-view as victim—the red flags were rising one by one. David said, "Do you think—"

The door swung open, flooding the room with light. Dressed in jeans and a Gap button-up, Diane entered. "There you are," she said. "What the hell has been—"

David sprang toward her, trying to block her from Clyde's view. "Not now. Get out! Who told you you could come in here?"

She shuffled backward as he pushed her. "The cops said it was okay, that you were just—"

"Keep this door shut," David growled at the officers. He slammed the door and leaned against it, one palm spread over an anatomical diagram of a lung.

Clyde's voice drifted around him, a miasma rising. "That one's special to you, huh?"

"No," David said. "I just don't want anyone disturbing us."

"Didn't see you jump to when that little pig from the blood bank showed herself to me. Not like you jumped for this one. Don't blame you. She's a pretty nurse."

David crossed the room and stood over Clyde. The glow of the X-ray box turned his skin a sickly blue, darkening the pits in his cheeks and the twinning tufts of hair that protruded ridiculously like an offset garland. He stared at Clyde, and Clyde turned away with a soft, dying whimper.

Empathy is not innate. It is a learned emotion, conditioned through trial and error, defeat and reward, forged in a Skinnerian oven. David sifted through forty-three years of instinct and socialization, searching for the string of a buried argument. The only way a person can know that someone else's pain matters is if someone has taught them that their own does. If no one ever showed that to Clyde, as a baby, as a child, then he had learned that his pain did not matter. And, more acutely, he would have learned that *things* in pain did not matter.

"Your pain," David said. "The awful pain on your chest. I'm sorry that happened to you."

Clyde watched him, rigid and sweating.

"The way you feel, the pain you feel—the women who you threw alkali on feel that also. That same pain."

Clyde's eyes watered. Tears beaded and stuck to his thick lashes. "My head hurts," he said.

David wondered what thoughts rattled through the corridors of Clyde's mind. "I need to go see some other patients. I'll check on you later."

Clyde turned his face away, staring darkly at the wall. "No you won't," he said.

David left him bound in the semidarkness.

CHAPTER 26

YALE was waiting for David outside Clyde's room, his arms spread. "Well, we're ready to take him off your hands. Press is cordoned, transport vehicle's waiting in the ambulance bay." He thrust a clipboard at David. "Please sign him out."

Diane paced the hall behind Yale, hands tucked into the back pockets of her jeans. His face still flushed, Jenkins congregated with a few officers farther down by the lobby doors. Murmuring to one another and shifting on their feet, they directed their stares toward David and the closed door of Clyde's room. Waiting like jackals for a whisper of opportunity.

David felt the crush of an ugly dilemma. What was already a difficult, complex decision was now enflamed by the agitation of the hospital board, the press, an angry city. He felt the myriad pressures in the heat rising to his face, and he fought to find the correct response. Something flared in him, bright and sharp, and he found himself saying to Yale, "I'm afraid the patient is not ready to be released."

The clipboard smacked against Yale's thigh. "No?" He flicked his wrist and the Rolex appeared. "Eight-fifteen. Your shift is over. Who's the next attending on call?"

"The patient is not improving at a rate that indicates he'll be ready to be moved tonight."

Yale opened his mouth, then closed it. He scratched his forehead with two fingers. Diane was watching David, a puzzled expression on her face.

"When is the earliest he'll be ready?" Yale asked.

"Eight tomorrow morning."

"And it's just a coincidence that that's when your next shift begins?"

"Yes. I'll brief the next attending to contact me in the event of any change in Clyde's condition, no matter the hour. If he has a miraculous recovery in the night that enables him to be moved, I'll come in immediately and sign off on him."

One of the clerks stuck her head out of the CWA but withdrew it quickly when David looked at her. Two nurses whispered to each other in the doorway of Twelve.

"You said you thought he'd be ready to be moved by now," Yale said.

"My patients don't always abide my expectations."

Yale dropped the clipboard on the tiled floor, where it made a startlingly loud bang. "If you insist, I suppose we have little choice."

Jenkins and the other officers stood in a flying wedge at the hall's end, looking foolishly formal.

A grin flashed across Yale's imperturbable face and vanished instantaneously. "We'll be here waiting."

Diane paced tight circles while David signed out to Dr. Nelson, a young attending who'd trained under him. She walked swiftly to keep up with David as he headed through the hospital toward the lobby, avoiding the ambulance bay so he wouldn't have to pass Jenkins.

"What are you doing, David?" she said. It clearly was an effort for her not to raise her voice. "We've released patients to custody in worse shape than that."

"If I release him," David said, "he's likely to die."

"Nobody dies of that kind of alkali burn."

David looked at her, his stomach twisted into a knot. "I'm not talking about the burns."

Removing his cell phone from his pocket, he ducked into the empty fluoroscopy room and had the operator put him through to the University Police. Diane sat on a gurney, waiting patiently.

"I need to reach Officer Blake. Urgently . . . Yes, I would appreciate it if you'd page him to this number." David rattled off his cell phone number. "No, I'd rather not say what this is regarding, but please tell him it's extremely important."

He snapped his phone shut and faced Diane. She made a circular gesture with her hand. "I'll just ask when this is over," she said.

He glanced at her clothes. "What are you doing here anyway? It's your day off. I'm not used to seeing you dressed."

"I'll take that the way it was intended."

It had been a long time since he'd smiled, and it felt good.

"With all the shit that went down this morning, how could I not come in?" Diane said. "I wanted to make sure you were still in one piece."

"And am I?"

Judging by her expression, he must have looked like something someone coughed up. He fisted his stethoscope on either side of his neck and tugged on it like a scarf. "That bad?" His phone rang.

"Blake here."

"Officer Blake, this is David Spier, the physician who treated Clyde when he came in."

"Oh. Oh yeah. Can I help you?"

"Where are you?"

"Can I help you with something?"

"Yes, I'd like to have an off-the-record conversation with you."

A pause. "Where would you like to not meet?"

"Are you in the area?"

"Yeah, I'm still on campus."

"Can you meet me right now?"

"Where?"

"My car is parked on the top tier of the PCHS lot. It's a green Mercedes. They're not letting press through to that area."

"I'll meet you there in five minutes."

David hung up and gestured for Diane to follow. They threaded through the lobby and out across the dark quad. Dr. Kingston, a white-haired senior member of the board, paused and regarded David judgmentally, but David simply nodded and kept walking.

Diane kept her eyes on the ground. "You really think they'd kill him?"

"I think Jenkins would, yes."

"What are you gonna do?"

"That's what I'm figuring out. But I just bought myself—and Clyde—twelve hours. And this guy, Blake, there's no love lost between him and Jenkins. I'm hoping he can help."

They reached the top tier of the parking lot, and David saw Blake leaning against the trunk of his Mercedes. He was glad Blake's police car was not in evidence.

David had parked at the far side of the tier, away from most foot traffic and passing cars. He unlocked the doors to his car, and they all got in, Diane sliding in the back.

Blake cupped his hand and ran it over his thick mustache. "What would you like to not discuss?"

"I appreciated your helping today in the ER."

Blake nodded, continuing to regard David a bit impatiently.

David took a deep breath. "I'm concerned that if I release Clyde to the LAPD, he'll be killed."

Blake's eyebrows rose and spread. "Jenkins *is* a live wire."

"I'm holding him through the night for medical reasons. Is there any way I could release him to your custody? To the university police?"

With a fingernail, Blake worked something out from between his teeth, his mustache bristling. "No. No way. He's in LAPD custody. He has to be released to LAPD."

"And they're taking him to Harbor for further treatment. In a transport vehicle."

"Yeah. A squad car."

"Probably Jenkins's?"

Blake studied David for a moment, his face textured and leathery under the light of the lampposts. "That's not quite how it would work," he said.

"How would it work?"

"*If* it was gonna work? Someone else's squad car. Jenkins following, off-duty or on. Yale and Dalton eating at a diner somewhere, somewhere with high visibility. A near-escape in a dark alley. A mix-up." Someone walked by and Blake turned away so his face couldn't be seen. "Of course, I don't much buy into conspiracy theory."

David realized he was sweating. He turned on the car and put the air-conditioning on low. Blake reached over and turned the key, then looked to see if anyone had taken note of the car starting up.

"Do I have any options?" David asked. "Could a judge do anything?"

Blake shrugged. "Shit, I'm no lawyer, but I'd doubt it on your time line. A case this big, there'd be a huge inquiry and investigation."

Diane leaned forward. "How about Sheriff's Medical at USC Med? We send critical patients there sometimes. Does that fall under a different jurisdiction?"

"If the patient is critical, as in *critical* critical, he'd get sent there and signed in to the Sheriff's custody. But he'd still have to be transferred."

"How?"

"By the city, actually. They'd send an LA City fire paramedic unit with a uniformed police officer over to haul him off. But LAPD won't let that fly. They're not gonna want to lose custody—it's a big fucking collar. They'll want him under their thumb at Harbor. Plus, the dude walked into UCLA—if they're walking at all, they go to Harbor, not County. And you can't bullshit this one. The LAPD chief would be over there with a second opinion from one of his guys before they'd let him roll to County." His eyes were a weary blue. Washed out. "Once you clear him, he's going to Harbor, all right. Unless you want to fuck him up more with drugs or something, make it so he *has* to roll out on a gurney."

David shook his head. "Can't do that."

"How about if we contact the Sheriff?" Diane asked. "Does he have any kind of intervening authority? Wouldn't he want the collar too? Could he send his guys over?"

Blake laughed a smoker's laugh. "Shit, you guys don't get it. You really think the Sheriff's gonna step on the Chief's ass like that? On *this* case? No sir."

Blake turned away as a security guard approached, and David quickly got out and regarded the man across the top of his car. He was relieved to see it was Ralph. "It's me," David said. "We're having an impromptu staff meeting." Diane cleared the fog from the back window and waved.

"Okay, Doc. Just keeping an eye out around here."

David nodded and ducked back in the car.

Blake shook his head. "Security jackasses." He pressed his hands together. "Is that it, then?" He started to get out.

"How about a psych hold?" David asked. "If he got put on seventy-two-hour hold, would he still have to be transferred?"

Blake cocked his head, silent for a moment. "I don't know. Let me look into that for you. My chief's throwing a party for his wife's birthday tonight. I can sneak over there once things wind down, bend his ear for a bit." He turned so he could take in both David and Diane. "If I'm looking into this, you keep a lid on things till I get back to you."

"Okay," David said.

"Keep your cell phone on." Blake got out from the car. Resting his arms on the roof, he leaned back in. "Hey. I'm just dispensing information, not recommendations. Got it?"

"Absolutely," David said.

The door slammed shut, and David took a deep breath and exhaled hard, puffing out his cheeks. He regarded Diane in the rearview mirror. "Where to, ma'am?"

"Why don't you let me take you to dinner? Somewhere real."

"I don't think I have the energy to go somewhere real."

"Fine. We'll grab a six-pack and some Taco Bell. Oh—and David? Just in case the press is on the lookout for the ER chief's car . . ." She flashed a grin. "I'm driving."

⊕

Diane drove a maroon Explorer, which was bad enough, and drove it too fast for David's taste. After they picked up some food, she'd raced up Coldwater Canyon to a brief, dusty plateau. They sat on the hood of her vehicle amid a clutter of taco wrappers, sipping beer and following the headlights' gaze out to the hazy Century City skyline. The August heat informed the evening cool, wrapping around them, fresh yet stuffy as only LA air is. Diane listened silently as David finished filling her in on the day's events.

She popped open her second Heineken and took a sip. "Wow. Sounds like an episode of *ER*. Never underestimate vengeance."

"I guess not." David let the beer dangle from two fingers and wondered if it made him look younger. He took a sip and remembered he didn't like beer. A car drove by behind them, its headlights briefly illuminating the windshield at their backs. "This is a nice area. There's a little Italian restaurant down that way." He pointed. "I just ate there last week."

"Oh? Who'd you go with?"

Reaching into the brown paper bag, he surreptitiously switched his beer for a Coke. He studied her as he took a sip. "I went alone."

She peeled the label off her beer, her fingernail lifting the gum from the green bottle. "I go out to dinner alone a lot too. A thirty-one-year-old resident. Kind of in that dead space between normal-age house staff and the older docs. I mean, it's not like I'm gonna date Carson. And you've made it clear you're *way* too old."

David smiled. "I'm sure you have plenty of options. For company, I mean."

"I suppose." She smiled self-consciously. "I've never really dated much. No real relationships, so to speak. Not that I haven't wanted to. I guess I'm something of a . . ." After a moment, it became clear she wasn't planning on finishing the sentence.

"Men are a stupid breed," David said. "They're intimidated by intelligence in a woman, particularly when paired with beauty. God knows why. Maybe it makes them feel less virile."

"I suppose that's a compliment."

"One subtle enough that you're supposed to pretend you didn't notice."

"I didn't." She sipped her beer again. The silence seemed to make her uneasy. "So, what else do you do? I mean, with your time."

He shrugged. "Read. Work. Take walks. Work. Masturbate." He looked over at her. "That was a joke."

"Really?"

He set the Coke can down beside him on the hood. "No."

Her eyes took a pensive cast. "It must be hard," she said. "Being alone after not being alone."

The blinking light of an airplane cut through the distant haze, descending. "It's the little things," David said. "It's always the little things, isn't it? Like now, I turn on the answering machine when I take a bath." He smiled sadly, to himself. "We had a good, solid marriage. Full of honesty and openness and all the things most marriages aren't. It was a real relationship, with a lot of caring and compromise. Did you know I was working the night she came into the ER?"

Diane shook her head slowly, as if afraid any abrupt gesture would knock David off course.

Bitterness overlaid the pain in his voice, hiding it beneath a sharper veneer. "An embolus. Why not a car, a plane, a fire? A goddamn embolus. Her slipping away and me just standing there with my useless, useless hands."

His hands, thin, smooth, and unlined, were indisputably the hands of a professional. No scars or thick calluses from the kind of work men toiled at year after year, hauling crates or fighting shovels into the ground. He was fortunate. Despite everything else, he had his work.

Diane's voice startled him from his reverie. "What do you miss?" She was staring out across the tree-darkened valley to the floating lights of the high-rises. Her face was heavy, somehow, weighed down with melancholy, or sadness, or both. "From your relationship. What do you miss the most?" A soft vulnerability hid within her curiosity.

The answer was there waiting, though he didn't know it until he started speaking. "I miss that feeling when you're out, and the night is softly lit, and you know that after the smiles and the glances and the red wine, you're going to go home and make love. That's what I miss."

Diane looked at him, a soft noise of appreciation escaping her throat, then they watched the hazy skyline together for a while, sipping their drinks.

David pulled out his cell phone, called the ER, and had the clerk put him through to Dr. Nelson. "How's the patient?" he asked.

"Looks fine. I just poked my head in. I'm doing my best to avoid any formal assessments."

"LAPD giving you any trouble?"

"Actually, no. They've retreated to the ambulance bay."

David thanked him and hung up.

"What time do you think Blake'll call?" Diane asked.

David squinted at his watch, a plastic digital thing from Longs Drugs. He wore bad watches to work because he constantly misplaced them; he had a drawerful at home. It was nearly 11:30 P.M. "Any minute."

"What's Plan B?"

"Depending on what Blake says, I can gather some other opinions. I have a friend on the board at Mass General—attorney. I'd rather not overexpose myself, but I do trust him. And Peter, of course. He's excellent with this sort of thing."

"What about Dr. Evans?"

"The last thing Sandy wants is a big fiasco, but if I don't come up with any better options by morning, I'll talk to her first thing."

"Can I ask you a question you probably don't want to answer?"

"You just did."

"Why are you doing all this? I don't mean to sound callous, but this isn't your mess."

"I can't release a patient when I believe he's going to be killed."

"But you're beyond your domain, David. Your job is to treat him and hand him over. You're a doctor, not a vigilante. A bunch of cops are probably fucking up some guy in custody somewhere right now. Why is this any more your business?"

"Because I can do something to prevent this."

"Not as a physician, you can't."

He finished his Coke and crumpled the can.

"Plus, what about Jenkins? If he's really as rash and

unstable as you think, what's to say he won't go after you?"

"He might."

"Who knows how far he'll push this? You're stepping into a different world here, David."

"So you disapprove?"

"God no. Not at all." She finished her beer and set the empty on the hood behind her. "There are no easy answers here. But I do know the dogma of a physician is the same as the dogma of a soldier. It's just better articulated. Think beyond the rules and oaths of the profession. Know what you're getting into. Then, whatever you decide, fine."

David's phone rang in his jacket, and he pulled it out and flipped it open. "Hello?"

"Blake here. Even if you throw a psych hold on your boy, he'd still have to be transferred, and since he's not critical, LAPD would be the guys to do it. But he could go to USC, not Harbor, since Harbor doesn't have a secure psych ward."

"So he'd end up in the Sheriff's custody?"

"If he gets there. And be advised—the Mayor's got this one in his roundhouse. His approval ratings are down. You do the math."

As if there weren't enough stresses already in play. "Thanks for calling back."

"I didn't."

David hung up and looked over at Diane. "A psych hold gets him to USC, but he'd still have to be transferred. In an LAPD squad car."

"Why don't we call Dash? Might as well see if a psych hold is even plausible."

Dash answered after four rings, his voice heavy with sleep. "Yeah?"

"It's David. Sorry to wake you."

"What's up?"

David explained the situation in its entirety while Dash listened in silence.

"Why didn't you say anything to me this afternoon?"

"I didn't want to get ahead of myself. Plus, I was waiting to get a better handle on just how real this threat was. What do you think? Do we have any options?"

"Well, clearly I'm not going to put him on a psych hold without a complete and formal assessment."

"Of course."

"And even if I determined he could only be released to a secure psychiatric facility, that doesn't get you around the transfer problem."

"Unless . . ." David pressed his lips together, thinking hard. "Unless you determined he was so unstable he had to remain in four-point restraints. Four-points would buy us an ambulance. And a supervising physician inside it."

"You know the cops will believe he can be transferred just fine in handcuffs." Dash exhaled long and hard. "I understand the predicament, David, but a formal psych assessment goes on record. There could be ramifications for the trial. He is highly unstable, but I don't know that he *demands* psychiatric supervision versus incarceration."

"Just come in for an official psychiatric evaluation. That's all I ask. I'll figure out how to get you past the cops and buy you the time you need. You *can* get him to talk . . . ?"

"I'm confident I can, yes. With some more time. But even if I can't, I've made assessments on uncooperative patients before, David."

"I'll meet you at the hospital now and get you in with him."

"I can't do it unless I'm the psychiatrist on call. It'll smell bad. In the paperwork and in the courts."

"Who's on tonight?"

"Bickle. Asshole clock puncher."

"Are you on call tomorrow?"

"Seven A.M."

"Meet me at Clyde's room."

"I'm not promising anything, David."

"I understand that."

David hung up and looked over at Diane, who was watching him intently. "Dash will make an assessment in the morning. *If* he puts Clyde on psych hold, and *if* he wants him kept in four-points, we're in the clear."

"And if not?"

"I get into it with my lawyer friend and Sandy."

"What do we do now?"

David leaned back, accidentally knocking one of Diane's empties. It rolled off the hood and shattered on the ground. "Wait until morning."

CHAPTER 27

THERE is no nighttime in an emergency room. Day or night, the clean-scrubbed halls have the same feeling of perennial waking, of intrepid alertness tinged with exhaustion and suffering, like the rung of some ever-glowing Purgatory.

Behind the locked and guarded door, Clyde lay in his own private torment, awash in the screams of a boy in a room nearby. After David had left, the cops had turned the lights back on in his room, despite his pleas. He winced frequently and with regularity, his forehead wrinkling now and again as if to fend off the tightening jaws of a migraine.

Despite the soft lining of the leather restraints, his wrists and ankles had reddened from his constant tugging. He twisted, his bare and blistered chest arching to the harsh, ceaseless lights of the ceiling. He let out a grunt, then settled back, spread and defeated, a dog waxing passive, a turtle flipped, Prometheus bound.

Whatever they were doing to the boy ceased, for there were no more cries echoing through the halls. A shuffling past his door, but the bar handle did not turn. Sliding the restraint of his lowered hand along the rail until it was even with his hip, Clyde turned on his side. He managed to get ahold of the drawstring of his scrub bottoms and the waistband fell instantly loose, revealing his money clip tucked within the small interior pocket. Because it was flat, nestled on the inside of his hip, and soft-padded with several singles, the money clip had survived the brisk patdown outside. The fact that he'd been swathed in alkali-soaked material had discouraged a more vigorous search.

He swayed back and forth on his rear end to bring the pocket closer to his bound, gloved hand, his fingers straining pronged and stiff. He snagged the ragged edge of a bill between his second and middle fingers and managed to pull the clip halfway out, but it caught on the fabric pulled tight by his shifting motion. The tin square containing the lozenge, pressed beneath the clip in his pocket, dug into his thigh with a sharp corner.

He released the money clip and wiggled several more times before timing a better grab, his fat thumb and forefinger clamping shut around one of the rearing horses, fake turquoise against hammered brass. Breathing in small, repetitive grunts, he slid his body down as far as the restraints allowed, pressing his rear end down into the mattress so he'd drag his loose scrub bottoms with him.

The money clip popped free.

He rested for a few minutes, his face a red, sweaty globe. He shifted the money clip in his hand, then wriggled his thumbnail into the slender groove that lifted the blade from the clip. The blade pulled slightly open, then snapped shut. He tried again and again until his thumb ached near the cuticle from the pressure. He wasn't able to get the blade far enough open so it would hold until he could reshift his hand and thumb it the rest of the way.

Finally, he raised the blade just far enough to slide his index finger beneath it before it could snap shut. When he released his thumb, the spring pulled the blade home, slicing down through the thin latex glove and his flesh. He bit his lip, eyes watering, and quickly repositioned his thumb and flicked the blade fully open.

A stream of blood found its way from the neat slit of the wound down over his knuckle. He turned the money clip in his hand so the blade protruded down toward the restraint. The leather cuffs themselves were far too thick to cut through without better leverage and a serrated blade, but they were connected to the gurney rail by a thin band threaded through a small buckle and hasp.

With some effort, he slid the blade between the restraint and the band, and turned the sharp edge up until it tented the thin leather strip. Rocking gently on the mattress, he began to saw.

At 3:17 A.M., a gurgling scream from Exam Room Fourteen sent both officers rigid on their feet in Hallway One. One fumbled at the door handle as the other stood back, already searching for an ER nurse.

Made unusually unsteady on his braced legs by exhaustion and a mild irritation at being called out of his warm bed at three in the morning to assess a shotgun wound to the groin, Peter was nearly startled off his feet by the scream. He froze a short distance up the hall, leaning in the open doorway to Procedure Room One.

The first officer swung open the door to Clyde's room, the gurney coming slowly into view, and the gruesome, twisted body strapped to it. Clyde's torso was literally doused in blood, broad streaks flowing down his arms and crossing his bare, burn-pocked chest. His head wavered drunkenly as he raised it to regard the cop, and then sank back to the pillow, eyes rolling to thin white bands.

The officer's voice hiked high when he spoke, approaching the bed. "Find a doctor," he said. "We have a suicide." The other cop's footsteps faded down the hall.

Clyde's body flopped listlessly, a caught fish losing life. The officer stepped forward again, adrenaline blooming red in his cheeks. The restraints all seemed to be in place. One of Clyde's cheeks, impossibly, was smudged with blood. His head lay still on the pillow.

The body tensed, then lunged at the officer with a bellow, arms swinging free and fast. The officer leaned back, fumbling for his pistol, but Clyde whipped his wrist around, armored with the hard leather restraint, and caught him across the forehead with the metal hasp. He pounced on the officer as he fell, and yanked the Beretta from the holster with a blood-slick hand. The officer raised his hand as if to deflect a bullet, but Clyde kicked him across the face instead, and he went limp on the floor.

Clyde darted to the door, shirtless and bloodstained, restraints still banded around his wrists and legs like cuffs and ankle weights. He sprang into the hall as the other cop bore down with a nurse. An old man wearing an oxygen mask lay on a parked gurney between them, awaiting transport to the wards. The cop noticed Clyde first and he yelled something, fast-drawing his pistol.

Fisting the Beretta, Clyde leapt at the gurney, his foot knocking the lever to release the brake when he landed, his momentum sending the gurney hurtling toward the cop. The old man rose with a moan as he flew forward, oxygen mask tangling around his neck. The front of the gurney struck the cop crotch level and his chest flopped forward onto the mattress as he fell, legs scrabbling on the slick tile. His gun went off, blowing out an overhead light, the recoil kicking it from his hands. Peter, who'd been shuffling up the hall behind the second cop and the nurse, ducked his head inside a doorjamb.

Rather than running for the exit, Clyde sprinted toward the heart of the hospital, sidearming the cop's head with a restraint-heavy wrist as he passed. Nurses and interns screamed, scrambling for cover. As Clyde passed Procedure One, Peter swung a leg out to trip him. The thick metal brace caught Clyde across the shins, spilling him onto the floor. Clyde tumbled once, crying out, his bare chest slapping the tile and leaving a bloody Rorschach. His face tightened as he turned and glowered at Peter over a shoulder, haunches already rising beneath him.

His feet slipped for his first few steps, then he hit a crazed sprint, patients and doctors leaping out of his way. By the time the security guards arrived, he had disappeared into the hospital's interior.

CHAPTER 28

HORACE Johnson McCannister, a high school dropout with mouselike facial features and a sharp osmotic mind, hummed as he pulled on his shoe covers. His feet had plenty of room at the bottom of the white plastic boots, and the elastic held the tops tight around his scrub bottoms, just below the knees. He always wore shoe covers now, having learned his lesson his first day as a Lab Tech II at UCLA's Center for Health Sciences, when he'd accidentally sawed into a swollen length of colon and splattered shit across his brand-new Rockports. His particular wing of the hospital's seventh floor, the Three Corridor, remained quiet when the med students weren't tinkering with bodies in the gross anatomy lab next door, and it was deathly still now at three-thirty in the morning.

He tossed his keys and cigarette pack on the counter and adjusted his surgical cap before turning to regard the two new bodies wrapped tightly in sheets before him. The prep room shone with metal—stainless sinks and cabinets, countertops and gleaming tools, and, in the middle, the scrubbed-dull embalming table. To Horace's back, the twelve-foot door to the anatomy crypt rose like a castle gate, a wooden rectangle with dark metal latches.

Plastic Surgery had requested ribs still attached to musculature for a 7 A.M. talk—an unusual lecture focusing on the innervation of the teres major. He could see already that one of the bodies was too obese to be of much use to the med students. He'd junk that one for parts and preserve the other intact. The obese body lay supine, wrapped like a mummy. He prodded the bulge of its stomach, debating where to dig in.

It would be a messy process.

Hands sheathed in thick blue gloves, he picked up his autopsy gown but hesitated a moment before pulling it on. He'd had two cups of coffee on his way over, trying to chase reminiscences of sleep from his hazy head, and he'd have to stop soon and take a leak. He opted to go now, before he got sticky.

Shuffling out in his oversize shoe covers, he headed down the empty hall to the bathroom and pissed long and hard, smiling to himself afterward while he fumbled in his autopsy gloves to zip up his fly. Walking back down the hall, he punched a four-digit code into the Omnilock and reentered the prep room.

If he sneaked a cigarette, all lingering traces of smoke would be long dissipated by the time the first students began to arrive in a few hours. He searched the counter, but his cigarettes were gone. Maybe he'd misplaced them on his way to the bathroom. Shrugging on a blue autopsy gown, he slid a surgical mask over his head. The built-in eye shield, a rectangle of clear plastic atop the mask, would be helpful once the sawing began.

He started with the obese body, electing to leave the smaller one for later. Moving it to the embalming table gave him some trouble, but he managed. He used trauma shears to free the cadaver from the white sheets. A bluing elderly gentleman with sagging jowls and a thick mustache, funeral-dressed in a dark suit. The rose in his lapel had wilted. Probably moved straight from the convalescent home to the parlor to the hospital. Once they arrived, bodies were brought to Horace's happy workplace by the freight elevators, which rode up and down the shafts on the backside of the passenger elevators. Hospital staff did their best to keep the bodies out of the patients' sight. Nothing chills the sick like a fresh reminder of mortality.

Horace pulled the clothes off the cadaver and tossed them in a corner. Then, humming Vivaldi's "La Primavera," he shaved the skull with a pair of barber clippers. He used a scalpel to peel the scalp, the fresh meat yielding a steady current of blood. The slant of the table caused the blood to flow toward the feet to a drain, which was hooked up to a sink against the wall. Bodies also yielded viscid fluids and tangles of tissue. Clogged drains here were a bitch and a half.

Once he had the skull adequately peeled, he began to cut a large circle around the top with a Stryker saw. The circular blade did not spin; it vibrated ever so slightly. Horace had, on occasion, slipped and touched the oscillating blade to his hand, but it wouldn't cut flesh, only hard surfaces like bone. The end of the saw heated up, sending up thin tendrils of smoke that he could smell through his mask—a pungent odor like burning hair, like the dentist-chair stench of a tooth being hollowed.

Once he finished, he popped the skull lid off, lifted the frontal lobe of the brain, and cut the connective tissue, starting with the optic nerve, then moving through the other nerves, the arteries, and finally the spinal cord. Wiggling his fingers beneath the brain, he gently peeled it up out of the head.

Passing a string under the artery so the brain dangled from the middle, he lowered it into a bucket filled with formalin and snapped the lid on quickly, clamping down on both ends of the string. Inside the bucket, the brain hung upside down in the fluid, a perfect natural specimen. Had he not suspended it, it would have sunk to the bottom and hardened with a distorting flat spot, and he never would have heard the end of it from neurobiology.

He switched to a pistol-grip Sawzall, an old-fashioned reciprocating saw. Pressure on the trigger sent the straight blade, which protruded from the saw's long body, hammering up and down. Horace sawed off the feet next, wrapping them in a red biohazard bag and dropping them into a top-loading freezer that ran the length of the east wall. The fire red wrapping would tip off the podiatrists that they were dealing with fresh material—ripe, bloody, and possibly contaminated.

Next he attacked the knees and elbows, severing the limbs about ten inches off the joints on either side but keeping the skin and muscles intact. There wasn't a big call for hands, so he left them attached. He dropped all four units in the freezer, praying that would buy him some time with the orthopedics guys, and turned to the big chore of the day—the musculature-attached ribs needed for the morning lecture.

The Sawzall got him through the ribs in short order, the soft organs throwing a good splatter across his gown, then he cut a quadrant around the shoulder and removed the lungs from the ribs with a scalpel. The table's blood gutters grew choked with debris. He bagged the specimen and set it aside, prepped and ready for the talk.

He decided to remove the spine as a favor to a professor in neurosurgery. Flipping the cadaver over, he sawed down three inches on either side of the spine, cutting through ribs and pelvis. He removed all organs from the interior, cutting through the mesentery and along the visceral cavity walls. He scooped out the bowels and rectum as one unit, trying to hold his breath, though the stench still managed to work its way into his system. The neurosurgeon wouldn't care that the brain was missing, so he kept the topless head attached to the spine. Having whistled his way through "L'Inverno," he stepped back to admire his work. It was beautiful. All the vertebrae were intact, from neck to ass.

Every body had so much to give. At times, Horace viewed his job simply as playing Santa Claus to the various medical departments.

He laced his hands and raised them above his head, cracking his knuckles. Things would slow down soon enough—this was the last week of summer session gross anatomy for the med students—and then he'd have the entire area to himself for a few blissful weeks until regular classes started up again in September. His gown sported a mishmash of fluids and bits of viscera, and an unidentified string of pink matter clung to the bottom of his eye guard. The saw swayed at his side, a warrior's tool.

It was time for body number two.

Body number two proved to be a woman, midforties, with a shock of bright orange hair. It was much easier to move her to the embalming table, and her vivid hair quickly succumbed to the clippers. Horace made a three-inch incision just below her clavicle and raised her carotid artery and jugular vein so they protruded from the cut like fat soda straws. A pump system was strategically positioned on a table nearby, one wide cylinder containing the alcohol-based, five-percent-formaldehyde solution. A tube attached to the pump terminated in an enormous needle, which he sank into the carotid. He knotted a string around the end of the artery so the needle wouldn't fly out when he turned on the pump.

Pressurized at about fifteen pounds, the pump activated with a low hum, and began pushing the urine-colored embalming fluid into the carotid. The fluid would work all the way through the circulatory system, deep through the tissues, pushing the old blood and body fluids out the jugular ahead of it. The entire process would take about twenty-five minutes.

Horace wiped his brow with the arm of the autopsy

gown, accidentally leaving a moist crimson smear across his forehead. The saws sat still and bloody on the counter against the wall, beasts slumbering after a feast.

It was time for a snack.

CHAPTER 29

THE phone rang, and David was instantly awake in his dark bedroom. "Yes?"

Peter's voice. "You'd better come in. It's Clyde."

"Did they kill him?"

A pause. Sirens in the background.

"No. He escaped."

At 4:27 A.M., the ambulance bay festered with cop cars. Four security officers jogged past, radios bouncing on their hips. David braced himself as he walked past the parking kiosk and descended into the ambulance bay. Sandy had reached him in the car on his way over and poked around the issue in her incisive, aggressive way. He'd been vague; he could tell the call had left her displeased and unsatisfied, and her tone had seemed to hold some unspoken warning. David had called Peter back so Peter could fill him in on the escape. The realization had not yet fully hit; David moved with a dazed calm.

An officer straight-armed David as he stepped through the sliding glass doors. David unclipped his medical badge and displayed it, as he had already done at the police perimeter by the parking kiosks. "I'm Dr. Spier. I run this division."

"All right, sir," the officer said. "Be advised this entire area is a crime scene."

David heard Jenkins yelling the minute he stepped through the swinging doors into Hallway One. Jenkins had cornered Ralph and was jabbing his finger in his chest. "You're the chief security officer. What the fuck do you mean you can't find him? He ran into *your* hospital!"

Ralph calmly pushed Jenkins's hand, finger still extended, to one side. "Listen, cowboy, this building has twenty-nine miles of corridor, three-point-one million square feet, and fifty-seven exits. It's second only to the Pentagon."

"We gotta shut this place down, move room to room with dogs and SWAT."

"That would take weeks. Plus he probably already slipped out an exit."

"This isn't exactly *Where's Waldo*. We're looking for a shirtless man covered in blood running around with a stolen Beretta. Figure it out."

David slid past them and found Yale, who was crouched in Exam Fourteen, his back to the door. A few men in rumpled shirts and ties poked through the cabinets and the gurney mattress. David circled Yale and squatted beside him. Yale was examining an empty blood bag, turning it slowly on the end of his pen.

"It was supposed to be picked up by the blood bank. They came down, but I was in with him. . . ." David squeezed his eyes shut tightly, regretfully. "That's what he smeared all over himself. To make it look like he'd attempted suicide."

Yale nodded. He was chewing gum, something strong-scented and fruity. He pointed with his pen to the severed leather band. "Restraints," he said. "Once you get through one, the other three are a snap."

David stood and regarded the empty gurney. Several strands of Clyde's hair remained behind on the pillow. A crime scene technician was lifting them with tweezers and depositing them in a clear plastic bag. "You can catch him again, right? It'll be easier this time?"

"He never even coughed up a last name."

David gestured to the technician taking hair samples from the pillow. "What about the forensics?"

"We can run a DNA on the hair fibers, but unless he's been arrested *and* had blood drawn in the last five years, it won't do us much good."

David's voice sounded increasingly desperate. "But you have fingerprints. . . ."

Yale shook his head slowly. "He was wearing gloves the whole time. We don't book them and lift prints until we get 'em transported to Harbor." Yale studied David through a cool, even countenance.

David felt his face go slack.

Yale turned his gum over in his mouth and snapped it once, loudly. "If he was well enough to escape, he was well enough to be moved to Harbor. Now either you're a liar or a shitty doctor. Which is it?"

The blood bag leaked onto the floor.

David felt as if Yale were looking straight through his head, studying the back wall of his skull.

"If you were gonna keep him here, you should have tied down your fort," Yale said. "Made sure the room was secure."

"But I'm a doctor. That's not my job."

Yale looked at him again, the same impenetrable shine in his eyes. *"Exactly."*

David took a moment to let the roiling in his gut settle. "Listen. Why don't we figure out who's to blame later and focus on finding him."

Yale looked rightly irritated.

"I know my way around this hospital better than you. Better than Security, even."

"Sure," Yale said derisively. "It's your family business."

David stopped short, trying to keep up with a sudden cascade of thoughts. "How do you know that?"

"The building's named after you. Even if I weren't a detective—"

"That's what Clyde said. He said, 'Spier, like the building.' I thought he was thinking of a *spire*. But he saw the SPIER AUDITORIUM sign by the cafeteria—it looks like that whole portion of the building bears my family name. Clyde's been around the hospital. A lot."

"Not a news flash. He did escape *into* the hospital."

David's face felt hot. He blurted, with sudden conviction, "He works here."

"You can't say that with any—"

"Come here."

Yale reluctantly followed David into the hall. David swung a nearby gurney over between himself and Yale, and set the brake.

"Try to move this," he said. "Go ahead."

Yale tried to push it out of the way, but it didn't budge.

"Peter said he shoved the gurney at the officer, but if the gurney was left in the hall with a patient on it, it would've been locked," David said. "The foot levers on the new gurneys have to be kicked to the right to release the brakes—that's not common knowledge. You couldn't figure it out just now—imagine if you were running and someone was pointing a gun at you. Clyde already knew how the gurney operated. From working here."

"A helpful hypothesis. But it's time for you to leave."

"That's why he ran into the hospital interior—he knows these corridors and knows where to hide. Or what if it's not even a detour? Maybe he injured himself to get in here."

"We're on it. And this is *our* job. Now it's time for *you* to stay out of *our* way."

"I think we can—"

"If you continue to compromise this perimeter, I'll bust you for noncompliance." Yale pointed down the hall. His face showed he wasn't listening anymore.

David turned and headed for the lobby. A SWAT crew jogged by with two German shepherds straining at the leashes. Through the small windows atop the swinging doors, he could see Dalton interviewing Peter. From Peter's gestures, it appeared he was conveying details of the escape. Across the lobby, Jenkins alternated between shouting at Ralph and bellowing into his portable, contacting officers around the perimeter of the hospital. "Be advised suspect is considered to be in the possession of a police officer's nine-millimeter," David heard him say. "Let's take him down."

David glanced in Fifteen as he passed; Don was playing the hero, tending to the injured officers. Clyde's blow had inflicted some damage, the hasp on the restraint splitting the skin above one officer's ear. As he finished stitching, Don told a joke David couldn't overhear—probably something involving golf or heaven—and the officer's laughter carried to David as he pushed through the doors to the lobby.

Jenkins had disappeared, leaving Ralph to direct police traffic through the lobby. David moved up beside Ralph. "Is someone watching Nancy?" David asked.

"Yeah, Doc. We got her covered."

"What would Clyde want to do if he was loose in the hospital?"

Two more dogs walked by, sniffing, their nails scuttling over tile, pulling SWAT guys behind them.

"Get his ass out of here, I'd think," Ralph replied.

"Which way did he head?"

"Found smudges of fresh O-negative blood in the Three Corridor. Doors back there are Omnilocked, but we only change the combos once a year, so the codes are around. Plus, people sometimes leave the doors propped open."

David thought of the convoluted hospital interior, the endless white corridors, and realized how hopeless it would be to try to find Clyde's hiding place.

Ralph shook his head. "I'd say our bird's flown the coop."

Dalton finished with Peter and strode over. His tie was yanked to one side, and he'd missed a button on his shirt, the small gap revealing a threadbare undershirt. "Congratulations, Doc. You've turned the ER into a crime scene. Now I have jurisdiction. Get out."

David looked over his shoulder and saw Peter talking to a forensic artist. She shaded some element of the sketch with the side of her pencil, thanked Peter, and headed into Hallway One, probably to see the wounded cop.

"Go home," Dalton said. "You've done enough." His face, for once, was firm and intense. "I'm not asking this time."

David nodded once, slowly, and headed for the door, passing Peter. Peter embraced him across the shoulders with one arm.

"How are you doing?" David asked.

"Fine, fine." Peter ran his fingers through his hair, attempting to smooth it down. It did little good. His voice was a touch shaky. "You never think about it, but a hospital is full of weapons. Prongs and hooks and blades. It's grotesque, really. Tools of healing turned outward." He coughed into a fist. "The way he looked at me . . ."

"You didn't hurt your leg tripping him?"

Peter waved off the notion. "It's steel-enforced, remember?"

"All right," David said. "I have to leave. They're making me leave."

Dalton had finished scribbling something in his worn notepad. He flipped it closed with a flourish, rammed it into his back pocket, and looked up, sighting David. "I'm not fucking around, Doc. I'm gonna check on our artist, and if you're still here when I get back, I'll have you forcibly removed from the building. Don't think I won't." He banged through the swinging doors into the ER proper with the heels of his hands.

Peter trembled slightly, perhaps because the lobby was cool.

"Are you sure you're all right?" David asked.

"Yes," Peter said. "Always."

David was headed for the door when he felt a hand on his shoulder. He turned, expecting Peter but finding Jenkins.

Stress had gone to work on Jenkins's face over the last few days. The skin had reddened, as if pulled taut across the bones, and his cheekbones projected in almost skeletal fashion. His voice came low and vicious. "You treated him. You held him so he could escape. From here on out, every girl that winds up maimed and blind is your fault." He took a step back, as if not wanting to remain near David for fear of losing control.

David looked at him, unsure how to react, afraid to respond. An adrenaline rush left him light-headed, his ears humming.

When Jenkins spoke again, his voice was deathly calm. His finger stabbed the air, pointing at David's face. "It's on your head now," he said.

CHAPTER 30

DAVID returned to his car in the PCHS lot and slid behind the wheel. It was 5:12 A.M. There was little point in his going home; he'd be unable to sleep anyway. He rolled down the window to let in the chilly air.

The flurry of activity around the hospital didn't seem to be slowing. Two UCPD cops strode past David's car.

"—sleazeball reporter dressed as a doctor tried to sneak in a mini-camera. Cranked the cuffs extra tight for his ride to the station."

One of the cops saw David in his car. "Can I see some ID?" he asked.

"Yes, I'm the chief of the emergency room." David flashed his badge. He thought he detected a note of recognition in the cop's eyes. And disdain.

"The ER's shut down for at least a few more hours, sir, and we're keeping this area clear. You're gonna have to leave."

"What time do you think they'll open the ER again?"

"I don't know. At least a few hours."

David drove slowly down the concrete tiers to the exit. A few cars were queued at the police perimeter, and David gazed back at the hospital, taking it in. The ER, David now saw with renewed clarity, was the most accessible part of the institution. And the most vulnerable. As he'd discussed with Dash, the attacks on the ER were probably not specific to the division but symbolic attacks on the hospital itself. Even if Clyde did work at UCLA Med, that didn't necessarily mean his employment was the starting point of his relationship with the hospital. Clyde had been terrified of Dash in a way that seemed to indicate perceived abuse at the hands of doctors. Which could have been his interpretation of a childhood trip to the hospital or the NPI. If only David had a last name for Clyde, he could run him through the hospital files and see what came up.

David was puzzled by Clyde's claim that he wanted "them" to be sorry for locking him in the dark. Was this merely a hallucination, or was it grounded in reality? And if it was reality-based, what did it have to do with the hospital? David had considered that Clyde's comments might be cover smoke—crafty manipulations designed to mislead investigators—but his presentation had been authentic enough.

A cop waved David through at the perimeter. Not wanting to go home, David drove to a gas station two blocks away, leaned against his trunk, sipped a cup of coffee—scalding in taste and temperature—and tried to order his thoughts. He felt the night chill through his thin shirt and realized that, though it was past five in the morning, he wasn't even tired. Seventeen years in the emergency room provided excellent sleep-deprivation training.

He threw away the empty cup and called Diane from his cell phone. She sounded wide awake. "I heard," she said. "Pat called me. It's all over the news."

"I'm going to need you to cover a bit for me tomorrow," David said. "Would you mind coming in?"

"Not at all. Do we have another attending in the morning?"

"Nelson."

"Fine. The media is stringing you up over this."

He fended off a stab of insecurity. "As well they should be."

"What does that mean?"

"I'm never going to apologize for treating him, obviously," David said.

"Obviously."

"But as you said, I stepped beyond my domain. Which is fine. I don't like boundaries, especially when other people are drawing them for me. But if I was going to assume responsibility for Clyde—and take that responsibility away from those who were actually entitled to it, however fucked up they may have been—I should have assumed *all aspects* of that responsibility."

"Like how?"

"Like instead of resenting security, I could have insisted it be tightened."

A pause as Diane processed this. "I guess we all dig ourselves into our own neat little areas of expertise, grow smug, and forget how many things we're *not* good at."

"My list is longer than I've been forced to consider for some time."

"So now what?"

"Now I have to see this through. That patient—and the fact he's on the loose—is still my responsibility." David hadn't said it aloud yet, and it rang with sudden conviction.

"So what are you gonna do? Track him down?"

"Yes."

"I'm not sure you want that mission."

"I *know* I don't want it. But that's irrelevant."

"Yeah," Diane said. "I guess it is." A pause. "What are you gonna do now?"

"Call Dash, fill him in, and let him know the assessment's off for the morning."

"Then what?"

"Sit here, drink shitty coffee, and wait for the ER to open up so I can get on this."

CHAPTER 31

A cleaner Horace returned a half hour later, munching on a Snickers. The cadaver had paled nicely, taking on a yellow hue. He threw the white sheets that had previously wrapped the bodies into a large rolling trash bin, followed by the woman's clothes. The man's clothes were not there, and he glanced under the table, puzzled, before concluding he must have thrown them out right after removing them from the body.

An I-beam ran overhead, continuing through a small gap in the top of the crypt door. Several chains dangled from the I-beam, and Horace slid one along its length, positioning it above the woman's body. The chain terminated in a pincer clamp, a unit with two jaws that crossed themselves and curved inward. Horace fitted the dull ends of the pincers into the embalmed woman's ear canals and hoisted the chain. The clamp tightened as it rose, the weight of the body pulled the pincers taut, and the cadaver jerked up to a sitting position. Horace raised her straight off the table until she was dangling from the I-beam, the weight of her body sustained by the two pincers digging into the holes of her skull.

Swinging the massive crypt door open, Horace returned to the woman's hanging body and slid it along the length of the I-beam, through the open door, and into the immense refrigerated room. To the left, about a dozen other bodies hung suspended from their heads, pale and naked. Storing them in this fashion ensured that their features wouldn't distort; a body left to harden on an embalming table had a plank-flat backside, which did little to help medical students who needed to explore the human body in its natural form.

Though Horace had long grown accustomed to the room, it was a gruesome place. Swollen blue tongues protruding from mouths, scrotums tightened to small walnuts between loose-dangling hairy legs, eyebrows perfectly plucked on wrinkled yellow foreheads. The donors, magnanimous givers to the cause of science, now hanging up with every inch of their bodies exposed. Each extra tuft of hair, each fold of the abdomen, each mole and birthmark. The same scrutiny would soon be applied to their insides.

Buckets around the periphery of the crypt contained brains and eyeballs, ready to be claimed by the various departments. Blue and red tubs, the type bought at Home Depot to ice down beers at summer parties, were positioned beneath the bodies to catch the ooze and drippings. Horace slid a red bucket beneath the woman and paused for a moment, nostrils widening. He rose, glancing around suspiciously. Beneath the overwhelming formalin and meaty odors, he had caught a whiff of something. Cigarette smoke.

The swaying bodies creaked and swayed as Horace walked slowly through them, searching. Once during his first week, he'd heard the crypt door swing shut behind him when he'd been hanging a squat Asian man. He'd pushed aside the panic, walking calmly to the door and finding that there was indeed a post to open it from the inside. Aside from that brief moment when he'd thought he was locked in with the cadavers, he'd never felt frightened inside the room.

Until now.

He walked along the far wall of the crypt, half expecting someone to jump out at him from behind a wall of yellowed flesh. He pushed aside the last cadaver in the row, a woman whom he could tell had been young and robust in life, but no one was hiding behind her.

Horace sank slowly to his haunches and gazed beneath the swaying feet. Aside from buckets and stained plastic tubs, there was nothing. The woman's body pivoted slowly on its chain, creaking. She was a fresh cadaver, and still draining. A thin stream of yellow liquid curved around the inside of her calf, dripping from her big toe into the red tub beneath her. Realizing he'd been holding his breath, Horace exhaled long and hard, rose, and walked out of the crypt.

Had he looked more closely at the woman's cadaver, he would have noticed a wisp of smoke rising from her foot. If he'd drawn nearer still, he'd have seen the small holes that had been burned into the side of her heel, just in front of the Achilles tendon.

With two cigarettes, held side by side.

Wrapped in an effluvium of formalin, Clyde sauntered past the gift shop and the security desk in a dark burial suit, the Beretta shoved in the band of his pants and pressed to the small of his back. The buttons that ran up the back of the jacket were misaligned, the gaps and flares of the fabric betraying the impromptu contortions he'd undertaken attempting to don apparel designed for the deceased. The combination of the suit's antiquated style and Clyde's robust build gave him the appearance of a vaudeville barker.

He caught a sideways glance from a six-year-old pulling an IV post, but neither of the guards at the desk looked up as he strode past, the glass hospital doors sliding open before him. The cops running the investigation had no photograph of him to circulate, but if the guards had looked closely, they might have seen dark spots on the shirt where the fabric clung to his weeping blisters.

The doors slid open before him and he stepped out, pulling the pack of cigarettes from the suit's damp breast pocket. He lit a cigarette—just one—with a match from the book nestled inside the clear wrapping and inhaled deeply, shooting a plume of smoke into the dark air of the plaza. In front of him, a massive lawn stretched wide, reaching almost to the top tier of the uncovered PCHS lot. The parking structure had many low walls, and exits leading to streets, paths, and gardens. The cops would have searched the cars that had remained there overnight, as well as those left along Le Conte.

His Crown Vic waited, hidden behind a Dumpster at the back of the old Macy's lot across the street, keys resting atop the left rear tire.

An officer jogged up the front steps, touching his cap. "Morning."

Clyde nodded, then, with an economical movement of his fat grubby fingers, flicked the cigarette butt aside. The cool air breezed around him as he walked forward into the open expanse of the plaza, the hospital towering behind him.

The sky was just beginning to grow light.

CHAPTER 32

POLICE officers were still moving about the hospital in clusters, but much of the activity had died down. The ER reopened at 7:45 A.M.; David was there waiting at the police perimeter, doing his best to hide his intense discomfort at the reporters pressing him for statements. The cops spitefully made him wait until eight to enter the hospital, as that was when his shift officially began. The gas station coffee, bad as it may have been, had certainly been caffeine-intensive, and he actually felt a few steps better than exhausted.

It would be a long, unrelenting day. After working a full shift, he'd have to run over to the Sunset Recreation Center for the meet-and-greet for the incoming class of residents. Aside from Diane and Dr. Nelson, the ER staff was curt with him. He wasn't sure if they held him responsible for Clyde's escape or if it was merely his own guilt at work.

Composites of Clyde had been posted in the lobby and the CWA. David removed one and gazed at it. The artist had failed to capture Clyde's dead, flat eyes, but she'd managed to sketch the mouth and chin perfectly. David stared at the wide neck and acne-scarred cheeks and felt a faintness ripple through him.

After making sure the floor was under control, he found Ralph in the rear hall of the ER. "Anything?" David asked.

Ralph shook his head.

David pulled the sketch of Clyde from his pocket. "Did you send these around to staff?"

"We posted them just about everywhere."

"I think we should circulate copies through the internal mail, make sure every single staff member sees this. We should write on it that Clyde is a possible hospital worker, so people give it more than a cursory glance."

"Yale told me about the worker angle," Ralph said. "But it would take me awhile to get a request like that through the bureaucratic bullshit."

"Put my weight behind it. See if that helps. If not, let me know and I'll get into it personally." David walked briskly through the network of halls across the hospital and into the connected Neuropsychiatric Institute. He unfolded Clyde's composite and examined it on the elevator down to the Badge Center in the basement. In order to move freely within the hospital, every employee of the UCLA Hospital was required to wear a photo badge. All pictures were taken passport style at the Badge Center, with a digital camera and a blue backdrop.

An obese woman manned a computer behind the terminal, her monitor cluttered with family photos and stickers featuring anthropomorphic animals. A plaque adhered to a bulletin board behind her read: SEXUAL HARASSMENT WILL NOT BE TOLERATED. BUT IT WILL BE GRADED. David shuddered.

The woman looked up with a wide grin. "Hello, Dr. Spier." She glanced him over, then waved a finger at him in scolding fashion. "I see you're not wearing your badge."

David found it difficult to force a smile. "You keep all employee photographs on computer file, right?"

"Did you lose your badge again? Do you need us to make you up another new one?"

"No, I have mine right here." He removed his badge from his coat pocket and brandished it at her. "I was wondering how many years back your photo files run."

"Five years, three months . . ." she recited proudly. She leaned over and checked a *Far Side* day-by-day calendar propped on her desk. ". . . and six days. Ever since we switched to a digital camera."

David laid the police sketch on the countertop and smoothed out the creases. "The man who escaped . . . I have reason to believe he works here at the hospital."

She picked up the sketch and shivered, her weight shifting beneath a stretched yellow sweater. "That's the guy, huh? The acid thrower."

"He said his name is Clyde, though I'm not certain he was telling the truth. Can you run a computer check and see if you can match the sketch to a photo?"

"Well, jeez, Doctor, I don't know. There's really no way to do that. I mean, it's not a big fandangled program or anything. I'd have to run through every entry click by click. And there are thousands of photographs in here. Plus, I can't run a search without a first *and* last name. That's how the badge search engine operates." She picked up the composite and stared at it, as if it contained the solution to the predicament. "Sorry, Doctor."

David took back the flyer, refolded it, and began to walk away before being struck by a new thought. The woman looked back up with the same wide grin when he returned. "Hello again," she said, with a short burst of laughter.

"You get a lot of people through here, I'd imagine, from all the departments, right? New employees and people who need replacement badges?"

"Yessirree. Why just this morning I've had five lost badges, including—"

"Would you mind running copies of this flier and

handing them out to people to pass around their departments? Just in case it gets lost in the mass mailing. Ask people to look at it, *really* look at it, and see if they remember this guy working here. Will you do that for me . . ." He glanced on the counter for a name tag, but couldn't spot one. When he looked back at her, she was holding up her badge proudly for him to read. ". . . Shirley?"

She seemed taken aback by the intensity in his face. "Um . . . it's not normally our policy to distribute non-badge-related information."

David took a deep breath. "I think the risk of more women becoming horribly disfigured probably outweighs this breach of badge etiquette. Would you concur, Shirley?"

The color seemed to wash out of her face, leaving only the two splotches of rouge that capped her cheeks. "Yes, Dr. Spier," she said tightly. "Though I don't see why you have to be so rude."

CHAPTER 33

DIANE'S scrubs shifted when she leaned over, the fabric holding tight to her body in spots—across the rounded band of her lower back, at the curve where her buttocks met her legs, on her right scapula—before fading back into folds and wrinkles. A wisp of hair had settled in a crescent along her cheek, the bottom point lingering near the corner of her mouth. She spoke a soft, badly accented

Spanish as she placed the bell of her stethoscope on the boy's distended belly. The father looked on, as did David from his eavesdropper's post at the door.

"*¿Dolor aquí?*" Diane asked, palpating the boy's midabdomen.

"*¡Ay, pinche cabrón bendejo maricón!*" the boy hissed through clenched teeth.

The father scratched his forehead, hiding his eyes. "He say yes."

Despite the shimmer of moisture rising in the boy's eyes, David couldn't help but grin at the exchange. He waited for Diane to finish and approach him, then lowered his voice. "Since Clyde knew where the kick-pedal release was on the gurney, maybe he has some job that involves transporting patients. I'm already covering the orderly angle. Can you think of any other—" David stopped when he heard hard footsteps on the tile, then turned and saw Jenkins and Bronner heading his way.

With a single brisk motion, Jenkins whipped a pair of handcuffs from their pouch on his belt and locked them around David's wrists. David looked down at them, dumbfounded. "What the hell is this?"

"Obstruction of justice. You had a suspect in here five days ago, August Fourteenth, with a gunshot wound from the Kinko's shooting. We've been looking for him for some time, but you deliberately misled us, giving him time to escape."

"Oh," David said, "this is brilliant. I thought we were through with that business." He had to raise both hands to scratch his nose.

"I reconsidered," Jenkins said.

"What the hell is going on here?" Diane asked.

Jenkins ignored her, continuing to address David. "We're taking you in. I'm gonna have a field day on your ass."

"On my ass?"

"It's a figure of speech."

"And a rather charming one at that."

"Save your breath for the station. You'll need it to tell us about the suspect you aided."

"Well, you see, there's this little thing called patient confidentiality. Your only out on that front is the Tarasoff ruling in '76 and it's less than irrelevant here."

"We'll throw you in a room with the Captain, see how quiet you are then."

"Captain Billings? Feel free. I haven't seen him since the Getty Center dinner in March. I'd love to catch up." David glared at Bronner, and could see the older cop was getting uneasy. "Plus, you're harassing me on a false civil charge, not a criminal one—you have no right to arrest me. If you pull me out of here mid-shift, I'll sue your asses. Loudly."

"You have the right to remain silent—" Jenkins began.

"Uncuff the attending physician immediately," Diane said. "Handle whatever grudge you have later. The other attending is on lunch, and I'm not qualified to run this department myself."

"Well, Ms.—"

"It's *Doctor*."

Jill came running down the hall, her yellow hair bouncing. "We have a horror show rolling in. A forty-year-old male sustained a penetrating trauma to the chest wall, ninety over sixty in the field, heart rate one-thirty, respiratory rate forty." She paused when she noticed the handcuffs around David's wrists. "Be careful with those hands," she said to Jenkins. "They're worth more than you are."

"Uncuff me," David said.

"—anything you say can be used against you in a court of law. You have the right to an attorney—"

Jill looked from David to Diane to Jenkins and Bronner, as if unsure to whom to address the medical information. "Two-minute ETA by ground transport." The familiar screech of gurney wheels, followed by the bang of the swinging doors. "Or right now."

Two paramedics sprinted toward David, pushing the gurney, the lead one shouting, "Code trauma! He was moaning and groaning in the rig, but we lost vitals in the ambulance bay. We got nothing."

A bent piece of rebar protruded nearly two feet from the man's chest on the left side. Strapped to a backboard, the man's head was secured with a C-collar. His visible flesh was pale blue.

David held up his hands, the chain tight between his wrists. "Uncuff me. Now."

"They were blasting out a section of the building across the street," the other paramedic said. "Someone forgot he was in there and let fly."

"Release him immediately. This is no time to fuck around," Diane yelled over her shoulder as she ran toward the gurney, meeting it halfway, only to turn and run with it toward Trauma One. David jogged after her into the resuscitation suite, handcuffs jingling, and the two cops reluctantly followed. Diane moved alongside the body. "No spontaneous respirations, no pulse, and he's cyanotic."

David reached his cuffed hands out and felt the man's stomach, pushing gently. It gave with a soft crunching sound, as though he were pressing on a bag of Rice Krispies. Air had escaped from the man's lungs and moved beneath his skin. "Crepitance," he said.

Several hands grabbed the backboard when they reached the wider hospital gurney.

"On my count," Diane yelled. "Three, two, *one*." They slid the man safely over onto the new gurney, and the paramedics backed out to make more space.

By the time David glanced up at the man's face, Diane already had him intubated and hooked up to one hundred percent oxygen. She helped the nurse scissor off the man's clothes. "We're gonna have to open him up. Someone get me a thoracotomy tray!"

People scurried about the body. The superficial veins had collapsed; they had a rapid infuser going on the right arm. Jenkins watched them working on the body, his face angry and distant.

"Someone find a line in the femoral," David said. A junior nurse responded, digging in the hip with a needle. She got a flash of blood in the syringe. "Good," he said. "Now feed a guide wire through the needle. Right, right." The nurse slid a blue number-eight French catheter over the guide wire into the vein. *"Don't let go of the guide wire."*

Six units arrived from the blood bank. Diane pulled on a gown and gloves. "Switch the saline for O-neg."

David turned and shoved his hands at Jenkins. "Enough already. Take these things off me. *Now*." Lab techs and nurses darted around them to get to the gurney.

The thoracotomy tray arrived, swathed in blue towels. Pulling the towels aside to reveal a forceps, rib spreader, rib cutter, and an array of gleaming scalpels, Diane paused and turned to the officers. David's hands were inches from Jenkins's chest, but Jenkins didn't so much as look down at them; he kept his cold, hard gaze locked on David's face.

Diane crossed her arms. "I can't do this without him," she said. "Get ready for a lawsuit."

The activity around the body seemed to stop. For an instant, all eyes were on David and Jenkins. Bronner broke the silence, stepping forward to unlock the cuffs. Jenkins tried to restrain him, but Bronner shoved him away fiercely. "You'd better settle down there, pup," he growled.

Jenkins's face was alive with emotion—rage, frustration, humiliation. He glared at Bronner, then turned and banged out through the doors. Bronner quickly unlocked David's cuffs and walked out also, his boots creaking.

David had his stethoscope off his shoulders and into place immediately. He set the bell over the man's left lung, then his right. Miraculously, there were no decreased breathing sounds—neither lung had collapsed. "What are our three major concerns with a penetration to the mediastinum?" he asked.

"Tension pneumothorax, pericardial tamponade, lacerated aorta." Using a squirt bottle, Diane doused the man's left side in Betadine, the antiseptic falling across the ribs like an orange drape. Her gloved fingers felt their way into position on the man's side, finding his fifth intercostal space. Using a scalpel, she sliced downward from the man's sternum, carving an arc that ran the length of his ribs. Blood gushed over her hands, coating her white gloves crimson as she continued to cut down to the muscle.

Jill's patterned scrub top, a cheery Amazon green number decorated with frogs, seemed oddly discordant. She leaned over with the spray bottle to clear the wound for Diane. A spurt of blood caught a poison arrow frog across the face.

A flash of aqua green scrubs to David's left. "Surgeon's stuck in a mess of an appendectomy," he heard the clerk say. "The junior surge resident is on his way down."

Diane finished scissoring through the intercostal muscles, then wedged a rib spreader into the bloody gap. The pronged tool was silver and ratcheted, and she flipped out the handle and cranked it like a winch. The man's ribs stretched, then snapped, sending a splattering of blood across her surgical gown and Jill's face.

"How's the left lung?" David asked.

Diane peered into the hole in the man's body. "Looks fine."

"Now feel your way in there. Check to make sure the aorta isn't lacerated."

She paused for an instant, her gloved hand hovering near the gap. David had walked her through this move on a cadaver, but she'd never had a live run. She looked up, her brilliant green eyes catching David's, and he nodded once, reassuringly.

Lowering her shoulder, she slid her hand into the man's living body.

"You feel the lung along the back of your hand?" David asked. "Bumpy and soft?"

She nodded. "I have my bearings."

Her arm disappeared midway to her elbow as she slid her hand down along the inside of the man's back.

David's hand twitched at his side as he mentally undertook the maneuver with her. "Did you check the aorta?"

She shook her head.

"How can you restrain yourself?"

Her eyes widened. "I've got it!" A smile bloomed on her face, a child's smile at sighting something wondrous. "Under my fingertips. It's firm and full of blood."

"Good," David said. "Now let's check for a pericardial tamponade." If the heart had sustained a trauma, which David guessed it had from the angle of the rebar, it was probably bleeding into the pericardium. And if the sac around the heart filled with blood, it would interfere with the heart's mechanism, preventing it from pumping effectively.

Someone banged into a rapid infuser and it nearly capsized.

"Where the hell is surgery?" Diane said. She readjusted her hand, and a soft sucking noise emerged from the wound.

"It's all right," David said. "Focus on the task."

Diane twisted her body so she could better maneuver her hand. "Got it! The pericardial sac is full and tense. The heart must've bled into it."

She removed her right hand to grab a tiny pair of scissors, picked up a pair of tongs with her left, and went back in with both.

"Okay," David said. "Grab the edge of the sac with the tongs and make a small vertical incision." He strained to look around her and saw blood spill into the chest. "Good. Now deliver the heart."

Her arm moving with exquisite care, she gripped the heart and pulled it out through the small incision, holding it in her hand. "It's beating," she said, ducking her head to see through the mess. "It's got a small hole."

"It's trying to push blood but can't. Put your thumb over the hole."

She adjusted her thumb, then turned and looked to David again. He held her gaze as they waited. Now that she'd plugged the heart's hole, blood should begin pumping more effectively. A nurse near the man's head looked up triumphantly. "I got a pulse!" A carotid pulse meant the blood pressure had just hit sixty.

"Me too!" another nurse exclaimed. "Femoral pulse!" The blood pressure had risen to seventy.

A wisp of hair fell across Diane's eyes, and she flicked it aside with a quick jerk of her head. Her lips were trembling ever so slightly—David was sure he was the only one who noticed. Her face had taken on the fervent, confounded cast of one in extreme grief or ecstasy. She held a man's beating heart in her hand, and her thumb plugging its hole was the only thing keeping him alive.

The junior surgeon jogged into the room. "Call OR," Diane said. "Tell 'em we're on our way."

The gurney took off with a lurch as Jill shoved it

toward the door, several others grabbing for the connecting gear and making sure it moved with the body.

Keeping her thumb firmly pressed over the hole in the heart, Diane threw one leg over the man's body as she hopped on the gurney. David stepped back as the gurney and its attendant mob swung out into the hall and rattled along at an impromptu sprint, the junior surgeon barking orders, nurses dragging rapid infusers on IV poles, and Diane straddling the patient's unconscious body, her arm inside him, seeming to ride the entire mob like a cowboy.

Looking up across the bobbing heads and waving poles, she caught David's eye. She winked just as the gurney turned the corner, and he realized he was in love with her.

CHAPTER 34

AFTER checking that Clyde's composite was indeed being circulated through internal mail, David rode up to the fifth floor and entered the ICU ward. It was busier than the last time he'd visited Nancy, two days ago. A frail woman called out to him from a bed, wanting more morphine, and he smiled at her as he passed. "I'm sorry, ma'am, I don't work in this department, but I'll get the nurse for you."

The curtains were drawn in a tight oval around Nancy's bed, like a coffin pall. The rattle of the rings woke her. She turned her face, and he did his best not to let his horror show despite the fact that she couldn't see him. If shock found its way into his face, it would find its way into his voice.

If anything, she looked worse, her burns resolving into wounds even more horrifying for their permanence. In the six days since the attack, her hair had fallen out along the front of her crown, leaving her with a coarse fringe of ringlets around the sides and back of her head. The large bolster on her right cheek had dried and turned gray, and the skin around the edges had yellowed. David didn't have a plastic surgeon's eye, but he doubted that the graft would take. Between her other bolsters, her patchwork flesh shone red, slick with residual Silvadene. In the midst of it all, her two eyeballs perched inside their sockets, shrunken and sightless.

"Who is it?" she said weakly, her voice a tiny rasp. "Who's there?"

"It's David Spier."

"Oh. I don't want to see you. I heard what you did . . . that you helped him . . . and now he got away." Her head drifted slightly on the pillow, a dying motion. "How could you?"

"I didn't help him," David said. "I treated him."

She drew breath raggedly. "I don't want to see you."

"Okay," David said.

"Ever again."

"Okay."

David backed up quietly and pulled the curtain shut.

Diane was back from surgery by the time David got downstairs. She'd already changed into fresh scrubs when David entered the doctors' lounge.

"This morning's incident with Jenkins gave me an idea," he said.

She gathered her bloody scrubs from the floor. "If it's

the handcuffs you're interested in, you'll have to buy me dinner first."

"Sadly, nothing so titillating. That patient we helped out who the cops wanted—?"

"Hell's Angel guy?"

"No. The guy Jenkins was yelling about. The bullet in the ass. What was ostensibly his name again?"

"Ed Pinkerton."

"Right." David went to his locker and withdrew the odd bookmark that Ed had left behind in the ER. It read: AMOK BOOKSTORE. THE EXTREMES OF INFORMATION.

⊕

David stopped at a bad *taquería* and wolfed down a burrito he was certain would give him acute GI distress. Driving toward the Amok Bookstore, he glanced down at the bookmark, double-checking the address. Located in a downscale-trendy area of Los Feliz, the storefront was small and unassuming, and David drove right past it and had to backtrack when he hit Hollywood Boulevard.

The book Ed had been reading, *Wiretapping and Electronic Surveillance*, implied that he'd be an asset in an effort to find someone. Plus, as an ex-con, he probably knew how to get done any number of things David could scarcely even name. He'd done Ed a favor, after all, and the man with the awkward flesh wound might be willing to point him in the right direction.

Even if Ed hadn't stolen his file, David would have had no way to get ahold of him without going out and tracking him down. David had not been surprised to find that he was unlisted—the only Ed Pinkerton in the area had turned out to be a ninety-year-old veteran of the Second World War—so he only had the bookmark to go on.

David parked at a broken meter in front of a shop that advertised inflatable sheep. He walked toward Amok, enjoying a small flare of pride at operating like a noir detective. Any notion of pride quickly vanished, however, when he entered and realized just how out of his league he was.

A twanging East Asian tune played over the speakers, interspersed with pleading in a foreign tongue and screams that David, who had heard a fair variety of screams at work each day, could not dismiss as staged. Wraiths of incense smoke curled in the air, dispersing, disappearing. The narrow store was lined with bookcases that displayed books cover-out, and a sinewy man in a leather vest leered across an old cash register at the front, tufts of grayish hair escaping from the V above the vest's buttons. Massive spiderweb tattoos worked their way up both his arms and clutched the balls of his shoulders. A bar pierced his septum, protruding a few centimeters beyond each nostril.

Several customers perused the shelves, indifferent to the ambient wailing. David pretended to do the same, though he could not shake the cashier's stare or the feeling that he'd been immediately recognized as an impostor. A book called *Jugular Wine*, positioned between *Red Stains* and the more respectable-looking *Sodomy and the Pirate Tradition*, caught his attention. He flipped through a few pages with a sort of horrified interest, then lowered the book and risked a look around.

A man too predictably clad in an overcoat shuffled through the front door to the counter, his nose glowing the broken-vessel red of a confirmed alcoholic. The tattooed cashier hunched over the counter, speaking in a lowered voice that David had to strain to make out. "Got something up your alley."

The alcoholic made some gesture that rippled his overcoat, and the worker pulled an unlabeled VHS videocassette from beneath the counter and slid it toward him.

David only heard bits and pieces of the cashier's next comment. "Buddy of mine . . . crime-scene guy in Tokyo . . ."

The alcoholic withdrew a hand from his overcoat pocket and tossed three balled twenties on the counter. The VHS tape disappeared with his hand into the same pocket and then he was shuffling back toward the door, never having uttered a word.

Setting down *Jugular Wine*, David couldn't help but register his amazement; he felt as though he'd just wandered into a particularly unsavory episode of *The Twilight Zone*. The books on the shelves, the background "music," the customers—they represented a seemingly vast undercurrent of society, people with alternative deviant needs and desires, not only buyers of such materials but creators, publishers, distributors.

Gathering his courage, David approached the cash register. "Hello," he said. "I'm looking for . . . well, I have this friend who—who shops here, and I've been—"

"Book records are confidential," the man snapped. "Kennie Starr found that out when he tried to subpoena records of Ms. Lewinsky's purchases at Kramerbooks in '98. So if you're going to, go ahead and serve me and get the fuck out."

David held up his hands and took a step back. "I'm not serving you anything. I'm not even making any inquiries about his reading habits. I was just wondering if you knew this guy. He's quite striking-looking. Very pale skin, bright red hair that he just shaved."

"Confidentiality is of the utmost importance to our customers," the man said. He sneered, revealing a set of perfect, glistening teeth. "Good friend, huh?"

"Look," David said. "He's not a friend." He knew he was losing ground, but he couldn't exactly reveal that he'd treated Ed without violating his patient confidentiality. "He's someone I met last week. I helped him out of a jam. I know he frequents this store, and I thought if you saw him, you could mention—"

"I don't involve myself in my customers' lives," the man said.

"There's nothing *involving* about it. I'll pay you to give him a message for me."

"I don't take bribes."

"Think of it as a delivery fee."

When the man leaned over the counter, the spiderwebs bulged. "I don't know who you're talking about. We have a lot of customers. I suggest you buy something or get the fuck out."

David elected to get the fuck out.

CHAPTER 35

REALIZING he was running late for the resident meet-and-greet, David raced back across town. His annoyance that The Eagles now qualified for the Oldies radio station was quickly replaced with dismay when the news cut in. "The Westwood Acid Thrower is still on the loose after a daring escape from the UCLA Medical Center last night. Sources indicate that ER Division Chief Dr. David Spier was in a standoff with the LAPD after he refused to release the suspect due to—"

An abrupt disquietude seized David. He clicked off the radio and drove in silence. His untainted career had not prepared him for being the center of controversy.

Now every decision he made would be before the glaring spotlight of the media.

Before going to the Sunset Recreation Center, he stopped at home and changed into a suit. Dinner was over by the time he parked and arrived at the banquet hall on the third floor. People were milling on the back terrace, enjoying the summer evening. An immense semicircle of a balcony, the terrace overlooked the UCLA track, its view broken only by the occasional tree. David was amused to find he'd coiled his stethoscope inside his jacket pocket from force of habit.

He nodded to his colleagues as he made his way through the crowd outside, taking care to seek out the new faculty members. Carson wore Birkenstocks beneath his slacks, and a wide grin. Near the bar, Don spoke in hushed tones to a busty blonde in a sequined dress, drawing close to whisper so their cheeks touched. Other colleagues seemed to huddle together after David walked by, probably discussing his treating "The Westwood Acid Thrower."

David ordered a cranberry juice and soda, and stood at the concrete balustrade alone, sipping his drink from a too-small red straw. Large overheads lit the track, a few remaining athletes toiling below through the tail end of a practice. The crack of a starting gun carried to David on the breeze, and he thought of days when he too ran and lifted and sweated and woke up unsore to do it all over again.

A soft hand on his shoulder broke him from his thoughts, and he turned to see Diane at his side, wearing a black wraparound dress. A single strand of pearls rested across her upper chest, kinking slightly over the lines of her clavicles.

"I know," Diane said. "You're not used to seeing me dressed. Any luck tracking down our friend at the seedy bookstore?"

"No. But I got to leaf through a coffee-table book featuring clitoral pierces, so the outing wasn't a total loss."

Diane grimaced.

Two attendings at the bar looked away quickly when David caught their eye. Being scrutinized by his own goddamn colleagues on top of everything else. His anger departed quickly, though; he'd made his bed. Turning back to the track, he saw that dark clouds had gathered by the mountains, threatening a shower. "I see Don's no longer with his wife."

"You didn't hear? He got one of those photo traffic tickets, the kind like in Beverly Hills where a camera snaps your picture at an intersection when you run the red light."

"Don't you mean *if* you run the red light?"

"Anyway, the picture showed up at home, and his wife opened it, and there was Don in the car with some nurse from peds."

"How'd you hear that?"

"From Dr. Jenner. They play golf together."

"Do doctors really play golf together? How wonderfully stereotypical."

Diane reached for the front of his shirt, then stopped herself. "You missed a button."

Everyone began moving inside for the post-dinner address. Having raced around for the past few days, David had neglected to prepare a speech. He was too tired to worry about it; he'd spoken at so many events, he'd be able to regurgitate something suitable.

A man in a red caterer's jacket shuffled along the edge of the terrace, plucking empty cups and bottles from the balustrade. David had noticed earlier, when the man had smiled, that his teeth were stained gray, probably from taking tetracycline at too early an age. He limped slightly, favoring his left leg. David glanced down—sure enough, a special shoe. Probably a childhood brush with polio. The vaccine was developed in the mid-'50s; the man looked to be in his late fifties—that seemed about right. If he was twelve when he contracted—

"David."

When he turned to face Diane, he was surprised to find the balcony mostly empty.

"You're zoning out on me. What were you thinking about?"

He shook his head, clearing his thoughts. "How our bodies are marked. How physicians are like detectives, reading scars and limps and intonations, seeing what we can glean about a person's past and present."

Diane looked disappointed. "Relevant to the past days' events, I suppose."

"Why? What were you thinking about?"

"Our conversation in the cafeteria." She folded her arms, a fluid, graceful motion. "I decided we'd both be stupid to walk away from this after a few half-assed dates."

He smiled as if she were joking, though he knew she was not.

"Come on. Your ageism aside, you think I don't notice how you look at me? How we interact? We both know it's more than professionalism, David."

"Well, it shouldn't be." He realized he was speaking loudly, and he lowered his voice. "I'm the division chief and you're a resident."

"I thought we were colleagues."

"We . . . we are."

"Besides, it's not like anyone can accuse you of sexual harassment. I'm the one who'd get hauled off on that count."

"Diane, I'm still your superior." He did not meet Diane's stare when she looked over at him. His tone became more assertive. "There are certain boundaries that shouldn't be crossed in the workplace." He felt his face flush and realized he was growing anxious. He wiped a line of sweat from his forehead with two neat strokes of his index fingers. "And besides, I just lost my wife."

She didn't look as though she wanted to touch that one. She let it sit with him, and it didn't sit well. It was a cheap excuse; he wondered how long ago it had lost its legitimacy. Was two years long enough to mourn? To let go?

"That's three excuses in thirty seconds," Diane said, "and I still haven't heard you say you don't feel the same way."

"Well, I don't think I really need to—"

"When's the last time you had a friend over for dinner?"

"What?"

"A friend. Just a friend."

"I don't know. I guess it's been awhile."

"David, you are the most heavily sublimated person I know. You work constantly, you're in a field that doesn't involve long-term care so you have no long-standing relationships with patients, you have very little personal time, and with the exception of our few nights out, you don't date. It's like you've pulled yourself into a protective little shell. Maybe you don't want to recognize the fact that you still *have* feelings."

His anger flared, instinctual and protective. "It's been a few years since your psych rotation, Dr. Trace. Why don't you back off the armchair analysis?"

Diane's face hardened, and he felt a sharp stab of regret. Frustration, sadness, and intensity were all part of her weekly routine, but this was the first time he'd seen her really pissed. He started to say something to mitigate the harshness of his remark, but a woman stepped through the French doors to the back terrace. "Dr. Spier, we're ready for you!"

"I'll be right there."

Diane refused to look down or turn away; she faced him, angry and vulnerable. He tried desperately to figure out what he wanted to say but could not, and finally it was he who turned away as he headed inside to deliver his address.

He moved through his remarks on autopilot. At one point, the room filled with laughter, and he was momentarily nervous before realizing he'd delivered a stock joke. Diane came in about halfway through and sat in the back.

As soon as he finished, she headed out with one of the new residents, a tall, striking brunette. David had to walk at a fast clip to catch her in the parking structure nearby. Diane was climbing into the passenger side of a red VW, the other resident at the wheel. A soft rain was falling, more like a wet breeze.

"Excuse me, Dr. Trace."

Diane paused, half in the car. "Yes, Dr. Spier?"

"I wanted to talk to you more about . . . about the case this afternoon. Would you mind terribly if I gave you a ride home?"

She thought for a moment, chewing her bottom lip. "I guess that's fine." She leaned back down. "I'll see you tomorrow, Marcy."

The friend nodded and pulled out, and David returned her wave. "Where are you parked?" Diane asked.

He looked around the wide lot. "To be honest, I'm not sure."

She shook her head but did not comment. She waited patiently as he walked around the lot with the alarm button depressed on his key chain, pointing it in all directions. Finally he heard a blip somewhere behind him and followed the noise back to his Mercedes. He debated opening the door for her, but decided that would be inappropriate.

Aside from her occasional directions, they drove in complete silence to her apartment building on Chenault. He pulled over to the curb and they sat silently in the car, studying the faux walnut dash.

Diane said, "Let me get a word in edgewise, would you?"

"Look," David said. "It's been a very difficult past few days and, for me, past couple of years. Lately, I've been trying to figure out how it all fits together, where I am in all this. As foolish as it sounds, I don't think I've really known where I am for a good long time, and I've only recently started piecing that together. And then this whole shitstorm hit with the escape. . . ." His voice trailed off and he realized he wasn't sure what he was saying. "You're right—I won't deny that I have certain feelings for you. But I'm not sure that those feelings are entirely appropriate."

"*Feelings* can't be inappropriate," Diane said.

"It's not that simple for me right now." He studied the steering wheel. "I'm afraid I'm a little lost."

She nodded once, slowly. "That's the first honest answer you've given me, so I'm gonna let you get away with it." Amusement flickered through her eyes. "For now."

"And I'm sorry I spoke to you so sharply."

"I'm sorry I was pushing you. That's not my place." She laughed. "Wow. Our first fight and we haven't even had sex. You really know how to cut right to the good stuff." Smiling, she put her hand on the door handle.

"So after all that, would it be entirely rude for me to tell you I think you're quite stunning?"

She considered. "Yes," she said.

"Okay," David said. "You're not stunning."

"You're not either."

David swerved out of his lane when he answered his ringing cell phone. He straightened the car and gave an embarrassed look around, but the road was empty.

Blake's raspy voice. "You paged me again?"

"Yes."

"Don't turn it into a habit."

"I'm looking into a few angles and if I . . . if I happened to locate the suspect and could bring him in or alert you, would you handle the arrest?"

Blake's laugh gave off a deep rattle. "Your planning didn't work out so hot last time."

"Would you?"

"Shit, yeah. I'll take the collar. And the book deal. TV movie. Talk-show circuit. This cop thing's only temporary. I really want to direct, you know."

"I'm serious."

"Well, shit, now that makes all the difference." A sigh. "Yes. I would handle the arrest—if you silver-platter it for me. But I can't interfere with an LAPD investigation without getting my ass in a serious sling. So short of you walking this guy in to me or giving me an *exact* location, save your quarter."

"All right. I just wanted to know who to contact if anything firm pans out."

"I'll be waiting with bated breath. Oh—and Doctor? Don't get yourself hurt."

David snapped the phone shut and laid it on the passenger seat. He turned off San Vicente, leaving behind the aisle of coral trees draped with nighttime mist, and threaded back through the quiet residential streets to his house. He cursed softly when he saw the flashing lights behind him.

He pulled over and waited, retrieving his registration from the glove box. A loud knocking at the window startled him upright. Jenkins. With a black metal flashlight. He'd hit the window so hard with the flashlight, David was surprised it hadn't cracked. Jenkins held the flashlight down near the lens, so the shaft could be snapped forward like a baton. Bronner appeared on the passenger side, his flashlight angled into David's eyes.

David took a moment before rolling down his window and then only rolled it down halfway. Without turning his head, he gazed into his rearview mirror, searching for other cars on the dark road. There were none.

"License and registration," Jenkins said.

"Can I ask what—?"

Jenkins turned, his boots crunching on pebbles as he headed back to the police car.

David sat quietly in his car, debating hitting REDIAL on his cell phone. But what would he say? He'd been pulled over for a routine ticket, no doubt. He decided to get UCPD on the line just in case Jenkins became violent, but as he reached for his phone, Jenkins reappeared.

"I'm giving you a fix-it ticket," Jenkins said. "You have a broken taillight."

"No I don't," David said. "I just had—"

"I don't think you want to harass a police officer. Do you, sir?" Jenkins ripped off the ticket and handed it over the glass.

David realized that Bronner was now waiting back in the car, and he grew even more tense.

Jenkins clicked on his flashlight and shined it into David's face from two feet away. David squinted into the light. "He knows right from wrong well enough to hide from the authorities," Jenkins said. "He's not *compelled* to commit these acts if he can plot and wait. This is a mind that is purposeful. This is a mind that is in control."

Jenkins's shadow loomed amorphous and large behind the powerful beam. When he spoke again, his voice was little more than a cold murmur. "This is a mind that you elected to defend." He clicked off the flashlight, and his eyes reflected back a glint from the dashboard lights.

David remembered his mother's hard-learned lesson from the young nephrologist who beat her—don't push a man on the edge—so he remained silent, but he readied himself to block a fist or flashlight butt coming at his temple. Instead, Jenkins pushed off the door frame. "You see about getting that taillight fixed," he said.

He headed back to the police car. As he passed the rear of the Mercedes, he swung the stock of the flashlight, smashing the taillight lens without breaking his stride.

CHAPTER 36

DAVID tossed his keys on the marble counter, closed the door to the garage behind him, let out an exasperated sigh, and hit the light switch. Nothing happened. He stepped forward into the living room, his hand scrabbling along the dark wall for another switch.

The voice came at him out of the darkness. "Don't bother."

David dropped his briefcase, the metal corner striking the hardwood floor, and he felt the flutter of papers settling around his feet. His eyes picked through the dark living room, coming to rest on the dark mass on the shadow of the leather chair.

"Why don't you sit down, Spier?" The voice was civilized and exceedingly calm. It wasn't Clyde, that much was certain. David wasn't sure whether he should be relieved by that, or more frightened.

"Do you want money?" David asked.

"Why don't you sit down?" the voice repeated. An arm rose from the formless shadow, indicating the couch across from the chair. David found himself obeying. He sat rigidly forward on the couch, trying to discern a face in the darkness. "It's come to my attention that you've been making . . . inquiries about me," the voice continued.

"Look, I don't know what—" David stopped. "Ed? Pinkerton?"

"That'll do."

David took a moment to gather his thoughts. "How's your wound? Is it healing?"

"Don't try to manipulate me," Ed said. "You're wondering: Am I going to hurt you? The answer: No."

"And why should I believe you?"

"You came looking for me, Spier. I didn't come looking for you." A moment of silence. "Why don't you have an alarm?"

"It's a safe neighborhood. Plus, we have Edison Armed Patrol."

"Yeah, they're doing a bang-up job."

"How's your kid?" David asked. "Your little boy?"

"Clever, Spier. We both know I told you I had a little girl. I always use the same lies. They're easier to keep track of." His affect was different from that he'd displayed in the ER. More shrewd.

"You used me," David said.

"I use a lot of people."

"But I went out on a limb for you. So you owe me."

"A phrase I wouldn't expect from you, Spier. What

have you gotten yourself into? A dead hooker in the trunk of your Mercedes?"

"You've heard of the Westwood Acid Thrower? He came in and—"

"So now you feel responsible," Ed interrupted.

Coverage of the case must have been even more detailed than David thought. "Yes," David admitted. "I do. This guy's out there disfiguring women."

"You want revenge." Halfway between a statement and a question.

"No, no. God, no. I want him located and locked up."

"Why do you think I can help you?" Ed's questions came out of the darkness at him, one after another, baseballs from a pitching machine. David was struggling to keep up, to pull concise answers from the muddle of his emotions and motives.

"You'd said you were on parole, and that book you were reading . . . you seemed accustomed to dealing with things outside the law. I don't know many people like that."

"Why don't you trust the police?"

"The first victim is a cop's sister. They're out to eviscerate the guy."

"And you don't think he needs eviscerating?"

"I think he's fucked up. Dysfunctional, possibly schizophrenic. I think he needs to be put under lock and key, and provided with psychiatric care."

"Lye thrown in women's faces. That's pretty evil."

David sat forward, shoulders hunched. "Evil comes in many guises. It can be banal. Why not pathetic?"

"And you want to . . . what?"

"I want to find him and get him into the hands of the right authorities."

"How?"

"I haven't figured that out yet," David admitted. "But

if I can get in touch with him, I think I can talk him in. Safely. He seems to trust me."

"A renowned physician like yourself taking a walk on the wild side." Ed's hands went to his shadowy head, arms bent to the sides. "Sometimes people have to pay consequences whether they make the right decision or not. You learn that in my line of work."

"What is your line of work? What exactly do you do?"

"Extreme shit." A rustling sound as Ed ran his hand along the fine leather arm of the chair. "Expensive shit."

"Why did you steal your chart from the hospital? It didn't contain your real name."

"Our bodies are full of clues, Spier. X rays and written records can be damning. You'd be amazed at what the FBI can use to ID a body—dental fillings, stomach staples."

"I'm not certain, but I don't recall any dental fillings in your ass."

Ed laughed, a loud, sharp laugh, and David felt a sudden relief. "Will you help me?" David asked. "Or point me to someone who can?"

Ed's shadow rustled, and David made out several shapes on the table beside Ed. Small and rounded. David wondered briefly if they were grenades. He found his surprising lack of fear to be empowering.

"I'll talk to you. Some. While I decide whether or not I trust you. If I decide I trust you, I might be willing to point you in a few directions. But first, some rules. I don't do violence. You saw my build—I'm not a fighter."

"Fine," David said. "I don't want violence."

"I have no involvement with the police. Ever. Is that understood? This thing gets out of hand, it's coming down on you. Believe me, I'll vanish." Ed waited for David to agree. "Now tell me about this guy."

"Overweight, disheveled, about 6' 1"."

"You'll have to do better than that. You want to play detective, Spier? Get observant. There are thousands of things you could've noticed. Was he clean-shaven? Did he have soft hands, rough hands, clean hands, dirty hands? Did he chew gum? Any scarring? Unusual facial features? Piercing? Tattoos? Length of hair? Type of shoes? Work shoes, cheap shoes, dress shoes, Velcro shoes? Did they match his outfit? Did he wear designer clothes? Did they have any paint on them? Plaster? Mud? Was he laid-back or intense? Were his clothes tight or loose? Did he have a watch? Did he wear it on the left wrist or right? Did he wear a belt? Pager? Cell phone? Rings? Necklaces? Did you undress him? Did you put anything in the property locker? Dumb as it sounds, cops sometimes forget to check it. What was he talking about? Any unusual remarks?"

David sat in silence for a moment, processing. Ed did not rush him. Finally, David said, "His speech was rambling and disorganized. He seemed extremely agitated, especially in the presence of a psychiatrist. He wore no rings or jewelry. A tattoo was reported by his first victim, but he didn't have one when he came in. He has bad acne and pitted fingernails. I don't know if he's right- or left-handed, and I don't remember his shoes. He wore hospital scrubs, loose, with no belt. They smelled faintly of cigarette smoke. The scrubs may indicate that he feels identified with the hospital somehow. My guess is, he works there. I don't know if he chewed gum, but his breath smelled of orange candy—very strong. His hair was thinning and greasy. His hygiene was terrible."

David's eyes were adjusting slowly to the dark, and he saw Ed nod approvingly. "You're a doctor. Use that. Give me more."

David pressed his hands together and rested his chin atop his fingertips. "Let's see. He wanted the lights dimmed, so maybe he has recurring migraines. His balance was off, and he slurred slightly. He might be obsessive-compulsive or delusional—he repeated what seemed to be ritualistic phrases and displayed concreteness of thought. He claimed he'd been locked up in darkness with snakes, and he mentioned lights and noises. His fixation on women, on punishing women, is extreme and conscious. And he seems to have deficits accurately interpreting the intentions of others."

"What does that mean?"

"He misinterprets benign questions as hostile, and this elicits aggression from him. For instance, I was checking his mental status, and asked him if he knew what month it was. He became hostile and asked if I thought he was stupid."

"If he doesn't understand something, it's an insult," Ed said.

"Precisely. Even when the presented cues—tone of voice, facial expression, conversational context—would lead an ordinary person to realize that the questioning is benign, even benevolent, he finds it antagonistic. Which means he finds himself constantly moving through a hostile landscape, where he perceives that people are antagonizing him. Imagine how that would be, if you thought people were always insulting you, attacking you. It would make you pretty aggressive."

A hint of irony crept into Ed's voice. "It sure would."

"He's also extraordinarily insecure and defensive, and he adamantly denies taking any drugs or pills, which leads me to believe he probably does. He seems simultaneously afraid and desirous of being alone, and betrays an intense fixation."

"On who?"

"On me."

"Better," Ed said. "Now we have a profile shaping up."

"So you'll help me?"

"No. I need more from you first. A fingerprint, decent photo, or at least a name."

"What can you do with that?"

"I have certain advantages over the police because I don't have to move through legal channels."

"I'm not asking you to do anything illegal or unethical," David said.

Ed's laugh echoed around the living room. "Everything's ethical. The question is: What kind of ethics?"

Ed reached over and plucked one of the items off the table at his side. He tossed it at David. David lost track of it in the darkness, and the object struck him in the chest and fell to the couch. "Ed? Ed?"

No sound in the darkness. David felt along the cushion, finally finding the thing Ed had thrown at him. A lightbulb.

David crossed the room, bumping into a lamp and nearly knocking it over, but he caught it by the thin metal post. He managed to remove the shade in the darkness and screw the lightbulb in place.

He turned the switch and was not surprised to find Ed gone.

Lying on the reading table were three other lightbulbs. Tucked under one of them was an unprinted business card, blank save for a phone number written across the bottom in black ink.

Sadly, it took one Jewish doctor more than ten minutes to screw in three lightbulbs. Afterward, David checked the doors and windows but was unable to find any signs of forced entry. No scratches on any of the locks. Whoever Ed Pinkerton was, he knew what he was doing.

Rather than sleep, David prepared a list of all Clyde's symptoms he had observed and then translated the more difficult terms into nonmedical phrases in case he had to show it to others. The list read:

nystagmus—pupils jerking
headaches
difficulty concentrating
clouding of consciousness
dysarthria—slurred speech
akathisia—restlessness
ataxia—drunken walking

Beneath that, David wrote some potential diagnoses, including CNS lupus, schizophrenia, schizoaffective disorder, brain tumor, Huntington's, Wilson's, metachromatic leukodystrophy, subdural hematoma, viral encephalitis or an obscure central nervous system infection, aqueductal stenosis, temporal lobe epilepsy, thyrotoxicosis, multiple sclerosis, drug toxicity, insecticide poisoning.

Given the vagueness of the information David currently had, it was impossible to narrow the list further.

He thought about Clyde's compulsive repetition, the counting backward from three. What did that represent?

David set down the pad of paper and checked his watch. It was close to midnight. He undressed in his bedroom. When he got into bed, he was struck by its vastness, and the empty space at his side.

He thought of his wife on the MICU bed, the monotonous hum of the monitor at her side. He thought of Clyde, an ugly, broken man shuffling through life, barely capable of looking other people in the face, and he wondered if he had a responsibility to emerge from the hibernation that had been his life for the past few years. His hard shell of Spartan regularity protected him, mostly, from the empty stretch of bed at his side. But it also shielded him from other, vital, things.

Though he'd been awake for nearly forty-five hours, his whole body was humming with energy. He lay for a few minutes with his thoughts, then threw back the sheets and got dressed again. The ride back to the hospital was dreamlike, the streets shimmering black and silver.

There was little activity in the ER lobby, and the examination rooms were mostly empty. Don had fallen asleep on a high stool in the CWA, slumped on the back counter. Nurses and interns lethargically filled out charts and shuttled them from tray to tray.

"Was there anything put in the property locker?" David asked, announcing his presence. "From Clyde?"

Don lazily raised his head, his eyelids heavy. "What?"

David continued, addressing the others. "Maybe something fell out of his pockets, or someone took something off him and stored it in the property lockers."

"Looking for clues, Dr. Spier?" one of the nurses asked. The others looked at him with barely concealed amusement.

"Was there?" he asked again.

A man David recognized as the lab tech he'd pulled in to help irrigate Clyde answered. "The property lockers are all empty. We didn't take anything off him, remember? And the cops confiscated everything that was left in the room."

"Why are you worrying about this at two in the morning?" Don asked.

David placed a hand on the counter, feeling the weight of the stares aimed in his direction. Meeting the fixed looks with resolve, he thought about how Clyde shied away from eye contact, how he found it threatening. What had Clyde said? *I don't stay around people anymore. Not people that can look at me back.*

The realization hit David with such force that he drew back his head. Where would Clyde have gone to hide out after his escape from the ER? Somewhere that people couldn't look back at him. Somewhere suited to a person simultaneously afraid and desirous of being alone. A place where he'd be among dead people. Dalton had mentioned that they'd found traces of blood in the Three Corridor—back by the freight elevators. The freight elevators were used to cart bodies up to the anatomy crypt on the seventh floor.

David took a step back, knocking over a tray of charts, and left the room at a brisk walk, leaving the others to exchange puzzled glances behind his back.

CHAPTER 37

DAVID entered through the anatomy lab, the wide rectangle of a room dotted with cadavers lying on elevated metal tables. The hatchlike doors of the dissecting tables had been left open. The bodies were exposed, their chests cracked, faces peeled, limbs sinewy and yellow. The stench of formalin hung in the air, a smell that reminded him of his own med school cadaver that he and his anatomy partner had jokingly named Hercules because of its scrawny musculature.

He paused above a body and peeled back the thin layer of bleached cheesecloth. The student had done a poor job on the cheek, making a mess of the masseteric fascia. The yellowed flesh of the jaw hung down like shredded chicken. David covered the face again and proceeded through the lab into the prep room.

The light switch clicked up loudly. Stainless steel counters and cabinets compounded the clinical light of the room. David reached for the large door to the crypt, and it pulled open with a soft sucking noise.

The formalin made his eyes water. The rows of bodies, dangling from hooks like sides of beef, the crossed scissor clamps pinching the ears—how could he have forgotten?

Holding his breath, he walked into the immense refrigerated room, unsure what he was looking for. His foot struck a bucket, and he looked down to see a detached brain swaying in the cloudy water, hanging from a taped string. He walked forward, his eyes picking through the bodies. His shoulder struck a corpse and set it pivoting slowly until it looked down at him, blue-faced and undignified.

He took his time, walking slowly up and down the rows, searching the floor between the red and blue plastic drainage tubs for any sign that Clyde had been there. In the back, a chunky cadaver was suspended from her oversized head. She'd retained fluids in her belly and extremities before dying. David stepped closer, examining the mid-sternal incision on her chest. A recent cardiac surgery. Probably died of heart failure. He glanced down, looking for the telltale linear incision along her inner leg from which they would have harvested her saphenous vein for the bypass.

Four emergency room restraints floated in the liquid that had pooled inside the tub beneath her. Hard restraints. David felt his heart quicken.

He crouched down and studied them.

He'd learned enough from old *Columbo* episodes to know not to handle anything and compromise evidence. He removed a pair of latex gloves from the pocket of his white coat and pulled them on.

Stainless steel abounded inside the crypt and the prep room. Many good surfaces, David imagined, off which to lift fingerprints. But it would be difficult; Clyde's escape was nearly twenty-four hours ago, and a decent amount of traffic moved through the area each day. Further disappointment set in when David remembered that Clyde had escaped still wearing his surgical gloves.

David finished perusing the crypt, found nothing else of note, and went out and sat at the small wooden desk in the corner of the prep room. He had little more to go on himself, so it didn't make sense to contact Ed. He'd just have to inform Yale and take the resultant reprimand for involving himself in the case further.

Reaching for the phone, he scooted forward in the chair, one of the legs knocking over a small metal waste bin. He leaned over and righted the bin, then retrieved a few pieces of crumpled paper and a banana peel from the floor. A small foil square had slid a short distance under the desk, and David bent down farther and reached for it, unsuccessfully.

It appeared to be the casing for a pill—Imodium, perhaps—torn from a larger sheet. The lettering caught his eye just before he touched it: Noblemen's Zinc Lozenges—*orange*.

David froze, his arm awkwardly extended beneath the desk. That was the smell he had picked up on Clyde's breath—the distinctive odor of orange-flavored medicinal tablets. He withdrew his hand quickly. Maybe the lozenge had been Clyde's, and he had eaten it here while he'd been hiding.

David dug quickly through the drawers until he found a packet of Sudafed. He removed a foil sheet and tried unsuccessfully to peel off the backing while leaving his gloves on. He removed a glove, then used his thumbnail to lift the corner of the foil, the print of his bare forefinger pressing firmly against the small square.

Even if Clyde had been wearing gloves, he'd have had

to take them off to get at the lozenge. Which meant that the discarded square under the desk—the plastic top with the foil half attached—would likely bear his fingerprint.

David felt the same rush of pleasure that a good diagnosis gave him. Pulling Ed's card from his pocket, he dialed the number and was greeted with three short beeps. A pager. The telephone number of the prep room phone was scotch-taped to the receiver, and David punched it in and hit the pound key. He'd barely hung up when the phone rang.

"Hello?" David heard nothing but silence. "It's David," he said. "David Spier."

"Look," said a gruff voice. "Just because I give you a phone number doesn't mean you have to call it at three in the fucking—"

"I have a fingerprint," David said. "I think."

There was a long pause. And then, "You'd better fill me in."

After David did, there was another long pause, and David thought he might've lost the connection. "Hello?"

"Still here. Listen carefully. *Do not touch the wrapping*. Find a pen or a ruler or something, and push it into a bag. Don't touch anything else in the room, and leave immediately. I'll meet you on the corner of Le Conte and Westwood in fifteen minutes. Stand near the curb."

"But what about the police? Don't they need to get here for a more thorough look?"

"I'll place an anonymous call. Right now. So clear out."

"Will you turn over the fingerprint to them if we get a—?" David realized Ed had already hung up. Down on his hands and knees, he carefully followed the procedures Ed had laid out, using a tweezers and a Ziploc specimen bag he found in a drawer.

Fifteen minutes later, he stood out on the corner of Le

Conte and Westwood, hands pushed into the pockets of his white doctor's coat, feeling as if he'd just stumbled into a Cold War thriller.

He clutched the plastic bag with the lozenge packaging in his pocket, watching the occasional car speed by. All of a sudden, the street was empty. A sheet of newspaper fluttered in the wind.

A red Pathfinder with tinted windows pulled into view, slowing as it neared David. David pulled the bag from his pocket and stepped off the curb. The opaque driver-side window glided slowly down, and Ed's hand reached out and plucked the bag from David.

"Look," David said. "I was wondering if—?"

The window slid back up and the Pathfinder pulled away, leaving David standing foolishly at the curb.

CHAPTER 38

THE bent metal lamp on the scarred tabletop gave off a low hum as the bulb flickered on and off. Beside it, Clyde sorted through a mound of generic gelcap pain relievers. His swollen fingers sifted through them, knocking the empty plastic bottle on its side. It rolled off the table, bouncing out of sight.

Behind him, the rain tapped against the window like hundreds of little fingers.

He dipped a moist soupspoon into a jar of instant coffee and brought it carefully to his mouth. He chewed the grounds slowly, scowling, then gulped water from an oversize McDonald's cup featuring Mark McGwire. His shirt was off, his flabby chest marred with weeping burns and small cuts, most of them well on their way to healing.

He grasped one red and yellow capsule, careful not to crush it, and gently twisted it so the two halves came apart. He dumped out the white powder and set the hollow capsule halves to one side. His lips moving quickly and silently, he repeated the procedure over and over until he had a small pile of empty capsules.

Reaching into the metal footlocker, he retrieved a carton of DrainEze and a bare razor blade. He popped the lid of the carton and sprinkled some of the solid-form alkali onto the tabletop. The little rocks glittered white and blue. He picked up the razor blade and sorted the alkali into thin strips, like lines of cocaine.

Licking his pink lips, he held an empty yellow gelcap half so its tiny open mouth was level with the table. Using the width of the blade now, he swept one of the alkali lines off the table, catching most of it in the capsule half. He repeated the process, filling a red capsule top. Careful not to spill, he fitted the red top over the yellow bottom and screwed it a half turn into place. Closing one eye and raising the perfect capsule between his thumb and forefinger, he appraised his work like a jeweler. He bent over the table, picked up the razor blade and another empty capsule half, and went back to his painstaking work.

There was still much to be done before sunrise.

CHAPTER 39

AT dawn, David pulled a pillow over his head and attempted to prolong his few hours of sleep, but the stresses of the past week pulled him from any thoughts of slumber. It was his first full day off since the attacks had begun, and he wasn't about to waste it in bed. Reaching for the phone on the nightstand, he paged Ed immediately.

He trudged into the study and removed the drape from the large brass birdcage. Two glassy black eyes stared out at him from beneath the fan of the bright salmon crest. The cockatoo's beak disappeared into its breast feathers, preening.

David sighed. "Hello, Stanley."

"Where's Elisabeth?" the cockatoo squawked. "M&M's. Where's Elisabeth?"

"Ran off and joined Cirque du Soleil."

The cockatoo's head tilted, then straightened. "Where's Elisabeth?"

"Moved to Memphis with a blues band." David took care not to spill any birdseed this time as he angled a handful through the bars of the cage into the plastic cup.

The cockatoo shifted from foot to foot, then dashed over and picked at the birdseed. Before David could leave the room, it raised its head again. "Where's Elisabeth?"

David paused by the cage. "Ice fishing in Alaska."

Taking the cordless phone and moving to the living room, he paged Ed again, then collapsed into a plush leather chair. Above the mantel hung a signed de Kooning print—*Woman I.* A violent depiction with rough, haphazard brush strokes, the painting portrayed an archetypal woman with a gleaming, devouring crescent of a mouth and a mess of broad, bloody strokes where her hips should be. It had been his mother's favorite painting.

Arrayed on the Oriental cabinet to one side were a Waterford vase and several photographs in silver frames. A picture of Peter with David's mother from late in her tenure as chief of staff—her head was tilted slightly back, suggesting royalty or aloofness. His favorite shot of Elisabeth, in the tub, only her head and knees visible in the wash of bubbles. A photo from the ER retreat to Catalina—David talking to Diane on the ferry over to the island, her smile just becoming a laugh. For the first time, it struck him as noteworthy that he kept a framed picture of himself and Diane on the cabinet with his personal photos. The mind moves before it is aware.

The phone rang and he picked it up on a half ring, eager to get an update from Ed.

"David, it's Diane."

"What's wrong?"

"It's Carson. We had a seventy-year-old stroke victim in early this morning. He was putting her in the sniffing position to tube her and accidentally snapped her neck. She died a few minutes later. David? Are you there?"

"Jesus, that's awful. How's he doing?"

"Not great. Dr. Lambert screamed at him for five minutes in front of the whole staff, called him a killer, and kicked him out of the ER. He was a mess. I'm stuck here all day, then I'm covering Marcy's late-night shift. I thought maybe you might want to—"

"What's his address?" David found a slip of paper and jotted it down. Carson lived in a little apartment complex at the top of Barrington near Sunset with which David was familiar. "I actually have to take care of some things around the hospital today. I'll stop by his place this afternoon—he could probably use some time alone now anyway."

"Okay. Swing by the floor if you get a chance."

"Will do."

"I've never seen Carson like this." A long pause. "I have to go figure out how to take a history from a deaf-mute."

David felt sick when he hung up the phone.

He dressed quickly and fixed himself a quick breakfast. He left the *LA Times* out on the doorstep, not wanting to see the day's blaring headlines, but he couldn't resist turning the radio on during his drive to the hospital. The news about the case was mostly high drama and rehash. He wasn't sure what to make of the fact that Ed hadn't returned his pages; he found himself second-guessing whether turning over to him a key piece of evidence had been a wise call. Maybe Ed hadn't even placed an anonymous call to the police, as he'd claimed he would.

David parked and hurried up to the seventh floor, pausing outside the anatomy lab.

Students milled in clusters, sporting backpacks weighed down with books. Inside, students were bent over cadavers with scalpels and tongs, slicing and prodding. In the corner, a frail student with a prominent Adam's apple enacted the timeless ritual of making the skeleton talk, manipulating the mandible so it moved up and down as he attempted a bad pirate accent. He stopped abruptly when he noticed David.

David had almost reached the door to the prep room when it swung open with a gust of formalin, revealing Yale and Dalton. A nauseated expression on his face, Dalton paused outside the door, leaning slightly on a chair.

Yale regarded David suspiciously. "What are you doing up here?"

"I was coming by to see the Lab Tech," David said. "There are a few maneuvers I'd like one of my med students to practice on a cadaver."

Yale snapped his gum. "Uh-huh," he said.

"What are you guys doing here?"

Yale said, "We got an anonymous tip to this location."

"You wouldn't know anything about that, would you?" Dalton added.

Unaccustomed to lying, David shook his head, hoping he looked convincing. "Find anything interesting?" he asked.

"Capone's gold. Lindbergh's kid." Yale flashed a quick smile. "O.J.'s other glove."

Dalton's look was firm and piercing. "We don't want to find you anywhere around this case, Doc," he said. "Remember that."

David stepped around them, entering the prep room and closing the door behind him. Horace looked up from the body he was working on, bloody saw in hand. A goofy smile lit his face. "Hey, Dr. Spier, how ya doing?" He offered David a blood-caked glove but then glanced down at it and withdrew it before David had to protest. Bits of gray matter clung to his eye shield, which he shoved atop his head with a forearm. His eyes were large, buglike, and somehow endearing. "Good to see you. Goddamn, has it been crazy in here. The kids are hyper because it's their last day of anatomy, on top of which the cops had me sealed out for four hours this morning. Dusting and picking and prying. Then the questioning." He rolled his eyes. "I guess after all that, they didn't find a single goddamned print they liked."

A police flier sat on the wooden desk, the composite of Clyde staring up from it. Horace followed David's eyes and nodded. "The cops brought that with them. I guess they went out through the hospital, but I haven't picked up my mail yet today."

"So he *does* work here?"

"Worked here. Crazy, huh? I always knew the guy was a few nerves short of a full plexus."

David's mouth went dry. "What's his name?"

"Douglas DaVella. He worked here up until a few months ago, as an orderly. His job was to bring the corpses up from the hearses and help me hang 'em."

So Clyde was a fake name, as David had considered. "What else did he do?"

"He ran specimens, got them to the appropriate labs."

That would mean he'd had a worker's pass, and would have known the codes to most of the Omnilock doors in the facility. Running deliveries—moving from stretch of corridor to stretch of corridor—would've taught him his way around the hospital. Transferring cadavers had been how he'd learned to operate a gurney; David had been wrong in making inquiries about the orderlies who dealt with patients.

Horace walked over and opened a cabinet below the sink, removing a plastic container of DrainEze. He plunked it down on the embalming table beside the cadaver lying inert and gray, a fresh hole sawed through its chest. "Trade secret." He grinned. "I have to special-order it. Which means Douglas probably stole it right from here."

"What was he like?" David asked. "DaVella."

Horace shrugged. "Not much into hygiene, if you catch my drift. For our lower-skilled positions, we like to hire people a bit disadvantaged." A glint of pride showed in Horace's face, the pride of a self-taught man who has pulled himself up the job ladder. "I'll tell you, he smoked with a vengeance, two at a time sometimes. You know, like trying to calm himself down. Willing himself to hold together. But he didn't."

"What happened?"

"He started coming undone. Showing up late. Not reporting back from runs. I found him once in the crypt, standing among the bodies. Wasn't doing anything weird, just swaying on his feet. Said the stillness calmed him."

"Any trouble with the corpses? Any of them . . . violated or anything?"

"No, no. Nothing like that." Horace drew back his head as if he'd just been exposed to a bad odor. It was the first time David had seen him wear an expression of disgust.

"Was he fired?"

"I finally had to let him go," Horace said. "I didn't have a choice," he added defensively. "Things weren't getting done."

David wondered if Clyde was avenging the fact he'd been fired. He'd told David, *I just want them to be sorry.* "Did he seem pissed off when you fired him?"

"No. Not really. Kind of sad, maybe."

"Did he interact well socially?"

"Boy, you ask a different breed of question than the cops," Horace said. David resisted the urge to ask him what Yale and Dalton had inquired about, letting Horace continue. "Douglas avoided students like the plague. Especially the girls. He liked to come in during off hours, when the place was empty." He gestured to the door, behind which the lab clamored with students picking at bodies. "They harassed him, now and then. Pretty upsetting, when you think about it, them being future doctors. But I'll tell you, doctors ain't the picture of empathy these days. Not like it used to be." He nodded deferentially.

"How would they harass him? The students?"

"Well, it didn't happen much, to be fair. But now and

then they'd stop him, try to get him to talk, assess his speech patterns, posture, things like that. You know how med students are—thought they were being subtle and helpful. He found the scrutiny unbearable. A girl tried to practice on him with her ophthalmoscope once. Reduced him to tears. She got apologetic after, of course, but it didn't seem to help." Horace's eyes traced over the split body before them. "Poor bastard."

When Horace looked up, David was surprised to see that he seemed upset.

"I've worked hard for this job. Hard like you wouldn't believe. And when Douglas started going loose on me, I had to protect my position. There was nothing else I could have done." His face looked tired, maybe from his working on guilt, or guilt working on him.

Before David could respond, Horace revved up the saw and turned back to the body. David left quietly.

He found Ralph down in the ER, leaning against a cart, arms folded across his chest. He seemed perturbed and didn't look over when David stood beside him.

"Goddamn cops," Ralph said. "Get a guy in that uniform, takes about two days before he's a USDA-certified prick."

"What happened?" David asked.

"They just want what they want, and they want it immediately. No consideration for the fact that I've got other responsibilities here. I'm running security for this facility, I'm not an errand boy for LAPD." Ralph jerked his thumb at his chest. "I was Third Battalion, Second Marines, Charlie Company. Two tours. Two fucking tours, and some doughnut-muncher expects me to how-high his shit."

"Who?"

"Yale. Dalton."

"What did they want?"

Ralph cast a look in both directions, and David took a

step closer so Ralph could lower his voice. The conspiratorial nature of the exchange diluted Ralph's anger considerably. "They confiscated records on a dude, name of Douglas DaVella," Ralph said. "He's a suspect, I guess. Used to work upstairs with Horace the Hacker."

"Oh? Anything interesting?"

Ralph homed in on David's interest like a dog spotting prey. "Oh no, Doc. You don't want to step into this too far. You're playing with a new brand of fire here."

David studied Ralph closely. "I was in over my head before I knew what was going on. I can either sink or swim. What would you do?"

Ralph rubbed his nose and it gave easily, the cartilage flexible from a few breaks. He studied David's face for a moment and seemed to reach some conclusion. "They were mostly after his address and phone and stuff," he said. "But the guy was a bit uneven. He had a couple of complaints filed against him. Nothing I investigated personally, but the records were there."

A few interns walked by without saying hello to David. For the first time, he appreciated the privacy his estrangement from the staff permitted him. "What were the complaints for?" he asked.

"He got a bit uppity once when confronted by a gal over in Human Resources. Something about him taking too many sick days. Turned out to be nothing. She claimed he got aggressive, but he was settled down by the time it was checked out. Afterward, she couldn't point to anything concrete. Then there was another complaint, from a patient over in the NPI, just before DaVella got fired. Guy's a real whackjob, I guess—six fingers on each hand. He said Mr. DaVella was trying to steal his meds, but the guy's a bit cuckoo for Cocoa Puffs, so no one took the complaint too seriously."

"What was DaVella doing over at the NPI? As a transporter of body parts, the psych ward should've been the last place he wound up."

"He said he got lost coming back from making a delivery to the Reed Institute next door. I know—it's kinda loose. But he was pretty cooperative during questioning, and the patient had some type of paranoid disorder, so it all kind of washed out."

"Who questioned Mr. DaVella?"

"A fellow named Tommy Jones was point on both complaints."

"Can I talk to him?"

"Moved to Baltimore. Divorced. Fell out." Ralph shrugged. "You know how that tune spins."

Diane swept past them in the hall, did a double take, and stopped. "Oh. Glad you're here. We need you in Four."

"I'm off today." David was anxious to get over to the Neuropsychiatric Institute to follow up on the complaint that had been issued there.

"I know, but it's Alberto," Diane said. "Sore throat. He said he'll only see you—you know how he is."

During the summer months, Alberto followed his father, who was a gardener for UCLA, around campus on his skateboard, causing damage to stairs, curbs, and himself. David had always treated him warmly, and Alberto sometimes made up excuses to come in and talk. David excused himself and headed down the hall, walking beside Diane.

"I hear they ID'd someone," she said. "You have something to do with that?"

He nodded. "Fill you in later. What time are you off?"

"Six. Then I'm on again at ten, filling in for Marcy."

"Okay. Let's meet over at Carson's around six-thirty. Make sure he still has his head screwed on."

⊕

"Ever try to suck your own dick, Doc?" The boy's smooth-skinned face looked up at David. Alberto wore his hair long in the back, and it bunched above the collar of his jacket. Sitting on the examination table with a beat-up skateboard across his lap, he looked even younger than his twelve years. His eyes always squinted, ever so slightly, as if needing constant protection.

"Not recently, no," David said. "I have a bad back." He walked over and closed the door, then studied Alberto. The boy was clearly sick, his face pale and tired, except where his lips were stained purple from some candy he must've eaten earlier. "Something you want to talk about?"

Alberto shrugged. "I tried once," he confessed. His heels drummed against the base of the examination table. "Does that make me gay?"

David touched Alberto's forehead—hot—then walked his fingertips up along the back of Alberto's jaw, feeling for swollen glands. "Why would that make you gay?"

Alberto pulled away. "Well, I like girls. I'm dying to get laid, even. I don't want to be gay." His eyes pooled with concern. "But, I mean, I almost had a dick in my mouth."

David inhaled deeply and held it for a moment. "Well," he began, in a textbook voice, "gender roles are a complicated and . . ." He paused, then rubbed his eyes with a thumb and forefinger. "No, Alberto, it doesn't make you gay."

The relief in Alberto's eyes was palpable.

"Now can we focus on your sore throat?" David felt again for Alberto's glands, and Alberto winced slightly when David found them. David grabbed a tongue depressor from a Pyrex beaker. "Open up. Open." Alberto refused, and David squeezed his cheeks gently until he complied. Red beefy throat, enlarged tonsils with exudate mucus—what David's mother would have called "angry throat." "Oh boy, kiddo. We have some activity going on in here. Does it hurt?"

"I had to spit into a bag last night because it hurt too much to swallow."

"Why didn't you come in?"

Alberto looked down. One of his untied shoelaces trailed along the tiled floor. "We don't got insurance no more. My dad got laid off, and I didn't want to cost him nothing more."

David crouched, resting his hands on Alberto's knees. "Alberto, listen to me. If you ever feel sick, you come in here. Don't worry about money. Okay? Now say *aah*."

Alberto opened his mouth, and before he realized what was going on, David had already swabbed him with the elongated Q-tip. He handed it to Jill outside. "Let's get a Rapid Strep on this."

He ducked into the doctors' lounge and called Carson but got the machine. Someone had taped Clyde's police composite to the wall, and David studied it as he left a message. "Carson, it's Dr. Spier. I hope you're doing all right. I'm going to stop by around six-thirty, and I hope we'll be able to talk then."

Jill met him in the hall on his way back to Alberto's exam room and walked alongside him. "It's positive," she said. "First strep of the day."

"All right. The patient has a penicillin allergy. He's also got no insurance, but I just met with a rep from Biaxin, and I stowed a bunch of samples in the locked drawer in Three. Would you mind grabbing them for me?"

David swung into the exam room and faced Alberto with a resigned smile. "You have group A betahemolytic streptococci, aka strep throat. I'm going to get you some antibiotics. You'll take one in the morning, one at night, for ten days. Now, this particular drug has a side effect. It'll give you a dry metallic taste in your mouth, so you'll want to get some Altoids or strong suckers so you can—" He froze.

Two minutes later, having paged Ed three times consecutively from the doctors' lounge, he had him on the phone. "I have something," he said.

"L' Ermitage. Twenty minutes."

CHAPTER 40

A man impeccably dressed in a charcoal suit with a shimmering blue tie, his gray hair coifed, paused in front of David. Still dressed in his scrubs and white medical coat, David slumped on a leather couch in the elegant cocktail lounge of the modern, upscale hotel. A fire flickered beneath the screen to his right, though it was August. Before him, on a simple glass table, sat a tray containing jars of wasabi peas, Parmesan twists, and herb-cured olives.

"Nice outfit, Spier," the man said. "I appreciate your not calling attention to us."

David literally did a double take as Ed shook his hand roughly and slid into the love seat opposite the couch, slightly favoring his left side. "Don't say anything loud," Ed said softly. "Don't raise your voice, don't act surprised. Just start talking."

David swallowed hard, finding his train of thought. "The orange zinc lozenges that Clyde was sucking—I think he uses them because he's taking meds that can cause a dry or metallic mouth as a side effect. Doctors usually recommend Altoids or zinc lozenges to cover it." David's voice was high and shaky; he could feel his heart hammering.

"Slow down. Calm down. Can't you use anything to cover the taste? Like gum?"

"You can, but generally something stronger is more effective."

The waitress came over, and Ed ordered a Sapphire martini, up, chilled, with three olives. David ordered cranberry juice.

"And guess which drugs most commonly have that side effect?" David said, as soon as she departed. "Psychiatric drugs. Sure, now and then an antihistamine like Claritin will dry you out, but classically it's antipyschotics—clozapine, Mellaril, Haldol, Prolixin, risperidone, Zyprexa—or antidepressants, like Paxil or Prozac."

David pulled a sheet of paper from his pocket and smoothed it on the cocktail table between them. "I made a list of Clyde's symptoms. Jerking pupils, headaches, difficulty concentrating, clouding of consciousness, slurred speech, restlessness, and drunken walking. These all pointed me to nervous system diseases and conditions."

"But you think these traits are actually drug side effects, not symptoms of a disease?"

"Exactly. I was so focused on the nervous system presentation, I neglected to write down other relevant traits. So I went back in my mind and tried to think of what I might have missed." Pulling a pen from his scrub top, David added *dry or metallic-tasting mouth* to the list. "Remember I told you he had swollen hands? Well, I recalled his neck was a bit swollen as well, which could indicate hypothyroidism. He left hair behind on the pillow when he fled, so it could be falling out. Acne and pitted fingernails should be on the list as well." He wrote down *swollen hands—hypothyroidism?; alopecia—loss of hair; acne; pitted fingernails.*

David glanced down at the potential diagnoses he'd written beneath. The new symptoms did not fit the symptom clusters for most of the diagnoses on the list. He drew a line through them all except *drug toxicity* and *insecticide poisoning*. But insecticide poisoning generally causes excessive salivation, the opposite of a dry or metallic-tasting mouth, so he crossed that one out as well. "We're probably dealing with a drug toxicity issue here. Whatever he's taking, he's taking too much of it and it's poisoning him."

David looked at Ed with sudden irritation. "And you—where have you been? What happened with the print? When did you tip off the police? Did you know Clyde's not even Clyde anymore? He's Douglas DaVella. He used to work at the hospital."

"No," Ed said. "Douglas DaVella died three years ago Sunday of colon cancer. He was a sixty-seven-year-old veteran of the Korean War. I ran the print, and the results came back this morning." Before David could say anything, Ed held up his hand. "I got the print results over to the police, as I promised I would. Our boy is indeed Clyde. Clyde C. Slade, to be precise. DOB January 2, 1963." He adjusted his wig with a subtle gesture that looked as if he were straightening his hair in the front.

"Holy shit," David said. "So he really *is* named Clyde. But how did he . . . ?"

"Clyde took Douglas DaVella over. Someone's social security number isn't placed on the social security death index when they die, it gets put there when their death benefit gets claimed. As far as the records go, no claimed death benefit, no dead guy."

"Don't registrars cross-index birth and death certificates?"

"Only by county, sometimes state. California does it statewide, but our boy Doug was from Virginia. He didn't move out here till after his tour in Korea. When he died, Clyde stole his social security number so he could apply for a job at the hospital under a false name. One might argue that showed premeditation, were one prone to legal arguing."

"How did you find out about DaVella?"

"Public Utilities Commission records. The cops always go the DMV route, which takes longer and is easier for criminals to deceive. But no one thinks to lie to the gas company. My scanner gave me a heads-up they were going after a Douglas DaVella, and my intelligence showed that Clyde C. Slade had changed his name on a gas bill to Douglas DaVella three years back, right after DaVella kicked. Unfortunately, he's not at that address anymore, and there's no new utilities listing for either name. So either he's living in some economy shithole where utilities are provided or he's got a new fake name. Back to square one."

"They got a current address on DaVella from security. I listened to the news on the way over to see if there was anything about an arrest. Or a shooting. Have you heard?"

"It was a fake address—some crib off Palms in West LA."

"How'd he get his paychecks?"

Ed shrugged. "Maybe he picked them up himself. All I know is, the address is a bust."

"How did Clyde know Douglas died? There could be a connection there. Maybe they lived in the same apartment complex."

"I'm checking it out, as, evidently, are the cops. Nothing yet."

"DaVella had two complaints filed against him when he worked at the hospital, one of them over at the Neuropsychiatric Institute where he wasn't supposed to be. He also had a violent reaction to one of our psychiatrists, who's black, and we'd hypothesized that he was afraid of shrinks or blacks. Now I'm thinking he's got a hang-up revolving around the NPI. I'm planning on checking it out when I get back to the hospital. The cops took the security records, but I can get at the medical records. In this case, I'm hoping, that'll give me the upper hand."

"Looks that way so far."

"What did you get on Clyde's background?"

"Thirty-eight years old. Spent his childhood shuttled from foster home to foster home. Eleven different homes in the first fifteen years of his life. Then he ran away. His juvenile record's expunged—which is odd for someone in his demographic, given the resources that takes—but he's got two adult priors. An indecent exposure and a 647.6."

"Which is?"

"Child molestation." He took note of David's expression. "Not like you think. It's not necessarily sexual. It can be anytime someone annoys a kid under eighteen. This was your standard Peeping Tom scenario. He was staring at a seventeen-year-old girl through an open window. They tried to get a resburg"—Ed caught himself and backed up—"a residential burglary, but they couldn't prove he crossed the plane of the window." He bit his lip. "It was a dusty sill, so they would've seen prints if he had. He just stood there and stared at her—freaked her out. It's pretty much just that and the weenie wagger."

"Who'd he flash?"

"A hooker."

"And she reported it?"

"She got picked up ten minutes later. She claimed she

was merely propositioning the UC—the undercover cop—to catch a ride out of the area, because there was a flasher on the prowl. When they rounded up Clyde, he copped to. Said he was just trying to scare her."

Ed leaned back, took a sip of his drink, and grimaced.

"You don't like martinis?" David asked.

"I hate them."

"So why . . . ?"

"Because two grown men sipping juice in a bar are bound to be remembered, just as a waitress might remember a man dressed in a thousand-dollar suit for ordering a Bud. Which is what I really want." He leaned back, crossing his legs daintily. He had indeed mastered the affect of a polished businessman. "Besides, one should always change one's habits. Habits are trails that lead back to you. Never drive the same route, never shop at the same stores, never order the same thing twice."

David realized from the expression on Ed's face that his brief speech was more than informational—he was consciously showing David that a trust and rapport was growing between them. Information was Ed's currency, and he spent it cautiously.

"I'm working a sting right now in the financial district. Thus the attire."

"I thought you were on the wrong side of the law."

"When you have a particular skill set," Ed said, "there are no sides of the law. Just things that need to get done." His tone changed quickly; the small talk was over. "So, now that we know that Clyde is, in all likelihood, taking psychiatric medication—too much psychiatric medication from the sound of it—how does that help us?"

"I can find out which drugs were prescribed for Douglas DaVella while he was at UCLA, who prescribed them, and what pharmacies they were called in to. That gives us a few trails. Plus, the NPI incident involved an alleged attempt on his part to steal a patient's meds, so when I look into that, it may dovetail."

Ed sucked an olive; the pimiento left the core with a popping sound. "I'm beginning to like you more and more. When can you get on that?"

"Right now. I'm off today, and I'll have someone cover my shift tomorrow."

"But you haven't taken a single vacation day in two years," Ed said. "Two years and fourteen days, to be precise."

"How do you know that?"

"You think I'd do anything for you without running you? I know how much you owe on your mortgage. I know that asshole Jenkins gave you a fix-it ticket last night, and that the word is it was a break-it fix-it. I know the only B you ever got in your life was in embryology your first year of medical school."

David smiled, impressed. "Goddamn embryology." He straightened up on the couch. "I have to proceed somewhat cautiously—too much time off in the midst of this could further damage my reputation at the hospital."

Ed arched a red eyebrow. "Still care about that, do we?"

"If it undercuts my effectiveness, yes."

Ed's pale face remained blank. "Let me keep shaking on the paper trail. Get back to me with any info about the meds—that front seems stronger."

"Do I need to . . . Should I pay you for any of this?"

"Free of charge for now. In my line of work, sixty percent of what I do ends up being favors for good people. Think of me as a guardian angel." He popped the last olive in his mouth and chewed it. "Plus I owe you for repairing my ass."

CHAPTER 41

CLYDE'S pate, visible through his thin veil of hair, glistened with sweat. With a final glance to the quiet upstairs window, he stepped from his car onto the curb. He kept his head lowered and moved swiftly to the apartment building entrance.

A kid with a deficient mustache and a blaring Walkman cleaned the floor with imprecise swipes of a mop. He'd propped open the front door, enabling a breeze through the lobby. Clyde waited until the kid made a dancing half turn toward the far wall, then scurried through the lobby and into the stairwell.

Flattening himself against the wall, he caught his breath, the redness slowly draining from his face. He mopped the sweat from his forehead with his T-shirt, leaving a crescent stain on the collar.

He turned and headed upstairs.

David called Diane in the ER on his way back to the hospital and filled her in as best he could. One of her college friends worked at the Drug Enforcement Agency, so Diane promised to follow up the prescription route before meeting David at Carson's.

David stopped off in the cafeteria to grab a sandwich and a Coke. As he waited in line at the cash register, he was acutely aware of the murmuring that seemed to follow him, the quick glances in his direction. The cashier's newspaper was pinned beneath a half-eaten, browning apple on the counter at her side, awaiting the next customer lull. The photograph on the cover was of David, sitting in the backseat of Jenkins's patrol car, looking as if he'd been arrested. The headline: TENSIONS BETWEEN SPIER AND LAPD ESCALATE. The fact that he'd joined the list of nefarious LA last names—Menendez, Furhman, Fleiss—elicited in him a mixture of embarrassment and alarm. It was as if he'd passed some point of no return and found himself suddenly lost.

David paid and went into the adjoining courtyard to eat in peace. A group of male nurses were playing pickup basketball on a worn wooden backboard someone had hammered up. David wolfed down the sandwich and was just on his way to the NPI when he noticed Peter wobbling across the courtyard and waving, holding a lunch tray in his other hand.

David caught up to Peter and walked patiently beside him, resisting the urge to offer to carry his tray. "How are you?" David asked.

"Oh, you know. I'm moving my procedure suite from across the street to upstairs from my office. Getting the damn thing up and running again has been something of a hassle, but aside from that—" Peter misstepped and grimaced, setting down his tray on a nearby picnic table. An empty wrapper blew from his tray, but he pretended not to notice. "Would you mind resting a moment?"

"No," David said. "Not at all."

Peter released his leg braces and they sat at the table, watching the men leap and pivot and shoot. One of the nurses took a low pass, biceps flexing beneath the cut sleeves of his scrub top, and shot a turn-around jumper from ten feet out. The ball missed wide and a flurry of legs and arms fought for it beneath the basket.

Peter watched the athletic melee. "Magnificent," he said. "So magnificent."

David cleared his throat uncomfortably. Peter waited patiently for David to find the words he was looking for. "You know how much I dislike being told what to do. . . ."

"I do."

"With this business with Clyde and the escape . . . Was that a classic example of my going too far over an ethical point?"

"You Spiers *are* prone to inflation," Peter replied. "But I think I know you well enough to say that wasn't the case here. From what I've pieced together, you perceived there were some real risks."

David rubbed his eyes hard and it felt divine.

"When your back is really to the wall, you rely on instinct," Peter said. "It's all you have left. I've had to do it countless times. Hour eight of a procedure. Combat surgery in Vietnam. You let go and you trust that your instincts are good." He reached out with an oversized hand and hooked the back of David's head. He shook it once, roughly, an avuncular gesture. "You have good instincts," he said. "You know that as well as I. Don't pick yourself to death."

David exhaled deeply, the tightness in his chest dissipating by degrees. "I just wish I'd handled him better. Clyde. Kept him secured and gotten him the treatment he needs."

A hard foul at the hoop led to shouting among the nurses.

"There's not always something helpful to be done for people," Peter said.

"I'm a scientist," David said. "I believe people can be fixed."

"People can't always be fixed, David. They're not machines."

"No, but they can be analyzed like machines. Their

posture and affect, blood work, and vitals. A good eye draws it together, finds what's broken, comes up with a protocol."

Peter laughed, a touch derisively. "You're so much like your mother in certain regards. Your instinct is there, your ethic, your proficiency. But not always empathy."

David recoiled. "What's that mean?"

"It means you're extraordinarily skilled and talented—God knows, more so than I—but occasionally you lose yourself in ethics and science. Sometimes it's better to feel your patients' pain and fear. Get dirty."

"You know," David said, "in this case, that's precisely what I did."

The nurses scrambled after a loose ball.

"People are wonderfully complicated, flawed creatures, David. Don't oversimplify them—for good or for bad."

A tall black nurse knocked the ball out of bounds, and it bounced over to Peter. He caught it easily and held it a moment too long before throwing it back.

He turned a wistful smile to David. "We're more than the sum of our parts."

CHAPTER 42

DAVID headed over to the Neuropsychiatric Institute, exiting the elevator on the sixth floor. He hit the buzzer to the side of the locked white door. A moment later, the door swung open, Dash all but filling the frame, arms folded across his massive chest. "There's been some whispering on the wards about the way you've been acting. Then you call me with this?"

"Did the cops come through here yet?"

"Yes. Filled me in on this DaVella business. Of course, they were pissed off when I didn't let them in. As you know, we don't disclose most patients' names." Dash eyed David, as if to make sure he'd caught the implication.

"I need your help, Dash."

"My shift is over. I'm on my way to my workout."

"This isn't trivial."

Dash sighed, a deep rumble. "You're looking for a patient with polydactyly, huh? On both hands?"

"Do you have a person fitting that description?"

Dash's head tilted in a half nod, half shake. "We might."

"I need to speak with him," David said.

"How do you know it's a him?"

David sighed. "You know what they say, Dash."

Dash's lips twitched, but did not form a full smile. "What's that?"

"Internists know everything and do nothing. Surgeons know nothing and do everything. And psychiatrists know nothing and do nothing."

Dash's booming laugh echoed a ways up the cold corridor.

"I'm asking you to *do something* here," David said. "If there was anyone who would ever respect patient confidentiality, it's I."

"You looked like an asshole, David. After the escape."

"I know," David said softly. "I know." He waited patiently for a verdict.

"Don't make me regret this," Dash finally said. He turned and entered the ward, gesturing for David to follow. They walked down the long corridor toward the reception desk encased in reinforced glass. Behind windows to their left, patients congregated in a recreation area.

A cluster of patients sat together, following a low-impact stretching workout on TV. The busty woman on-screen leaned forward in a hamstring stretch, grabbing both feet. Most of the patients could barely get their hands to their ankles. An attractive woman in her twenties shuffled aimlessly through the room, her paper slippers shushing on the tile. An older man with tardive dyskinesia sat alone at a table, his lips popping out in a rapid series of puckers, his fingers making choreic movements, as if playing the piano.

A nurse sat down across from him and engaged him in a game of cards. His straining lips loosened into a momentary smile.

Dash steered David past the reception desk down another locked corridor lined with seclusion rooms. The seclusion rooms were always kept lit, so staff members could observe the enclosed patients through the small sliding windows in the doors.

Dash paused outside a door and tapped it gently with a knuckle. "Give a holler if you need me," he said. "I'll wait out here." He walked a short distance up the corridor and leaned against the wall.

David gripped the knob and slid open the tiny window. The room, no larger than eight by ten, was entirely white. A wiry man paced along the far wall. He paused, his head snapping up at the sound of the window sliding open, his tight, close-set features quivering. He swept his hands through his hair with deft, quick gestures.

David stepped inside and eased the door almost shut behind him. The white walls reflected the overhead light harshly. David folded his hands out before him, keeping them clearly in the man's view. "Hello, I'm Dr. Spier. I work over in the emergency room."

"I'm Dean Lograine," the man said. He offered a six-fingered hand, which David shook cautiously. "My friends call me Mouse. My enemies too."

His gown was patterned with snowflakes, as had been the one Elisabeth had worn on her final day. David found the similarity unsettling. Over each of Mouse's nipples, a stain had spread through the fabric, the size of a quarter—breast discharge, a side effect of some psychiatric meds.

"I came by to follow up on a complaint you made a few months ago, against a Douglas DaVella."

"So you believe me that guy came in here was harassing me something awful and I told him to go stuff it. Stuff it I said but he kept on and kept on about my meds like he was asking everyone and he seemed scared really scared and angry just to be there."

"Where did this take place?"

"Out in the rec room. Arts 'n' crafts. We were doing arts 'n' crafts. Popsicle-stick men. Ever make those?"

"Yes," David said. "Though I'm not much of a craftsman."

Mouse threw back his head and laughed. And kept laughing. Finally, David interrupted him. "Do you remember any specifics of your conversation with him?"

"He saw me taking my morning meds and he came over and asked me what they were for. And I told him I'm manic, a bit manic, but there's a downswing to that, you know, not just all high flights of fancy, and so I get depressed and sometimes, only sometimes, I've been known to get agitated and the meds keep me from getting agitated or anxious or violent." He flashed a toothy grin. "Don't worry. I won't get violent now."

"I'm not worried," David said. "If you don't mind my asking, what medications are you on?"

Mouse spat in the corner. "Do you have any Tic Tacs?"

"I'm afraid not. If you don't mind my asking," David repeated slowly, "what medications are you on?"

"I don't mind, not at all. *Not at all.* That's what he asked too. I'm on risperidone and Cogentin and lithium."

"And what happened? Between you and Douglas DaVella?"

"He tried to steal my pills. But I fought him I didn't want him to I need those pills to keep me glued together you know that's what they're for to arm against delusions and hallucinations and . . . and . . . and . . ."

"I can understand why that would be upsetting," David said. "Did he say why he wanted your pills?"

Mouse regarded David, and his close-set eyes glowed with a sudden clarity. "He said he didn't want to be violent."

If Clyde had in fact given Mouse a reliable answer, the ramifications were fascinating: Clyde was self-medicating to try to cure himself. And poisoning himself by overdosing.

"But I bit him," Mouse continued. "And then the orderlies came and tackled me. But I wasn't lying. He tried to steal my meds."

"But no one believed you."

"Of course not." Mouse's words trembled with indignation. "They told me I was delusional."

"Thank you so much," David said. "You've been a tremendous help."

He backed up to the door until he felt it against his shoulders, then he reached behind himself for the handle.

"Hey, Doctor?"

David paused halfway out the door. He leaned back in the room. Mouse pulled his gown down tight across his chest, and David noticed for the first time that he had gynecomastia, increased breast tissue pushing out two bumps in his thin gown. Another side effect. Mouse released the gown and regarded David with a piercing stare.

"We take medications and do these things to ourselves, to our chemistries, to be well. It's *courageous* of us. We are willing to tamper with . . . tamper with . . ."

David nodded at him, a brief, sad tilt of the head, and closed the door.

He followed Dash back to his office. "There is definitely something going on with Clyde and the NPI," he said. "Remember how agitated he became when you were introduced by title, and then there was this incident with . . . Mouse . . . and Mouse reported that Clyde seemed scared and angry when here."

Dash closed his office door and unbuttoned his shirt. Beneath, he wore a tank top that barely stretched across his torso. He retrieved a gym bag from the corner, which he hefted with some exertion. "I'd agree—he probably has some phobia about the place."

"Maybe Clyde witnessed something here when he worked at the hospital," David said, following Dash back out to the main hall. "Something traumatic to him."

Dash leaned forward and hit the elevator's DOWN button. "Doesn't explain why he'd go to all that trouble covering himself with a fake name *before* he worked here." He readjusted the bag's strap across his shoulder as the elevator dinged and opened.

"Diane's following the prescription trail as we speak. I'm checking medical records this afternoon. Any way you could check NPI records?"

Dash's hesitation showed in the four lines that momentarily etched across his forehead. "I'm only playing with a half deck here. You want to bring me up to speed?"

By the time David finished filling him in, the elevator had hit the ground floor and Dash's face was far less placid. They walked in silence through the lobby. Stepping out into the warm afternoon, they headed for the track.

"Is there any chance someone like him could be rehabilitated?"

"What are you trying to do here, David? Assimilate him back into society?"

"What's the prognosis?"

"Not good," Dash said. "Delinquency problems, withdrawal, bad history of adjustment. Expunged juvie record would indicate early age of onset. Add the gender bias to that, and it don't look pretty."

"I think he's striking out against rejection, abandonment. As you said earlier, he perceives he's protecting himself."

"Of course he does," Dash said. "But there's more. Assaulting women gives him a satisfaction he doesn't achieve in any other aspect of his life. It's an accomplishment, David. It allows him to replace chronic feelings of inferiority with feelings of empowerment and pride. He's ugly, stupid, and profoundly asocial. He never knew what having control felt like until he seized that alkali and let fly."

"So maybe if he's given some control in his life . . ." David said. "If he doesn't feel like he's constantly threatened . . ."

"And how about when he is?" Dash asked. "I had a teenager call me a nigger at the grocery store for taking the last carton of orange juice. We live in a routinely hostile world."

David eyed Dash's bulging arms. "Brave kid."

They reached the field and Dash threw down his weighty bag and began to stretch out his arms.

"So you believe he has deeply ingrained psychopathology *and* his prognosis is bad," David said. "Sounds like a candidate for an insanity plea if he's brought to trial."

"There are a lot of people with severe mental and emotional problems who can still distinguish right from wrong."

"Which means?"

"Which means he might be psychologically insane, but in his case, that probably won't translate to legal insanity. The courts present us with two options—drooling psycho or nutcase—and they rarely if ever fit. If a violent person pleads insanity, it reduces them to a status of non-personhood, a passive victim of brain disease, whose behavior is senseless and unintelligible. This is facile and despicable, and unfortunately, the better option. But it's probably not open to Clyde. He's insane *and* criminal. No get-out-of-jail-free card."

"It doesn't matter if he's in legitimate need of psychiatric care? He can't go to a high-security hospital like Patton?"

"There are eight times as many mentally ill people in prisons as there are in state mental hospitals. Does that answer your question?" Dash took note of David's expression. "I'm just being realistic. If he's captured, it becomes a legal game. Has he shown goal-oriented activity? Yes. Has he attempted to avoid detection? Yes. The M'Naghten Rule still holds, and Clyde fits both criteria to be sentenced harshly—he knew the nature and quality of the acts he was committing, and he knew they were wrong. If memory serves, he made both of these facts abundantly clear in your conversation with him in the ER. So yes, he will, in all likelihood, wind up in prison. And you'll be the prosecution's star witness." He regarded David with a tilt of his head. "Unless you decide to take up perjury."

"No, I think I'll pass on that one."

"This case has all the elements for a good scapegoating. Heavy press coverage, benevolent victims, an inarticulate, unattractive assailant. He'll be locked away as soon as they can jam him through the courts."

Dash crouched, removing a discus from his bag. He was still the Nigerian record holder in the discus, though David had never been certain of how noteworthy that distinction was.

Dash entered the discus circle and practiced a few rapid pivots, his feet shushing over the concrete. The sun lent the surrounding grass a metallic sheen. Dash paused, breathing heavily, and faced David again. "And since I'm already on my soapbox, let me whine a bit about our lovely prison system. Rape is an institutionalized practice. Massively underreported."

"I'm aware that prisons aren't a good place to summer, Dash."

"My point is that someone like Clyde is particularly ill equipped to handle it. The acute deprivation, the constant abuse—he'll be ripped apart. Look what happened to Jeffrey Dahmer."

"What *did* happen to Dahmer?"

"Bludgeoned to death with a metal bar." Dash hurled himself into the spin, his enormous body moving quick and graceful, and unleashed the discus with a grunt. It shot from his grip, arcing across the clear blue sky.

David let out a long, weary sigh. "Well, odds are the cops'll shoot him anyway."

Dash stood, hands on his hips, and watched the discus hit the grass and skid to a halt. When he turned back to David, his eyes were deeply sorrowful. "In some ways," he said, "that might be more humane."

CHAPTER 43

THE shadows were beginning to lengthen by the time David arrived at Carson's apartment complex, a two-story '70s stucco sprawl. The grounds were a confusion of stairs, patios, and short outdoor halls.

Two guys in UCLA baseball caps sat in their fenced-in porch on crooked lawn chairs, watching a game of some sort, judging by the roar of the crowd that emanated from the TV. A video game unit was perched on a shoebox at their feet. The controls, attached to curling gray cords, looked complicated, with many buttons and dials. David remembered the Atari joysticks with their single red buttons and suddenly felt quite old. A female newscaster broke in on the TV, promising more details about the escaped "Westwood Acid Thrower" after the game. David leaned around a mountain bike hung vertically and asked to be pointed to Apartment 4B.

"Right down there, man," one of the guys said, pointing around a can of beer. A flicker of recognition crossed his eyes, and he glanced back at the TV. "Hey, aren't you—?"

"Yes," David said.

He rang four times before Carson answered, wearing a ripped pair of gym shorts and no shirt. His hair was even more disheveled than usual, and his nose and eyes were a weary red. He looked simultaneously glad and ashamed to see David.

"Dr. Spier. I got your message, but this isn't really the best time." Nonetheless, Carson stepped back and let the door swing open, and David followed him in.

The square living room was filled with boxes, scattered clothes, and an old TV on a fruit crate. There were no chairs, so David followed Carson's lead and sat on the stained beige carpet, his back to the wall. They faced each other across the length of the room. A worn cardboard box to one side evidently served as Carson's dresser. An open suitcase sat barely visible in the hall, a few pieces of clothing thrown in haphazardly.

"I haven't really had time to move in," Carson said.

"When I was a resident, I earned a little under four thousand dollars a year. Elisabeth and I had just gotten married, and our big treat was going for a walk in Golden Gate Park once a week and buying licorice. That was really splurging."

"I have loans out for med school," Carson said. "Not abject poverty, but I ain't living *la vida loca* either." He wiped his nose with his forearm. "You look like you haven't slept in days."

"As you know, there's been a lot going on."

"Yeah. With me too." When Carson spoke again, his voice trembled. "I should have cleared her C-spine with X rays."

"Did she come in in a collar?"

Carson shook his head.

"Did Dr. Lambert order an X-ray series?"

Carson seemed to recoil at the mention of Don's name. "No."

"She was a stroke victim, Dr. Donalds. This wasn't a head trauma. There was no way to tell her C-spine was compromised."

"I just did it too hard. Her bones were old and brittle. The last guy I tubed was the starting center for the football team—he had a neck like my waist. She was *seventy years old.* I should've handled her more carefully."

"That's probably true," David said. "But it was an honest mistake, the kind of mistake that happens in a hospital. I might have made it myself as a medical student."

Carson raised his head. "Really?"

"Yes," David lied. Carson watched him for a moment. The room was poorly lit—the soft evening air barely filtering through a yellow curtain—and David couldn't make out his face clearly. "UCLA is a teaching hospital," he continued. "There is no teaching process that doesn't progress through trial and error. We have as many checks and balances in place as we can, but we learn with our hands *in the body*. Being a physician is different from being an accountant, a lawyer, a mechanic. When we slip up, the cost sometimes gets paid in human life. That's what we sign on for. We're not beyond error. We're not beyond causing pain when we misstep. Or death.

"You certainly need to learn from this—you'd be a fool not to—but this was not compromised care. She was a seventy-year-old stroke victim, for Christ's sake, and you had to get her tubed quickly."

Carson's lips trembled. "I saw her daughter on my way out." He lowered his eyes behind a hand, and his breathing quickened.

"And you'll see more crying family members over the course of your career. But you'll also see some who are elated because you just saved a child, a parent, a sibling."

"Dr. Lambert told me to take some time off. He said I should—"

David glanced again at the half-packed suitcase. "Dr. Lambert doesn't make the decisions in my division." He stood and faced Carson's lowered head. "You're a fine physician. With fine medical instincts. Don't make us lose a good doctor over something like this. It could have happened to anyone."

When Carson raised his head, his eyes shone, red-rimmed and moist. Before he could respond, the doorbell rang. David took the liberty of answering it and found Diane outside, tapping a notebook against her thigh. "Is he all right?"

"Seems to be holding up."

"Can I see him?"

"You know what?" Carson's voice was cracked and wavering. He did not rise. "I appreciate your both stopping by, but I could use a little time by myself right now."

Diane leaned around David. "If you need us," she said. "Page away."

David stepped outside and pulled the door gently shut behind him. They walked down Barrington, side by side. Diane opened her notebook, a hint of excitement creeping into her voice. "So, get this. When Clyde—or Douglas—worked at the hospital, he had a prescription for lithium carbonate. Eskalith, to be precise."

David readjusted his stethoscope across his shoulders. "Well, the patient in the NPI whom I just interviewed—he said that Clyde tried to steal his medication once. And guess what one of his meds is?"

"Lithium."

"That's right. Evidently Clyde thought it would help control his emerging violent urges."

"But its primary use isn't to control violence. It's for mania."

"I know. But it can help against violence. It's been used to treat aggression in prison inmates and the mentally retarded. But the extent to which lithium actually controls violence isn't important. What's important is Clyde *thinks* it helps control violence. If he's after lithium, we have a paper trail. Who wrote the prescription?"

"Well, that's just it," Diane said. "Dr. Warren."

"Dr. Warren? An orthopod prescribing lithium?"

"I know. I checked it out with him. He's never heard of Douglas DaVella, of course. Clyde must've gotten ahold of his DEA number somehow."

"Well," David said, "Clyde must've made plenty of deliveries to Orthopedics. Horace does a lot of cutting for them. Joints and whatnot. It would have been easy enough to lift a loose prescription off a counter somewhere and copy down a DEA number."

"Why didn't he just go see someone and get drugs prescribed legally?"

"When he came into the ER, I asked him if he was on any drugs, and he became intensely defensive. I'd guess he's ashamed of the fact he needs help. Scared to admit it outright. It's not uncommon, especially for someone presumably uneducated. So he forged a prescription."

Diane added, "And his meds would've all been covered by his employee health plan. Eskalith doesn't come free."

"But he gets fired—"

"—goes off the health plan—"

"—can't afford drugs—"

"—believes that this affects him—"

"—and begins acting drastically," David finished.

Diane whistled. "Holy shit."

"What are the signs of lithium toxicity, Dr. Trace?"

"Upset stomach, difficulty concentrating, clouding of consciousness, hair loss, weight gain . . ." She paused. "It's as bad as Dilantin."

"What else?"

"Excessive thirst, metallic taste in the mouth, GI distress, acne, frequent urination." She paused, shaking her head, a faint smile crossing her face.

"Slurring of speech, swelling of hands, psoriasis of the

fingernails, nystagmus, ataxia, hypothyroidism," David added. "There are many more, of course, but these seem to be the relevant ones."

"But one thing doesn't make sense," Diane said. "If he lost his prescription coverage when he was fired months ago, then why was he displaying signs of lithium toxicity just last week?"

"Because he's still taking it."

"But my friend at the DEA said there have been no prescriptions of any kind filled in the past three months for either Clyde C. Slade or Douglas DaVella. So how's he getting it?"

"Maybe he's been stealing it." David made a mental note to tell Ed about this possibility.

Just south of the post office, they turned into a park composed of two converted baseball fields. Range Rovers and Land Cruisers pulled up and dogs bounded from tailgates—dalmatians and Rhodesian Ridgebacks and Great Danes—and headed for the large lawn ahead. David had forgotten about the dog park, and found himself entertaining the idea of trading in his wife's cockatoo for a Labrador. A golden retriever nuzzled Diane's hand and she laughed, crouching to scratch behind its ears. Its owner, a young Hollywood type in a tight black Kenneth Cole T-shirt that showed off his prodigious biceps, used the opportunity to strike up a conversation with Diane, while David stood by dumbly.

When Muscles finally strode off to join the other dog owners, Diane and David headed for the field. David felt a tug at his sleeve and looked down to see a hand covered with paint, the fingernails and rough cuticles flecked white and green. It belonged to a disheveled kid in his midtwenties with a long, pointed goatee and a pair of glasses with a green thumbprint at the edge of one of the lenses. The kid wore Tevas and a ripped Berkeley T-shirt, also splattered with paint. Even the greyhound dog at his side was speckled with green dots.

"Hey, Dr. S!" the kid said amicably.

"Hello, Shane."

"Hey, man, I'm sorry about Elisabeth. She was one of the good ones."

"Yes. Yes she was."

"If she hadn't come to my opening at that shithole gallery on Cahuenga, I'd still be running the coasters at Magic Mountain."

The greyhound sped off and began furiously humping Hollywood guy's leg. David watched with perverse amusement.

"Oh, shit," Shane said, running over to retrieve his dog. "I'll see you around, man," he called over his shoulder.

Diane and David hiked up in the bleachers overlooking the former baseball diamond and watched the dogs wrestle and chase objects. The brief discussion about Elisabeth, compounded by his sleep deprivation, had unsettled him. He knew Diane could see it in his face and was grateful she turned to the more pressing matters at hand.

"Now," she said. "Your turn. What have you discovered?"

David filled her in, telling her about meeting Ed, discovering the lozenge wrapper, and discussing matters with Horace, Ralph, Mouse, and Dash. The information came flooding out. He realized how much he missed having Diane as his confidante and colleague, being able to talk openly.

"You certainly pulled out all stops," Diane said. "Are you sure you want to get involved to this extent?"

"Yes," David said. "I can pursue this in ways that the cops can't."

"Your diagnostic eye."

"It sounds ridiculous, I know, but I have a sense of this man."

"You think the police are still out to kill him?"

"Yes. But I think I can find my way to him first."

"And then what, David?"

David watched Shane's greyhound zipping across the open field. "I guess I turn him in to the authorities I trust and hope he can get the kind of rehabilitation a person is entitled to. In a hospital or a jail."

Diane watched him closely. "Dash said his prognosis is bad."

"It's terrible. But that's irrelevant. We don't always fight these battles to win them."

Diane made a popping sound with her lips, then took a deep breath. "There's no outcome here that you want to feel like you made happen."

"No, there's not. I guess I have to find the most acceptable version of defeat."

They sat for a while, watching the dogs run. David enjoyed the brief respite, knowing he had to return to the hospital soon and begin slogging through records. As dusk encroached, the park cleared out until only a confused miniature poodle remained. It stood on second base until its owner collected it and carried it off, and then, save for the soft whistle of the wind through the chain-link backboard, the park was silent.

"Well, I need to go home and catch some sleep if I'm gonna go back on at ten," Diane said. She rose to go, but David laid his hand over hers.

She sat back down, putting her heels up on the edge of her bleacher plank and hugging her knees. The sky had dulled to a heavy gray, perhaps in anticipation of rain. The smog wreathing Westwood made a beautiful filter for the setting sun, scattered petals of violet and orange.

"You're not stunning," he said.

"I know."

"I don't think about you when we're not together." He leaned forward, hands laced together. The skin on his knuckles was hard and cracked from overwashing. "I don't love the way your hair collects around your neck. Your eyes aren't the most deep and exquisite I've ever seen."

When he finally looked up, her face was soft and unlined, like a Renaissance angel's. Her eyes, slightly misty, sparkled like green gems.

"I don't think about you either," she said.

Leaning over, he pressed his lips tenderly to her forehead. He held the moment, his eyes closed, before breaking off the kiss. A strand of her hair clung to his face for an instant before blowing free.

They looked at each other, confused and a bit breathless.

CHAPTER 44

THE Medical Records Office hummed with an all-hours vibrancy. A young clerk leaned back in his chair behind the counter, listening to the Dodgers game on the radio and flipping through a worn Michael Crichton paperback.

He didn't so much as look up when David slid into a seat at one of the computer terminals and began punching the keys. To access the confidential records, he typed in his user name and then his password—Elisabeth's maiden name. His password, which he'd kept for the past four years, struck him for the first time as dire and slightly pathetic, so he changed it to PINKERTON, in keeping with his new respect for security matters. On the drive over, he'd called Ed to set him on the trail of stolen lithium.

He entered the database and typed in CLYDE SLADE and Clyde's birthday. The search engine seemed to run for an eternity, the cursor turning into a ticking clock icon that stared out at him like a miniature eye. No results.

Sheffield tripled, and the radio roared with applause.

David tried CLYDE C. SLADE. Another tedious wait, and again, no results.

He pushed out from the terminal and crossed to the counter. "Excuse me."

The clerk held up a finger. "Hang on."

"Listen, I really need—"

"Just lemme finish this page."

David set aside his irritation. "Crichton, huh? I enjoy him."

The clerk slid a bookmark between the pages and looked up. "Pretty cool stuff. I dig his range. Doctors to dinosaurs."

"I was hoping you could tell me how far back these records are computerized."

"I don't know. Like twenty years."

Not far enough back to include relevant records, if Clyde was indeed harboring a childhood grudge against the hospital. "I need to look for a pediatrics file that's probably older," David said. "Where would it be?"

"Medical Records Storage. Culver City."

"Any way I could get it tonight?"

"No. Sorry." The clerk thrust a form across the counter at David. "Fill this out. Usually takes four to six days."

"Can I go down there myself?"

"Nope. They're closed. It's not run by the Med Center—it's just some warehouse that stores old files for companies."

David jotted down Clyde's information on the sheet

and passed it back. "I don't have four to six days. This is an absolute emergency, and I'd really appreciate it if you could put a rush on it and get this file for me first thing tomorrow."

"Okay, I'll do my best." The clerk glanced at the name. "The cops were down here asking about records for this guy," he said. "Anything related?"

"Did you give them access?"

"No way. Not without a court order and my boss's signature."

"Okay." David slid his card across the counter. "I'd really appreciate it if you would page me the minute that file hits this office."

Returning to the computer terminal, David typed in DOUGLAS DAVELLA and tried to be patient as the clock icon stared out at him cheerily.

⊕

The clock radio jarred Diane from her nap, blaring "La Macarena," a song she thought had been consigned to "Achy Breaky Heart" obscurity. With a groan, she slapped at the top of the radio until she hit the appropriate button, and slid out of bed. She'd barely napped for an hour before being awakened for her night shift.

Lowering her feet into a pair of slippers, she shuffled to the bathroom and turned on the shower so hot water would be flowing by the time she finished brushing her teeth. The fact that she didn't drink coffee made her that much more reliant on a hot shower to get her rolling before a long shift. She undressed and regarded her body in the mirror as she brushed, turning sideways for a better view of her rear end. Behind her, the showerhead coughed a few times, then the water steadied again.

She climbed into the steaming shower with a groan of pleasure and turned her face up into the flow, running her hands through her hair. The water went from clear to a cloudy white.

Diane screamed, jerking back out of the spray and knocking over a metal shower caddy propped in the corner. Shampoo and conditioner bottles spun on the slippery floor. She stepped on a can of shaving cream and went down, feeling her razor dig into her hand. Her face felt as though it had been set afire. She shoved the translucent shower door open, knocking it from the tracks, and fell out, the railing along the side of the tub digging into her stomach. As she scrambled from the shower, she opened her eyes momentarily from instinct, and screamed even louder, her hands scrabbling over her face. The smell of rank flesh filled the air and she recognized it instantly. It was the same smell that had lingered about Nancy's and Sandra's faces when they'd stumbled into the ER. Alkali. Somehow, it had gotten into her water supply. That meant it could flow from the sink faucet as well.

She pulled herself up from the bath mat, felt her way to the toilet, and raised the lid. She forced her eyes open again, for an instant, and saw through the tears and excruciating pain that the water was clear. Lowering her head, she leaned heavily on the rim, splashing water up into her face continually with one hand and alternating prying her eyelids apart with her other, trying to get her breathing back under control. Though she felt no burning in her mouth or throat and could taste nothing unusual, she hocked and spit, a cord of drool dangling from her bottom lip. The pain in her face did not seem to be subsiding.

She flushed the toilet, saw that the fresh water spiraling in was also clear, and leaned farther down, scooping it up over her face. She tried desperately not to think of the alkali eating its way through her flesh, focusing instead on treating the injury as if it were someone else's.

She flushed and irrigated for about another four minutes, preparing herself to make the dash to the telephone. Her bedroom phone was the closest, but the one in the kitchen had a sink nearby. She should start filling the sink while she dialed—there was a wash rag draped over the faucet she could use to plug the drain. Once the water was running, she'd have to force her eyes open again to check that it was clear.

Continuing to splash herself with water from the toilet, she envisioned the route to the kitchen. Out the bathroom door, right down the hall, dodge the small table with the vase set against the left wall, six paces to the kitchen door, then around the central table to the countertop. The dial pad was on the inside of the telephone receiver; 9 was the second button up on the right side, 1 the top left.

The pain came in waves, like tiny fragments of shrapnel flying in her face from a series of explosions. Her harsh breaths, strengthened with groans, fired through her chest as though she were finishing a marathon. Grinding her teeth, tensing her entire body, she drew her legs up under her and prepared for the blind sprint.

Douglas DaVella's records popped up on-screen, and David scanned through them eagerly. DaVella had come into the ER for a standard physical after a fender bender in '87—no significant findings—and he'd seen a gastroenterologist in '91 for irritable bowel.

Clearly, they hadn't cross-referenced medical files with employee records when Clyde had worked at the hospital as Douglas DaVella. That made sense, given patient confidentiality and logistical considerations.

David jotted down DaVella's social security number, date of birth, and address—*1711 Pearson Rd.* He'd just noted that the address was in Venice when his pager went off, its text message alerting him to get down to the ER immediately.

CHAPTER 45

WHEN Pat ignored David, he thought it was merely residual ill will from their confrontation earlier in the week, but the entire staff was stiff with him as he made his way to the Central Work Area. He couldn't find the attending on call, so he tapped a nurse on the shoulder as she passed. "Can you tell me what's going on?"

"You haven't heard?" She had a cruel, stupid face and wore too much eye shadow.

"I guess not," David said.

A medicine intern looked up from his paperwork. "There's been another attack, Dr. Spier."

David felt the air leave his lungs all at once. "On who? Who is it?"

The CWA was full, but no one answered. They stared with dull, implacable eyes, or turned back to their charts. *"Who is it?"* he said again.

The medicine intern angled his head toward the door to Hallway Two and David walked out at a fast clip. Bronner slumped in a chair near the door to Exam Eight. Jenkins stood over him, sipping coffee from a Styrofoam cup.

Jenkins looked at David with more concern than

anger, which sent David's anxiety through the roof. He strode toward the door and shoved it open.

Diane lay on the bed inside, her forehead and right cheek blistered in streaks and patches. A series of raised white bubbles ringed her right eye.

David stepped forward, dazed, his hand swiping the air several times before finding the back of a chair. He leaned. A tingling warmth spread across his face, and he blinked hard several times to strike preemptively against tears.

Diane looked away. "That bad, huh?"

He knew his voice would be unsteady, so he waited a moment to speak. "No," he said. Fighting to keep his emotions from overwhelming him, he crossed to her bed, dragging the chair along with him. She still didn't meet his eyes. He wanted desperately to touch her, to caress her face, but could not. Her hair, still wet from saline irrigation, had darkened the pillow. He took her hand, and she let him.

He sat at the side of her bed.

"You just missed plastics. Can't do anything acutely. Probably have some scarring, but no disfiguring contractions. Neosporin and Silvadene, blah blah blah. Wait and see. Should be fine." Head still turned, she laughed to herself, a nasty little laugh. "Wait and see."

"Ophthalmology?" David asked, still not trusting his voice to form longer sentences.

"Hourly Pred Forte, Cipro four times a day. Mild corneal epithelial erosion, faint anterior stromal haziness, no ischemic necrosis of perilimbal conjunctiva or sclera." She shook her head. "Words. Lots of words."

"Prognosis?"

"I should have little or no corneal scarring." She raised an index finger and twirled it lazily. "Whoopee."

David exhaled, relieved. "You're very lucky."

"*Lucky*. God, do we sound that stupid to people who come in here? I don't feel *lucky*, David."

He weathered her burst of anger quietly. She was entitled to it. After a moment, he asked, "Where did he . . . ?"

"Emptied out medicine gelcaps, filled them with alkali crystals. Then, he broke into my place, unscrewed my showerhead, and stuck them behind there. Hot water melts the capsules. Presto. Liquid alkali."

"Who thinks of that?" David asked in disbelief.

"I hate to confess I find it somewhat ingenious. If he'd just packed the showerhead with straight crystals, it would've clogged up, or I would've noted the immediate change in water color. Of course, it was slightly diluted, which is why I can see you right now."

He picked at the skin of his cuticle, drawing blood. "That bastard. That *sadistic* bastard." He stood up and paced around the room. "This is my fault."

"This isn't your fault, David." Her face remained turned away. "Pardon my manners, but I don't really feel like being comforting right now." Her voice softened, though she still didn't turn to him. "It's a fucked situation. Let's use it for what it's worth. You told me he sensed you and I were close when I burst in on you in his room in the ER. He probably did this to piss you off or get back at you for something. I'd guess that *I'm* actually irrelevant."

David stared at the back of her head, admiring her, still waiting for the heat to leave his face.

"It's a more elaborate setup," Diane continued. "Not to mention a tedious, time-consuming one." Her voice colored with acrimony. "Our little boy's growing up."

David tried to think, but couldn't find his way through the jumble of his emotions. He walked over and stood beside her bed. "Look at me."

"No." Her shoulders began to shake.

"Diane. Look at me."

Her voice, tiny like a child's, was wrenched high. "I can't."

Crouching, he reached out and touched her unmarred chin, ever so gently, and turned her face to his. The blisters were slick and shiny with cream, and they leaked a pale yellow fluid.

She tried to turn her face away, but he didn't let her. Her lips were trembling so hard she could barely speak. "I look repulsive. I must look repulsive to you."

"We're beyond that, Diane." His voice was hard, reprimanding. She wavered on the verge of tears, her face fighting itself. "I've scraped out bedsores," he said. "I've packed infected abdominal wounds. I've cut into gallbladders that spilled green bile. I've seen enough of the human body for six lifetimes—seen enough to know not to take it literally." He leaned forward, his face inches from hers. She met his stare, her eyes green and smooth. *"You are as beautiful as you have ever been,"* he said.

She reached up with trembling fingers, took his hand, and pressed it to her chest.

The gray sky had given way to showers. After ducking the press outside the hospital, David drove home carefully; the anomalous bursts of rain of the past few days had brought the oils to the surface of the roads. He watched the windshield wipers beating double time, trying to let them clear his mind. Puddles spotted the dark streets like pools of oil. The roads were deserted; the rain had even driven the dogged Tibet picketers from the sidewalk outside the Federal Building.

He had wanted to stay with Diane through the night, but found he couldn't. He held a reservoir of strength for such things—pain steeped in personal emotion—and for the past two years, his wife's memory had drawn steadily from it. Thoughts of Diane worked on him from the inside, guilt and fury searing him.

He thought of Clyde's dull, flat head, the odd, decaying odor of his body, like rotting wood, the fat fingers that rubbed and slid among themselves like rodents clustering for warmth. David imagined him holed up in a dark room, lurking and plotting and healing, wrapped in a blanket of unutterable sorrow. Clyde's wiring was off. He was broken.

David's medical ethics seemed distant right now, stolid and brittle like shelf things. He recalled Yale's aspersion—*you don't know much about how things work on the street*—and it stung like a virgin blow. David had been a child playing with a loaded gun. The most painful thing of all was that he'd suffered none of the consequences himself. Diane had.

The Mercedes's tires whipped through puddles, sending water hammering up on the undercarriage of his car. Through the bleary windshield, he saw flashing red lights ahead on San Vicente. An ambulance had pulled over near the lawned median, beside a car that had skidded off course and smashed into one of the gnarled coral trees.

Digging in the pocket of his white coat for his stethoscope, David pulled over behind the ambulance. A woman lay on her back in the grass, two EMTs kneeling over her with a backboard.

David sprang out, his shoes pooling with water as he splashed through a puddle to his trunk, where he kept his father's old-fashioned leather doctor's bag for emergencies. "Do you need any help?" he called out.

One of the EMTs delicately wrapped a C-spine collar around the woman's neck and secured it with a strap across her forehead. "We got it covered," he said.

"Did you check her airway?"

"We got it under control, buddy."

David pulled to a halt, his stethoscope dangling from his hand. "I'm an ER doctor."

On a three-count, the two EMTs raised the backboard and headed back to the open doors of the ambulance. A moment later, the vehicle was off, siren screaming.

Behind him, David heard the pinging open door alert from his car. The ambulance faded slowly from view. He stood in the rain, the crashed car steaming before him, water dripping from his hair and running over his lips.

He didn't feel much like going home.

CHAPTER 46

DAVID pulled into the garage and made his way back through the house to his bedroom, removing his clothes as he walked. He stood at the foot of the bed in his boxers, watching through the bare window as the rain came down in sheets.

Bed felt soft and divine, even more comfortable for the storm brewing outside. He put in his earplugs and burrowed beneath the covers. A roll of thunder rattled the windowpane above his head, but not loudly enough to wake him.

As he slept, rain drummed softly on the roof.

A lick of lightning lit the sky, throwing the outline of David's window, a skewed, yellow rectangle broken at the bottom by the waving tips of fronds, against the far wall. A few moments later, another low rumble vibrated through the air.

When lightning lit David's window again, the outline cast against the wall was broken by a man's silhouette. Wide and distorted, it remained perfectly still above the frenzied waving of foliage shadows. The lines of the silhouette were so distinct that even the water dripping from the man's oversize head was visible. The black form seemed to float on the far wall, hovering over David's sleeping body.

It flickered on the wall for only a moment before the room fell back into darkness.

His slick loafers skidded on the kitchen linoleum, and Peter felt his balance go. He let himself topple over stiffly, so as to keep his legs straight and out of the way, and broke his fall evenly with his arms and chest. If there was one thing he knew, it was how to fall well.

Getting up, however, was usually a bit more difficult. He took stock of his limbs. His right kneecap, exposed between the two strips of metal that ran down the length of his leg, throbbed a bit. Lying on his side on the cold kitchen floor, he tugged at his pant leg and it hiked up over his calf before catching on his brace. A few more tugs and his knee came into sight. It would swell nicely, but the skin was not broken. Even so, he'd probably have to dig his ortho cane out of the closet and use it for the next few days. Which he hated.

Peter turned back onto his stomach, his breath stirring a few toast crumbs near the base of the counter, and pushed himself up and back onto his stiff legs. A nearby stool gave him the grip he needed, and he walked his hands slowly up its metal back, careful not to let it skate out, his legs sliding to vertical beneath him.

His pant leg remained stuck up over his knee, the fabric tangled in a bolt at the joint. He wiped the sweat off his forehead with a cupped hand and began the slow waddle back to his bedroom, trying not to think about what would happen when he was seventy. Or eighty.

His hands found their familiar places, places where the wallpaper had been worn thin, the counters polished to a shine. Leaning against the bathroom counter, he brushed his teeth. When he turned to his bed, he noticed the thin water stain left across his pant thighs from the counter.

He removed his shirt and belt, then unbuttoned his pants, and let them fall. The tangle over his right knee remained, and he worked the pant leg out from where it had wedged in his brace. Shuffling a few steps to the bed, he turned and sat, then released the catches near his knees that permitted his braces to bend. Breathing hard, he removed his shoes and tossed them toward the closet, where they landed in a pile of stretched, distorted footwear. He lifted his feet from the puddle of his pants and then, finally, removed the leg braces. Red indentations lay in bands across his thighs and along the outsides of his heels. Near these indentations, the skin was dry and cracked, and his eyes rolled back in his head as he rubbed them.

He lifted his legs into bed, assisting with his hands, and wiggled to get himself under the covers. He noticed he'd forgotten to close the blinds, and he stared at his own reflection in the dark window, confronting an inexplicable sense of unease that took a few moments to dissipate. Given the steps he'd have to go through to get back up, the window was a good ten minutes away.

The nightstand lamp, on the other hand, was only an inch out of reach. He had to roll over to get to the switch. A soft click and the room was bathed in darkness.

He fell into a deep and immediate sleep.

⊕

Dalton swung open the front door, wearing a threadbare red-and-white striped bathrobe. He saw Jenkins standing out in the pouring rain, and lowered his hand so his gun rested against his thigh.

Water pasted Jenkins's hair to his head. He blinked twice to clear it from his eyes, but made no move to enter. "You look like a fucking candy cane," he said.

"You drove over here at two in the morning in the rain to tell me that?" One of the girls called from down the hall, and Dalton leaned away from the door. "It's okay. Go back to sleep!" He reached out, fisted Jenkins's shirt, and pulled him inside. Jenkins followed him into the kitchen.

Dalton turned on the light and a mouse scurried under a cabinet. He removed two Old Milwaukees from the refrigerator and sat at the table. "Don't knock the robe," he said. "It was Kathy's. I like sl—" He slid one can across the table at Jenkins and opened the other. "It was Kathy's."

Jenkins had pulled his chair out from the table so he faced the wall. He slouched in the chair, his posture unusually lax. Dalton waited patiently. After a while, he finished his beer and reached across the table for Jenkins's, which sat full. He was halfway through that one before Jenkins spoke. "I can't see her," he said.

"Nance?"

He nodded. "I can't go in there anymore. I tried yesterday, but I got to the curtain and couldn't pull it aside. She called out, asked who was there, and I turned and left."

Dalton sipped his beer. He cleared his throat but didn't speak.

"My little sister," Jenkins said. "She meant more to me than anything in the world."

The only noise was the quiet ticking of the cracked plastic clock above the sink.

"I wish she was dead," Jenkins said. After a moment, Dalton realized he was crying. He was an inexperienced crier, all gasps and jerks. Dalton walked slowly to the light switch and flicked it back off, then returned to his seat.

"Thanks," Jenkins said.

They sat quietly in the darkness, Dalton occasionally sipping his beer.

⊕

David awakened at three in the morning, and it was as though he'd never fallen asleep. The same images had followed him from exhaustion into sleep, and then back out again. Diane dabbing ceaselessly at the weeping wounds on her face. Their kiss at the park. Tame as it had been, his kiss with Diane had been wonderful. It had also been unsettling, and he suddenly realized why. He had grown accustomed to feeling other people's flesh only when examining them. He asked himself whether some part of him was as fearful of human contact as Clyde was.

After forty minutes of lying in darkness, David rose from his bed. He sat in the living room and tried to read a medical journal but could not concentrate. Changing into workout clothes, he went into the garage and ran on the treadmill for a half hour. After his shower, he lay in bed again, studying the ceiling, the plants scraping softly at the dark window overhead.

At five, he fell into a fitful sleep, full of jerks and tremors. He awoke several times, bathed in sweat, the sheets wrapped around his legs. At six o'clock, he rose and showered again, went to the study dripping wet, and raised the drape from the cockatoo's cage.

He watched the bird slowly awaken, like a mechanical toy coming to life. "Where's Elisabeth?" it asked. "Where's Elisabeth?"

At six-thirty, a sudden and irresistible urge to do laundry seized him. He grabbed the hamper from his bedroom and sorted his laundry carefully by color, washing the dark blues with the blacks and browns, and leaving the light blue scrubs for the next load. As he awaited the washer's chime, he sat in the laundry room and watched the appliance vibrate and hum.

When he finished, he stood over the warm mound of clothes on his bed and began to separate the items. With the slow automatic movements of a robot, he lined the socks in pairs, stacked his boxers, folded his shirts in tight military rectangles.

His scrub bottoms were all folded identically, and he laid one pair on top of another until they rose like a smooth blue tower. One of the pant legs was a half inch out of line with the others and he pulled it out and refolded it, refolded it, refolded it, his hands working in short concise movements until they began to tremble and then the stack blurred before him and he turned to sit on the bed, using one hand to lower himself slowly, and the sobs seized him from the chest up, his breath coming in short choking gasps, and he covered his eyes with a cupped hand though there was no one there to see and wept for the first time in two years.

CHAPTER 47

DAVID double-checked the address he'd jotted on a slip of paper as he pulled the car to the curb near the intersection of Butler and Iowa. It was 1663 Butler Ave. The West LA Division police station would have been another dull city building if the curved entranceway hadn't been tiled a fantastic reddish-orange.

David parked in the lot across the street beneath the red-and-white metal tower he'd sighted from Santa Monica Boulevard. He'd heard similar structures referred to on TV shows as repeaters; they were presumably used for radio contact between police vehicles. The sky, gray and heavy from last night's storm, looked as though it might not return to its summer blue without another downpour.

His head swimming drunkenly from his sleepless night, he crossed the street to the station. He had to push hard into the heavy glass doors to get them to swing. Probably bullet proof. The lobby smelled of dust. Two desk officers manned the sprawl of the wooden counter, one facing away from the entrance, typing hypnotically on a computer. A Dr Pepper machine hummed against the near wall, bookending a row of mustard-yellow chairs. A sign proclaiming INVESTIGATORS hung overhead, with an arrow pointing down a hall. The main desk officer, a black woman in her late thirties, stood with one hand on a cocked hip, arguing with someone on the telephone.

David realized he'd never been in a police station. Ever.

A bulletin board labeled WEST LA PREDATORS hosted several crime-alert flyers, a composite sketch of Clyde staring vacantly from the one pinned dead center. A stack of extra flyers sat on the nearest yellow chair, and David took one of Clyde, folded it, and slid it into his pocket.

He headed for the men's room at the end of the lobby, wanting to take a moment to brace himself. The bathroom floor and walls were overlaid with yellow and avocado-green tiles. The fierce lighting made the whole room shine like a dentist's office, and he left before his incipient headache could gain momentum. He waited patiently at the front counter while the woman ignored him, directing her considerable energies toward the telephone handset.

"That is the way it works, sir. You are to come down here if you'd like to file a report. That is all we can do. . . . Listen to me. Listen to me. Listen to me. That. Is. All. We. Can. Do." She glared at the handset suddenly, as if it were to blame for the fact she'd been hung up on. It clanged loudly back into place beneath the counter. Then she looked up at David for the first time. "Yes?"

"I need to speak with Detective Yale."

"Was he expecting you?"

"Yes. Well, no, but I think—"

"Well, which is it? Yes or no?"

"Look, Officer, my name is David Spier. I'm a physician at the UCLA emergency room. I wanted to talk to him about the alkali throwings. He said to call anytime."

She glanced David up and down. "I don't see no phone."

"I thought it would be better to handle this matter in person."

She picked up the telephone and wedged it between her cheek and shoulder. Assuming she was making some sort of inquiry call, David strolled over and pretended to study the Dr Pepper machine. Her trademark hang-up nearly rattled the windows.

"Hey, you. Doctor-man. Go down this corridor. This one. You're going to go up to the second floor. No. No. Stop. That door. Okay." She hit a button beneath the counter and the door in front of him buzzed.

He pushed through and made his way upstairs to find another lobby with another counter. A gruff officer was waiting for him, reeking of coffee, the edge of his brown mustache darkened by a recent beverage. "Well, well, well," he said. "If it isn't Dr. Kevorkian." He looked behind him, presumably for someone to laugh at his joke.

"I'm looking for Detective Yale."

"Detective Yale is in court this morning and won't be reachable." He pawed his hand down over his mustache and wiped it on his cheap slacks. "I can handle whatever matter you have."

"I'd really prefer to speak with him."

"Then come back tomorrow."

David inhaled deeply, drumming his fingers on the countertop. "How about Detective Dalton?"

"Detective Dalton took the afternoon off."

"Where is he?"

"I can't tell you that."

"I was told by both men to contact them immediately if I had anything important to tell them."

The officer looked unimpressed.

"You know what this is regarding," David added.

"If you have anything important to discuss, you should discuss it with me." The cop saw he was getting nowhere and heaved a coffee-stale sigh. "All right, *Doctor*. Dalton's up at the Academy. You'll find him behind the graduation field."

David got turned around three times trying to find his way, but finally drove up a hill and saw the metal sign stretched between two stone towers with Spanish tile domes, LOS ANGELES POLICE ACADEMY spanning its width in gold letters. A series of stucco buildings and terraces reminiscent of a grandee's hacienda, the Academy worked its way up the slope of a hill. A sentry post stood near the base of one of the stone towers, and a blond guard manned the booth. David heard the crack of gunfire from a nearby shooting range.

Feeling a bit uneasy, unsure if access to the Academy was restricted, David approached the sentry. "Hello," he said. "I was hoping you could point me to the graduation field."

Her smile, fast and radiant, reminded him of Diane's. "Absolutely, sir. It's right up here." She raised a gloved hand and pointed.

He nodded his thanks and trudged up the hill, turning left onto the wide field. Down at the end, he noticed a picnic ground and recognized Dalton's slump near the immense barbecue pit. As David drew close, two girls came into view, sitting behind Dalton at a battered picnic table. They sat perfectly still, a few badly wrapped presents in a small pile before them. A breeze kicked up, and the younger one shivered.

David paused, knowing he shouldn't intrude.

Dalton pulled a two-liter bottle of Coke from a plastic bag, which promptly blew away in the wind. He chased it down and turned back to the barbecue, only to find the hot dogs on fire. He poured some Coke over them to put them out, and pulled them from the blackened grill onto a paper plate. David backed away, but Dalton spotted him before he could leave unnoticed.

Dalton wore a red flannel shirt and a pair of jeans, mended badly at one knee. The left leg of his jeans flared at the ankle, maybe from a gun. "Still want to help the sick fugitive, Doc?"

David did not respond.

"This is personal time for me," Dalton said, turning back to the soggy hot dogs. "My little girl's birthday party."

"I'm sorry," David said. "I wouldn't have come if I'd known. I was told you were at the Academy, so I figured it was work-related." He leaned over toward the girl, hands on his knees. "How old are you?" he asked.

Dalton nodded at his younger daughter. "Go ahead and answer." He glanced back at David self-consciously.

"Ten," the girl said. Her face, stained with food, was

downturned and sad. Her older sister didn't look much happier.

A homemade cake sat lopsided on a sheet of cardboard at the end of the table. Dalton slid two burnt hot dogs, moist with Coke, into buns and set the plates in front of the girls. The older daughter pried at the hot dog with a glittery pink fingernail, and the burnt shell crumbled a bit.

"Go on," Dalton said. "It's not that bad." He fixed himself a hot dog, took a bite, and pretended to enjoy it.

The girls stared at their plates. The little one looked as if she might start crying. A volley of gunshots echoed in the background, and the children jerked in their seats.

"I'm going to talk to the man for a moment, girls," Dalton said. He nodded at his ten-year-old affectionately. "You can go ahead and open your presents."

He strode off toward the graduation field, and David followed. Arms crossed, Dalton faced him. "What?" he asked.

"I'd like to put our differences aside and offer whatever help I can," David said.

"After you've been questioning our judgment? Getting in our way?"

"I know you were doing what you thought was right—"

"Doc, I make thirty-two thousand dollars a year after taxes. What the fuck do you think I do things for? The money?"

"I don't care anymore," David said. "I just want to help."

"What, now that someone *you* like got hit?"

Dalton must have seen the pain in his face because he looked down at the ground. A recently discarded cigarette smoldered in the grass, and Dalton stubbed it with a savage twist of his foot. David could see on the side of his shoe where he'd colored the worn leather with a brown pen.

"Why should I work with you?" Dalton continued. "You're the guy who tells the jury this guy needs to go to the nuthouse."

"Why don't we catch him first, then decide what to do with him?"

"Still *we*, huh? Seems to me you got a Jesus complex, Doc. And let me tell you something. It's stupid to think you can save anyone else. That's a lie reserved for films and shitty novels." Dalton studied the tip of his shoe. "There's no *we* about this. Yale and I have it under control. Don't get involved."

Dalton's eyes were hard and intractable. To make any progress, David knew he'd have to deal with Yale. The detective at the station had said Yale was in court—maybe he was back by now.

Dalton turned to check on his girls. The hot dogs sat on the plates before them, uneaten.

"I'm sorry to have bothered you," David said. He extended his hand and after a moment, Dalton took it.

"Jenkins isn't a bad guy, you know," Dalton said. "He thinks like you do. You gotta cut out disease."

He did not release David's hand, and David did not pull it away. "Cutting is always a last resort," David said.

"I'd say we've reached the last resort," Dalton said. "Wouldn't you?"

David was too spent to argue.

"Me and Jenkins," Dalton continued, "we just figure enough shit goes wrong in the world without someone planning it."

Dalton's younger daughter began to cry, drawing his attention. She lowered an unwrapped Barbie doll into her lap, as her older sister tried to console her. Dalton dropped David's hand and jogged over.

"What's wrong?" David heard him say.

The older girl glared at him. "She already has a Doctor Barbie. Mom would've known that. Mom used to keep track of stuff like that."

Dalton crouched in front of his younger daughter and squeezed her thin little ankles. She wiped her tears with a tiny fist. "I'm sorry," she said. "It's not that. I don't care about that." Another volley of gunshots echoed over from the range, startling her upright, then she continued crying. The clouds clustered dark and ominous overhead. Rain would soon ruin Dalton's little picnic.

Dalton looked up from his crouch, a bit shyly, and nodded. David returned the gesture and left him with his family.

⊕

The desk officer at West LA cocked her head and glared at David with annoyance. "No, Detective Yale hasn't come back in. Why don't you leave a message?"

"Please tell him—"

"I know, I know. Dr. Spier stopped by. Fine. Thanks."

David left and sat in his Mercedes in the parking lot across from the station, keeping an eye on the entrance. He listened to the radio for a while as he waited. Boredom began to set in after about a half hour, and he debated leaving and finding Yale later.

A knock on the driver's window startled him. He turned to see Yale crouched over, a barely perceptible smile on his face. David rolled down the window.

"Can I help you?" Yale said.

"I'd like to talk to you about some things."

"Specifics are helpful."

"The case," David said. "In private."

Yale took him upstairs and enclosed him in an interrogation room, complete with an observation mirror. He left him in there alone about fifteen minutes, probably enacting an intimidation strategy he'd learned in some noirish detective course. David studied the carving in the wood table beneath his hands. *Tyrone's waiting for your sweet little punk ass. Inquire in LA County Jail, Cell 213.* High school etchings with a street vernacular.

Into the back of one of the chairs, someone had etched the three wise monkeys wearing gangsta shades—see no evil, hear no evil, speak no evil. An apt trio of mascots for an interrogation room.

Finally, Yale entered. He pulled up a chair opposite David.

"I want to help you catch him," David said. "And don't tell me to talk to the Public Information Officer. I can help you. Let me help."

When Yale stood up and paced behind him, David resisted the urge to turn and keep him in sight. "And what do you want?" Yale asked.

"I want the guarantee you wouldn't give me earlier. That Clyde won't be taken into an alley and shot."

Yale let out his breath in a long rush. "I don't get you. This guy has attacked your colleagues and now your girlfriend, and you're still hell-bent on protecting him. When do you get mad?"

David felt his face color with intensity. "I'm mad already. But that's not relevant."

"When do you want revenge?"

"I'm not about revenge. I'm happy to leave that to Jenkins. And Clyde."

"He's escaped. No longer under your care. Why do you still give a shit?"

"I want to deliver him to the authorities safely, as he would have been had I not contributed to his being in this position." David leaned forward, hands resting on the table. "Listen. I'm going to have access to a lot of information. Would you rather I shared it with another law agency?"

Yale circled around and sat opposite David again. "I can't give you a guarantee—now or ever—but I can tell you this: This case has become too much of a media circus for Jenkins to be allowed latitude within it. The Mayor's been cracking the whip. We have pressure coming at us from all angles. Things will go by the book. And if you don't trust my interpretation of the political situation, trust my selfish nature. Shit is not coming down on my ass. Jenkins's sister took it from the wrong end, and that is certainly unfavorable, but I am not having my case fucked up. There was a time when Jenkins might have had an . . . outlet . . . but that time has long passed." He let his hands slap to the table.

He and David regarded each other for what seemed a very long time.

"If a cop shoots Clyde in self-defense, or in defense of some other victim, would that be okay with you?" Yale asked.

The harsh realities of the case hammered David even through his haze of exhaustion. Clyde had whipped the city into a hurricane frenzy. Considering all the forces at work felt like sifting through the aftermath of some natural disaster. Every new bit of information seemed only to increase the burden on David's shoulders.

David weighed Yale's question cautiously. "No. But it would be acceptable."

"What are you offering me?"

"I have access to Clyde's medical records. I'm the only one he's really spoken to, and I believe he's attached to me in some ways that might prove helpful down the line. I can assist you in navigating through the hospital bureaucracy should the necessity arise. Anything new I discover, I give to you."

"I don't want you interfering with our investigation."

"I'll stay out of your way."

Yale settled back in his chair with a sigh. "I'm still gonna treat you like the dirt dog you are in front of my colleagues because I don't want them to know we're dealing."

"*Are* we dealing?"

"Not yet." Yale slid a business card across the table. "This is my pager number. Only talk to me."

"My preference." Still no pact, but it seemed they were making headway. "How did he get into Dr. Trace's apartment?"

"She's listed. There are two Traces in the area, and the other one's not Doctor. The front door of her complex is a simple bar lock, can be picked with half a brain and a tilted credit card. Used a regular pick set on her apartment door. No prints, smudges consistent with latex gloves. SID couldn't even find a partial. We found he dropped a couple extra doctored capsules in her Tylenol bottle, in case she popped a few of those first." Yale chewed his lip, his features softening. "It seems we all underestimated this guy."

CHAPTER 48

DAVID stood at the counter in Medical Records, staring down at Clyde Slade's file. He'd spent about an hour at the station, filling in Yale but withholding the theories he wanted to flesh out more in his own mind. And of course, he'd made no mention of Ed. On the drive home, he'd received a page from Medical Records, informing him Clyde's file had arrived.

Again, the clerk was listening to the Dodgers game, staring at the radio as though that would enhance the experience. He broke off his intent focus to glance at the skimpy file. "Not much there, huh?" he said.

David flipped open the file, revealing a single sheet. The note at the top: *Admitted 8/13/73 for NPI study under Dr. J. P. Connolly.*

A tingling swept across David's body: the feeling of nailing a difficult diagnosis.

August 13. The day of Nancy's attack. Clyde had been admitted for the study twenty-eight years before—to the day. He would have been ten years old. The study was a likely source of his fear of the Neuropsychiatric Institute and of Dash as its representative. Maybe the date had been an unconscious trigger, a precipitating event for Clyde's assaults. Psychologists refer to the phenomenon as the anniversary syndrome—people entering depressions on the anniversaries of the deaths of their loved ones, post-traumatic stress victims feeling their anxiety escalate on the anniversaries of the original trauma.

The study's lead researcher, Dr. J. P. Connolly, had been a world-renowned psychologist. A close friend of David's parents, he had grown somewhat cantankerous in the final years of his life. He'd passed away about a decade ago.

David glanced down the page. The only other note indicated a respiratory infection Clyde had sustained in September of '73—the reason for the file's existence in Medical Records as opposed to the NPI's.

David picked up the phone and reached Dash at the office. He took a few steps away from the counter, lowering his voice, though the desk clerk seemed immersed in the ball game. "Hi, Dash. Did you look for that NPI file I asked you about?"

"Despite my better judgment. Nothing came up under either name."

"I found a peds file for Clyde Slade. Shows he was entered in a study run out of the NPI by Connolly in August of '73."

"That's odd. There's nothing here under Slade—I did a thorough search. Hang on a sec, I'm logged on right now." The sound of keyboard strokes. "Nothing about a Connolly study in August either. Of any kind."

"Why would files be missing?"

"I don't know. Restricted, maybe. Or Connolly could have kept his files at home. He did have funding from a variety of sources."

"But shouldn't there at least be copies at the NPI?"

"Yes. And the journal in which the study was published. But there's nothing."

"All right. Thanks for your help." David hung up, his enthusiasm undercut by the nagging sense of something askew.

⊕

The walkway was as David remembered it as a child, a thin path twisting through gardens to the front door. The gardens themselves, however, were hardly recognizable, so overgrown were they with weeds and patches of sourgrass. The trademark marigolds drooped in limp clusters, baked brown by the heat.

David had not been to the Connollys' house in over twenty-five years. He recalled dark leather furniture, thick carpeting, and the pervasive, comforting smell of a pipe. When he knocked on the front door, a distant, warbling voice sounded from within. "Just a minute, please."

Mrs. Connolly's estimate was overly ambitious; it took her nearly two minutes to get to the door. Clutching a tissue that had been worried to shreds, she gazed up at David. Old and quite frail, she wore a heavy cotton nightgown decorated with flowers. The skin of her arms draped in wrinkled sheets over her bones. "Yes?"

"Hello, I'm David. Janet Spier's son." David realized too late that he'd neglected to mention his father.

"Oh my goodness." The woman's eyes grew watery. Her hand described a fretful arc in the air with the tissue. "David, I haven't seen you since God knows. I just can't believe it. How handsome you are." She reached out and stroked the front of his white coat once, reverently.

"It's good to see you, Mrs. Connolly."

"I remember you used to run around wearing your mother's white coat. It would be down to your shins." A faint, sad grin etched itself on her face. "I was so sorry to hear about her."

"Thank you. My father too."

"Oh dear," Mrs. Connolly said. "Oh dear."

"And I'm sorry about your husband. I don't believe we've spoken since he passed. Dr. Connolly was a great psychologist."

"Yes." Her head bobbed with tiny nods, perhaps a Parkinson's tremor. She stepped back, opening the door. "Please come in. It's been so long since I've had a visitor. What prompted you to stop by?"

"I . . . I actually wanted to know if your husband kept any of his old files and records."

Her face fell with disappointment, and David could have killed himself for it. "Oh, of course. You stopped by on a work matter. You must be awfully busy."

She turned and shuffled slowly back into the musty interior of the house, steadying herself by setting her trembling hands on counters and the backs of chairs.

"My J.P. kept all his files and records. They're in his study, every last one of them, organized by date, color, size. He was very protective about them, but I'm sure he wouldn't mind Janet Spier's son having a look around."

She raised her arm up in the air with a giggle, and David recognized, for the first time, the younger Mrs. Connolly he remembered. He followed her patiently down a long, thickly carpeted hall, gripping her arm gently from behind. She paused before a door. "You'd better open it, dear. It sticks. I'm afraid I don't have the strength anymore."

David found he had to throw a little shoulder into the door to get it open. Dr. Connolly's office sat virtually untouched. A magisterial desk and leather chair, a wall of filing cabinets, rows of meticulously organized medical journals. A thick film of dust covered everything, and the smell of pipe smoke that David recalled still tinged the air.

Mrs. Connolly stood in the doorway for a moment, taking in the room. "I haven't seen the inside of this room in some time." She shook her head once, as if throwing off sad thoughts, and forced a smile. "Take your time, dear," she said. "I'll be in the living room, watching the TV."

David waited to make sure she safely navigated the dark hall, then closed the door and surveyed the room. Dr. Connolly kept his office impeccably organized, and David located the relevant files in the cabinets in no time. *Fear's Legacy—1973.*

He pulled out the two general files and set them on the desk. Swirls of dust lifted from the leather blotter and refused to settle. The abstract sat at the front of the first folder. It was titled FEAR'S LEGACY: SORROW, DISTRESS, AND ANGER.

> Fear arousal can be obtained using several stimuli, including but not limited to: noise; sudden change in illumination; sudden unexpected movement; rapidly approaching objects; height;

strange people; familiar people in strange guises; strange objects and strange places; threatening animals; darkness. Often, two or more of the above items can be combined to achieve a higher degree of fear arousal (i.e., darkness and the noise of a growling dog's rapid approach). When confronted with fear, children respond in three distinct and predictable ways: They grow immobile, or "frozen"; they increase their distance from one type of object (snakes, loud noises, flashes of light); they increase their proximity to another type of object (mother figures).

Twenty-seven boys between the ages of six and ten were selected from foster homes, orphanages, and delinquent holding facilities. Each subject was removed from his "home" for a period of six weeks and taken through a twelve-phase series of fear-arousal experiments, four trials a day, seven days a week, increasing in intensity. Each set of subjects lived together through the six-week trial, barracks-style, so the contagious effects of fear might also be analyzed. All trials occurred within a controlled environment.

Feeling a growing sense of nausea, David paused to rub some dust from his eyes. Dr. Connolly had chosen children without families. That way, there were no parents to complain. No one to notice if the children deteriorated emotionally as a result of the experiments, or developed abnormal attachment patterns. Further, the study evinced bad science. There was no control group—Connolly had selected children who already, in all likelihood, were emotionally fragile. The experiments were biased before they even got off the ground.

Remembering Dr. Connolly's kindly blue eyes and his

well-trimmed white beard, David could not recast him as the perpetrator of these experiments. But his mother had told David cautionary tales about Dr. Connolly, who had deteriorated in his later years beneath the burden of tongue cancer and a rapidly diminishing reputation. He'd become reclusive, holing up in his house. For the last three years of his life, the professional community heard from him only in the form of his letters to psychology and psychiatry journals, angry diatribes decrying the work of more-renowned rivals.

David's mother, he recalled, had gone to great lengths to distance herself from the man. Now he knew why. The study had taken place during his mother's tenure as chief of staff—he was appalled and surprised she had permitted it. When he glanced back at the abstract, he felt the soothing glow of relief. *Results were inconclusive, as the study was terminated on October 15, 1973.* David's mother had, in fact, stopped the experiments. The paper continued:

> However, several of the results are worthy of note, perhaps for incorporation into future studies. We found that once the subjects reached a state of acute distress, they were not easily comforted. In social workshops following the trials, they were permitted to role-play with dolls, interact with nurses, and draw pictures. We noted an increase in hostile behavior following each trial, particularly hostile behavior directed toward the nurses, who carried out the logistics of the experiments and acted as attachment (mother) figures. The subjects seemed to hold the nurses at fault. Those subjects who did not act out their aggression harbored a tremendous amount of latent resentment.

Through each six-week trial period, the subjects tended to develop along one of two distinct routes, either becoming intensely clinging and anxious, or growing increasingly emotionally detached. Those who became detached expressed three central beliefs: (1) The attachment figure would not respond to calls for support and protection, (2) They did not judge themselves to be the sort of person toward whom an attachment figure would respond in caring fashion, and (3) Their actions had no consequences on the external environment.

All three beliefs are reinforced by operant conditioning. As the subjects were rewarded randomly and punished randomly, they came to view themselves as powerless within their environment.

Some intense bonding occurred between subjects during off-hours between trials. When one subject perceived that another could offer comfort or respite from fear, an intense, almost obsessive relationship developed, reminiscent of collective confabulation, the shared fantasy worlds that sometimes develop between castaways and POWs. Through these relationships, the subjects attempted to wrest back some means of control over their lives.

The next few pages had been ripped out. Feeling slightly light-headed, David pushed back in the chair, sending up a miniature cloud of dust, and returned to the filing cabinet. The subsequent alphabetically arranged files were bulky and labeled by name—all males: JOSH ADAMS, TIMOTHY DILLER, FRANK GRANT. David scanned them, his finger coming to rest on the tab reading CLYDE SLADE.

He pulled the file, returned to the desk, and sat staring at it, gathering his courage. Katydids shrilled in the darkness outside the window.

He flipped open the file to reveal a bad Polaroid atop a stack of papers. Clyde, age ten, squinting into a background light. His posture was uncomfortable and defensive—head lowered, shoulders hunched, skinny arms dangling awkwardly at his sides. The points of his shoulders were visible through his threadbare T-shirt. David recognized the dark flat eyes and wide nose, but little else.

The top papers contained Clyde's history, most of which Ed had already told David about. Moved from foster home to orphanage to foster home. Beneath the history were Clyde's clinical results. He had grown increasingly withdrawn throughout the study, the document reported, displaying a fair amount of latent aggression toward the nurses. The experiments had been conducted against Clyde's will; he had begged repeatedly to be left alone, to be permitted to return to his last foster home. His requests were recorded merely as data. He had no parents to lodge more persuasive complaints or to demand that his rights be protected.

The following pages consisted of self-reports, clinical observations, and the results of physiological exams, including a precocious series of skin conductance tests. A few wrinkled drawings remained at the bottom of the stack. Drawn with the fat, simple lines of a coloring book picture, they all featured the same guideline figure: that of a nurse. The nurse's outline was clearly defined, right down to her patronizing smile and white cap. Clyde had used mostly red crayons, turning the simple sketches into gruesome depictions. Vicious slashes colored the nurses' faces, markings pressed so firmly down into the pages they left indentations and even tore the paper in spots. Their heads were covered with layer upon layer of color, until they resembled bloody blurs. Many of the nurses' breasts and genital areas were likewise ravaged with red.

A note at the bottom read: *Particularly fierce and impassioned.* And below that: *Film Reel #23.*

Dread spreading inside him, David looked up and located the dusty old projector in the corner. The cupboard above the filing cabinets seemed to stare back at him. He opened it to find reel upon reel of sixteen millimeter film, labeled in black marker. He found Reel #23. A screen pulled down from the ceiling in front of the window, unleashing more billows of dust. The light switch clicked off loudly, filling the room with shadows.

David blew the top layer of dust from the projector, plugged it in, mounted the take-up reel, and threaded the film. He pulled a chair around beside the projector and, bracing himself, flipped the switch.

Ten-year-old Clyde Slade, brought into a seclusion room with a timer on the wall. He wears a child's hospital gown. A nurse sits in a chair centered in the small room, staring at the wall like a statue. He goes over to her and takes her hand, but she pulls it away, keeping her stoic stare leveled at the far wall. A loud wavering shriek sounds from hidden speakers, so sudden it startles David back in his chair. On the screen, Clyde begins to cry and attempts to pull himself into the nurse's lap. She moves only to repel him, shoving him off. Clyde sits on the floor, hands pushed over his ears, mouth bent wide, his cries not even audible beneath the shrieking. The noise ends. By the timer on the wall, it takes Clyde over three minutes to cease his frantic sobbing.

And then a loud mechanical voice intones, "Three, two, one. Step back from the door." The loud sound of the door's bolt being unlocked, and Clyde scrambles to freedom.

Clyde's ritualistic phrase, his private mantra, was actually the hard-conditioned cue given to him as a child that his fear was about to end. He used it still to alleviate anxiety.

The film cut out and David wiped the sheen of sweat from his forehead. Seconds later, the seclusion room appeared again on the screen, this time with the lights off.

The outline of the nurse in the chair is barely visible. Clyde is led in, though he pounds at the door as soon as it is closed behind him. *"Please! Please!"* He runs to the nurse, who again moves only to push him firmly away. The door opens and another nurse enters with a large rectangular box. She opens it and dumps what appear to be harmless garden snakes on the floor. Clyde shrieks and tries to run away but the snakes quickly spread out through the small seclusion room. The second nurse pushes them toward Clyde.

David closed his eyes for a moment, but Clyde's wails still came. *"Please! I'll be good."* And then: a final terrified strategy— *"I'm sorry. I'm sorry."*

When David viewed the screen again, his mouth was dry and sour. Clyde turns to the wall, burying his face in the corner as the snakes curl around his feet. He murmurs to himself, something inaudible, though David knew he was counting down from three over and over, anticipating. Finally, the second nurse collects the snakes and the mechanical voice sounds, "Three, two, one. Step back from the door." Clyde sprints for freedom.

At the beginning of the next trial, Clyde crosses immediately to the seated nurse and bites her leg. She rises and administers him a quick but vicious spanking before returning to her stonelike perch on the chair. When a series of blinding lights begin to flash in the white room, a wet spot spreads down the leg of Clyde's trousers.

Trial after trial followed on the reel of film. Experiments with animals, with people in threatening poses, with motorized contraptions that sprang open like jack-in-the-boxes, but with no warning. By the final trial, Clyde had resorted to sitting against the far wall, face blank and dazed. He made no attempt to approach the seated nurse. They brought in a snarling German shepherd on a chain and held it inches from Clyde's face. Clyde seemed hardly to notice it. The scene cut out and the end of the film flapped in the reel.

As the reel continued its mindless rotation, David sat in the darkness of the study, breathing dust. A long vacant block of time passed as the film slapped the reel and the katydids chirped. Finally, David peeled himself from the leather chair and clicked the lamp on the desk. With the quiet, precise movements of a priest, he put away the projector and the screen. He jotted down the names of the subjects and their dates of birth. Clyde's file, the general files, and a few reels of film he took with him.

The rest of the house was dark and smelled of mothballs and fragranced powder. Mrs. Connolly had fallen asleep in the living room, a quilted blanket at her side. *Dr. Quinn Medicine Woman* flickered across the TV screen, muted. David crossed silently and pulled the blanket up around her. She stirred as he reached the door.

Her voice was gentle, and it warbled slightly. "David?"

"Yes, Mrs. Connolly?"

"Did you find what you needed?"

"I did."

She smiled, though sadness found its way even into that. "We always appreciated what your mother did for us."

A quick flare of unease. "What do you mean by that?"

Her eyes gathered an acuity he had not before noticed. It quickly faded. David wondered for the first time if her usual demeanor was an affectation.

"He was a good man, wasn't he? My J.P.?"

David felt a slight tingling in his face at her avoidance of the question. "Yes, he was."

He closed the front door gently, leaving her to fall back into sleep.

CHAPTER 49

THE nameplate on Sandy's door, like Sandy, was bold and straightforward. It read simply: EVANS. CHIEF OF STAFF. No first name, no appended M.D.

Though it was late and the halls had fallen quiet, light shone from beneath Sandy's door. An informal pool among members of the Board rode on how many consecutive nights she'd work past 10 P.M.

David knocked, and she called out for him to enter. She was sitting at the end of the long conference table at which she liked to work; her desk sat empty and untouched at the other end of the office. Her face lit with the glow of a green-shaded banker's lamp, she pored over papers. She looked up at David and smiled. He was one of the few people at whose entrance she smiled. He was aware of this and made uneasy by how much it flattered him.

"David, what's this I hear about you nosing around the hospital?"

"I've been following the trail a bit."

"Make sure you don't follow it too far away from the ER. There is a division to be run. You could also stand not to ruffle any more feathers."

He ignored her remark and his resultant irritation, not

wanting to be sidetracked. "Dr. J. P. Connolly did a fear study in 1973 at the NPI. Are you familiar with it?"

Sandy pulled off her glasses and set them neatly on a stack of files. "Yes. I am."

"The NPI has no records of it. None at all. I tracked it down at Dr. Connolly's house. Pretty grim."

"It wasn't unusual for the time, David. You'd be surprised."

"Then why did my mother terminate it?"

Sandy averted her eyes, just for a moment, but it was such an uncharacteristic motion that David noticed it. "If memory serves, the science was sloppy from the get-go."

"Your memory serves well. Particularly for a study that took place thirty years ago."

Her green eyes gleamed cold and marblelike. She tapped her forehead. "Like a steel trap."

"It had some interesting methodology too, wouldn't you say?"

"Just because you and I now look at a study like that with disdain, you'd better remember it was not such a marked departure from the standard of the day. It may be hard to believe, but that's how many experiments were back then. I'm not kidding. Go back. Take a look at fear and separation studies from the late '60s, early '70s."

"Are you aware that Clyde Slade was a participant in that study?"

Sandy flushed, shocked. It was astounding how quickly she regained her composure. "I was not."

"I think something else happened. Something to do with the study. There were pages ripped out of Connolly's files. I think the hospital removed the copies from the NPI and expurgated the files I found at Connolly's. I think if you wanted to, you could talk to some people and figure out a way for me to see what's missing."

Sandy's lips pursed—they were just beginning to texture with wrinkles. "Seems you're out of your bailiwick here, Doctor."

"There are lives at stake."

"How do you know that whatever information is or isn't missing from those files is at all relevant?"

"I don't. But if it is, and you withhold it, think about what that means."

"Ah. A directive." Sandy's cheeks drew up in a half squint. "Don't pry too deep, David. You might not like what you find."

"In light of what we're dealing with here, I'll handle it." He paused by the door, tapping it with his fist once in a soft knock. "I'll check in with you tomorrow."

Sandy had already gone back to her papers. "I know where to find you, David," she said. "Should I want to."

For the tail end of her recovery, Diane had been moved to the VIP section of the prestigious ninth floor. She'd be ready to be released the day after tomorrow; her doctors thought it wise for her to remain on site so her eyedrops could be applied regularly and Silvadene spread over her wounds.

The elevator doors clanged open, and David stepped into the clean tiled hall. The door to Diane's room was ajar. David entered and closed it gently behind him.

Diane gazed through bleary eyes at the small clock on the wall. "Eleven o'clock, huh?"

"It's ten."

"Oh. Either way, you look exhausted. Go home and get some sleep."

He felt a pull toward the door—a necessity to pursue, to investigate, to undo—but he could not move. Diane's face was shiny with antibiotic creme and, inexplicably, even more beautiful for its scars. They seemed to highlight her elegance, like the black spots on the water-smooth red wings of a ladybug. "I wanted to see you."

"You saw me yesterday."

She looked down, picking at a thumbnail. The swelling on her face had begun to weep. She patted her blisters with a square of gauze. David looked in the trash can beside the bed; it was full of soiled gauze pads. She'd spent all day sitting up here, mostly alone, trying to staunch the fluids leaking from her face.

It took him a moment to find his voice to continue. "I wanted to see you again."

"Don't you dare. Don't you dare feel sorry for me." She raised the heel of her hand to her eyes but couldn't touch her face. He knew her tears were burning her. "Goddamn it," she said softly. "Goddamn it."

He crossed to her and sat on the bed. She found his hand and squeezed it so tight he could feel his wedding band digging into his other fingers. Carefully, he brushed the hair off her forehead, sweeping it back from her face. He took the stained gauze from her trembling hand, threw it out, and pulled a fresh pad from the box on the bedside tray.

He dabbed at the blistering on her right cheek, her forehead, around the socket of her right eye. Her hands went limp in her lap as she let him work, wincing from time to time. He shifted on the bed, moving closer to her. Her left cheek and chin were unmarred, the curved bow of her lips perfectly smooth. He moistened a clean square of gauze with some saline and swept it along the elegant line of her jaw, cleaning her.

Her breathing was sharp and shallow. Through the swelling around her eye, her iris shone, ice-green and pristine. She turned, a sudden shy movement, and her lips were against his, impossibly soft. He felt the gentle suck of her breath in his mouth and the room seemed to swirl around him, smelling of disinfectant, Silvadene, and a distant trace of her perfume. She cringed against the pain of her face moving against his. He started to pull back but she moved her face forward to keep it pressed against his, kissing him still as the salt tears burnt tracks down her wounded cheek.

CHAPTER 50

CLYDE had been taking the pills more and more, but they didn't do what the book promised they'd do. He stayed in bed mostly, rising to drink and piss and reheat beans in a dirty pot. He'd stopped feeding the cat. He took to urinating in jars again and carefully labeling each jar with the time and date.

The ancient Zenith TV in the corner got terrible reception. Now and then, if he angled the antenna just right, he could get the audio on a porn channel, though static still blotted the screen.

He gathered his dirty sheets in a ball between his legs and sat in bed, looking out the window and fishing pickle after soggy pickle from a wide jar. When he finished his sloppy crunching, he tilted back the jar and drank the sour, green-tinged juice. The juice left his lips stained a fishy gray, as it had his left hand to the wrist.

Leaning the mirror against the base of his bed so he could see his reflection, he smiled at himself and practiced talking. He spoke gently and softly, reaching out to touch his water-spotted reflection. Sometimes his voice was drowned out by grunts and groans from the TV.

At night, a few girls walked past the window, their giggles carrying into his dirty apartment, and he looked around, pupils jerking, as if seeing the room for the first time. The mounds of dirty clothes, the halved capsules piled on the pocked wooden table, the grease splatter up the kitchen wall above the stove.

He cried for a little bit without gasps, just a slow leaking of his eyes, then rose and stood in the middle of the room in his white underwear. He pulled on some loose scrub bottoms and his yellowed Adidas sneakers. Hunting around, he found an old button-up shirt under the bed. He pulled it out and shook it to rid it of cat hair. Laying it on the bed, he flattened it as best he could with a swollen hand.

He pulled it on and looked at himself in the mirror. He fixed the collar, twisting it back into place. He practiced a smile, then murmured a greeting to himself. In the kitchen, a jar atop the refrigerator was filled with change. He poured it on the floor and counted the few silver coins out of the wash of copper.

When he left the apartment, he made sure to turn all three deadbolts.

The bar at the corner had tinted windows and a torn green awning. He shuffled inside, eyes on the ground, and climbed onto a bar stool with considerable effort. He rested his hands on the bar, but then looked down at them—swollen with pitted nails—and put them in his lap.

The bartender, an older lady with wrinkles and blush, slid a rag up the counter. "What'll it be?"

He lowered his eyes, his hand clutching the ball of quarters in his pocket. "Water," he said. "Two waters."

She made a disappointed clucking noise. "We're not a welfare office. You don't order something soon, we'll ask you to leave."

A blush bloomed beneath his pocked cheeks. His button-up shirt clung to his body, dotted with sweat. "Sorry," he said. "I'm just thirsty. So thirsty."

"Then buy a goddamned beer," she muttered, as she filled two glasses with water from the tap.

An attractive blonde sat on the stool two over from him, turned toward a girlfriend. The water glasses banging down on the bar in front of him nearly startled him off his stool.

The bartender looked regretful when she saw his expression. "Look, I'm sorry. You can take some time and finish those up before you go." She moved down the bar to serve other customers.

He sat alone in his little bubble—a man on a bar stool at a bar—breathing heavily, murmuring to himself, counting down from three.

He drained one glass of water, then the other.

His thumbnail was so severely pitted it had begun to flake. The skin beneath it had reddened, like an enormous hangnail. He worried it with his teeth for a moment, head angled down, and chanced a look at the blonde to his left.

She turned with a jangle of bracelets, mouth open in a bark of a laugh from her girlfriend's joke, and then she spotted him.

Her face changed. The light in her eyes vanished. Her lips drew together and curled in disgust, distorting her nose.

Her eyes said: You do not have a right to view me.

They said: You are something soiled and rotting.

They said: You are not fit to mate.

He looked quickly back down at the bar, hand rising to his head to block his eyes from hers. He felt a clump of hair give under his soft fingertips and drift down, landing on his shoulder.

"Disgusting," she said.

A strong hand on his back. A male voice. "Hello, ladies,

is this guy bothering you? Are you bothering these women, pal? Whew, how 'bout you go take a walk through a car wash?"

Laughter.

"What's the matter, you don't answer when someone asks you a question?"

Clyde's lips moved, but no sound came out. They mouthed: *Sorry. I'm sorry.*

He stood, sensing the large male presence, and stumbled toward the door, uneven on his feet.

"Drunk fool," the blonde said.

As he reached the door, he heard the male introducing himself to the two women.

Leaning on lightposts and mailboxes, he made his way to the Healton's Drugstore about a block and a half from his apartment. The large white sign with blue Gothic lettering glowed into the night. It was something of a neighborhood beacon; when sitting in his bed, Clyde could see it through his window.

He couldn't afford a carton of cigarettes, so he bought a pack, counting out the coins on the counter before a frustrated worker. The chiming bells on the closing door seemed inordinately loud.

He walked back to the bar and stared at the people inside, barely discernable through the dark window. A few weeks ago, he would have endured such a rejection, dissolved it in the blackness inside him. But not anymore. Now he made sure that someone answered to him. Answered with their own pain. Their own fear.

He wandered away from the dark window, his lips moving to keep up with the rush of thoughts through his head. He found himself before the two-story house for retarded adults. The house that was no longer his own.

He moistened his thick lips and whistled a few beckoning notes.

Some time later, he found himself within the protective shell of the scorched Chevy, sitting on the brittle and lumpy newspapers that composed the driver's seat. He watched the house ahead, waiting for the nighttime signs of life, waiting for her to come downstairs and discover what he'd done.

He smoked the pack straight through, two cigarettes at a time.

The light went on in the room upstairs. A wait. The back door opened and she appeared. Same bunny jumpsuit, same messy ponytail positioned too high on her head.

He rocked slightly in the car, his hands gripping segments of the broken steering wheel. When he looked to the side, his pupils beat once, twice, unable to hold in place.

With a whooshing whistle, she stepped down off the porch, activating the motion-sensor lamp. Her hands fluttered up to her face as she gasped, her eyes widening until he could see the whites even through the spiderweb crack in the windshield.

The scraggly dog lay on its side in the tall weeds of the yard, its head bent back across the neck, broken. A trickle of blood ran from a wound at the base of its throat, where a jagged bone had punctured the flesh.

Her mouth bent wide, wavering. She sank to her knees.

He drank her tears.

He got out from the Chevy, slamming the car door behind him. She kept her gaze on the dead lump of fur, even as he walked toward her drunkenly.

Her hand trembled as she reached for the dog. She began to pet the coarse hair covering its ribs, her hand moving soothingly while her breath came in sharp gasps.

He stood over her, tall and powerful, the lamp casting

his shadow across her face. She cowered in her bunny sweatsuit, but at last looked up at him, cringing. She smelled of tuna. Sounds came from within the house—an inner door closing hard, then the rapid beat of footsteps.

He fled, his feet dragging through weeds and broken bottles, leaving behind the light and the people. His breath came in animal grunts, sounds of exertion or of sobbing. He turned to squeeze his wide body through a missing slat in the wooden fence at the yard's edge and then he staggered toward home, his face flushed a deep red, almost matching the splatter of dog blood across his button-up shirt.

CHAPTER 51

THE ER bustled. Broken legs, hemorrhaging wounds, a Rorschach blot of vomit on the tiled floor of Exam Seven. Don had been called in to provide double coverage in the rush, and he and David spun from room to room, pushed, prodded, and pulled by residents and nurses. David didn't have time to check on Security, but he knew they were working double-time outside, fending off the almost constant influx of media. The flurry of press surrounding the hospital over the past week made him feel increasingly claustrophobic.

At one point, David had tried to go up to see Diane, but he'd been pulled into a food poisoning case by an anxious medicine intern. It was already past lunch, and neither he nor Don had had a moment to sit down. A college kid who'd been in a motorcycle accident came in DOA, and Don was walking a medical student through the gestures with the defibrillator.

Stepping on a pedal to turn on the sink, David rinsed his hands and shook them dry before sliding on another pair of gloves and stepping back into the hall. He pivoted quickly, dodging a cooler that a smiling orderly wheeled past him from the ambulance bay—probably a heart on ice. When he stuck his head in the CWA, he saw the board was filled, a Magic Marker tribute to bad doctor scrawl.

"Someone call the blood bank and get a few units on the way for Jefferson in Fifteen Two," he said to a passing nurse. "Where's Carson? Has anyone seen Carson? Someone call him and get him in here. And get urology on the phone again—they're dragging their feet on Kinney in Four because he's MediCal." He glanced down Hallway One and saw, through the small windows atop the swinging doors, Don speaking to a man in his forties. Don held a hot dog in one hand and was chewing between words; the man's face was lowered and he held his head, as if in great pain. It took a moment for David to put it together—the man was the father of the student who'd died in the motorcycle wreck, and Don had just informed him of his son's death. While eating a hot dog.

His temper flaring, David stormed down the hall. He forced himself to calm down, knowing that it would make matters worse for the father if he made a scene. Instinctively, David thought to grab Diane to see to the father, before remembering why she wasn't working.

Don was finishing as David approached. "So, again, I'm really sorry to have to bring you this news."

David struggled to keep his rage from finding its way into his voice. "Dr. Lambert, would you mind if I had a word?"

"Not at all." Don gave the man's elbow a cursory squeeze before following David back into Exam Fourteen.

David closed the door and took a moment to get his breathing under control while Don watched expectantly, hot dog in hand.

"Do you think, Dr. Lambert, that you could refrain from eating while informing people of deaths in their families?"

Don popped the end of the hot dog in his mouth. "Sure. Whatever."

"This is not a *whatever* issue. I know you do this every day, but he doesn't." David jabbed an angry finger in the direction of the father outside.

"Oh come on. Look, Dave—"

"David will do just fine."

"Let's not make a big deal out of this. I've been on my feet all day. If I'm hungry and cranky, that doesn't help anyone, least of all my patients."

"So eat in the doctors' lounge."

"I would, but I haven't had time to get back there."

Someone rapped on the door. "Be there in a minute!" David said. He turned back to Don. "Then wait to eat, or if the agony is too much for you to bear, come get me, and I'll take care of dealing with the family members."

"That man just lost his son. Do you really think my not eating a hot dog is going to make things easier for him? I doubt he even noticed." He crossed his arms. "Look, you brought a bunch of shit down on yourself lately. The press is beating you up. The board's on your ass. Don't take it out on me. This is preposterous."

"No, Don. It's shitty care."

"You are *always* on my ass. What are you worried about? Do you think if I'm gone for an extra ten minutes, or I'm eating a hot dog, that someone's gonna sue your precious department?" He shook his head. "Well, rest assured. Everything I do can hold up in a court of law."

"Since when is that the gauge by which we judge our level of treatment?"

Don did not respond. On his way out, David grabbed a roll of gauze from the counter and tossed it at him. "You have mustard on your lip," he said.

He found the man sitting stunned in a chair in the lobby, people bustling around him in all directions. His face had reddened and he was breathing hard, as though fighting down a panic attack.

David crouched and looked up into his face. "Mr. Henderson? Robert Henderson?"

The man's eyes flickered, but there was no look of recognition in his face.

"Why don't you come back with me for a minute?" David said. "We can find a private room."

With a hand in the small of Henderson's back, David guided him back to Fourteen. The sleeves of Henderson's yellow Carhartt jacket extended down over hard, calloused hands. A white outline, the shape of a tin of tobacco dip, had been worn into the back pocket of his jeans.

Henderson sat on the bed, paper crinkling beneath his legs. He turned his hands over before his eyes, as if checking to see if they were real. His face, slightly sunburned, was wrinkled beyond its years from hours spent working outside. His face quivered, as though he were about to cry, then stiffened again. David sensed that Henderson did not cry very often.

David slowly became aware of his own discomfort in the face of Henderson's suffering. He was inadequate at this—the comforting. As a diagnostician, as a technician, as a scientist, he was exceptional, but in this department he was lacking. There was nothing for him to *do*—no action to take, no medicine to administer, no test to run. If these past few days had driven anything home, it was the fact that people suffer from events beyond their control. Often, they make all the right choices and suffer anyway. Again, he found himself wishing Diane were here to console Henderson.

"Kevin was gonna be the first one on my side of the family to graduate college," the father said. "Was making good grades too. His mom's been working double shifts to help pay. I been trying too—to work steady. He was a good kid. A good fucking kid." He swiped angrily at a tear with his cuff. "Don't know how I'm gonna tell his mom."

"Do you live with her?" David asked.

Henderson shook his head. "She's up in Seattle. Remarried."

"Would you like me to call?"

Henderson shook his head. "I should do it." He sighed, puffing out his cheeks. "You have kids?"

"No."

"Well, if you do, have mean ones. Good kids, good kids are the ones that die. You get a fuckup like me, I'm gonna live forever." He lowered his eyes into the fork of his thumb and index finger. "That kid was the best thing I ever did in my life. I hope I told him. I hope I told him enough."

David sat quietly, uncomfortably. "I don't know a single person who gets everything said to those they love. It sounds like you said so much more than most of us do." His pager went off—a text message to pick up a package at Sandy's office—and he felt a quick flare of necessity. His desire to leave Henderson to jump back on Clyde's trail shamed him. He turned off the pager and sat with Henderson for a few minutes, glad he had chosen to remain.

"You have to go?" Henderson asked.

"No."

Henderson lowered his shoulders, his hands twitching on his knees. Receptive. Needing. He looked up at David, his face starting to come apart. "Can I?"

David moved over and embraced him, and Henderson keened openly for a while. It took him a few moments to raise his head again, then David sat by his side, the stain of Henderson's tears drying on the front of his coat. The two men stared at the wall.

"Me and my old man, we never talked much. All growing up, we never talked about anything, like . . . you know. He was a man's man. When I got divorced, I was hurting, you know, something awful. Peggy's a great gal—she just finally figured out what she deserved, I guess. But when she left me, I decided I wasn't gonna fuck around no more. I was gonna tell people how I . . . you know, how I felt. So I took a whole weekend and wrote a letter to my father. Told him how much I . . . how much I loved him, what he meant to me, all that stuff. I wrote it and rewrote it and rewrote it. Spent the whole goddamn weekend at the kitchen table. And finally I finished it—eight pages—and I went over there and gave it to him. He read it, right there with me standing there watching him, then he handed it back to me and you know what he said?"

David shook his head.

" 'Nice letter.' " Henderson laughed, a genuine laugh. " 'Nice letter.' " Grief washed through his eyes again. "I hope I told my boy enough," he said.

CHAPTER 52

THE humble room that served as the chapel barely fit ten chairs. A stained-glass window lit the front, and bad paintings of clouds decorated the walls. English and Spanish copies of the New Testament leaned from a small box adhered to the wall.

David sat on a chair in the middle row, one foot perched on the genuflecting pad before him, the occasional sound of a rolling gurney audible in the hall outside. The manila envelope he'd picked up moments before from Sandy's assistant sat in his lap, unopened. Sandy had written on it: *David—the enclosed is all public record.* Covering her ass, as always.

Henderson's open weeping had unsettled him, and he stared at the tacky chapel walls, thinking of the ways he'd weathered his own losses. An image came, whitewashed and ethereal. Elisabeth blow-drying her hair, naked so she wouldn't overheat, her dress draped across the bathroom counter. She'd caught him looking, smiled around the comb she held between her teeth, and closed the door with a foot. The aching reached a place inside him it had not in months, and he wondered which intimacies had allowed it its inroads. He thought about lying beside his wife, feeling her warmth along the full length of his body. They used to sleep forehead to forehead sometimes, curled beneath the sheets. Through a brief chink in his scientist's armor, David caught himself wondering if we go anywhere when we pass, and if so, what things we miss the most.

He wondered if he would ever allow himself to know someone so intimately again. He wondered why it took a smattering of alkali to eat through the monotony of his life and reveal it for what it was.

He opened the manila envelope and pulled out the two pieces of paper it contained. The first was a photocopy of a newspaper article.

PSYCH STUDY TERMINATED AFTER RESULTANT AGGRESSION IN CHILDREN

A psychology study at UCLA's prestigious Neuropsychiatric Institute was terminated after several alarming incidents involving its subjects. Chief Investigator J. P. Connolly was not available for comment, but NPI Chief of Staff Dr. Janet Spier described the study's focus as "examining children's responses to stimuli, that parents and educators can better create healthy, supportive environments, and avoid unhealthy ones."

David felt a growing sickness. Mrs. Connolly's comment—*We always appreciated what your mother did for us*—had snagged on a raised suspicion in his mind. He scanned farther down the article, looking for information betraying the extent of his mother's involvement in what was quickly betraying itself as a cover-up.

The problems arose when the first set of subjects were released from the study and returned to their homes. Several of the boys were observed by foster parents to be more aggressive, disrupting the home environments with persistent fighting and temper tantrums. After one boy broke a foster sibling's nose, his "mother" phoned the Chief Investigator and lodged a formal complaint. "We shut the study down immediately," Spier said. "While we stand behind its meritorious and conscientious nature, we also recognize that certain minor problems have resulted in assimilating the subjects back into their social environments, so we decided to halt and recalibrate."

The study, which was to run for three months, was shut down after nine weeks.

The other piece of paper was a photocopy of a check for $40,000, signed by the UCLA Medical Center's treasurer. Dated two days previous to the article, it was made out to Happy Horizons Foster Home. Clearly, some aspect of the study had gone terribly awry—something worse than a broken nose—if the foster home owners were being paid off so grandly.

David's nausea reached a room-jarring pitch as he contemplated his mother's involvement in such a matter. It was probably she who had ordered the files cleared from the hospital, wanting to leave behind no paper trail. His head buzzed with shock. The full force of epiphany would come later, he knew; this was only the tug of the retreating surf, drawing back and back and back.

The foster home's address, listed on the check stub, was *1711 Pearson Rd.* The same as Douglas DaVella's.

David slid the papers back in the envelope and sat quietly, trying to untangle the implications of what he'd just read. He breathed slowly and evenly, taking advantage of the surprisingly effective surroundings of the chapel.

David's earliest memory was of visiting his father at the hospital. He'd followed him around the entire day, tugging at the edge of the white coat. When he'd gotten bored, his father had inflated a latex glove and drawn a face on it for him. He couldn't remember how old he'd been, but when he'd walked by his father's side, he'd only come up to his hip. His father had rested his hand on his shoulder, as he always did.

A nurse had stopped his father, flipping some pages on a clipboard and needing advice. A bad trauma had come in—a motorcycle crash—and the body approached them on a gurney. David had made out only the gruesome red mess of the face before his father's hand rose from his shoulder and shielded his eyes, cool, protective, and rough from overwashing, pulling his face in tight to his white coat, never missing a beat in his conversation with the nurse.

He wracked his brain to recall an equally warm memory he had of his mother but found none. He remembered only briefer, colder images—how she wouldn't meet his eyes when he'd had chicken pox, as though something about his weakened state shamed her; the way his palms had sweat when he'd called to tell her about his low mark in embryology; how she wouldn't address Elisabeth at the dinner table when she broached medical topics.

Still, he was horrified by her complicity in covering up the study. And she was not alive for him to confront, question, or accuse. He'd always held her medical code of honor to be impeccable. That she'd been cold and withholding in her personal life, and a sharp-edged politician, had always seemed separate from that somehow. He should have known that in a field as absorbing as medicine the lines would eventually blur.

The bedrock had shifted beneath his feet. David had no choice but to desert it and seek more solid ground, to accept the injustices of the past and work at redeeming the present.

The door opened and someone sat in the chair beside him. He gradually came to realize it was Diane. He looked over. Her face was wrapped loosely in gauze. "*I am not an animal,"* she joked in a creaky voice. *"I am a woman."*

"You shouldn't cover your wounds," he said, his voice tired and flat.

"I know," she said. "But I don't want to scare the patients."

"You are a patient."

"Oh," Diane said. "Oh yeah." She put her feet up on her chair and hugged her knees to her chest. "What are you doing in here? You're a Jew. And an atheist."

"How'd you find me?"

"Jill said she saw you duck inside."

"How are you feeling?"

"I feel pretty. Oh so pretty. It's a pity how pretty I feel." Diane's monotone matched David's pretty well. "They let me out of my cage, at least. Said I should be ready to go home tomorrow." She pointed to the manila folder in David's lap. "More notes from the underground?"

He told her briefly about Connolly's study, then handed her the folder. She read it slowly, then set it down. She didn't say anything for a few minutes as they stared at the tiny stained-glass window ahead. David realized it depicted a tree. A man came in and uttered a few prayers, his lips moving soundlessly. He departed quickly afterward.

Diane patted the bandage gently over her cheek, as if trying to alleviate an itch. "This keeps getting messier."

"It's just that with the attacks, the cops, bullshit hospital politics, the media all over me . . ." He rubbed his eyes. "It's all been wearing on me enough. And now to learn my mother bears some responsibility for these assaults . . ."

Diane's eyes sharpened. "From what do you draw that conclusion?"

"The experiments took place under her tenure."

"It sounds like she stopped them when she caught

wind. You know damn well that the NPI chief of staff can't oversee every study run over there."

"She covered up the experiments that created him."

"*Helped* create him, David. Only helped. There were twenty-seven other kids in that study. None of them are throwing alkali."

"If you'd seen those films—"

"They sound awful. I'm just saying you can't shoulder this one too. Your trying to is an act of arrogance. A lot of psych studies were questionable before the Ethics Board tightened up. And besides, who's to say that your mother or even those experiments have any specific culpability? Nature versus nurture. Causation versus correlation. Genes versus environment. You're wading into some pretty murky philosophical waters."

"My mother taught me a lot of things," David finally said. "Probably more than anyone else. She was as tough as they come, tough to the point of being obdurate and unfeeling."

"That toughness also gave her her career in an age when women didn't have careers like hers," Diane said. "People's best traits are often also their worst. That's true for most of us."

"But you have to own up," David said. "You're permitted to stumble as long as you rectify. She never did. That study was wrong. There's no way around it. *It was wrong*. And she knew it. She covered it up."

"Well, you hardly have time to mope about that *now*."

He wiped his hands on his scrub top, and they left a sweat stain. "What am I supposed to do?"

"Go check out that address, for one thing. You have double coverage today—you can probably sneak out a bit early."

David nodded. "Happy Horizons. Sounds like a '50s retirement facility."

"Are you keeping the cops at bay?"

"For the time being."

"Clyde has clearly been exacting revenge for being run through those experiments. You need to get a better handle on what, specifically, he's after."

"The million-dollar question is: Then what?"

They studied the stained-glass tree, sorting their respective thoughts.

Diane touched her good cheek with her fingers. "If you were the kind of man who strictly wanted to see him punished, there would be an easy solution."

They looked at the tree a few moments longer.

"But then I probably wouldn't love you," she said.

CHAPTER 53

WHEN David stepped on the decrepit front porch, it sagged as though about to give way. The address on the side wall, composed of rusting numerals, read 17 1, the middle 1 having fallen off. The placard by the doorbell read PEARSON HOME FOR THE DEVELOPMENTALLY DISABLED. The adjacent lot stood desolate and empty, save for a heap of trash and a burnt-out old car up on blocks that looked somehow haunted in the twilight.

A woman in a ratty sweatshirt opened the door, pinning the screen with her knee. She wore her hair in a high ponytail, a young style for someone who looked to be in her late thirties. Behind her, an overweight man with Down's syndrome sat cross-legged on the floor, folding and refolding a section of newspaper. "Can I help you?"

"Hello, I'm David Spier—I'm a doctor at UCLA. A man named Douglas DaVella used to live here. I was hoping you could put me in touch with someone who knew him."

"Oh sure. Doug was my dad, kind of. He passed on a few years back. He and his wife, Sue, used to run a foster home here. That's where I grew up." She smiled proudly. "I started working here after high school, and we switched the place to a retarded home in '86—more money available for that kind of stuff, you know."

"How do you mean?"

"The government subsidizes it when you take in kids, or people with disabilities. Not a ton of money in it, but it's a living. And you get to, you know, help people."

The man on the floor behind her made an incomprehensible noise.

"Okay, sweetie." She walked over and handed him a new section of newspaper, which he began assiduously folding. She smiled at David self-consciously. "He's a handful sometimes, but it's twenty-five hundred a month."

"That seems like a good arrangement," David said. "Did you live here in 1973?"

"Yup. I was . . ." Her head tilted back, her tongue poking at her lip. "Nine."

"Do you remember an incident that year involving a study run at the Neuropsychiatric Institute?"

"Yeah. But we weren't supposed to talk about it. Still aren't, I suppose. But you're from the hospital, didn't you say? I guess you know already."

"Pretty much," he lied. "I just wanted to talk to someone to flesh out the details."

"Would you mind if I took a look at your ID?" She

smiled ingratiatingly. "I'm sorry; we do get all kinds through here."

"No problem." David pulled his UCLA badge from his pocket, and she examined it before stepping back from the door.

"Why don't you come in? Keep your voice down, though. It's quiet time. Except for those who did the most extra chores last week. Isn't that right, Tommy?" She ruffled Tommy's hair, but he remained fixated on the newspaper.

David sat on a plush maroon chesterfield. The house smelled strongly of cooked vegetables and ammonia. The mantel was decorated with well-dusted porcelain figurines and a collection of Jesus plates. "I'm Rhonda Decker, by the way."

"Nice to meet you, Rhonda. Thanks for inviting me in."

Tommy rose and walked into an adjoining bathroom, and David and Rhonda pretended not to hear him urinating.

"When the study started, Doug didn't think much of it. They paid good—a grand a kid, I think—and he never dreamed they'd do anything harmful to any of them. Two kids went off and did the study. Frank Grant and Clyde something. It was an awful, awful thing. That's a vulnerable age, especially for kids like us. If they wanted to study fear in kids, they could have asked just about any one of us about it and we could have answered. We didn't need snakes and lights and stuff to scare us. Not us."

"Did Frank and Clyde have problems when they got back?"

"Frank wasn't back for long. He got moved somewhere else, down to San Diego or Oceanside or something. But the other kid, he did some awful stuff."

"Like what?"

Tommy returned and stood beside David. He rubbed the top of David's head, and David took his hand and held it, mostly because he wasn't sure what else to do with it. Rhonda stood and handed Tommy the Business section, and he sat and happily resumed his folding.

"That's what we weren't supposed to talk about. They gave some money, so we wouldn't talk to the press, or other foster homes that were involved in the study. They didn't want to admit anything to the others, you know. Liability and stuff. I guess I can understand."

"I'm a representative of the hospital, so that arrangement doesn't apply to me." The limits and conditions of David's honesty, he was discovering, were different from what he'd have hypothesized during a calmer week.

Rhonda took a deep breath. "The other kid, Clyde, he used to wake up the younger kids in the middle of the night and, well, sort of torture them. Doug had no idea this was going on. Not until later. Doug was a good parent to us."

It seemed that, despite the fact that DaVella had rented him out to the hospital, Clyde still felt a certain attachment to him. It was, after all, DaVella's name he had chosen to steal. "How would Clyde torture them?"

"Well, there's an upstairs room with exposed rafters. We had three kids in there, five to sevens. Clyde used to string rope over the rafters and make a noose, then dangle the kids just above the ground, so their tiptoes could barely reach. He'd sit there, holding the other end, watching them struggle. The thing that was most awful was, the other two kids had to watch. He'd rotate them, one a night. They were showing up all exhausted at breakfast, none of them sleeping at all, waiting up scared all night. Imagine that, lying in the dark, trying to sleep, but knowing what's coming. . . . It must have been terrifying."

Clyde's own reversal of the experiments. Inflicting fear on others. Empowering himself. He'd certainly succeeded with his alkali assaults at the hospital. Not just by frightening the women he'd attacked, but in creating an environment of intense alarm and anxiety all through the Med Center. The same hospital that had once victimized him the same way.

Rhonda shook her head, her eyes clouding. "None of them would tell, either. Scared, I guess. Doug noticed red marks around one kid's neck but thought it was from wrestling. And then Jim Kipper died. Clyde dangled him too long and he just . . . died. Doug heard the body hit when Clyde relaxed the rope. Ran in there. The two other kids were crying. Clyde was in shock."

"What did he say?"

Her cheek twitched below her right eye. "He said he was just trying to scare him."

The same thing he'd told the cops about why he'd flashed the hooker. David tried not to let his emotions show in his face. It had been the Med Center that had expunged Clyde's juvenile record, in order to protect the cover-up from future investigations. And the Med Center had paid off DaVella specifically not to alert the other foster parents, so it wouldn't be opened up to paying other settlements. They'd taken kids already terrified of the world and their place in it, and turned up the volume of their fear, yielding remarkable results for the study. Then they'd released these kids back into society, traumatized and angry, and taken no steps to ensure their safety or the safety of those around them.

And David's mother had helped cover it up, providing spin control. His emotions, loose and searing, were of little use right now. He tried to refocus.

"They took him off to a youth detention center," Rhonda was saying. "You know how that goes. Vicious cycle picks up speed."

"Have you noticed anything strange around the house lately?"

"Oh, you know. Bad part of town, so the usual. Spray paint. Mail rifled through from time to time. Someone killed a dog out in our lot last night, but the cops thought it was a cult thing."

"Last night? Who found it?"

"One of my girls. Layla. Like from the Clapton song."

"Can I talk to her?"

"I think she's napping, but I guess I could wake her up."

David followed Rhonda up the stairs and into a cozy room, almost a large garret. A crude but charming rainbow was rendered in paint on the far wall. A child's desk sat in the corner, beside a single bureau. A retarded woman lay on her bed, facedown, wearing a dirty pink jumpsuit, snoring delicately. Rhonda sat beside her on the bed, plucking the fabric. "I can't get her to wear anything else," she whispered with a smile.

David pulled up a chair as Rhonda rubbed Layla's back in tight circles. "C'mon, sweetie, wake up. A man wants to talk to you."

Layla rolled over and sat up, yawning so wide David could distinctly make out her dangling uvula. Her face was puffy from sleep and, maybe, from crying. "Hi."

"Hi there. How are you?"

"Tired."

David smiled. "I am too. I wanted to ask you about the dog you found."

Her eyes welled instantly with tears. David admired her quick vulnerability.

"My dog. He got illed."

"What do you mean *your* dog?" Rhonda asked.

" 'Othing. Just that I iked im."

"Did you notice anyone out there watching you when you found him?"

Her eyes went to Rhonda. "No."

"Are you sure?" Rhonda asked.

"I idn't do anything." Her breathing quickened into jerks, threatening to grow to sobs. Rhonda's presence clearly made Layla less forthcoming.

"We didn't say you did. We're not blaming you for anything at all." David turned to Rhonda and said quietly, "Is there any way I could see her alone?"

"No, sir," Rhonda said. "I know you're a doctor and all, but I don't leave my girls alone with anyone."

"Okay. I understand." He turned back. "Have you seen anyone else around? Hanging around the place?"

" 'Ometimes he ooks at me from his car."

"From his car?"

"We get perverts drive by from time to time," Rhonda said. "Teenagers poking fun."

"Is that what you meant?"

Layla again cast a nervous glance at Rhonda, then nodded heavily, her full cheeks bouncing with the movement.

"Are you sure?"

"Yes."

"Nothing unusual or scary at all. No men hanging around?"

A big head shake.

Rhonda checked her watch, then ruffled Layla's hair. "Okay, sweetie. Why don't you go and round up the others for dinner?"

Layla shuffled out.

David stood up, noticing, for the first time, the exposed rafters. A coldness moved through him. "Was it here? Is this the room where Clyde tortured the boys?"

Rhonda nodded. "Obviously, we don't tell the kids that."

David stared around the room, feeling an irrational sense of awe. The rafters were lower than he'd imagined. "How often did he do this to them? More than a few times?"

Rhonda nudged the chair toward David with her foot. "See for yourself," she said.

Unsure what she wanted him to look at, he climbed on the chair, bringing the top of the rafters into view. Every few inches down the center rafter's length, shallow grooves had been worn in the wood. The kind of grooves a hanging body would make.

CHAPTER 54

DAVID had spent very little time at home the past few days, so it was with a sense of relief that he pulled into the garage and entered his house. A light was on in the living room, and the house smelled of popcorn.

He tensed, until he recognized Ed's voice, calling, "Honey, you're home!"

David threw down his keys on the counter by the garage door and walked into the other room. Wearing a wife-beater tank top and a pair of paint-splattered jeans, Ed lounged on David's couch in front of the television. His hair was just starting to grow back, giving the top of his head an orange sheen. He held an open Amstel Light, a bag of microwave popcorn, and the remote control to the television. "You need to go grocery shopping," he said. "Nothing in the fridge."

"Please," David said, sitting down beside Ed with a sigh. "Make yourself at home." He reached over and touched one of the paint dollops on Ed's jeans, checking that it was dry.

Ed put a ragged workman's boot up on the coffee table. It was worn through the heel, almost all the way. A green sock showed through.

"I think it's time for some new boots," David said.

"These *are* new boots," Ed said. "They're beat up because I pulled them behind my truck for a half hour this morning."

"So they'll blend with your new getup?"

"You got it."

"Are you ever going to tell me what you do?"

"Probably not."

"You didn't just happen to walk into that Kinko's, did you?"

"No," Ed said. "I was tagging the guy for something else. All of a sudden, he was committing an armed robbery and people were at risk."

"I thought you didn't like to get involved. With violence."

"I don't. But sometimes we don't have a choice, do we?" Ed broke off his knowing look. "So what do you have for me? I've been waiting eagerly for the Spier update, and the news, for once, is a few steps behind."

David filled Ed in on his progress as best he could. Ed listened attentively, asking occasional questions. When David finished, Ed regarded him with an expression of amused respect. "Go go Gadget," he said.

David reached for Ed's beer, took a swig, and handed it back.

"Do you think Clyde's aware of your mother's role in this?" Ed asked. "Has he connected you to her?"

"We shouldn't rule it out, but I don't think so. He recognized my name from the Spier Auditorium but didn't seem to link it to any other *person.* I would guess a more significant recognition of my name would have shown."

"So he holds the hospital *in general* responsible for

victimizing him." A small smile played across Ed's face. "The alkali attacks are a pretty unique revenge strategy."

"I think those experiments etched into his experience what he already knew as a kid who'd spent his life shuttled from home to home—power is in the hands of those who *scare*. By attacking Nancy and Sandra, he scared not just them but every young woman in that Medical Center. Now he holds the reins."

"I suppose that's one definition of power."

"That's the definition the study taught him. For all these years, he's been locked in a terrified preadolescence. Now he's slowly finding his way out of fear. Even the nature of his attacks are changing. They're more complex, more specific. The attack on Diane probably had to do with me—maybe he was jealous of my affection for her, or maybe he felt I betrayed him in some way—but it also shows that this man is capable of growth."

"He's capable of getting what he needs too." Ed clicked the remote, turning on the television and VCR, then clicking PAUSE. The frozen video appeared to be a store's security camera recording. "There have been eleven pharmacy burglaries in LA County in the past three months. Mostly morphine and Percocet—those accounted for five of the break-ins. Three times, Vicodin was taken, and one guy stole condoms. Talk about being desperate to get laid."

"That only adds up to nine. I thought you said there were eleven."

"I was getting to that. Lithium carbonate was taken in mass quantity from Healton's Drugstore on May fifteenth. Eskalith, to be precise."

"How much?"

"About five hundred 450-milligram tablets."

David whistled. "That should be enough for six months at a normal dose."

"Evidently not, because our boy came back. Last night."

"The dog was killed by the Pearson Home last night, too."

"Well, Healton's was smart. They installed a security camera after the first break-in. Caught this on tape." Ed pressed the PAUSE button, and the screen unfroze. A few moments of silence, then the figure of a man appeared outside the store. He picked up a nearby trash can and hurled it through the window. Lights came on within the store; alarms flashed. The man staggered inside, and David recognized him for the first time. Clyde. He stumbled into a display pyramid of sodas, sending them rolling up the aisles.

"Looks pretty hammered," Ed observed. "There's your ataxia, huh?"

Clyde stumbled to the pharmacy door and found it locked. Rearing back, he kicked it in, the jamb splintering.

"Powerful guy," Ed said softly.

Clyde entered the small back room of the pharmacy and emerged thirty seconds later, a few pills falling from his pockets. He grabbed a carton of cigarettes from above one of the cash registers, then staggered out of the frame. He reappeared a moment later, cradling a few items to his chest, shuffled out the door quickly, and was gone in the darkness.

The small timer at the bottom of the screen indicated that the entire break-in took Clyde less than four minutes. Ed sighed. "Estimated police response time to that area is twelve minutes. Pacific Division is over on Culver and Centinela, but they might as well move it to Venice Beach since that's where all the cops hang out. Checking out the chicks on Rollerblades."

"Was that a bottle of Gatorade he grabbed?" David asked.

Ed nodded slowly. "You said excessive thirst was a side effect. Polythirstia."

David smiled. "Poly*dip*sia. Is that all he took?"

"A few cans of beans. More lozenges." Ed ran his hands over the red stubble dotting his scalp, making a harsh rasping sound. "And two containers of liquid DrainEze."

David leaned back on the couch, exhaling loudly. He rubbed his eyes. "Goddamn it."

"Cheer up. We got some good news from this tape."

"Like what?"

"Think."

David's voice sharpened again with frustration. "Why couldn't they have just caught him at the goddamned drugstore?" He stood and paced around the living room, running his fingers through his hair.

"This does us no good." Ed snapped his fingers. "Sit."

David walked back and sat on the couch.

"This is emergency surgery, Spier, and we've just had a complication. We're going to keep our cool. We're not gonna panic like a candy striper. Now . . . what does the tape tell us?"

David took a deep breath before speaking. "The lithium toxicity has progressed. Clyde burned through the pills he stole at a dangerous rate. I'd guess his blood level is up over two point zero. His balance is even worse than when we saw him last."

"Which means?"

"Which means . . ." It struck him. "Which means he probably couldn't operate a vehicle." He took a deep breath. "So he probably walked to the drugstore, since taking a bus would have been too visible."

"Very good, Spier. He lives within walking distance. We now have an area pinned down. Is this drunken-walking thing permanent?"

"No. If he backs off the pills, it'll resolve. His coordination could be significantly improved within twenty-four hours."

"Okay, so it is possible that he may be more mobile in the future. What else?"

"Well, he stole food too, so that probably means he's low on money."

"Good. He was laid off three months ago, and he doesn't strike me as a meticulous financial planner. So he's probably overdue on rent." Ed smiled and tossed a piece of popcorn in his mouth. "Pissed-off landlords like to talk."

"So how do we go about that?"

"We?" Ed shook his head. "Oh no. This is the stuff I can't get involved in. Grunt work. Door-to-door. It's too visible. I'd suggest you turn all this info over to Yale so he and his boys can start following up on it. You'll just have to trust him." He smiled playfully. "Time to unleash the hounds."

CHAPTER 55

THE full moon cast the palm fronds' shadows against the wall at the base of David's bed. He watched them dip and bow like distorted puppets. A horn blared up on Sunset, followed by the squeal of brakes. David listened for a crash, but there was none. Clearly, the earplugs weren't helping, so he removed them and set them by the alarm clock on his nightstand. It was 10:27 P.M.

He'd paged Yale over ten minutes ago.

He reached for the phone, dialed 411, and asked to be put through to the listing. He was surprised when he got an answer. "Healton's Drugs. Help you?"

"Yes, how late are you open?"

"Midnight."

"Can you—"

"And not a minute later. Got that? Doors lock the instant the second hand clicks."

"Yes," David said. "I understand. Can you give me your address please?"

After heaving a weighty sigh, she complied, and David jotted down the address on a notepad. A run-down part of Venice, close to the intersection of 5th and Broadway. And a few blocks away from the Pearson Home for the Developmentally Disabled.

A hefty coincidence.

The drive took less than fifteen minutes. David slowed as he neared the drugstore, taking in his surroundings. He passed several weedy lots where buildings had been torn down. In one, a group of men huddled around a burning mattress. It became increasingly evident why the police's response time to this area was so slow.

David pulled into the Healton's parking lot. Though the front of the store was well lit, he had some misgivings about leaving his Mercedes unattended. He took his cell phone with him rather than leaving it in the car.

Fourth of July drawings still decorated the building's large windows—flags and firecrackers depicted with thick, messy paint. The window Clyde had broken was backed with plywood and covered with garbage bags that sucked in the wind. The inside smelled of Clorox and Band-Aids. The tabloids at the unmanned checkout counter screamed out in vivid colors: WESTWOOD ACID THROWER STILL ON LOOSE AFTER DR. DEATH AIDS HIS ESCAPE! Beside it loomed a photograph of David entering the hospital, taken at paparazzi distance.

Aside from a few food aisles to the right, the drugstore featured health, cleaning, and home improvement products. David happened on a pair of heavy-duty earplugs and grabbed them, figuring he'd give them a try. He walked up the aisles until he arrived at the row of lye products. Drāno, Red Devil Drain Opener, Liquid Plumr, and, there at the bottom, DrainEze. Industrial strength, the label advertised.

The harsh female voice startled him. "We're closing up. If you're gonna buy something, bring it to the register."

David turned to find an elderly woman in a hand-knit sweater, her face wrinkled and smeared with makeup. She smelled distinctly of baby powder.

"Hello, ma'am. I was hoping you could—"

"Don't you 'hello ma'am' me. I'm trying to close up now. Buy what you're gonna buy or else get out."

Pulling a copy of the police composite from his pocket, David followed her surprisingly fast hobble up to the cash registers in the front. "I'd really appreciate it if you could take a look at—"

He halted. Through the front windows clouded with the smeared decorative paint, he made out movement around his car. A shadow seemed to orient itself toward David and freeze, as if aware of David's gaze. Then the figure flashed away into the night.

David stepped out through the doors, and the old woman was there instantly behind him, locking him out. A man, stocky like Clyde, was walking up the deserted street, hands shoved into the pockets of a torn jacket, loose shoelaces trailing. Fleeing, yet trying to remain inconspicuous. He did not look back. David jogged a few paces to keep him in sight.

He followed the man at a distance of about half a block, wondering if he was, in fact, Clyde, and if so, how he had spotted David. Had he been staking out the drugstore? The pair of earplugs grew sweaty in his hand, and David realized he had inadvertently stolen them. The man turned a corner into one of the deserted lots David had noted on his way to the drugstore, and David picked up his pace, trying unsuccessfully to keep him in view. He passed a dilapidated phone booth, the black receiver dangling from its cord inside the four shattered walls. When he turned the corner, he realized the man had entered the empty lot beside the Pearson Home.

Broken bottles, gravel, weeds, and a few chunks of concrete left over from the demolition. A scorched car sat up in blocks in the middle of the lot. Nobody in sight.

Cautiously, David stepped off the street and entered the dark, deserted lot. He noticed a slat missing in the fence at the periphery and headed toward it. An opening to another street. His Brooks Brothers loafers crunched gravel underfoot as he walked slowly forward. His mind raced with all the reasons it was foolish for him to be out here in this neighborhood in the middle of the night pursuing a dangerous fugitive, but something drew him forward, a deep-seated compulsion.

Clyde had been careful so far to attack only those who couldn't effectively fight back; David hoped he was too timid to go after an able-bodied man.

David stumbled over a beer bottle, and it shattered against a rock with a dry, popping sound. He paused, leaning on the hood of the torched car.

Through the myriad cracks of the windshield, he saw two eyes glinting in the darkness. His mouth went instantly dry, and his voice seemed to catch in his throat on the way up. "Clyde?"

The door creaked open. David stood frozen, one hand resting on the car hood, as a rustling figure got out and slowly took shape in the darkness. The door closed with a bang, then Clyde stood over him, his face dark and shadowed.

The two men faced each other, David looking up at

Clyde. Excitement mingled with fear, kicking both up a notch.

Clyde calmly drew back a large, puffy fist and struck David in the face. David's head snapped down and to the side, a splattering of blood leaving his mouth and spraying across the car's hood. The punch made a dull thud, that of a dropped orange hitting asphalt. The action was oddly matter-of-fact; the men had observed it as it occurred, as if they were both somehow detached from it. Clyde made no move to strike David again.

Slowly, David raised a hand to his mouth and pressed it to his split lip. He had felt no pain, just a sudden pressure. His stomach churned.

He turned back to Clyde, careful to keep his head lowered so as not to make eye contact. The thought of Diane's soft whimpering the first time she kissed him in the hospital room brought on a sudden, intense rage, but he fought it away. Anger did him little good here, as it did little good on the ER floor.

Only Clyde's large stomach and chest were within his view. The sickening and frighteningly familiar combination of body odor and orange candy-coating hung in the air.

It occurred to David how surreal it was to be threatened physically and how ill equipped he was to handle it. He'd been in one fight in his life—Daniel Madison in third grade over a stolen Sandy Koufax baseball card. The ass-kicking Daniel administered had convinced David subsequently to pursue other avenues of conflict resolution. And to root for the Giants.

"You don't know," Clyde said, his words a slur. "You don't know how scary I can be."

"Yes, I do," David said. Clyde might strike him at any moment. He tried to figure out where he'd hit Clyde if he had to defend himself. Neck? Crotch? "But you're in danger. I can help. I can bring you in myself, and make sure you're taken care of."

"I'm not a game." Clyde's voice, deep and raspy, was pained. "You'd better leave me alone."

"Clyde, listen to me." David's voice was shaking, though he was doing everything to keep it even. "I saw the films of the fear study. I know what they put you through when you were a kid, and how wrong it was. I understand why you're angry—you have every right to be angry." He sensed Clyde's shape relaxing slightly, shoulders starting to lower.

"No one's born with problems like mine," Clyde said. "Someone made me."

"If you come with me, we can talk to the authorities together and explain everything that's happened to you," David continued, in as calm a voice as he could muster. "But as long as you're out here and wanted, you put *yourself* in danger."

"I'm not in danger. They're the ones. They're the ones who are scared of *me*."

"Clyde, I know there's a part of you that doesn't want to do these things to people. I know there's a part of you that wants to be better." Wording the question like a statement, trying to pick up ground. David stared up at Clyde's shadowy face, framed in silhouette by the glow of a distant streetlight.

"I tried to go into a clinic," Clyde said. "To stop the feelings that were starting to come. I wanted them to make me better. To give me . . . *things* . . . to make me better." Fear crept into his voice. "But I got to the parking lot and saw them with their white coats and I couldn't. My hands were sweating. I dropped my orange bottle, but it was empty."

The orange bottle—for prescription drugs? Clyde's cryptic words were confirming connections David had already made. Connolly's study had left Clyde terrified of doctors. Or at least of receiving treatment. That's why he'd been trying to cure himself.

"How about if I went with you?" David asked. "To get help?"

A voice, small and defiant, like a child's. "No."

"If you won't go with me to get help, I have to believe you're not very serious about getting better."

A low humming sound broadened into a sob-stained cry. David waited silently, shocked, as Clyde wept and then fell silent. After a pause, Clyde said, "People talk at me but their voices don't have any color. They're metal and cold. They scrape my ears." His words were distorted from crying, but his tone was more gentle. Confessional. "It's like there's darkness everywhere and in my eyes until someone smiles and then it gets light." A mournful pause. "It hasn't been light in a long time."

David tried to collect his thoughts.

"I'm not filled inside," Clyde continued. "It's like straw instead of skin, and ropes instead of veins. I'm rotting. I'm rotting from the inside out, but I still move around in my body." Clyde beginning to cry again. Rocking on his feet, muttering. "Three, two, one. Back from the door." Calming himself. When he raised his head, his eyes gleamed, sharp-focused and angry. A forged connection—vulnerability followed by intense animosity.

David took a small step back. "There are people who can talk to you." He made sure not to mention psychologists or psychiatrists. "Make you feel better. Plus your wounds—your wounds from the alkali—those need to be treated as well."

Clyde turned and spat. "I can taste my rot. It's like there's a dead rat in my throat and it's melting."

"That's a side effect," David said, "and another reason

you need help. You've been poisoning yourself with the drugs you're taking."

Clyde's shadow stiffened, rearing back, and David realized he'd made a terrible mistake.

"I don't take drugs." The fist drew back calmly again, like a piston, and drove down into David's face.

David came to with gravel in his mouth. Using the front bumper of the car, he pulled himself to his feet and spit out the gravel on the hood. His mouth was warm and salty; when he studied the gob of spit in the moonlight, he saw it was dark, lined with blood.

The vice-grip of a headache seized him suddenly and intensely, pulsed three times, then dissipated. He slid up on the hood, careful to miss his spit, and sat with his feet on the front bumper. His pants were ripped and bloody at one knee. He caught his breath slowly, blotting his split lip with a sleeve and going through a neuro checklist. He didn't have any weakness or altered sensations, and there seemed to be no clouding of his mental facilities. He thought about getting himself to the ER to be checked out, but continued toward the missing slat in the fence on the far side of the lot. Halfway there, he noticed another slat that had been shoved aside, farther down the fence. This one appeared to lead not to a street but an alley. David was fairly certain the slat had been in place before his confrontation with Clyde.

He headed over and stepped through the fence without first scanning the alley. He was tired, aching, pissed off, and no longer cared to slow down for the sake of taking precautions. A homeless man shuffled from behind a Dumpster, approaching David in threatening fashion, but David lowered his hand from his bloody lip and froze him with a glare.

He trudged out from the alley and found himself on an empty street of run-down apartments. Dilapidated cars were parked along the curbs—Chevettes with tinted windows, El Dorados on sunken shocks, trucks with soil scattered in the beds. On the apartments, screens hung off windows by single pegs; clean patches of wood were visible where decorative shutters had recently fallen off. David walked along the torn-up strips of grass intended to decorate the sidewalks, not really sure for what he was looking. He paused at the corner of the street, staring at the row of quiet, decaying buildings. Insects chirped somewhere nearby, though there was little vegetation.

The realities of the situation struck him. He was alone, in a bad part of town at night, searching the streets for an assailant.

David turned purposefully and began the long walk back to his car. Beside an overturned Healton's shopping cart, a man slept on the sidewalk, drawing deep, shuddering breaths. David circled him, passing beside a car.

A parking permit hanging from the car's rearview mirror caught his eye: UCLA MEDICAL CENTER. Expired in May, three months ago. The month Clyde was fired.

David froze, peering at the car. A chipped brown Crown Victoria. On the dash sat an empty box of Nobleman's Zinc Lozenges and a loose twenty-gauge needle, still in its plastic sheath. Wrappers and soda cans covered the backseat.

Carefully sidestepping the homeless man, David headed for the run-down apartment building closest to the car. He ran his finger down the list of names on the mailboxes, searching for Clyde's to no avail. He did the same at the apartment building next door. And the one next door to that. He was just about to give up when a name caught his eye. Slade Douglas. Apartment 203.

The lobby featured a circular couch with the stuffing

showing and a large dead fern. The carpet covering the stairs was worn through in the middle. A shattered lightbulb littered the landing between the floors.

A bare flickering bulb was all that lit the second floor. Maroon carpets and brown peeling wallpaper made the hall seem darker than it was.

David paused outside the door to Apartment 203, then slowly drew his eye close to the peephole. A large form, coming directly at him.

He sprang back, nearly tripping over his feet, and darted for the alcoved doorway to Apartment 202. As Clyde's door swung open, David pressed himself flat against the neighboring door. He heard three dead bolts lock, one after another, then Clyde swept past him, banging into a wall. Clyde stumbled down the hall toward the stairs, pulling on a torn jacket and muttering under his breath.

Loud footsteps on the stairs, then all was still. David realized he'd been holding his breath, and he let it out in a rush. He felt light-headed.

Walking back outside, he headed out of view along the side of the building, in case Clyde returned. He paged Yale again, this time to his cell number, then switched his phone over to vibrate mode. Peering up the street, he wondered where Clyde had gone. Probably to spy on David again, to make sure he'd left the area.

Pacing impatiently beneath a fire escape, David waited for Yale's return call. None came. He'd just decided to page Yale again when the muffled cries of a woman caught his attention. Looking up the side of the building, he saw he was standing beneath Clyde's window. The muffled cries were in all likelihood coming from Clyde's apartment.

David's face went slick with sweat. The breeze kicked up, and he lost the sound of the cries momentarily, before it died down. Ed had pointed out that police response time to this area was slow. Clyde could return and resume torturing, or even kill, whoever was up in his apartment before a 911 call could be responded to. And Yale hadn't even called back.

David walked back and forth beneath the fire escape, the cries overhead driving him to a near-panic. His mind stumbled through terms—*suppressed evidence, search warrants, unlawful entry*—searching for something to guide him, but he was forced to acknowledge that his legal expertise was derived almost entirely from bad movies. A pained, stomach-deep grunt overhead drove him to action.

David pulled on a pair of latex gloves from his back pocket, then jumped up, grabbing the fire escape ladder and yanking it down. He climbed to the first landing, then the second, the structure creaking beneath him.

Peering through Clyde's filthy, cracked window, he saw little more than an unmade bed. The reflection of the glowing Healton's Drugstore sign shined in the glass, and David turned to look at the store, visible beyond the empty lot. In front of the store, bathed in a cone of light, sat his Mercedes, in clear view from Clyde's window. David grimaced at the distinctive tilt of the headlights—his car stuck out glaringly from the surroundings. Clyde must have recognized it pulling up, and realized David had come looking for him. The Pearson Home was also distinctly observable from Clyde's apartment. It struck David as noteworthy that Clyde had never left the vicinity of the Happy Horizons home in which he'd spent part of his childhood. Clearly, he derived some comfort from being nearby.

The woman's cries brought David's attention back to the dark apartment. He carefully removed a long shard of glass from the cracked window and reached through, lifting the catch. He pushed the window up and slid inside, resting the shard on the sill.

The first thing to catch his attention was the odor of decay—nearly unbearable. Thousands of motes swirled in the artificial light filtering through the window.

The woman's muffled screams continued, rising in pitch and frequency. David felt an overwhelming sense of embarrassment as he crossed to the moaning mound of clothes and pulled away a crusted sweatshirt to reveal the amorphous, static-bathed shapes of a couple fornicating on an overturned television set. The riddle of the cries was solved. David closed his eyes, feeling himself flush. He could not help but picture Freud's somber, astute face.

He started for the open window, but then paused. He was inside now. Whatever laws he may have violated were already broken. He might as well look around and see what he could glean about Clyde Slade, aka Douglas DaVella, aka Slade Douglas, while he waited for Yale's call. He ran through a quick checklist in his mind of what he should look for. DrainEze. Lithium. Evidence.

He stepped farther into the apartment, surveying it. Clyde obviously had been removed from normal socialization for some time. Burnt and cracked pots and pans covered the small counter that served as the kitchen. Among them sat hardened clumps of bread that Clyde had molded into sculptures. They resembled decaying gingerbread men. Toothpicks protruded from the sculptures, decorative flags or voodoo pins.

David almost tripped over the cat bowl, overflowing with mush and teeming with flies. The odor was riper here, more fresh. He turned and saw, sprawled along the top of the kitchen pantry, a partially decayed cat. It had been dead for weeks, and the flies and maggots were at it.

With a nervous stare at the door, David quickly entered the bathroom. On the interior doorknob hung a child's hospital gown that looked to be the one Clyde had worn during Connolly's study. David stared at the filthy mirror, dotted with bits of pus from popped zits. The toilet was splattered with stains. Diarrhea—an early side effect of lithium toxicity. The medicine cabinet was empty, except for a massive bottle of generic aspirin. Aspirin meant more trouble; when taken with lithium, it raised the lithium blood level and thus the likelihood of toxicity. If Clyde did indeed suffer from migraines, that would explain why he kept so much aspirin on hand. David briskly searched around the sink, but was unable to find where Clyde stored his stolen lithium.

He pulled aside the frayed shower curtain. The entire bottom of the tub was lined with jam jars, lids screwed on tight, stacked five or six jars high. David raised one to the light and saw the yellow liquid inside. Urine. Clyde was saving his urine. The date and time was etched on a label on the side in black pen. David looked over the jars with increasing amazement. Clyde had been saving his urine, off and on, for months. A few jars were filled with clusters of hair, and others with fingernail and toenail clippings. One held a collection of scabs. David tried to swallow, but his throat clicked dryly.

The best he could come up with to assess the contents of the tub was a weak parallel to Freud's anal stage, and to the fetishizing nature of recently toilet-trained two-year-olds. Flushing the toilet and becoming upset at where it all went. Fixation at an early stage of development. Maybe Clyde was holding on to some part of himself. Himself at an earlier age? David shook his head, irritated. Too facile an explanation.

Stepping back into the main room, David approached the large wooden table. Several books were stacked to one side, and he noticed the Louise M. Darling Biomedical Library stamp on the fore edges—Clyde had stolen them from the hospital. David laid the books side by side. A *Merck Manual*, a DSM-IV, a *Physician's Desk Refer-*

ence, a dictionary, and several psych textbooks. One of the pages of the *PDR* was dog-eared, and David flipped to it.

Not surprisingly, it was the section on lithium. Several bullet points detailed its possible uses: to control mood swings and explosive outbursts, and to help patients combat aggressiveness and self-mutilation. One phrase, "may also help control violent outbursts," had been circled in red. Clyde must have mistaken *violent outbursts* to mean outbursts of violence rather than intense, brief tantrums. Certain words were underlined, and David flipped through the dictionary and found them marked there correspondingly.

Driven by senseless compulsions that he didn't understand, Clyde was—with some degree of sincerity—trying to prevent himself from committing acts of violence, and poisoning himself in the process. It was, above all else, a display of wish fulfillment, a desperate hope that magical pills could heal him and dissolve his violent urges. Clyde had managed to galvanize some of his few and pathetic resources to this misguided end.

Beside the books, stubbed-out cigarettes lay clustered on a small plate, a few wayward butts scattered across the table like shriveled white worms. Most of them were mashed together in twos, as if they'd been smoked that way. Clyde had probably developed a heavy dependence on nicotine to reduce his anxiety and improve his concentration. Two cigarettes at a time would certainly maximize those effects.

David leaned over a sheet of notes that Clyde had scrawled, most of it phrases he'd evidently culled from the med textbooks. Clearly, much of the reading was above his level; Clyde had drawn up lists of words he didn't understand. David studied his writing, considering whether Clyde was dyslexic. At the bottom of the page were several phrases. *Nic wether toda. Helo ther. Hav a nice dae.* Variant spellings of *dae* were written beneath—*day, daye, da.*

Clyde's desperate attempt to wear a mask of sanity.

Beneath the table was a large metal footlocker. David shook it, and it gave off a metallic jingle. There was a smudge of blue liquid near one of the built-in locks, which David took to be alkali. He hadn't sighted DrainEze in the kitchen or bathroom; Clyde probably kept it secured in the footlocker. Searching for the footlocker key in the messy apartment would be hopeless. Instead, David pulled a toothpick from one of the bread sculptures on the kitchen counter, jammed it in the footlocker keyhole, and snapped it off. That should be enough to keep Clyde away from the alkali until the police arrived.

Near Clyde's bed, on an upended orange crate that served as a nightstand, David found a rusted numeral—the 1 he'd noticed missing from the Pearson Home's address. It served as a paperweight, pinning down a yellowed, damaged photograph of Happy Horizons. The house had not been significantly altered over the years. These fetishized objects from Clyde's childhood home—how did they fit into his psychopathology?

Taped to the wall by the bed, a headline torn from the *LA Times* proclaimed FEAR COURSES THROUGH UCLA MEDICAL CENTER. Clyde's goal accomplished. Staring at the headline, David wondered how sincere Clyde's attempts to cure himself were.

The longer David was in the apartment, the more acutely he sensed his own approaching panic. He was breathing hard, glancing at the door every few seconds, and feeling an immense urgency to leave, but the information he was uncovering was riveting and invaluable. He had no idea when Clyde was coming back; he shouldn't push his luck.

He turned, regarding the rest of the room to see if there was anything else he might have missed. In the corner, a desiccated snapdragon leaned from an ice-cream carton, soil spilled around its base. Something seemed odd about it, and it took David a moment to figure out what. The stalks and leaves were angled toward the kitchen rather than the window. The plant should have been leaning in the direction of its sunlight source, not toward the dark apartment interior. It must have been recently moved.

David walked over and crouched above the plant, pulling it away from the wall. It hid a heating vent set into the crumbling plaster. The vent cover tilted from the hole easily, revealing an orange bottle of pills. Falling to his knees, David reached inside and removed it. He lined the arrows and popped the white top. It was full of pale yellow pills. Eskalith. 450 mg.

Clyde's self-consciousness about taking meds was so great, he hid them even within his own apartment. As if he couldn't bear to have them in plain view.

David replaced the meds, set the vent cover back into its hole, slid the plant into place, and headed for the window. He heard a key hit the lock of the front door and felt his gut go slack. One bolt turned, followed by another slide of the key, and then the second. David was halfway to the window before it hit him that he didn't have nearly enough time to get out. There was nothing big enough to conceal him, so he flattened himself against the wall behind the bed, in the shadowed corner beside the window. Save the darkness, David was in clear view.

The third dead bolt slid with a thunk and the door swung open. Clyde's outline filled the doorway, a few swirling locks of hair framing his head like a halo set afire. He swayed a moment on his feet, then stepped inside.

David remained completely inert, afraid even to exhale.

Clyde shuffled in, slamming the door behind him and

throwing a dead bolt, and headed directly for David. If he turned on a light, David would be completely exposed. Clyde's pace quickened as he neared David, then he lunged forward. David fought the urge to draw his arms up protectively, but Clyde fell to the bed, face pressed to the mattress, and lay still. After a few moments, he began to draw ragged, uneven breaths.

David remained in a panic freeze, head drawn back to the wall. A bit of light from the distant Healton's sign fell across Clyde's back, making the chain around his neck glint. David eased out a breath.

With painstakingly slow movements, David took a step toward the window. Then another. He was just lowering his foot when his cell phone vibrated.

Clyde rolled over, his head rising lazily from the mattress. David sprinted for the front door, rather than risk scrambling out the nearby window. Sensing Clyde's struggle to rise from the bed behind him, David turned the three dead bolts furiously, trying to find the correct combination to unlock the door. Several times, he twisted the bolts and yanked the door, but it wouldn't open. He heard pounding footsteps—Clyde charging him with a roar—and he ducked to the side, Clyde's weighty body smashing into the door and splintering several panels. Clyde collapsed on the floor, stunned. The door dangled lamely, jarred loose from the hinges, though the dead bolt remained buried in the frame on the other side. David grabbed the hinge side of the door and yanked it farther open. He leapt through the gap into the hall as Clyde stirred and snatched at his ankle, missing it.

David flew down the hall, hearing Clyde crash through the wreck of the door, and took the stairs two at a time. He sprinted through the lobby, Clyde bellowing behind him. Though David knew he was faster, he sprinted with a blind, panicked speed. Through the gap in the fence, across the empty lot, tripping and fumbling for his car keys in his pocket. He did not hear Clyde pursuing him.

David reached the light-bathed parking lot of Healton's, his Mercedes sitting out like a showcase vehicle, and unlocked the doors with his key's remote control. He slid into the car and squealed out onto the street, banking a hard left over the curb. He could not resist a look out the window as he passed the abandoned lot, and there, halfway across and pulling to a halt near the scorched car, was the shadowy form of Clyde.

Something glinted in his hand—maybe a gun, maybe not—and then Clyde stopped, standing frozen in the dark lot like a misplaced statue, watching the car speed away. David would be haunted by that image—Clyde's quiet form in the lot staring out at him with something calmer than anger, something like interest newly kindled.

He did not let up on the accelerator until he was several blocks away, then he realized his cell phone was vibrating in his pocket. He fumbled for it and flipped it open. "Where the hell have you been?"

Yale's voice was calm as always. "Take a deep breath. I was in an interrogation. What's going on?"

"I tracked down Clyde . . . to his apartment . . . he came home . . . chased me . . . 1501 Brecken Street, Apartment 203." David knew he sounded frantic, but he couldn't get his breathing back in control.

"You tracked him *yourself*?" The sounds of Yale moving on the other end of the line. "Is he at that location now?"

"No. I don't know. He knows I know where he lives. He chased me, but stopped a few blocks from his house."

"I've got the area Clyde's bedded down," Yale yelled to someone else. "Get me Pacific on the line. Let's move, let's move!" Mouth back to the receiver. "Where are you?"

"I'm in my car. Driving."

"Is he chasing you now?" The beat of Yale's shoes on the floor quickened.

"No. He stopped."

"All right. We're moving in. Clear out of the area immediately."

David's heart was racing, and he felt a line of sweat working its way down the inside of his biceps. "Check the area around Clyde's apartment, including Healton's, the Pearson Home, and the empty lot beside it. I'll call the hospital, alert security, and have someone get upstairs with Diane and Nancy in case Clyde's heading over there. I'll go to the hospital now. I'll be in Diane's room."

"Fine. I'll send a unit upstairs too. Don't leave there. Keep your phone on. And Spier? You're in deep shit if this goes sour. You broke our deal."

"How can I break a deal you never accepted?"

Yale hung up without responding.

CHAPTER 56

JENKINS had gotten the call and driven over immediately. He'd flown across town, sirens blaring, drawing a nasty look from Bronner when his cup full of tobacco spit sloshed over onto a knee.

Bronner stood by the curb, scrubbing at the Kodiak stain with a thumbnail. Jenkins broke through the crowd of press, shoving roughly and dodging questions, and bolted up the stairs. A crime-scene technician tried to stop him in the hall, but Jenkins straight-armed him into the wall. Yale met him at the shattered door of Clyde's apartment and placed a splayed hand on his chest, walking backward as Jenkins continued to advance. "We're sweeping for evidence. Watch your step. SID doesn't want us all through here. We don't know if he's—*back the fuck off, Jenkins*."

Five heads snapped to attention. Then, the Scientific Investigation Division went back to work, dusting and marking. One held a jar of urine to the light; another flipped the pages of the DSM-IV with gloved hands.

Dalton shuffled over from his position at the window, stepping between Yale and Jenkins, resting his hand lightly on Jenkins's stomach and walking him a few steps back.

"You listen," Yale said. "I'm keeping you in the loop on this as a favor. Calm the hell down or you're gonna blow leads. Is that what you want?" He took a step forward, glaring at Jenkins over Dalton's shoulder. *"Is that what you want?"*

"No," Jenkins said.

"All right. Me neither. But save your bull-in-a-china-shop routine for speeders and jaywalkers. This is my case. And I'm gonna bust the POS, for your sake and your sister's, but don't you fuck it up by being such a hard-on, or I'll make a few calls and you'll be shoveling out stables for the mounted unit."

Jenkins's eyes narrowed. "Sorry," he managed.

"We missed him. Dr. Spier tracked him here and called in the address. We came over with SWAT to serve the warrant, but by the time we got here . . ." He gestured to the broken door. "No sign of Clyde C. Slade. We have units out around the area, but nothing yet."

One of the cops popped the locks on the footlocker and raised the lid, revealing a container of DrainEze nestled among syringes, Pyrex beakers, and other medical paraphernalia. When Jenkins caught sight of the alkali, his lips pressed together until the pink left them.

"Place is a fucking monkey house," Dalton grumbled. "Jars of scabs and shit. That reek we're all relishing—it's from a rotting cat in the kitchen."

A technician snapped a photo, and Jenkins tensed up at the flash.

"Don't worry," Yale said. "By the time we're through with this place, we'll know at what grocery store he buys his TV dinners."

A technician sifting through the contents of a vacuum-cleaner bag paused to sneeze. Yale grimaced at him. "Great. That's just great."

"So what's the call?" Jenkins said. "What now?"

Dalton flipped open his notepad. "DMV came back with expired registration to an old address. A '92 Crown Vic, bought at a sheriff's auction."

"Irony," Yale said. "Rich." Hands on his hips, he turned and gazed at the half-open window. A shard of glass had been carefully balanced on the sill.

"He had citations and parking violations up the yin-yang, but the car was never impounded. I assume he still has it, but we've found no sign of car keys." Dalton surveyed the wreck of the apartment. One of the technicians, on his hands and knees picking through dirty clothes, stopped to fan himself. "Though you could lose a refrigerator in this joint. But I think he bolted, took his car. We already called it in."

"The good doctor sticking his nose in again," Jenkins said. "Fucking things up."

"His ass is covered, though," Dalton said. He sighed, irritated. "It's within his rights to walk around, ask questions."

"Unless he broke in here," Jenkins said.

"He knows better," Dalton said.

Yale walked over and lifted the shard of glass from the windowsill. He slid the pane down, revealing the hole the displaced shard had left, just above the latch. "Does he?" he asked.

CHAPTER 57

PETER was sitting at the edge of Diane's bed, his legs straight-braced out in front of him, when David entered the room. An ortho cane leaned against the base of the bed, but David knew better than to ask about vacillations in Peter's condition. Peter moved to rise. "Please," David said. "Sit."

"Nonsense," Peter said. He turned around, gripping the bar at the foot of the bed and backing himself slowly onto his feet, then he pivoted, faced David, and shook his hand gravely. "Good God, what happened to you?"

Diane craned to see around Peter. "Your lip, David. Did he attack you?"

David walked over to Diane, hesitated for a moment, then pushed back her bangs and kissed her on the forehead. She looked surprised by this show of tenderness. Peter did not.

"Don't get affectionate on me," Diane said. "I might not recognize you."

David turned to Peter. "I'm so glad you were in the ER when I called."

"Motorcycle versus streetlight," Peter said. "Crotch rockets indeed."

"What took you so long?" Diane asked.

"I've spent the last hour buttoning down the ER and dealing with security."

"Why?" Diane asked.

"I've just come from Clyde's apartment. I tracked him there and we had a confrontation. I escaped and gave Yale his address, but he probably fled before the cops got there. I thought he might come here."

"You went alone?" Peter sank slowly back onto the bed. "Are you mad?"

The question hung heavily in the silence. A loud rapping startled them, and David tensed as the door swung open. Yale, Dalton, and Jenkins entered the room, looking extremely displeased. Jenkins closed the door behind him firmly.

"What are you doing barging in here?" Peter said. "This is a patient's room." He struggled to stand, and Jenkins took note of his efforts with a calm disdain.

"We'd like to talk to you alone," Yale said to David. David noted genuine anger in his voice—it seemed more than a front for Jenkins's and Dalton's benefit.

David crossed his arms. "You can talk to me here. I don't mind if they're here."

"We do."

"Then you can talk to me in the presence of my attorney."

"Listen to me, you motherfucker," Jenkins growled. "How about we jack your ass on the burg you committed at Clyde's pad, stick you in the general population at County, and have a big bad jig try you on as a condom. How about that?"

Yale turned neatly on his soft leather shoes, facing Jenkins. "Out," he said softly. Jenkins did not move, and Yale walked over and opened the door. "Out," he said again.

With a glare at David, Jenkins straightened his shoulders and walked from the room. Yale closed the door and nodded at Diane. "I apologize for that."

"I should hope so," Diane said. "That's the first time I've ever been exposed to that kind of fucking language."

"I take it you didn't find him," David said.

"You stepped in it proper this time, Spier," Dalton said.

David studied Yale; he seemed to be struggling between the competing needs to vent his anger or arrive at a more constructive state of affairs. "What do you mean?"

"I mean, you fucked up," Dalton said. "Our best bet for catching him would've been you finding the address, getting the fuck out of Dodge, and calling the police so we could sitting-duck his alkali-throwing ass."

"That's what I was planning to do," David said. "But I thought there was a woman trapped in there."

Yale looked puzzled. "Well, you thought wrong," he said. "And even if you were correct, you should have left her in there rather than risking your civilian rear end."

Dalton ticked off the counts on his fingers. "Obstruction of justice, interfering with a police officer, burglary, contaminating a crime scene."

"Contaminating a crime scene?" David said. "But how? I wore gloves."

"Gloves. Great." Dalton crossed his arms. "Did you breathe near anything? Pick your teeth? Lean against a wall? Scratch your head? Flush a toilet? Turn on a sink? You don't have the slightest idea of how to enter a crime scene. *Gloves*." He shook his head disdainfully. "You've been fucking up this investigation since day one."

"I've been trying to work with you from the beginning." David caught Yale's eye and Yale turned his head slightly left—barely a shake. David should make no reference to the fact that he and Yale had spoken off record in the past.

"That's not your fucking job, Doc," Dalton said. "And in fact, we might just clink your sorry ass to keep it out of our way."

"I think you have it wrong," David said. "I have more on this than you do."

Heads swiveling, Peter and Diane watched the exchange with surprised interest.

"Then you'd better fucking spill, because if one more woman gets—"

Yale held up his hands, arms spread. A humorously saintly pose. Everyone calmed and looked at him. "Listen," he said quietly to David. "If I arrest you, it'll be a big hassle and your lawyer will ride my ass for years. To be honest, I don't have the time right now—or the resources—to commit to that."

David resisted the urge to respond, sensing that Yale was working an angle of some sort.

Yale turned to Dalton. "He's involved whether we like it or not. We might as well use him. At least he's a *resourceful* pain in the ass."

Talking cop to cop as though David were not in the room.

"He'll talk," Dalton said. "He'll have to talk."

"But in the interest of time, I say we give the bastard an out on charges and get what he's giving immediately. If he wants to agree to it. If he doesn't, we'll go the arrest-lawyer route."

"I'll agree to it," David said, a bit too quickly. He hoped Dalton would perceive it as his being scared, rather than his implicitly picking up the line of Yale's agenda.

Dalton's soft, misshapen face seemed to shift as he assessed David.

"There's a lot I'd like to fill you in on," David said.

"Fine," Dalton finally said. "You're now our most overeducated informant. Spill."

"Let's talk about this privately," Yale said, indicating Diane and Peter.

"No," David said. "They can contribute."

Dalton pulled his notepad from his back pocket and flipped it open. "Let's take it from the top, Doc. And include that shit about the woman you thought you heard."

Yale held up a hand when David opened his mouth. "Details," he said.

David told Yale and Dalton the events of the past few days, fabricating only when necessary so he wouldn't have to mention Ed. David was grateful to them for not making light of the porn mix-up. For the most part, they listened attentively, Dalton shaking his head now and then. When he related his discovery of Connolly's study and his mother's cover-up, he noticed Peter's shocked expression. Diane blanched at his description of his confrontation with Clyde. When he finished, everyone appeared to be in a state of mild shock.

"What happened tonight when you got to his apartment?" David asked.

"He cleared out before we got there," Dalton said. "Took his car. Thanks to your intervention, he's now roving. We got a whole new world of variables."

"You wouldn't even know where he lived to begin with if it wasn't for me."

"SID lifted some vaginal secretion from his sheets, so we're questioning the female apartment residents and some hookers in the area to see if we can obtain more information about that," Yale said. He paused. "What's wrong?"

"I guess I'm just surprised he's had any sexual contact. He's a real loner."

Dalton studied David angrily. "You feel sorry for him, don't you?"

"I think he's pitiful."

Dalton gestured to Diane, keeping his eyes on David. "Pitiful. That's it, huh?"

Yale shot him a sideways look. Wrong approach. David wasn't the type to get worked up over having his manhood questioned, and he was impressed that Yale realized that. "I'm answering your question," David replied evenly, "not starting a playground fight."

"And this experiment shit. I bet you think that explains him."

"This man, as a child, was systematically exposed to snakes, darkness, and blinding lights, and denied attention, affection, and nurturing. That he lacks gentleness is not his most surprising quality. Nor that he's dysfunctional."

Dalton's cheeks colored with anger. "Dysfunctional," he repeated disdainfully. "Do you have any idea how elusive this man is? We see it all the time—a guy can't keep up his own hygiene, or interact with people, but when it comes to eluding capture or injuring others, he's a regular fucking Kaczynski. Never underestimate what obsession can accomplish. This guy's bent his entire life to one aim—harming women."

"More than one aim," David said. "He's also been trying to cure himself."

"This guy's a nutcase, and you're buying what he's selling. If you didn't have your Ivy League credentials, I'd say you weren't the sharpest stick on the heap."

David felt his anger flare, bright and sudden, fueled by exhaustion and stress. "This is not a thriller, or some movie of the week," he snapped. "We're not dealing with Hannibal Lecter, or Norman Bates. This is a man—a sick man, with predictable and definable psychopathology."

"Sick or not sick—it doesn't get him off the hook," Dalton said. "He knows what he's doing. We see fuckers like this all the time. Out of prison every time some dipshit liberal judge gets a tingle in her conscience, then another girl gets raped, another family killed. I don't give a *shit* if he had a tough childhood."

"Here's an idea," Diane said sharply. "Why don't you both stop beating your chests and do something productive?"

Peter rested a hand on Diane's shoulder, but she shook it off.

"Ms. Trace," Dalton said, with exaggerated patience.

"It's *Doctor* and don't condescend to me because my face is fucked up."

"I agree with Dr. Trace," Yale said. "This pissing contest is getting us off track. Let's cut the shit and get into it."

"Okay," David said. "Fair enough." He turned to Dalton. "Listen, I am not suggesting that anything in Clyde's childhood does or doesn't get him off the hook. I'm suggesting it's what we need to bring him in. His past doesn't excuse him. It explains him. And if we can figure it out further, it might help predict him."

Dalton finally met David's eyes. Some understanding seemed to pass between them. The politics were now irrelevant. They had to get on the trail and sort all that out later.

"Let's start with the drugs," Yale said, glancing down at his notepad. "Is there any way to determine how much lithium carbonate Clyde is taking?"

"The urine jars in the bathtub are labeled by date and time," David said. "Take the most recent one and send it to a lab. Lithium is cleared by the kidneys, so it'll show up in the urine. That'll help us gauge his level of toxicity."

"Could he die from lithium poisoning?"

"It's difficult to say. When it comes to psychiatric drugs, the dosage variance between patients can be immense. But I would say that if Clyde keeps up at this pace, it'll shut down his kidneys. As it is, he might already need hemodialysis."

Peter leaned heavily on his cane. "Or perhaps he needs

to take the rest of the pills at once and have a nice long sleep," he said.

A thoughtful silence.

Dalton jerked his head toward Peter. "I like this guy," he said.

"Did you find the pills?" David asked. "Behind the heating vent?"

Yale nodded.

"Looks like your wish won't come true, Peter," David said. "He left his supply. He's off the meds again. You know what that means?"

"A return of his faculties and motor skills," Diane said. "He'll regain his balance. He'll become more lucid, probably within twenty-four hours."

David looked down, working his cheek between his molars. "And, possibly, more violent," he said.

"We should stake out drugstores in the area in case he tries to break in for more drugs," Yale said. "If he tries to steal more alkali, that might provide an opportunity to catch him."

"There are other trails now, too," David said. "I have the names and birth dates of the study's other subjects. Since the abstract mentioned there was intense bonding between them, it could be a lead. I also have Clyde's file that shows all the addresses he lived at as a child—can you look into those too? We should check out people who worked at Happy Horizons, other kids he overlapped with. Maybe he's in contact with someone. Plus, he mentioned trying to go to a clinic once to get help. In case it's true, maybe we should check that out too."

"Wait a minute." Dalton held up a hand. It was large and weathered, like a baseball mitt. "We need all files and films from that study. We'll follow you home and pick them up." He said it as though expecting David to object.

"Okay," David said. "We can make copies."

Diane seemed to emerge from a separate train of thought. "The fact that Clyde hit you isn't sitting right with me," she said. "It seems so out of character."

"Surprised the hell out of me. So far, he's only attacked women, and even then from something of a distance."

"He attacked two cops in the course of his escape," Yale said.

"He didn't attack them. He injured them trying to escape *from* them. There was no emotional motive or release there. But me—he wanted to assault me."

"I'll buy that." Yale slid his cheap pen neatly behind his ear. "So then, what enabled him to stray so far and aggressively from his previous pattern of attacks?"

"I think the empty lot and the Pearson Home are comforting to him."

"Why?"

"That house is a place of empowerment to him. It's the place where he was able to inflict fear rather than be victimized by it. Once I spotted him outside Healton's, he may have drawn me into the lot to attack me. Being in the vicinity of the house may have helped him work up the nerve to hit me. I doubt he would've attacked me in public."

"There are more concrete reasons for that," Yale said. "No witnesses. No one to interfere or help you."

"True. But I think my hypothesis is strengthened by the fact that Clyde shows a clear fixation on that house. He took Douglas DaVella's name. He collects items from the house—you saw the photograph and address number by his bed. Plus he still lives within a few blocks of the site. As an adult, he selected that area for a reason. Clearly, it's his comfort zone. He's been clinging to it all these years."

Dalton chewed his cheek, his lips making a sloppy O. "I'd agree. Healton's is two blocks away. And he cashed his checks right over there on Lincoln."

"So by that logic, wouldn't he attack someone in the house?" Yale asked.

"I don't think so," David said. "That doesn't fit into the revenge aspect of his psychopathology. That house never did him wrong, so to speak. The hospital did. To oversimplify, I'd say he draws comfort and empowerment from the house and area around it, and uses that as a springboard to launch his attacks elsewhere."

"And he could be angry that the house was taken away from him," Dalton said. "Maybe he's pissed off that he got removed from his sick-fuck nirvana when he strung up the kid and got shipped off to a youth detention center."

"Again, something he could blame on the experiments and the hospital."

"And so he'll be even more pissed he's been driven from the area *again*."

"Probably so."

"We'll keep the units in that location on alert," Yale said. "Just in case."

"I doubt he's dumb enough to go back," Peter said.

"It's a base we have to cover. The bulk of our work is proving what we already know. It's tedious, but it helps us sleep at night."

"Our jobs are similar that way," David said. Once the words were out of his mouth, he expected to be rebuked by Yale or Dalton, but was pleasantly surprised.

"You said you believe he's been evolving, becoming more bold and aggressive," Diane said.

"Unusually so," Yale interjected.

"Any way we can figure out that trajectory and intercept it?"

"I think that's our top priority," David said.

"The primary aim of his attacks is to scare people," Yale said. "There's got to be something there, something we can use."

Dalton turned his red, weary eyes to his watch. "Right now, I want to get my hands on those films and files." He turned to the door, prompting David with a tilt of his head.

Peter fiddled with his leg braces. David looked over at Diane, and she tapped two fingers to her forehead in a mock salute.

When David turned back, Yale was standing right beside him. Yale pulled a stick of gum from his pocket and popped it in his mouth, bending it Doublemint-commercial style. He fixed his sharp, indecipherable gaze on David. "We work together now," he said. "On everything."

"All right," David said. "I get it."

"You'd better get it," Dalton said. "Because if you fuck up again . . ." He pointed at the closed door, behind which Jenkins waited. ". . .we're gonna sick Bad Cop on you."

CHAPTER 58

FEELING slightly schoolboyish, David called Diane when he got home to say good night.

She said, "You're not stunning."

He hung up the phone and lay on his back, staring at the ceiling and thinking about Clyde. It sruck him that, when talking to Diane, he'd slowly gravitated to the middle of the bed, rather than leaving his wife's side untouched as he usually did.

He should have been exhausted, but he was wired, still

riding his adrenaline high. The clock blinked 3:30 A.M. He'd have a little more than three and a half hours to sleep before getting up for his morning shift. He couldn't even count how long it had been since he'd had a respectable night's sleep. He closed his eyes and forced himself to clear his thoughts. He was just drifting off when the phone rang. He fumbled for the receiver, then answered. "Diane?"

"Almost," a voice said. Suddenly, an awful screaming came through the phone, the sounds of someone being tortured. David bolted up in bed, slowly placing the initial voice as Clyde's. He reached for the answering machine on the nightstand and clicked RECORD. The screams continued, followed by a woman's intense pleading.

"Hello?" David's heart was pounding. Nothing engendered panic like exposure to it. "Hello? Who's there? Are you all right?"

The noise stopped instantly, and David heard only labored breathing. He tried to put his thoughts in order. How had Clyde managed to take someone captive? The screaming had cut off abruptly—maybe it had been recorded. Why would Clyde awaken him with a woman's screaming? To scare him. To scare him *off*.

David's voice sounded weak, and he had to clear his throat to start over. "Clyde. What have you done? Listen to me. What have you done?"

A silence during which David imagined Clyde relishing the fear that had shown in David's voice.

"You said you were gonna help me and you didn't. You're like them, like the others. You've seen what I can do to them." Clyde's voice firmed with pride. "The hospital was shut down because of me. Security guards to protect people from *me*. They're scared. And you'll be too."

A woman's scream, prolonged and wavering.

The sheets around David were stained with his sweat.

David fought to keep the fear from his voice, because he didn't want to give Clyde the satisfaction. He got up and paced circles around the room, the phone pressed to his ear. "Do you have someone with you, Clyde? Is someone there?"

"Yeah." He laughed. "Yeah. Someone's here. I got her. It's your fault. I did this because of you."

"Clyde, listen to me. This is very important. If you harm another person—*one other person*—I won't ever try to help you again. Do you understand me?"

A pause, and then a statement, ringing with the clarity of conviction. "I'll. Never. Stop." The line again filled with the woman's wrenching cries, then cut out.

David turned on a light, suddenly spooked by the dark bedroom, and paged Ed. Then, he called Diane's room.

She answered the phone, her voice cracked from sleep. "Hello?"

Relief poured through him. "Clyde called. He might have had someone captive." David's reflection in the window stared back at him, frightened. "Just lock your door. And call security. Have them post a guard at your door."

"Okay. I'll call someone to stay until I get out of here in the morning."

"All right," he said. "All right."

"Are you going to tell the police?"

"I have to." David cursed under his breath. "They'll probably think I instigated this somehow."

"Well," Diane said. "Didn't you?"

After they hung up, Ed called back. He sounded wide-awake. "Something's off," he said, when David finished recounting the call. "I doubt this guy is capable of holding a captive. Plus he no longer has his own space. Was there any background noise?"

"I don't know," David admitted.

"Make me a recording of the call before you turn it

over to the cops," Ed said. "Drop it in your mailbox. I'll drive by and pick it up."

Yale returned David's page immediately, listened with a quiet intensity, and said he was on his way.

David found an ancient dictation recorder in his study, and dubbed a copy for Ed. He'd just finished when Yale arrived, and he handed off the answering machine tape at the front door. Yale's face reflected David's own exhaustion. Their exchange was wordless. David watched Yale striding to his car, his impeccable posture undiminished by fatigue or the late hour. David waited for him to drive away, then dropped the copy of the tape in his mailbox for Ed.

When he got back inside, he double-locked the door. After inserting a new tape into the answering machine, he slid beneath the covers, but only stared at the ceiling again, his heart pounding as the early light of morning spilled through the window. The phone rang at 6 A.M. and he readied his hand over the answering machine RECORD button before answering. His voice sounded weak and shaky, even to himself. "Hello?"

"Don't worry about it," Ed said. "Clyde's not holding any captives. He played you a bootleg copy of the Bittaker-Norris torture tapes."

"I . . . I'm sorry?"

"Lawrence Bittaker and Roy Norris. They raped and tortured girls in the back of their van, and recorded their screaming and pleading."

"But . . . where . . . ?"

"You can get the tapes at any number of places. Like the Amok Bookstore, which I believe you're familiar with."

"Certainly a good place to find tools to scare the shit out of people," David said.

"Make sure you let the flatfoots in on the joke so they're not running circles all day. I'll be enjoying myself thinking about what it'll do to your ego to tell the police you recognized the recording after playing it a few more times. They'll think you have some pretty perverse interests." In the background, a computer monitor hummed. "When I come over to install security equipment, remind me to set a phone trap on your line so we can trace incoming calls."

"You're installing security equipment for me?"

"Don't make me repeat myself. I'm laconic *and* impatient."

David thanked Ed and set down the phone. He was not looking forward to calling Yale and stumbling through a fabrication about how he came to identify Clyde's recording.

He stared at the ceiling, trying to bring it back into focus.

CHAPTER 59

DIANE'S footsteps echoed in the parking structure, the dull yellow glow of the lampposts turning her legs to elongated shadows on the concrete floor. The hospital had changed the arrangements; now all female employees parked in the PCHS usually reserved for the attendings. Because it was outside, well lit, and nearer to the hospital, it was a safer choice than the distant, enclosed P1 lot.

Even so, the pre-dawn quiet of the structure tinged the air gloomy and cool, as though the rising sun couldn't compete with the chill of silence. Diane heard the cars rumbling by on Le Conte, though a tall line of trees blocked them from view.

As the top tier of the parking structure provided the only access to the hospital, it was crammed with cars. A physician pulling out in a dark green BMW mock-saluted her, and she returned the wave, feeling slightly self-conscious about the gauze wrapped around her face. Though the bandages she wore were soft, they felt harsh against her raw skin. She practiced a smile beneath the wrap, testing the pain.

A few minutes ago, she'd finally been cleared by ophtho, and she was relieved to be out of the hospital room. Before this week, she'd never suspected that boredom could be such an intense affliction.

A fresh-faced security officer passed her with a nod and an obligatory double take. "Ma'am, would you like me to see you to your car?" he asked. "There's been some trouble lately."

Evidently he thought she was a patient. An ironic smile touched her lips beneath the gauze when she realized he was right. "I'm aware of that," she said. "Too aware, in fact."

A glimmer of recognition moved through his eyes, which she noted even through the dusty gray dawn air.

"Oh," he said softly. "I'm sorry."

Diane smiled again, a hidden, ineffective gesture. "I'll be fine. My car's the next level down." She raised an arm, pointing.

He glanced down the narrow concrete stairs at the line of cars he'd just patrolled. "I'd really prefer to escort you down." He was standing rigidly, shoulders back, chest forward. The posture seemed to match the "ma'am."

"You're right," Diane said. "You probably should."

They headed toward the thin, open set of stairs that led down to the next tier. His cheeks were flushed in neat, almost prepubescent circles. "Ma'am?"

She tilted her head slightly, a gesture she'd picked up to show she was listening. Now that she'd lost half of her face.

"I just want you to know, we're doing everything in our power to nail the bastard," he said. "Don't you worry."

When she felt the pain through her cheeks, she realized she'd flashed another useless, reflexive smile. "Thank you," she said. "Officer."

They emerged from the stairs. A few cars spotted the spaces sporadically; it was the farthest tier from the hospital, and usually abandoned. Her hand rustled in her bag for her keys. She heard a thud behind her and the sound of a body striking asphalt.

When she turned, she nearly collided with Clyde. She gasped once, a sharp, screeching intake of air, and then his meaty hand was pressed over her mouth, hard, the bandages grinding into her wounds. Something metal flashed in his hand—a twenty-gauge needle—then she felt the point against her throat.

Shock and pain were one and the same—sudden, intense, all-enveloping. Clyde's face was inches from hers, wide and thick.

From the corner of her eye, she saw the guard lying on his back on the ground, unconscious, a contusion blossoming across his temple. Beside him lay a sock where Clyde had dropped it. Judging from the few stray rocks that had spilled out, the sock's end had been weighted with white gravel.

"You move," Clyde growled, "you'll be eating through your throat."

Their closeness and position couldn't help but recall intimacy. His face was richly textured—the fat curl of his nostrils, the deep, pitted acne scars, the sparse patches of stubble and random, curling hairs. His loose belly pressed into her, filling the hollow of her back-drawn torso. A rich smell emanated from his pores, the smell of clogged sweat and sliced, low-grade meat gone slightly bad. He wore a pair of dirty green scrubs, and she felt the soft roll of his penis against her thigh.

She was sucking air through her nose, moistening his index finger. Her face was hot with pain and fear.

"Close your eyes," he growled through clenched teeth. "Didn't you learn your lesson?" The force of his words sent a soft spray across her face.

She closed her eyes, her chest pounding, her breath coming so hard she thought she might hyperventilate. The smell of him choked out the air. She felt him growing hard through the thin fabric of the scrub bottoms.

When he spoke again, his voice was different. Harder, more confirmed. "You can open your eyes now," he said. "I don't give a shit. I'm not scared of you. Or the guard they put here to protect people from me."

It took her a few moments to force her eyes open. He was even closer, the tip of his nose brushing the bandage of her cheek beneath her eye.

"You scream, I'll carve you up even worse. My little jack-o'-lantern." A smile spread his thick lips into a grin. "You tell him," he said. "You tell him I did this to you."

Slowly, he released the hand over her mouth. Diane's eyes flickered to the security guard, but he still lay perfectly still. Any other guards would be at least several tiers away, and even if one of them could hear an interrupted cry over the noise of the cars on Le Conte, the needle's tip remained, pushing into her larynx.

Clyde's laugh came as a shudder, a grunt that blew back her bangs. His breath was sour and rotten. "I'm gonna show you just how unafraid I am," he said.

His hand disappeared from view, down to his waist. He pulled at the drawstring of his scrubs. She opened her mouth to scream, but his eyes flared wider, dead and cold, and the needle pushed deeper into her neck, threatening to break the skin.

She tried to bring into focus a rape prevention class she'd taken in college, but its calm setting seemed distant and oddly irrelevant. A stream of maxims cascaded through her brain, and she tried to focus. What were the three steps she'd been taught? Something facile and probably defunct. Her scrambling mind grabbed on to the catchphrase: *Fight, Personalize, Intimidate*. She was too overpowered to fight.

"Listen," she whispered, her voice trembling. "My name is Diane Allison Trace. I was born in Los Gatos, California. I swam in high school."

His nostrils flared and his eyes seemed to withdraw into their deep cavities. "Don't," he said. "Don't. *Shut up*." The slur had returned, blurring his words together.

"My mother died of breast cancer when I was eight, and I lived alone with my father." Diane fought off the panic sobbing that threatened to interrupt her speech, but her voice still wavered, filling with fear. "He sold insurance. Now he's—"

Clyde slammed his hand over her mouth, gripping it hard, drawing her lips and cheeks forward in a half fist. She felt skin sliding, wounds breaking open, hot razor blades of pain lashing across her face. His other hand gripped the back of her neck, hard. His hands seemed to encompass her whole head.

His eyes were clouded, his forehead wrinkled under a fresh sheen of sweat. His mouth fought itself away from a frown. "I don't care," he said. He released the back of her neck and ripped his scrub bottoms down roughly. His forearm flexed against her stomach as he worked himself up. She sobbed against his hand, mucus leaking down onto his fingers.

She prayed for a car to drive by, but it was the bottom tier of the lot and mostly deserted. Any scream would be terminated by the needle.

He turned her around, bending her roughly over the

trunk of her car. He yanked her scrubs down, pressing up against her. She started to scream finally, not caring anymore, but his other hand quickly blocked the cry before she could put anything into it.

He bent her head back, and she saw his reflection in the rear window of her car, hunkered down behind her, sweaty face colored red with fear and excitement. He kicked her legs wide and reached with the hand holding the needle to pull down her underwear, but she thrashed on the trunk, preventing him.

Thoughts streamed through her head, and she clamped her concentration around one, holding it. *Step three: Intimidate*. She felt a sudden, cold lucidity.

She made herself go dead still and tried to say something calmly, though it was muffled by his hand. He stopped laboring behind her, confused by her abrupt shift in demeanor. "Huh?"

She repeated herself, her voice calm and quiet beneath his hand.

He released his hard grip on her mouth but kept his hand hovering over it, in case she tried to scream again.

"All right," she said. "You win."

He stared at the back of her head, nonplussed.

She continued in the same low, assured voice. "You can fuck me."

He withdrew from her, ever so slightly.

"In fact, I want you to fuck me. But let me tell you something." She squirmed in his grip, twisting to face him. "You'd better fuck me long and hard." She glared at him, trying to pierce his eyes with her own. His face loosened, anger giving way to fear. She felt him going soft against her. His hand hovered, then withdrew.

She knew her words—aggressive and sexual—would strike at the heart of his vulnerability. An incisive psychological attack was her last chance, so she continued.

"I need a man with endurance," she said, spitting out the words. "I hope you're up for that. I hope you're man enough to fuck me how I need to be fucked."

He released his other hand, baffled, and leaned back, pulling his weight off her. She reached back, yanking up her scrubs, not yet daring to scream. A crescent of sweat darkened his shirt at the collar. His face had turned pasty, almost totally devoid of color. He was mumbling to himself nervously, "Three, two, one. Step back from the door."

His putty-fat cheeks quivered, then drew tight. He tried to say something to her, but the words came out a jumbled mess, an animal's low-throated bellow. Reduced again to the pathetic creature he was.

He slapped her once, hard, across the face, and scampered across the lot, struggling up and over the concrete wall, the posts of his legs kicking in the air.

Pain ringing through her slapped cheek, Diane waited until he dropped to the other side, then cried out as loud as she could manage.

She sank down to the ground, bumper digging into her back, and tried to hold her throbbing face in her hands as she wept with relief.

CHAPTER 60

DAVID and Diane sat in perfect silence at their ends of the telephone. Listening to the quiet hum of the line, David watched the minute hand of the bronze clock in his study make a full rotation, then another. He was running late for his morning shift.

Diane had just relayed the news of her near-rape, leaving him stunned. For the first time, the thought of Clyde elicited in David a cold, vengeful rage. The perfect dark outside his bedroom window mirrored his mood.

"I'm leaving now for the hospital," he finally said. "Can I come see you?"

"No. I don't want to see anyone right now." A long pause before she spoke again, her tone more recognizable. "You've got the night shift tomorrow, right? You can come upstairs and see me then. I'm the new permanent addition to the ninth floor. Me and a bad Monet print they hung across from the elevators."

"And the wounds?"

"Reopened. It set me back a few days, that's for sure. Won't help with the scarring either."

"No. No, it won't."

"He told me to be sure to tell you about his attacking me. He's using me to threaten you. To hurt you. To get you to back off."

"I wish more than anything he'd come after me."

"That probably would have been less effective."

He considered this.

"Hey, David? I know that what you found out about the study has replenished your store of empathy, but don't expect that from me. The first time, with the shower, well that was awful. But this. This was so much more personal. His smell, his dead eyes. There was nothing there behind those eyes. Nothing. He's already dead. Death masked in flesh and bones." He heard her breathing for a moment on the other end of the line. "I think if the police found him first and shot him, well that might be all right with me."

"Right now," he said, "I'd have to agree."

"You don't mean that."

He wasn't sure if objecting would have been specious, so he didn't.

"With all my involvement since his escape, I don't know how much good I've done," he said. "It seems like I've only made things worse."

"I guess it's better to make a mistake than do nothing. Isn't it? Isn't it?"

"Yes," he said slowly and with little conviction.

They breathed together for a few moments.

"I'm thinking maybe I *should* leave things in the hands of the cops," he said. "They're used to this game, these stakes. I have an ER to run. If I'd just focused on that from the beginning, neither of us would be in this mess."

"Well, you do what you have to do." Diane sounded disappointed, though he couldn't tell if that had to do with him or the miserable position in which she'd found herself. Again. "I have to change my wrappings. I'll talk to you later."

He hung up the phone and felt the bitter, distinct sensation of defeat settle over him like a noxious rainfall.

The cockatoo immediately became animated when David withdrew the drape from the bronze cage, preening itself and gnawing at its black claw. Dressed in his white coat, ready for work, David regarded the bird with weary irritation.

"M&M's," it squawked. "M&M's. Where's Elisabeth?"

"Resurrecting the Russian economy."

David angled the seed carefully into the cup, but some fell anyway. Grumbling to himself, he crouched and tried to pinch it up off the floor.

"Where's Elisabeth?"

David brushed his hands off above the small metal

trash can in the corner. "Leading a nudist hike on the Appalachian Trail."

"M&M's," the cockatoo squawked. David headed from the room as the bird continued to hop about the cage. "Where's Elisabeth? Where's Elisabeth?"

David paused by the door, hand on the frame. "She's dead," he said.

CHAPTER 61

THE ER was a madhouse. Broken arms. Unusual rashes. A few flu cases. Three patients asked David about the cut on his lip. Carson still hadn't returned—when David called, he got his machine. "I wanted to check in on you and remind you we're a med student short," David said, after the beep. "We need you here. I hope we'll see you soon."

David's alienation was high-school apparent. His colleagues only spoke to him in brief, informational exchanges, and the nurses and interns had taken to not meeting his eyes when they spoke with him. He'd always been a popular attending, so he'd found his rapid estrangement from his own staff over the past five days to be unsettling. With both Carson and Diane missing from the ER, he felt suddenly without allies. And the press had ensured that his plight in the division was mirrored elsewhere. Alienated. Vilified. His reputation shattered.

David barely had time to update the board before a family of five came in on stretchers after their van overturned. Don was supposed to be providing double coverage, but David had to dispatch a nurse to find him in the cafeteria. By the time Don showed up, David and the two residents had everyone stable. Without apologizing, Don retreated to the CWA, where he lounged at the back counter, checking his stocks in a twice-folded section of the *LA Times*. Knowing that his general stress level had stretched his own patience to the point of snapping, David elected not to confront him.

Despite his vigorous efforts, he had trouble finding his way back into his routine. He continued seeing patients, somewhat distracted, thinking of Clyde's flat eyes sunk in his doughy face, the way he'd stood in the abandoned lot and calmly watched David drive away. He was relieved that Ed planned to install security devices in his house.

The sleeplessness caught up with him eventually, making him irritable and more intolerant than usual. A wailing toddler came in with a pro wrestling action figure's head wedged up his nose. An overwrought Beverly Hills mom with tonsillitis droned on at adenoid pitch. David found himself taking less time with patients than he ordinarily did.

Jill caught up to him washing his hands in Trauma Twelve. "That urine came back for McKenzie in Six, you've got a—"

"Slow down, Jill."

"—food poisoning in Two, and there's a football player with a ruptured spleen in Four."

"I have my hands full, Jill. Where's Dr. Lambert?"

"We haven't seen him for about fifteen minutes."

"Fifteen minutes? Again? Are you kidding?"

Throwing his stethoscope across his shoulders, David stormed toward the doctors' lounge, drawing several stares from workers and patients. He flung the door open, and it struck the wall with a bang. Black marker in hand, Don was standing by the far wall near the composite of Clyde. Target rings were drawn around Clyde's face, beneath which was written: WANTED DEAD OR MAIMED—$1000 REWARD.

Don's deep blush grew visible even beneath his five o'clock stubble. He cleared his throat, lowering the marker. "Look, Dave—"

"You've been missing from the floor for fifteen minutes—*again*—and I catch you drawing pictures like a sadistic little bully."

Still flushed, Don slid the marker into his pocket. "I didn't write that," he said.

David felt drunk with fury. "Don't insult my intelligence."

"You've been a bit on edge lately, Dave. Let's not jump to hasty conclusions."

"Get the fuck out of here." Gripping Don firmly around the biceps, David pulled him toward the door. "I want you out of my ER. Right now."

Don pulled his arm roughly from David's grasp, but kept walking toward the door at David's prompting.

"All right, Chief," Don said. "I'll let you flex your muscles and be the big ethical guy again since it worked out so well for you last time."

Ignoring him, David guided him through the door into the ER, his hand on the base of his back, hurrying him. By the time they reached Hallway Two, Don's uncomfortable expression and David's propelling him toward the door made the situation quite evident. Nurses watched with gleeful interest; patients stared; a girl with a teddy bear tittered. The phone rang and rang in the CWA, but no one reached for it. Don slapped David's hand from his back and walked faster toward the swinging doors.

David's face still burned with anger. When Don

paused at the hall's end, David raised his arm, pointing at the doors.

"Imagine that," Don said. "A guy who pulled the plug on his own wife without hesitation getting all worked up over some acid-throwing psycho."

David seized Don and hurled him through the exit. Don's feet tangled as he struck the swinging doors, and he slapped to the lobby floor, the doors fanning his red face. A news photographer popped up from his recline in one of the triage chairs, snapped several photos, then grinned as if he'd just captured Big Foot humping the shooter from the grassy knoll.

An overweight woman with a bun looked up from her needlepoint. "Oh dear," she said. The doors stopped swinging, hiding both Don and the woman from view.

David turned back up the hall and faced the myriad staring faces. One of the nurses began to applaud tentatively, but stopped when no one joined in.

David headed slowly back to the board. "Next patient," he said.

"A fucking disgrace is what it is," Sandy barked. The elevator stopped at the second floor with a ding and everyone cleared out, though plainly it was not everyone's floor. When the doors closed again, she threw the EMERGENCY STOP switch and glared at David, lowering the turkey sandwich she gripped like a football in her right hand, careful to hold it clear of her maroon silk blouse. David gestured for her to wipe off the few crumbs that dotted the corner of her mouth, and she all but swung at his hand.

Don had called her after retreating from the ER. Sandy had come running from the cafeteria and followed David through the corridors, failing in her attempts to keep a lowered voice and drawing looks from everyone they'd passed. David had moved through the halls purposefully. Something had rekindled inside him, and he felt an overwhelming sense of freedom. He'd been weathering Sandy's reprimand without the feelings of remorse and shame he would have expected.

"You've done it this time, and there's nothing I can do to cover your ass," Sandy said. She shook her head. "Your mother must be spinning in her grave."

"My mother is hardly in a position to spin disapprovingly."

Sandy cocked her head in condescending fashion. "Maybe that's what this is all about." He didn't give her the satisfaction of a reaction, but she raged on, undeterred. "Manhandling a colleague. Hurling him out of the ER in front of his staff and patients."

"My staff," David said.

"Well, maybe not anymore. The board will be convening tomorrow at nine in the morning, and you'll need to appear. They've been less than thrilled at your new controversial self as is, so this is only fuel to the fire. You finally did it. You gave them something tangible." She flipped the switch, and the elevator continued to rise. "You know damn well that as a physician—and particularly as a chief—you are a representative of this hospital everywhere you go."

Something crossed tracks in David's mind. Clyde's intense and growing fixation. The dark waters of motive. He waited for something to resolve but couldn't discern it, and Sandy was still yelling.

"You've turned this business with Clyde into a three-ring circus." Her cheeks were getting flushed. "The Mayor called me this afternoon. The *Mayor*, for Christ's sake."

"You don't think I know this, Sandy? You don't think that I, of all people, am aware of the stakes here? At all levels? You're not the one getting strung up by a reactive press. I've been under a magnifying glass *every day* of this thing. You think I'm doing this for my own enjoyment?"

"Your motives aren't relevant here, David." Sandy took a deep, angry breath. "I've been urging you to take some time off for a long while, and it would have served you well. But you stayed here, and you fiddled around with this case, and you crossed the line, despite my attempts to help you quietly and keep you within the bounds of discretion. And I'll tell you something else. If you keep pushing this—with the cops and the media and the private eye routine—your future at this institution will be jeopardized."

The elevator opened again, and David stepped out. He turned and faced her from the hall. "Listen, Sandy, you can handle this however you want, but let me tell you something. Don Lambert is a lazy piece of shit, and I'm tired of putting up with his incompetence. I am a physician. I am trained to take care of people, and that's what I'd like to do—*my* way. I'm tired of smug, second-rate physicians; I'm tired of the HMOs; I'm tired of so-called medical professionals more interested in punishment than repair, and while we're at it, I'm tired of you and your legal considerations. So thanks for the recommendation—I will be taking some of that vacation time, starting right now, to pursue this case and set things right, because I might be the only one who can. And if you or the board are displeased with that, you be sure to tell someone who's actually interested."

The doors shut in Sandy's surprised face, and David headed down the corridor to the ICU. The halls were still and silent.

"She's been having a tough time," the ICU nurse said. "And she hasn't had any visitors lately. Should I tell her you're here?"

"No," David said. "That's all right. She actually asked I not visit. I've just been concerned."

The nurse gave him an odd look.

"Are the skin grafts taking?" David asked.

"Some are, some aren't. Right now, our primary objective is making sure she doesn't get septic."

Nancy's looks were the least of their concerns.

"I was just dropping by to let you know that I'm not going to be around for a while. The hospital." He was surprised by how difficult that was for him to say. "But if there's anything I can do to facilitate Nancy's treatment, please let me know."

"Thanks, Doctor." The nurse touched his arm curtly, then pivoted and headed back to the nursing station.

Twilight crept through the windows, turning the room gray and ashy. The curtains were spread to Nancy's bed, ever so slightly, and David could see through the gap.

The front half of her crown was little more than mottled flesh, the hair having all fallen out. Her eyeballs had shriveled further, and the sockets were oozing a thick pus. The skin of her face was the worst of all—most of the grafts had not taken, and the flesh hung loosely in gray and yellow squares, a grotesque patchwork. A cheek wound had begun to contract, drawing her right nostril down toward the corner of her mouth.

Her lips, cracked and oozing, moved slowly; she was murmuring something to herself.

David wondered whether the plastic surgeons were working on her as fastidiously as they were on their other patients. There was little reason to risk complications and infection from plastics work; after all, Nancy would never have to see her own face again. Probably a blessing.

To think this was all caused by a confused, pathetic man and a beaker of alkali. Nancy would probably survive, and drag out the rest of her days in pain, hidden from her own sight and the eyes of others. Clyde's perverse turning of the tables.

The mindless embolus that had claimed Elisabeth's brain seemed almost humane by comparison.

Nancy's lips continued to whisper, and when David realized what she was saying, his mouth flooded with saliva as it sometimes did before he vomited.

"I wanna die," Nancy was saying. "I wanna die I wanna die I wanna—"

David drew back quietly and headed for the door, feeling his pulse race.

A man sat on a visitor's chair beside the last unoccupied bed in the row, his shoulders hunched, his hands dangling between his legs. Jenkins. David had not noticed him on his way in.

Jenkins wore a blank stare, his cheeks hollowed with grief. David paused before him, his breathing slowing. Jenkins's eyes moved slowly up to David's face, but showed no glint of recognition. Jenkins lowered his head again, studying the tiled floor. "What the fuck are you doing by my sister's bed?" he murmured.

Across the ward, a woman cried out in pain, and Jenkins flinched, the skin around his eyes drawing up in a squint. He did not look up.

"I shouldn't be there," David said. "But you should."

David reached out his hand, an offering to be taken or slapped away. A moment passed, then another. Jenkins's shoulders vibrated once, an intimation of a sob. He reached up with a trembling hand and grasped David's. Then he leaned forward, his weight pulling on David's arm, his face downturned, both hands gripping David's so tightly the skin of his knuckles turned white.

Motionless, he hung from David's hand, clinging to sanity, a man receiving an unexpected blessing. After a moment, he stood.

David left quietly as Jenkins headed to his sister's bed.

CHAPTER 62

DASH pulled off his sweatshirt and draped it over David's couch, where it sprawled like a gray blanket. He put his feet up on the table, and David worried momentarily it would give under the weight of his legs. Dash flipped through the bad photocopy of Connolly's abstract—Yale had taken the original—and let a grumble escape his chest.

Someone had leaked the story of the torture-tape call, causing a fresh influx of reporters to sweep through the Med Center grounds. David had all but waded through reporters on his way to his car after work. News of David and Don's dispute in the ER had not helped to abate the media frenzy. David had returned home to find a photographer camped out across the street and six messages on his answering machine from trashy TV "news" producers and more legitimate reporters. David's problem-resolution instincts had been firing inside him, phantom synapses—to call Sandy, to protect the hospital, to spin control. When he'd closed and bolted his front door, an intense burst of stress-lined relief had hit him; at least for the duration of his time off, he was no longer a part of the medical establishment. For the first time in his life.

Dash set down the abstract on top of the stack of other materials he and David had spent the late afternoon reviewing, and gripped his shoulder, working it with a thumb—an athlete's habit. "Have the detectives finished running down the other subjects?"

"Most of them. Three suicides, five are in prison, and three have been completely lost track of. Probably homeless. Or dead."

"Connolly certainly raised the bar on sadistic separation studies." Dash leaned back and laced his hands behind his head. "Those kids were never given a fair chance. Love, respect, care—these are not negotiable luxuries for children. They're fundamental needs."

"I know, but how can we *use* all this? To get to Clyde."

"I think you have several pieces of the puzzle," Dash said. "One: He wants revenge for this study. Two: He's learned that to inflict fear is to hold power." He let out a ticking exhale. "You see the problem."

"No."

"Well, the people directly responsible for the study are dead. He's probably not a sufficiently abstract thinker to go after grant committee members and the bureaucrats who enabled the study. So what does that leave him?"

"The hospital."

"Precisely. But how can you elicit fear from an institution? You can't. So he attacks some nurses and doctors, tries to run a current of fear through the hospital, but that's not personal or sufficiently satisfying. That's why he's evolving. He wants to exact more. But he doesn't know how."

And evolved he had. He'd varied his attacks, and switched their location. From a cowardly, unseen hurler of alkali to a rapist attempting to dominate a woman directly.

David recalled Sandy's words in the elevator that had struck something in him: *As a physician—and particularly as a chief—you are a representative of this hospital everywhere you go.* "Me," David said. "He can frighten me." He stood. "Of course—I'd been mostly viewing his obsession with me and his attacks on Diane as warnings. As his attempts to get me to back off, since I've been pursuing him. But that's entirely wrong. He's only switched his focus."

"What do you mean?"

"If he's interested in revenge on the hospital, I'm the perfect object of his vengeance. I'm the highest-level employee of the hospital he's had contact with. My last name is all over the Med Center. And he perceives me as threatening him in my attempts to locate him—something that surely must recall the persecution he felt as a child in Connolly's study. Why else would he call me in the middle of the night and play a recording of a woman being tortured? Why else would he attack Diane? To scare me. But he doesn't want me to back off. He wants to involve me more. He wants me to be diminished."

"I suppose it makes sense. A movement from the general to the specific." Dash crossed his legs, letting a size-seventeen foot dangle over his knee. "What are the ways to instill fear in you? To threaten or injure you directly, or to threaten those you love."

"I'll have to call Yale and see if we can get some protection on people close to me."

"Okay. Who?"

"Diane . . . Sandy . . ." David was embarrassed that he couldn't think of anyone else.

"I assume there's already protection on Connolly's wife."

"I believe so, but I'll double-check."

"How about men?"

"No way. He doesn't have the balls."

"He attacked you."

"On his turf. In his comfort zone. He had to lure me near that house. Plus, I walked into that attack—he didn't plan it."

"He attacked the security guard who was with Diane."

"Yale said the kid looked barely older than an adolescent." David shook his head. "I have to say, despite Clyde's emergence from timidity, I still doubt he's acquired the courage to attack a full-grown man." David rubbed his temples, straining to think of other names. "The only other person I'm close to who he knows about is you." David looked at Dash's barrel chest, the ridges of muscle capping his shoulders. "And he'd be an idiot to try that."

"Let's keep in mind that you and those around you are not necessarily his only targets. While you're certainly appealing to him, there's nothing to say he's not still planning other attacks on nurses and docs."

David moistened his lips, which had grown dry. "If there was some way to provide an opportunity for him to inflict fear, maybe we could lure him."

"Well, what are the ways you could draw someone like Clyde? The appearance of vulnerability. Who appears vulnerable? Old ladies. Kids. Women."

"We wouldn't risk anyone in those categories, except female cops, maybe. Besides, how do you make someone look susceptible to being scared?" David shook his head dismissively. "Maybe there's a play to be made at locations that are meaningful to him. He's been driven off his own turf. The only other area we know is of interest to him is the hospital. Maybe we could tempt him there."

"If you think he's that stupid. Security's been cranked up *another* notch after his attack on Diane. He's got to know he's playing increasingly bad odds there."

They sat quietly for a few moments, digesting their respective thoughts. The phone rang, and David heard the machine pick up in the bedroom. "Hi, Tom McNeil from the *LA Weekly*. I've received word that you're actually in contact with the Westwood . . ."

"I could try to manipulate him if he calls back," David said. "Actively draw his interest. If he threatens me, how can I respond to make him more likely to contact me again? If I can agitate him, maybe he'll give up more information. Should I act really scared or not scared at all?"

"I'd imagine your being immune to his attempts to scare you would be more galling. If you taunted him, even, that might draw him in. But don't overdo it. He's not beyond being scared off himself." Dash paused. "There are risks."

"Aside from the obvious?"

"Yes. Every intervention so far has driven him to a higher level of violence. When he's foiled, he comes back with something more bold. The more bold he gets, the more fear he's able to generate. Think of it as an intensifying addiction."

"What can I do about that?"

Dash shrugged, a massive, shifting movement. "Probably nothing. I'm just making something clear. You're the one who's been raising the stakes."

CHAPTER 63

OUTSIDE Sandy's office, Don shot his cuffs and readjusted a gold cuff link with a practiced flick of his thumb. A female resident walked by, full in the ass and tight in the waist, and he watched her until she disappeared around the corner.

"Come in," Sandy called out, before he could knock. The door was solid, windowless.

Seated at her conference table, she continued to sort through mounds of paperwork, not looking up. "What can I help you with, Dr. Lambert?" she asked.

"I wanted to let you know that I'm going to actively pursue assault charges against Dr. Spier unless this matter is handled expeditiously in-house."

"Don't split your infinitives, Dr. Lambert," Sandy said. She removed her wire-rim glasses, set them on a folder, and rubbed her eyes. "It spoils the illusion of eloquence you seek to cultivate." The smell of his aftershave permeated the room. Sandy finally looked at him. She whistled. "Where you going all dolled up?"

Don adjusted his tie nervously. "I'm on my way home from the opera. My date is waiting in the car."

"Well, I hope you left a window cracked."

Neither smiled.

"So you've been worrying this all night like a canker sore, have you?" Sandy put her glasses on and studied him. Her icy blue eyes matched the starched collar of her shirt. "What do you propose we do?"

"I think he should step down as chief of the division."

"That would be convenient for you, wouldn't it? But inconvenient for the board. We'd be unable to find a qualified replacement—how did you put it in your corporate way—*in-house*."

Don's voice rose in pitch. "This isn't about career advancement, it's about misconduct and a complete disregard for professionalism. He assaulted me in front of patients and staff. Assaulted me. Over something I didn't do. He's coming unwound. He's barely ever in the ER anymore, and I heard he left early today."

"He left early?" Sandy whistled, feigning astonishment. "Maybe we should report him to the Medical Board."

Don stared her down.

She sighed heavily, then her face resumed its usual businesslike cast. "The board is airing the issue tomorrow," she said dourly. "Rest assured, we are viewing this incident seriously."

"Well, I hope action will be taken before this gets . . . loud."

Sandy searched for a pen behind her ear and found it. She tapped it against her lips, which had drawn together in something of a scowl. "For seventeen years at this institution, Dr. Spier has been a physician beyond reproach. Do you know what that means? To be beyond reproach?"

"Of course."

She regarded him dubiously. "Your concern in this matter has been duly noted." She glanced back down at the papers in front of her. "Good night, Dr. Lambert. You don't want to keep your date waiting."

CHAPTER 64

AFTER calling Yale, David crawled into bed. Yale had spent the day shaking leads with Dalton and had turned up little of consequence. Happy Horizon's records had not been well kept, and the detectives were having some difficulty tracking down the children Clyde had overlapped with during his time there. From information collected at Clyde's apartment, they'd compiled a list of the places Clyde had stopped at regularly—Ralph's Groceries, 7-Eleven, Healton's—and they were keeping an eye on them.

After David filled Yale in on his conversation with Dash, Yale told David a unit had been sitting on Mrs. Connolly's house, and said he'd see about getting another car freed up to cover Sandy. Hospital security had been watching Diane's room.

Though David could barely keep his eyes open, he called Diane.

"Hey, Rocky," she said.

"You heard."

"Don puts out a loud whine."

"How are you doing?"

"I've had better weeks."

"Do you want me to come in and see you?"

"Sorry," she joked. "Visiting hours are over."

"I'm not a visitor."

"Are you something more permanent?" she asked.

After he hung up, he lay back and let his muscles go lax. A revving sports car up on Sunset reminded him of the earplugs he'd accidentally stolen from Healton's Drugstore. He retrieved them from his pants in the laundry, returned to bed, and put them in. They were surprisingly effective. He closed his eyes, pulling the sheets up to his chin, and drifted on the blissful silence. He was asleep in seconds.

Through his sleeping stupor, he became vaguely aware of a distant ringing. It repeated itself at intervals, then he was awake and momentarily lost before the familiar glow of the alarm clock reminded him he was home. The ringing returned. The doorbell. Muted through his earplugs. And some kind of rasping.

Why was someone ringing his bell at 3:30 in the morning? Grabbing the cordless from its cradle, he padded to the front door, leaving his earplugs on a hall table.

He peered through the peephole at Jenkins and Bronner. "Yes? Can I help you?"

"Please open the door, Dr. Spier."

David cracked the door and peered through the gap. "What does this concern?"

"Dr. Spier, *please*." Jenkins's voice had an edge of

concern in it, enough to cause David to open up. Both officers stood back toward the edge of the porch. "Can you please step out onto the porch?"

"Look, I'm not really sure—" David noticed Bronner leaning to the side, trying to get a better angle to see around him into the dark foyer, and he stopped short. Resisting the urge to look behind him, David stepped out into the cool night.

Jenkins grabbed David's arm, his hand encompassing his biceps, and pulled him back, eyes locked on the open front door. "We got a 911 call alerting us to this address about fifteen minutes ago," he said.

David shook his head. "Well, everything's fine. I've been sleeping for hours. It must have been a prank."

His declaration did little to wipe the intense concern from the officers' faces. Jenkins was working his lip between his teeth, his arms steeled and rigid.

"What?" David asked. "Why are you so alarmed?"

Jenkins unholstered his pistol. "The call came from within your house."

David swallowed hard, but the spit caught in his throat.

Pistol drawn, Jenkins toed the door the rest of the way open and inched inside. "Stay outside," Bronner growled. He turned on his flashlight, unholstered his pistol, and, crossing his arms at the wrists, followed Jenkins into the house.

David stood out on the porch in his boxers, shivering in the cold. After a moment, Jenkins hissed at him from within the house. "Lights! Where's the fucking light switch?"

David inched inside, and clicked one of the switches by the front door, concealed by the braided trunk of a tall *Ficus benjamina*. A cone of light from the ceiling softly illuminated the antique table and the couches, just enough to see that the room was empty and undisturbed.

Jenkins and Bronner looked relieved, but did not

lower their guns. They did a brief walk-through of the other rooms, using flashlights, whispering, and searching in closets and behind furniture. There was no sign of forced entry. Finally, they headed down the long hall toward the study and master bedroom.

The beam of Jenkins's flashlight illuminated the birdcage in the corner of the study. The drape had been removed, and the small wire door hung open. The cockatoo was missing. Jenkins and Bronner looked at David interrogatively, and he nodded solemnly.

David remembered the strange rasping which, in addition to the doorbell, had awakened him, and he felt the hair along his arms prickle. His bedroom.

He pointed to the slightly ajar bedroom door to which the hall led, and Bronner and Jenkins slunk toward it, pistols aimed at the small strip of blackness that ran the height of the jamb. Jenkins gestured as if he were flipping a light switch, and David mimed its location within the bedroom. Angling his gun to cover the left side of the room, Bronner toed the door so it creaked open, then he and Jenkins burst in, flashlights sweeping the interior.

A sudden stillness. David heard Bronner make a noise low in his throat and he stepped into the room just as Jenkins flipped the switch. He blinked against the flash of light.

But not before he saw the bird pinned wide, unfurled across the wall facing David's bed, its wings and feet tacked to the wall with surgical scalpels. A blood splatter sprayed the wall to one side.

The cockatoo's bright pink crest was stained and matted, its feathers shredded and broken. A small square had been excised from its throat with one of the scalpels, and blood drained from the hole down its feathers. Its voice box had been removed, a crude surgical procedure.

A shudder wracked through David as he stared at the

bloody tableau. Clyde had pinned the mutilated bird to the wall while David had slept feet away.

Had David stirred, Clyde might have killed him. The stolen earplugs may have saved his life.

The beak quivered, then opened weakly. The bird was still alive. It rustled feebly against the scalpels impaling its wings, its head and feet rasping gently against the wall. David crossed to the wall, and pulling a scalpel free from Stanley's wing, unceremoniously ran the edge across the bird's throat. Because its syrinx had already been removed, the blade ran deep through the throat, severing the windpipe. The cockatoo ceased its movement against its pinnings.

David fisted the scalpel and drove it into the wall, where it stuck.

Bronner and Jenkins lowered their guns slowly. Jenkins's face had reddened, his cheeks flushing with color.

David's breath left him in short spurts, reverse gasps. "Innovative," he managed. His legs were shaking, so he donned his white coat, wrapping it around himself like a robe.

Bronner lowered his flashlight with a faint groan and hoisted his pants. "I'll have Dispatch contact SID, and Yale and Dalton. I'll keep an eye on the front." He looked at David. "Don't touch anything else." He left Jenkins and David with the blood-splashed wall.

"Not his usual MO," Jenkins said. "He's getting bolder. More courageous." He chewed his lip.

David nodded. "We're right on track."

He followed Jenkins to check the garage. On the side of the Mercedes, Clyde had written ASHOLE in what appeared to be red spray paint. Jenkins shined his light beneath and inside the car, then took a step back.

They went back into the living room to wait for Bronner's return, and Jenkins flipped all three light switches, using a pen. David noticed immediately that the de Kooning was missing. He pointed to the blank space above the mantel.

Jenkins raised his eyebrows.

"A painting," David explained. "A de Kooning."

"I didn't have him pegged for a collector." Jenkins's joke was an offering of sorts. David's laugh was genuine. When Jenkins smiled, the harshness left his features. "Motive, motive, motive," he said. "Assuming he's not aware of its value or . . . artfulness, why did he take it?"

"It was a modern piece, a somewhat violent depiction of a woman."

"I see."

David felt momentarily like a pervert. He thought of the drawings Clyde had made as a child, the crayoned revenge he'd exacted on the study's nurses. Clyde probably found the de Kooning to be pleasing. The notion that David's taste in art was similar to Clyde's was not comforting. That the painting had been his mother's lent the theft a certain irony.

"Worth a lot?" Jenkins asked.

"Yeah," David said. "Now I'll have to deal with insurance. My penance for being part of the medical establishment." He ran his fingers through his hair.

Jenkins peered around the impeccably decorated living room. "Right."

The vase sat crooked on the Oriental cabinet, and David walked over and reached to straighten it.

"Don't touch that," Jenkins said.

David froze. "Sorry." He studied the small collection of photographs arrayed around the base of the vase, focusing on the shot of him and Diane from the ER Catalina retreat. His eyes lingered on the picture of Elisabeth in the tub, before skimming across the rest of the silver frames. One of the photographs was missing; there were normally five.

David crouched and peered behind the cabinet. Some loose change, several clusters of dust, and the silver gleam of the frame.

"There's a picture frame back here," he said. He pulled a pair of latex gloves from his pocket. "Can I get it?"

"Let me." Jenkins took the gloves from David, pulled them on, and moved the cabinet a few inches out from the wall. He grabbed the frame by the corner and held it up for David to see. The photograph of Peter with David's mother. Janet Spier, the steel gleam in her eyes, her chin raised in what David had previously thought regal fashion, but now recognized as a symptom of her deeply ingrained sense of superiority. Peter's smile, deferential yet confident, his arm across Janet's shoulders.

There was a smudge on the glass over Peter's face, and David knew, even before he leaned toward the frame and inhaled the saccharine odor, that it would smell of the orange-flavored lozenges.

Clyde had studied the photograph before he'd taken the de Kooning and, in replacing it, had accidentally knocked it behind the cabinet.

A flash of Peter after Clyde's escape, still shaken after he'd tripped Clyde in the hall. *"The way he looked at me . . ."*

David and Dash had neglected to add Peter to the list of potential victims. David doubted that Clyde had grown bold enough to attack a man, but it now occurred to him that a disabled man might be a possibility, as the boyish security guard had been. And Peter was a representative of the hospital. Depending on the extent of his surveillance, Clyde might even know that Peter was David's close friend.

"Do you think we could get some protection on Peter Alexander?" David asked, pointing to the photo.

"That's up to Yale," Jenkins said. "And the Captain.

But I'll radio Dispatch and have someone swing by now to check the welfare."

"I'd appreciate that."

Jenkins called in the request, then he and David stood in silence as they awaited the other cars, not wanting even to sit on the couches in case that would disturb evidence. It was an awkward silence.

"How was Nancy?" David asked.

Jenkins shrugged. "Awful," he said. "She's awful." His head bobbed in an intimation of a nod. "What are you gonna do? What the fuck you gonna do?" He raised his hands, then let them fall to his sides. The silence of the room was deafening. "My first day on the job, we were responding to a radio call," he said. "Domestic violence. Some crackhead out in Central had shot his wife. I got there with Dalton—me and Dalton were partners before he got promoted. Kicked in the door. Lady was laid out in the kitchen. Sawed-off shotgun from about two feet. What was left of her head was pasted to the refrigerator. The thing is . . ." He paused and took a deep breath, his nostrils flaring. "The thing is, she had a newborn. The baby had been playing in the other room, but it found her. Crawled across the damn apartment. It was nursing on her when we showed." He lowered his head. "That's the kind of thing you're supposed to see in a war. Bosnia, or some village in Vietnam. Not in an American city." He shook his head. "Not here."

A few cars pulled up front, blue lights flashing. Coming in the open front door without knocking, Yale announced his arrival with a sharp snap of his gum. He was dressed for the office at a Wall Street firm. Behind him, Dalton looked more aptly like someone roused in the middle of the night. His stained tie was jerked hard to one side, Rodney Dangerfield style, and he wore unmatched socks.

David followed them silently back to the bedroom. Yale appraised the scene silently, then gestured with two fingers for David and Dalton to follow him into the bathroom. He leaned into the shower and turned it on as hot as it went. The head sputtered a few times, then the water turned cloudy. Using his pen, Yale flicked the head to the side, and the water sprayed onto a bar of soap. It fizzed, then dissolved rapidly under the alkali.

"Looks like our boy had plans for your pretty face," Dalton said.

"No," David said. "He knows I've been unscrewing that showerhead every time before I turn on the water. *That's* what he wants—my anxiety."

Yale worked his gum as they headed back into the living room, where Jenkins was just signing off a radio call. "Everything clear on Peter Alexander," Jenkins told David.

Yale threw open the front door and nodded, and the Scientific Investigation Division poured into the house, toting bags and boxes.

Yale lowered his hard, cool eyes on David. "I'm gonna take a look around," he said. "Then why don't we have a chat at the barn. Get out of these boys' hair." He turned to Jenkins. "We got it from here." Yale winked at Jenkins, and Jenkins headed slowly for the door.

"Officer Jenkins," David called out. When Jenkins turned around, David said, "Thank you."

Jenkins nodded once before ducking outside.

CHAPTER 65

WAITING in the back of the detectives' generic sedan while Yale, Dalton, and the SID went over the house, David paged Ed on his cell phone. Ed was seemingly at a club or bar of some sort when he called back, leaving David to wonder when, exactly, he slept. In the background, Gloria Gaynor's "I Will Survive" blared. For Ed to hear him, David had to raise his voice. Ed grew upset once David described the night's events, displaying an endearing sense of responsibility.

"I just got the security equipment delivered this afternoon. I was gonna install it at your house tomorrow. I've been on a stakeout all night. Fuck, I'm sorry."

"It's okay," David said. "We can get it done today. Nothing truly awful happened. Besides, this might give us a good lead."

The sky was just beginning to lighten when Yale and Dalton emerged. On an ordinary day, David would just be getting ready for work. At a stoplight, they pulled alongside Dr. Woods, the lethargic gastroenterologist, in a BMW. His eyes first found the removable police light on the dash, and then he did a double take at David in the backseat. David raised his hands together, as if they were handcuffed, and waved. Woods's jaw was just beginning to drop when Yale pulled forward, leaving him at the stoplight.

David told the detectives about the picture frame and

said he'd added Peter to his list of potential victims. Dalton threw a weary look in Yale's direction. "Captain's been chafing at all the OT as is. We're gonna have to kiss some serious ass to get another unit for Peter Alexander."

Yale took a turn a little too fast. "Pucker up."

When they pulled up to the station, David waited patiently to be let out. The *LA Times* dispenser showed a color photo of Don's fallen body in the ER waiting room, David looming unpleasantly in the background. Front page. It was too bad that no media had staked out David's house through the night; they might have seen Clyde breaking in.

They headed directly upstairs; David was relieved not to have to deal with the contentious desk clerk. Yale's and Dalton's desks were pushed together so they faced each other as they worked. A stained coffee mug at the edge of Dalton's desk proclaimed WORLD'S GREATEST MOM. Next to it were the film reels of the fear study.

David gestured to the reels. "Did you take a look at those yet?"

Dalton sat back down heavily. Yale pushed his fingertips together and pressed them over the bridge of his nose. "Late last night," Yale said softly.

Dalton's thumb fidgeted on his cheek. "The shit they did to those poor little bastards . . ." he said. "No kid should have to go through something like that." A series of crayon streaks stained Dalton's shirt near the pocket, and David thought again of Dalton's picnic at the Academy. He found something poignant in the crayon streaks, as he did in Dalton's rumpled shirt, though he wasn't sure what or why.

"Are you done speaking with the other subjects?" David asked.

"A few we're still running down. Nothing's rang the cherries."

"He's so withdrawn," David said. "I'd say it's a long shot that he's had real contact with anybody."

"Aside from you," Yale said. He flipped through his ever-present notepad. "He used surgical scalpels on the bird. Correct?"

"Yes."

"Any special kind?"

David shook his head. "He had plenty of medical supplies at his apartment. Maybe he took them before he fled. The needle he wielded at Diane—I saw a similar one in his car. For all we know, he's got a Dr. Mengele funhouse in his trunk."

"You were right about the urine sample," Yale said. "Our guy at County Med said his kidneys were clearing a lot of the stuff. He estimated something like a 2.3 blood level. That mean anything to you?"

David nodded. "That's bad. Really bad. But if we're correct in our assumption that he's no longer taking lithium, it'll be lower by now. It must be, for him to have driven over and broken in." He paused and moistened his dry lips. "Some pretty dexterous maneuvering."

"Why didn't he attack you? He's bigger and certainly a more capable fighter."

David suspected the latter remark was intended as a dig, though he found it merely accurate. "I think he's more interested in scaring me. First the torture tape, then the attack on Diane, then this. The phonetic graffiti on my car is probably intended to humiliate me. Diminish me further."

"Fits your theory," Dalton said. "Lucky for you, huh?"

"Actually, I'd be thrilled to figure out a way to make him come after me more violently. Better likelihood of catching him."

Dalton stood up and ran a hand through his already tousled hair, his cheap button-up shirt pulling untucked at the side. He chuckled to himself. "You've got balls, Doc," he said. "I'll give you that."

"The key is to instigate him consciously and intelligently," David said.

"I'd have to say you've been doing that from the get-go."

"But if I could provoke him in a way we could channel . . ."

"Then what?"

Before David could answer, Yale did. "We could designate his next victim. The question is: How do we place a fitting stimulus to prompt him to make a move?"

Dalton sat back down, the effort pushing a grunt out of him. "Female cops going UC as nurses?"

"But where? We haven't turned up shit over in his neck of the woods, and as you said, he's gotta know we'll nail him if he steps on Med Center grounds again."

"A nurse might be a step back for him," David said. "He's already attacked people further up the hierarchy of influence at the hospital."

"Maybe he'll go after that bitchy chief of staff. Who's on her?"

"Bicks and Perelli," Dalton said. "They'll have it covered. Perelli's the Police Olympics freehand shooting champ."

"Clyde's not going to attack someone with visible police protection," David said. "He may be getting bolder, but he's still essentially a coward. And besides, I still think I'm a more appealing target. We could wait for him to contact me or come after me again."

"Waiting," Dalton said, "sucks."

"For the next few nights, I'm putting a unit on you," Yale said. "If Clyde calls again, make sure you record it. I assume it's okay with you if we start taking steps to trace your incoming calls?"

"Yes. Fine. Can you do it immediately? I imagine he's gonna call to soak up my reaction to Stanley." At their blank looks, David added, "The bird."

"You named your bird *Stanley*?" Dalton said.

"My wife did. Clearly she had lapses in taste if she married me."

Yale cracked a grin—the first David had seen. "Unfortunately, even with your approval, we have to jump hoops," Yale said. "Every major post–O. J. Simpson investigation's gotta squeak. With the political pressure on this one, we can't sneeze without the DA checking in. We'll have to subpoena the phone company, get a search warrant for subscriber information. A couple of days minimum."

"Why didn't you start this already?"

"We did."

It was David's turn to smile. Dalton took a sip of coffee, his face showing he'd forgotten to refill the cup since yesterday. David emitted a monstrous yawn.

"When the last time you slept?" Yale asked.

"I'm fine."

"I'm not asking if you're fine. I'm asking the last time you've strung together more than a few hours of sleep."

"I don't know. Five, six days. I can handle it. During internship, I was on call every other day and every other weekend."

"You were a young buck then. I'd guess you didn't look *this* shitty."

"No," David said. "Probably not."

"I'm gonna take you home to get a few z's. You're no good to us blurry."

Dalton drew his hand down the front of his face wearily, distorting his features. "We have our own world of shit to get back to. Combing evidence from Clyde's apartment. Car tips. Ex–foster home kids. Drugstores. Trying to press something useful from Forensics."

David's pager went off, beeping loudly. It was Sandy. His watch read 9:23. He'd missed his appearance before the board. "I have to return this," he said. "Sorry."

He withdrew his cell phone from the pocket of his white coat, and walked a few paces off so he could have a semiprivate conversation.

Sandy picked up the phone after a half ring. "Where the hell are you?"

Two cops led a heavily drugged prostitute into a nearby interrogation room. She twisted in their grips and tried to bite them. "Things are . . . complicated right now."

"Well, you've succeeded in making them more complicated. The board is rightly pissed off that you're not here. The meeting is progressing, whether you're here to defend yourself or not. And you're being depicted in even less flattering fashion than you deserve. And this morning's *Times* photo isn't exactly salve on our PR wounds." An angry pause. "You're doing an excellent job sabotaging what was shaping up to be a great career."

"I appreciate your keeping me in the loop," he heard himself say. His voice was cold, clinical, detached. Sandy hung up without saying good-bye.

He nodded to Yale and followed him down the stairs. The irritable black desk officer looked at David, then elbowed her counterpart—an obese man with a Wilford Brimley mustache—in the ribs.

"Ask him," she said. When the man shook his head, it set his jowls jiggling.

David and Yale passed the counter.

The woman elbowed her partner again. "Ask him," she repeated.

Wilford Brimley looked up with what David imagined was uncharacteristic shyness. "I got this heart murmur . . ." he said.

David slid his stethoscope into place and leaned over the counter.

⊕

David sat quietly in the passenger seat of Yale's car as they headed back to his house. Dalton had stayed at the station, running down leads on the phone. The sky was gray-brown, the clouds overhead indistinguishable from the haze of pollution. David tried to imagine his life if the Board voted for him to step down as division chief. He'd always lived with a presumption of irreproachability, probably a flaw he'd inherited from his mother. Events of the past week had knocked him from his armor, and dressed him in the trappings of visible failure. Maybe this was a good place from which to start over. To pick up the fragments and build something new from them.

Not surprisingly, he next felt a mentor's pull to get Carson put back together.

Yale said something, pulling David from his reverie.

"Excuse me?" David asked.

"I said, don't worry. We *are* gonna nail him. We have the whole department on the lookout for him and his vehicle. Ninety-eight hundred officers. He must have the vehicle hidden away, but every time he takes a drive or steps out in public, he's playing Russian roulette with five bullets."

David's mind slowly caught up to Yale's words, taking a moment to awaken. "You're more confident than Dalton."

"Dalton is accustomed to fate, chance, and the world conspiring to fuck him. I'm not. Clyde is no longer an unknown suspect. He's now an identified, wanted, violent felon, and he's starting to unravel. He's taking bigger and bigger risks, like going to your house. He's playing an endgame now. There's no question we'll nail him, and in my mind, there's no question we'll nail him soon." His hands fisted the wheel, then loosened. "There's really only one major uncertainty."

David rested his head against the glass. "What's that?"

"How bloody it gets before it's over."

They rode in silence the rest of the way to Brentwood. As they turned onto Marlboro, David recognized Ed's red Pathfinder across the street. The police cars had all left. "Want me to come in?" Yale asked. "Check for alkali throwers under the bed?"

David glanced at Ed's Pathfinder warily. "Thank you, I'll be fine."

"Do you have a weapon?"

"No," David said, opening his door. "No."

Yale leaned over so he could see David's face. "Keep your doors and windows locked. See about an alarm system. Call me with any sign of anything out of the ordinary. I'll check in with you every few hours. We'll have a car on you by nightfall."

"Thank you," David said.

A new lock greeted David at his front door, which stood slightly ajar. When he entered his house, Ed was on all fours behind the ficus wearing a woman's halter top—nicely filled out—and a leather miniskirt. A pair of patent leather pumps sat at the edge of the carpet. Next to two Nextel phones on the counter lay a Kate Spade purse.

Ed turned toward David, revealing a faceful of makeup and a luxuriant blond wig. "Not a word, not a fucking word," he said. He spliced two wires together and attached them to a keypad.

"Darling," David said. "Your mascara is running."

Adjusting his wig, Ed stood and approached David. He moved differently—high on his toes, shoulders drawn slightly back, chin raised. Feminine. When he went undercover, he really went all out. "I was on a job. I came straight over."

"What, on Santa Monica Boulevard?"

"Bomb threat at a drag rave. I know, it sounds like a Roger Corman movie."

David laughed. "Everything under control?"

Ed shrugged. "Nothing happened. That's what I get for taking a job from worked-up queens."

"At least you got to get dressed up."

Ed's face registered that he found little humorous about the situation.

David pointed to his wig. "I think it's safe to say you can remove that now."

"Oh. Oh yeah." Ed pulled off the wig and flung it on the carpet. "I came over as soon as the cops left, so put the brakes on your commentary. Now listen, here's what we did. I switched your Schlage locks to Medeco—double-cylinder, one-inch hardened dead bolts with six-pin tumblers and brass revolving collars. I set up a triangular-patterned, infrared, dual-beam break around the perimeter of your property line. It'll give off a beep to let you know when someone's on your property."

He paused to glare at David. "Keep your eyes off my tits and pay attention. Next, we have a Radionics security system setup, run off this keypad. It employs passive infrared through the interior and at the windows, which are also outfitted with glass-shatter sensors. Delayed entry and exit is not to exceed forty seconds. If the system is breached, it'll call out on POTS—plain old telephone system—with a backup cellular dial in case someone takes out your hard line. Your code is your birthday, including the four-digit year, plus the number seven. Got it?"

David nodded.

"Your little shrub collection out front provides excellent concealment for intruders. I'd rather you went with a cleaner look."

"You do landscape design?"

Ed pulled a compact out of the purse and began vigorously removing his eye shadow. "Honey, I do it all."

"What about the phones? The cops can't get the paperwork through to trace calls for a few days. Can you get a tap on the line?"

"Yeah. As soon as I go back in time to the 1950s." Ed picked up one of the Nextels and punched in a number, shaking his head. "Nobody uses taps anymore. I have a Lucent technologist on the inside." He changed his voice to a drawl. "Yeah, hey there. Your baby brother calling. Listen, I'm trying to find mom's new phone number. Here's her old one: 310-555-4771." David's telephone number. "I'm gonna stay with her about a week. . . . No, to be safe, I'd like to stay with her a week—twenty-four hours isn't enough time for us to catch up. . . . Thanks, bro." He hung up and smiled at David. "Your number's red-flagged for seven days."

"Shouldn't we let the police know we've done this?"

The smile left Ed's face instantaneously. "Absolutely not. This is an inside guy I'm using. I have to keep his ass covered. We're trading legality for speed, here." Ed screwed the keypad into the wall behind the ficus and slipped into his stilettos with a pained grimace. "If Clyde calls, let me know immediately and we'll be able to trace the location he called from."

"Thank you," David said. "I . . . thank you."

Ed nodded at him on his way to the door. "I'll send you a bill. You'll send me a money order."

"How much?"

Ed turned, touched two manicured fingers to his lipsticked mouth, and blew David a kiss. "Honey, you don't want to know."

David retrieved the morning paper, sitting in his leather chair and reading the two front-page articles on "The

Westwood Acid Thrower." He noted with amusement that they'd selected a less-than-flattering photograph of himself, captured mid-sentence during his speech at the resident meet-and-greet, to go along with Clyde's.

For the first time in several months, he turned on the television, but news updates of the manhunt cut into the programming every fifteen minutes and he finally turned it off and gazed at the blank space where his mother's de Kooning used to hang. His exhaustion was too charged to give way to sleep.

He sat quietly, snipping and removing the stitches from his healed knuckle. When the phone rang, it nearly startled him off the chair. He dashed back to his bedroom so he could record the call if necessary. After taking an instant to catch his breath, he picked up the phone with a trembling hand. It was only the dry cleaner calling to remind him he'd had clothes ready for pickup since last Monday.

He hung up, gazing at the light swirl of fingerprint powder on the plastic receiver. After trying to sleep, then disconsolately flipping through the latest *New England Journal of Medicine*, David called the ER. Carson still had not come in.

David couldn't rest. He was well on his way to his first glaring professional setback, and Clyde was still on the loose. At least there was one thing David could fix. People stared at him from their cars as he drove up to Carson's building; he wondered why until he saw his car's reflection in a store window, ASHOLE lettered across the side in red. He couldn't help but laugh at the expressions of pedestrians and other drivers.

The newsman on the car radio cheerily announced, "Dr. David Spier's position as UCLA ER division chief has become tenuous. Apparently, the board convened this morning over allegations that he attacked a fellow physician. The hospital has not issued a statement. Spier has been at the controversial center of . . ." David's lack of irritation and unease about the report surprised him pleasantly.

He managed to find Carson's apartment easily this time. Wearing boxers and a ripped T-shirt, Carson opened the door. His face, unshaven and darkened with exhaustion, showed little reaction. David followed him inside wordlessly, and they sat on the floor of the living room again, facing each other. Near the window stood a large bong, which through some tacit agreement, he and Carson pretended not to notice.

"When are you coming back?" David asked.

"I don't know that I am," Carson said softly. "I'm not sure I'm cut out for this." He looked away, his face striped with the shadows of the cheap venetian blinds. "Who's gonna want me to work on them now? If they knew, if patients knew, they'd never want to be in my hands. Under my care." His fingers slid up into his mop of blond hair, disappearing. He held his head and studied the light filtering through the window.

"Forgive me for being harsh," David finally said, breaking the silence. He brought his hands together and laced them into a temple. "But you need to pull your head out of your ass."

Carson blinked several times in rapid succession.

"This self-indulgent wallowing is for lovesick schoolboys. You're a physician. Your job is and will be to make difficult calls in the face of life and death *and to live with them*. I've seen hundreds, maybe even thousands of young doctors, and I know who's cut out for this and who isn't. If you walk away, you'll grow to hate yourself by small, vicious increments."

Carson's lips quivered, ever so slightly.

David continued, "When we spoke the other day, you

expressed ambivalence about your return. I've decided I'm not going to leave that decision to you. You need to come back. It's your responsibility to the division and to yourself. Recent events have forced me to learn anew that the world can be a miserable, difficult place. We can't afford to lose a good physician. Not ever, but especially not this week."

Carson looked at him, his eyes moist.

"I'm taking a few days off, starting now," David continued. "I want to know that you're in the ER in my absence." He stood up and dusted his hands. "I'm not leaving until you get dressed, get in your car, and start your drive to the hospital."

Carson stared at him for a very long time. Then he rose and headed back to his bedroom to change into scrubs.

CHAPTER 66

DAVID sat in the still of his bedroom, back against the headboard, files and papers scattered across his lap. He watched the palm frond shadows wave across the newly scoured blood-tinged wall at the base of his bed, and knew with a sudden and vehement certainty that the telephone was about to ring. He watched the bobbing shadows of the plants and waited, breathing softly, as the clock ticked on.

The phone rang and he set aside Connolly's abstract, which he'd been rereading. His voice was surprisingly calm when he answered. "Yes, Clyde?"

The voice, low and sloppy, rattled with phlegm. "You saw. You saw what I left you?"

David's voice was entirely calm. "I did. And?"

A confused pause.

"If you think sneaking into my house and killing a canary are gonna get me upset, you have another think coming. You're gonna have to do a lot more to scare *me*, Clyde."

Some murmuring: "Back from the door. Three, two, three, two. From the door." Clyde fell quiet. The silence stretched itself out and out, and just as David was certain Clyde had hung up, he spoke. His voice came low and growling. "I'll make you quiver," he said. "I'll make you beg."

"Try it," David said.

The sound of Clyde spitting came through loud and clear. When he spoke again, his voice was eerily calm. "It's gonna get worse. A lot worse."

A chill ran through David's body from his scalp to the soles of his feet. Good, he thought. Then let's play.

The line had gone dead.

His heart was pounding—good competitive bursts of adrenaline.

When Ed returned David's page seconds later, David simply said, "Bingo." Ed called back three minutes later and said, "Pay phone at the Chevron at Venice and Lincoln. Clyde's old stamping grounds."

"What? He hasn't left the area? I've got to head over. I'll call Yale now."

"And say what? Based on an illegal phone trace, you have reason to believe that an escaped felon placed a phone call from a gas station? Don't bite the hand that's dealing you, Spier. That's our deal."

"So what do we do?"

"First, we slow down. We figure out what new information we've gleaned from the phone call."

David started to protest but held his tongue, remembering the last time Ed walked him through this exercise and the helpful information it yielded. "Okay. . . . He's probably hiding in an area near the pay phone."

"Why?"

"His face has been on the cover of the *LA Times* six times in the past week, plus there's an APB out on his car. It's daytime, so there's no way he'd risk a big trip. The farther he travels from his hiding place, the higher risk he runs of being spotted."

"Unless he knew the call was being traced and is purposefully misdirecting the investigation."

"You're right," David said. "That's an option."

"What else?"

"He was no longer slurring when he spoke. That means he probably hasn't been taking lithium, just as we hypothesized, so his blood level is dropping. That makes him more menacing physically, because his balance problems will disappear. He'll be able to run and drive more effectively, as we already surmised. Plus, it makes him more menacing psychologically, because whatever benefit the lithium was providing in reducing his violent tendencies—if it did at all—is now gone."

"And perhaps he filled up his tank," Ed added, "which would explain why he was at the gas station. We're assuming he doesn't have any money, but if he does, you might look at new apartment rentals in the area."

"He's an addicted smoker. If he'd risk going out for gas, he'd probably also risk heading out for cigarettes. I'll go down there with his newspaper photo and ask around at 7-Elevens and Quickie-Marts. And the gas station too, obviously. First thing that yields, I'll call Yale. Then I'll have a concrete reason for red-flagging the area for the cops."

"And if you spot Clyde? What are you gonna do?"

"Talk him in."

"Oh that's right. I forgot how well versed you are in hostage negotiations and combat tactics."

"Sarcasm suits you better when you're in drag, Ed."

"I am not fucking around here, Spier. Watch your ass."

The small concrete storage unit stayed cold, so cold Clyde curled into the fetal position on the cigarette-burnt cushioning of the front seat of his car, his abundant rear end pushed against the driver's door, the cool Beretta pressed to his cheek. The ocean was far enough away that its hypnotic sounds were lost beneath the hum of electric lines and the whir of passing cars, yet close enough that the chill had crept off its surface last night and slunk its way through the streets of Venice, a malicious mist.

Clyde turned and grunted, adjusting his arms under his head. Frustration and then anger found their way into the small noises he made as he shifted. He got out of the car and circled it a few times in the enclosed space. He pulled two cigarettes from a pack of Marlboros in the glove box and smoked them until the cherries singed his lips. Using the tip of the pistol, he slid his dirty T-shirt up and gazed at the pattern of alkali burns across his chest. They looked fearsome, with white, dead skin flaking off around the edges, but they were healing well.

Opening the trunk, he gazed at the mix of oddities he kept stored there. Surgical tools, spare scrub tops and bottoms, a container of liquid DrainEze. Unscrewing the DrainEze cap, he sniffed the alkali solution, then set it on the ground. His hand, tumbling through tire irons and stained towels, found and clutched a Pyrex beaker. He slammed the trunk lid, then set the beaker and the DrainEze on it. Two thick metal runners for the roll-up storage door ran across the ceiling. Around one of them, he'd looped a length of rope. He'd left a makeshift gag dangling from the noose at the rope's end. A recipe for fear.

His call should have drawn David by now—a phone trace, or at least caller ID, would be in place after his last call. Retrieving the pistol from the passenger seat of the car, Clyde walked over to the roll-up storage door, inches away from the front bumper of his Crown Vic, and slid it up a few inches. Daylight streamed in like a gold twinkling river, pooling around his wide calves. He gazed down at the light for a few moments, transfixed and smiling, before taking a knee and peering out of the unit. Dangling from a hasp was the broken combination lock he'd smashed with a tire iron to gain entry to the unit. The lure.

Squinting into the bright light reflecting off the white quartz gravel, he peered down the row of boxy, garage-style units with bright orange metal doors. The strip of storage spaces terminated in the back of a 7-Eleven. A large cracked sign set up on posts—POPPY'S SELF-STORAGE—angled toward the road to entice drivers-by. Across the street, cars crammed into lines at the Chevron station's pumps.

The loose skin of Clyde's face drew up around his eyes in a half squint, half scowl when he spotted the olive Mercedes, ASHOLE lettered on the side. Right on schedule. It pulled over into the lot and Clyde watched it, his mouth pulsing slowly as if working a cud of tobacco, his hand tightening around the Beretta's stock.

David stepped out of his car and headed toward the 7-Eleven. He paused for a moment, his eyes sweeping across the storage units. Clyde bounced slightly with excitement. A family of four pulled into the parking lot about fifteen feet away from Clyde's hiding place and noisily began loading items into the storage unit next door. Clyde's bouncing slowed. Stopped. His meaty hand sneaked through the gap in the roll-up door and snatched the incriminating broken lock from the hasp. He eased the rolling door down until it tapped the concrete, then gripped the inside handle and set all his weight down against it.

He waited in the darkness.

David exited the 7-Eleven, peeved at the teenager behind the counter with a faceful of pierces. The kid had barely bothered to look at the photograph before saying he'd never seen Clyde before. The Chevron worker across the street had been equally unhelpful—he'd recognized Clyde's photograph only from the news. David's heart had quickened when he'd spotted a dilapidated Crown Vic at the curb, but closer examination had revealed it was not Clyde's.

POPPY'S SELF-STORAGE sign drew David's eye again. His feet crunched on the quartz rock as he made his way across the lot. A man struggled to unload an antique bureau from a Jeep, his family watching with concern. David offered to help, but the man waved him off, his face red and sweaty. A manly man. See you in the ER with a slipped disk.

At the bottom of each unit was a hasp, and each hasp housed a lock. Except one. David walked over to the empty hasp and crouched before the roll-up door. Some of the paint was chipped behind the hasp, as if it had been struck by a blunt object.

David grabbed the door handle and yanked upward, but it barely gave. He crouched so as to get his legs into it and pulled, but again, it scarcely moved. Probably jammed.

He headed back to his car, squinting to cut the glare coming off the ground.

The drive to the Pearson Home took only a few minutes. Walking distance for Clyde, as David had estimated. He pulled over to the curb and got out. Up the street, a few kids clicked bright yellow spray cans and further assaulted the beat-to-shit phone booth.

David's feet crunched across the gravel and broken glass of the abandoned lot beside the building. A figure moved in the upstairs window, behind a rippling curtain. Wide and dancing. Layla.

David came to the scorched car and, on an impulse, climbed in. When he slammed the door, the glove box fell open. Inside was a heap of cigarette butts, filling the interior. Mashed together in twos—the way Clyde smoked them. A quickening of David's heart.

David looked up at Layla's shadow dancing awkwardly behind the curtains. *'Ometimes he ooks at me from his car*, she'd said. Kind and controlling Rhonda Decker had misunderstood, misdirected. This car. This broken car. It hadn't been chance that Clyde had hidden here the night David pursued him from Healton's. It was his hideout.

What dark thoughts rushed through Clyde's head when he sat here and stared at his childhood home? Coveting. Watching girls dance in the very bedroom where he'd once strung up boys and relished their fright.

The reek of stale nicotine filled the car. David reached over and felt a cigarette butt on the top of the mound. The cotton filters were soft and spongy. He picked one out from deeper in the pile, knowing the smell would taint his fingers and not caring. Dry and brittle. It crumbled under pressure from his thumb. His heartbeat quickened with excitement.

The top cigarettes were newer. Though David was no smoker, he'd guess they'd been smoked within the past day or two. Yale and Forensics could figure that out.

Clyde *had* stayed in the area, in his hideout, smoking and watching, despite the great risk of getting caught. His pull back to his childhood home must have been stronger than David imagined.

His pager vibrated, startling him. The telephone number to Diane's room at the hospital, with 911 punched in after it.

Heading back to his car, he dialed the number on his cell, trying to quell the panic rising in his throat. It rang about nine times, but Diane didn't answer. As he squealed away from the curb, he had the hospital operator put him through to Ninth Floor Reception, but no one picked up there either, the voice mail kicking in after four rings. Maybe Clyde had drawn David across town with the phone call so he could attack Diane back at the hospital. Growing increasingly frantic and speeding up, David had the operator put him through to hospital security, whom he alerted. Then he called Peter's office.

"Dr. Alexander is in with a patient, can I take a message?" the office manager intoned.

"It's an emergency. Pull him out." David ran two red lights as he waited for Peter to pick up. "Peter, it's David."

"I'm glad you called. What's this nonsense about police wanting to follow me around everywhere I go? I told them—"

"We'll talk about that later. I just received a 911 page from Diane's room, but when I returned it, there was no answer. Security's on their way up, but I was wondering if you could check in to make sure nothing's wrong. I'll be there in"—David checked his watch—"fifteen minutes."

"Of course. I just wrapped up a vasectomy, so I'll go now. When I get there, I'll call you on your cell phone."

"Thank you." David hung up and raced across town, honking for slower-moving cars to get out of his way.

Two women screamed at him, their moving mouths visible through their fast-retreating windshields, and one innovative gentleman in a Chevy flipped him the bird. It seemed an eternity to get across town to Westwood Village, and David pounded the steering wheel, waiting for the light to change at Wilshire and Westwood.

He zoomed up Westwood and made a screeching right onto Le Conte. He recognized Peter's distinctive gait as Peter waddled slowly back from the hospital toward his office, his cane moving in concert with his right leg. David tried to read his demeanor from a distance. Peter did not seem to be alarmed—he even nodded casually at a crew of lunching construction workers as he passed them by. David pulled his car over and hopped out, hailing Peter just as he made his way beneath the scaffolding flanking the building.

Peter watched David approach, mopping his brow with a handkerchief. "Everything's fine," he called out. "Diane wasn't in her room because she checked out this morning after a good set of exams. She's safe and sound at home as we speak."

David stopped a few feet off the curb. "Then who paged me?"

A loud revving behind him. Peter's face changed instantly, his bushy eyebrows drawing apart and up. "Move!" he cried out.

In dreamlike slow motion, David pivoted and saw the chipped brown Crown Victoria peeling out from an alley onto Le Conte, Clyde's wide figure hunched over the wheel, pistol-bearing hand extended toward the windshield. The alley was no more than fifteen yards away, and the vehicle bore down on him quickly. For an awful instant, David's legs froze. He felt the pounding of his heart in his ears as the car barreled toward him, and then he turned and dashed for the cover of the scaffolding.

The deafening report of a gunshot. The bullet cracking the air beside David's head as it sailed past. He did not turn; he kept his eyes ahead, focused on the next four steps, which would bring him to the curb.

The car seemed to fill the air behind him. David dove off the street into the safety of the scaffolding, knocking over a toolbox and rolling to a stop between a sledgehammer and two sturdy 4-by-4s. The Crown Victoria hit the curb about ten feet away, one tire popping. It hurtled at David, plowing through the scaffolding, snapping the rails like toothpicks and sending chunks of wood airborne. A sharp pain seized David's left side, and he felt himself go momentarily light-headed. A raised wedge of plywood intervened just before the Crown Victoria could crush David, tilting the car to one side so the remaining inflated rear tire could no longer find purchase.

Clyde revved the engine to a deafening pitch, the back tires spinning and sending up showers of splinters and dirt, then the car suddenly quieted, the steaming front grill so close to David's face he could have reached out and stroked the grimy metal.

The scaffolding leaned and creaked fearsomely overhead, but did not collapse.

Behind him, David heard Peter rustling in the debris. He felt moisture spreading through his shirt around the site of his pain, but he did not tear his eyes from the car. A bullet had penetrated the window in its lower left quadrant, spiderwebbing the glass around it. Clyde's face, pressed forward against the steering wheel, drew suddenly back, and the flat eyes, accented by the bright red smear of a forehead gash, stared at him.

The pistol had tumbled from Clyde's grip on the car's impact with the scaffolding, and it lay on the dash against the windshield, gleaming in the diffuse sunlight. David's and Clyde's eyes seemed to fall on the weapon simultaneously, and Clyde lunged for it with a meaty hand as David anticipated he would. David's hand had been sifting through the debris as if of its own volition, searching for a plank or some suitable weapon. It closed on the handle of the sledgehammer.

David drew himself to his feet, pain seizing his left side in a fiery grip, as Clyde fumbled the pistol across the dash. Clyde finally grasped the pistol firmly. As he brought it up, aiming at David through the once-shattered glass of the windshield, David drew the sledgehammer back like a baseball bat, and hammered it sideways at the nose of the hood, directly between the two square headlights.

The air bag inflated with a boom, knocking Clyde's arms back up in his face and pinning him to his seat. David went weak with pain, the sledgehammer dropping from his grasp. The crack of a gunshot echoed within the enclosure of the scaffolding, and the air bag went limp. Clyde clawed and shoved his way through the material and out the door, landing on all fours. The gun skidded from his hand.

A streak of bright yellow on Clyde's forearm. The information shifted and fell into place. The freshly spray-painted phone booth by the abandoned lot. Clyde had been watching David. He'd placed the fake distress page from the booth right around the corner from the Pearson Home, then followed David back to the hospital.

Clyde's head rotated to face David slowly, mechanically. His eyes moved past David, finding Peter, then returned to David. Standing, Clyde wiped the blood from his brow, his eyes widening with the intensity of his rage. His face was twisted, flushed a deep red. Wrathful. He let out a cry, an unintelligible expression of fury. His hands curling into fists, he advanced on David, who remained rooted to the spot.

Someone knocked David to the ground from behind

with a sudden, forceful blow. Pain screeched up his side and his mouth filled with sawdust. He rolled over, looking up at the dark figure of a man towering protectively over him, his workman's overalls unbuttoned and hanging down, the dark, twisted form of a swastika tattooed across his chest. Zeke Crowley.

Clyde's expression changed to one of nervous alarm. He backpedaled a few steps, stooping to pick up the Beretta, and sprinted off up the street, turning into the alley from which his car had sprung.

Zeke looked down at David. "Motherfucker," he said dolefully. "Motherfucker."

It took David a moment to realize that Zeke was gazing at David's side. For the first time, David looked down and saw the length of splintered 2-by-4 protruding about ten inches from his side. The shard was no more than two inches at its thickest. Blood had colored David's shirt black around the puncture site. David's eyes moved dreamily back up to Zeke's. "Could you please call me an ambulance?" he said calmly. "And, if you wouldn't mind, check on Dr. Alexander there behind you."

Peter's gruff voice. "I'm fine." Peter's bespectacled face staring down at David. "I wish we could say the same for you."

A group of spectators had gathered along the wrecked scaffolding, clustering around Clyde's abandoned car. A reporter was already snapping photographs—how did the press arrive quicker than the police? David gripped the shard protruding from his side so no one would be tempted to pull it out. Straining, he tried to feel behind him to see if the point had penetrated the other side. When he spoke, his voice was even weaker. "Call Detective Yale at the West LA Police Station. And keep the crowd away from the car. That's evidence."

Zeke faced the crowd, his throat cording with muscle

as he yelled. "Someone call the hospital. Tell them a doctor got hurt. Tell them it's the Jew doctor."

"I'm afraid," David said, just before passing out, "that won't sharply narrow it down."

CHAPTER 67

DAVID monitored his own pulse, two fingers laid across his wrist, as the ambulance screeched to a halt outside the ER. Though the screen near his head flashed his exact heart rate—98—he found something calming in feeling for himself.

"Ready, Doctor?" one of the EMTs asked, and then the back doors swung open and the gurney slid out with David on it, the legs snapping down into place.

The glass doors opened as they approached, impervious, heavenly gates. The length of wood protruding from David's side seemed oddly humorous to him, like a shot-through-the-head-with-an-arrow hat. As they rattled through the lobby, Jill recognized him and leapt up from her chair, spilling a cup of coffee across the triage desk.

"Dr. Spier? Are you all right?" She turned and shouted up Hallway One, "Clear Procedure Two!"

They banged through the swinging doors. A scramble of faces, and then Don standing overhead, the stifling smell of his aftershave permeating the hall. A nurse tried to pry David's stethoscope from his hand, but he didn't let her.

Don's face registering concern. "Dave—Jesus!"

Carson ran through the CWA as the gurney swept into the procedure room, his disheveled hair bouncing with his steps. He fought through the sea of nurses and interns, taking David's hand.

David squeezed his hand reassuringly. "What do we do first, Dr. Donalds?" he said weakly.

Carson took a step back. "I don't . . ."

Don pushed Carson aside with a glare. "Carson, get out of here. This is a serious trauma. We can't have you mucking around like before."

Through the arms of two nurses, David saw Carson's face wilt. Someone hit the brakes and the gurney slid to a halt.

"Dr. Donalds will be treating me," David said.

"Bullshit," Don said. "I'm not having that kid in here. Not after what happened last time."

"He will be my physician." David's voice was uneven from the pain, but firm.

"We don't have time for this right now, Dave," Don said, readying a syringe. "He's a medical student."

"And I'm the chief," David said sternly. "At least for now. Get out of Dr. Donalds's way."

Don lowered his hands, irritation flickering across his handsome face. "And who's going to be the attending on this case?"

David managed a smile. "I am."

Carson's voice cracked when he spoke. "Look, I don't think this is such a—"

A nurse leaned over David, then an IV needle dug into his arm. "I am not presenting either of you with a choice," David said.

"Fuck this," Don said. "Let him kill you. What the hell do I care?" Storming from the room, he shot a latex glove at the rolling trash bin, but it flew wide and landed on a counter.

"Dr. Donalds," David said. *"Dr. Donalds."*

Carson's eyes slowly found focus. "Yeah?"

"What do we do first?"

"Check vitals?"

"How are we looking?"

"We're looking good." Carson slid his cold stethoscope along David's side, checking his lungs. David inhaled without being prompted.

"What do you want to ask me?"

"Do you have pain anywhere else aside from the entry site?"

"No," David said.

A note of confidence crept into Carson's voice. "I want a Foley in, let's see if it nicked a kidney."

"Exactly." David clenched his teeth to fight down the next wave of pain as the nurse reached for a urine catheter. "But you may want to think about giving me something for the pain first."

"Shit. Morphine." Carson turned to the nurse. "Five mgs."

"Let's start with two," David managed. "We can always step it up."

"Two mgs. And someone get that Foley in."

A flurry of hands at David's pants, and then his penis laid bare in a gloved hand.

"Listen for bowel sounds," David said. He sensed the nurse readying the catheter to shove up his urethra and wished the morphine had kicked in. Carson took his hand. The nurse's arm tensed, and the pain set David's body ramrod straight in the gurney. Pat appeared from nowhere and wiped the sweat from his forehead with a moist roll of gauze.

Carson set the bell of his stethoscope on David's stomach.

"Lower," David said. When he released Carson's

hand, the white imprints of his fingers were visible. "Lower."

"Good bowel sounds," Carson announced.

"No blood in the urine," Pat said. "I'll send it for a UA."

"Dr. Donalds, why do we send urine for a UA?" David asked.

"To check for microscopic blood."

"That's right. Next step, next step," David said. "Where are we going next?"

"We're getting you a CT to see if the shard penetrated the abdomen wall?"

"Is it a question, Dr. Donalds?"

"We're getting you a CT to see if it penetrated the abdomen wall," Carson said with more conviction. His head snapped up. "Let's move him."

Nurses scrambled around David's body like industrious rats. The gurney started moving again, heading over to radiology. Someone's arm brushed the protruding shard and David cried out in pain. His face felt as if it were on fire. Sweat ran into his eyes. He tried to slow his breathing.

They slid David onto the large white scanner and the room was cleared. He began the slow, lonely journey through the quietly whirring machine. He felt peaceful and drowsy, either from the morphine or the calm, hypnotic movement of the scanner.

When he emerged, he saw Carson through the window, peering into the computer monitor, looking relieved. The machine printed out a few sheets of CT cuts, which Carson picked up and snapped into an X-ray box. He stepped back into the scanner room with the sheet of CT cuts, finally allowing himself to smile. "Missed your large bowel by a few centimeters," he said. "No perforation, no free air. You're looking at a deep flesh wound. Why don't you take a look?"

Still lying on his back, David raised the sheet above his head so he could view it through the overhead lights. Carson's read was accurate, but before David could agree out loud, Carson had already turned to the others and said, "Let's get him back to Procedure Two."

Another hallway ceiling, and then through the doors and back into the procedure room. David's hands hovered protectively around the protruding shard. The pain was rising through him in waves, deepening the lines of his face.

Snapping on a fresh pair of gloves, Carson turned to one of the nurses. "Another two mgs of morphine," he said.

"I don't think that's really necessary," David said.

The nurse paused, needle near the port of David's IV.

"Another two mgs of morphine," Carson repeated, ignoring David.

David smiled weakly. "Congratulations, Dr. Donalds," he said. "You are now acting like a physician."

After the second morphine injection, David felt only pressure when Carson gripped the shard firmly with two gloved hands. Had David been less drugged, the sucking sound it made upon being extracted would have been disagreeable.

He lay back, watching the walls slide around as the nurses irrigated him with sterile water. "Don't even think about ducking out on the sutures like you usually do, Dr. Donalds. You're going to tie every last one of them if it kills me. Which it might."

Carson had gotten through the deep tissue sutures and was working on the superficial ones when Yale and Dalton arrived.

David smiled at them sloppily.

"We're getting awfully tired of running around after you and picking up the pieces," Dalton said.

"Yes," David said, grimacing as Carson slipped with

the needle. "I can imagine it's quite trying for you." He pointed into his open wound. "Try to approximate the edges better. There you go. Perfect." He glanced back up at Dalton, who was beginning to look a bit green. "Did you catch him?"

"We have thirty units sweeping the area, but he seems to have disappeared on us again," Yale said. "The Tibet protests had our traffic units tied up at the Federal Building, so it took over ten minutes to get a unit to the scene. The Captain's apoplectic, the Mayor's foaming at the mouth, and Clyde is gone, baby, gone."

Dalton hitched his pants, his grimace indicating that the gesture took considerable effort. "My guess is, he's still in Westwood, holed up somewhere. We've locked down the Village pretty well and are beating the bushes. Some of the boys are starting to go door-to-door. Oh, and we found your painting in his trunk. The mangled naked lady. Looks like she got a bit more mangled in transit."

"That's fine." David tried to grin. "It was my mother's. I've grown less trusting of her taste."

Carson continued to work on David's side industriously.

"You want to fill us in here, Evel Knievel?" Dalton said.

"I went out to Venice to show Clyde's photograph around some other places I thought he might have gone. Gas stations, 7-Elevens." David's head was reeling from the morphine, but he fought his thoughts back into focus. "I stopped by to take another look at the Pearson Home. I discovered he's been back there, hanging out in that scorched car in the lot. I found what I think are recently smoked cigarettes in the glove box, mashed together in twos like Clyde smokes them."

"The fucker was right there," Dalton said. "I don't believe it."

"You should be able to determine how old they are, right? The cigarette butts?"

"I'd imagine." Yale nodded at Dalton. "We'll get some SID guys over there."

"I think he was watching me there," David continued. "He sent me an emergency page—Diane's number—from the phone booth right around the corner from the Pearson Home. Then he followed me and tried to run me over the minute I got out of my car."

"From the looks of his vehicle, he's been hiding out in it the past few days," Yale said. "We're not sure where, but we found an unusual white gravel stuck in the tires' tread. Same type of rock he used to weight the sock he hit the guard with when he attacked Dr. Trace. Looks to be fake quartz."

With the morphine, David's face felt loose. "There's a storage facility called Poppy's at Lincoln and Venice. It's got a white gravel lot. Look around there." Carson looked up at David reverently, but David gestured at his wound with his head. "Get back to work."

Dalton removed his notepad from a back pocket and, with a self-conscious glance at Yale, jotted down some notes.

Yale touched the end of his nose with a knuckle. "Are we gonna keep pretending you're gathering all this information yourself?"

"Yes."

Dalton broke the resultant pause. "You were wrong about him leaving all the DrainEze behind at the apartment. He kept a spare in the trunk."

"Well, he doesn't have it anymore," David said. "And at least no one got hurt."

Dalton's eyes traced over the gash in David's side. "Right."

"Clyde's been slowly deprived of his necessities," Yale

said. "Pushed out of his apartment, forced to leave behind his car. He has no drugs, no alkali. That makes him more desperate. He's out of resources, so he'll have to steal or surface. A car, meds, some food, something, and we'll nab him then."

"Do you have men on those people I red-flagged?" David asked.

"We have a unit at Mrs. Connolly's around the clock, and one at the chief of staff's house nights. Mrs. Trace is being covered too—"

"Dr. Trace," David said faintly.

"—but your buddy Peter Alexander is being a stubborn pain in the ass. He says he doesn't need protection, that he's perfectly capable of taking care of himself."

"Infuriating," David said. "But not entirely surprising. We *have* to keep him covered. Clyde's seen him on two occasions—during his escape, and just now when he tried to run me over. Both times were antagonistic. Is there anything we can do?"

Dalton shrugged his familiar shrug. "The guy refuses, the guy refuses."

"I'll see if I can talk some sense into him."

"Good luck."

"We need a more extreme plan," David said, "so I picked his next victim."

Dalton scratched his cheek with the end of his pen. "Who?"

"Me."

"I don't know," Yale said. "Your theories haven't exactly been airtight. I thought you said he wanted to scare you, not kill you. Trying to run you over in a car would qualify as the latter, I believe."

"That's because by going to that lot and poking around—near the house that is his sanctified ground—I committed a violation so great I probably pushed him over the edge. That was the first time I've seen him close to that enraged, including when he was dragged into the ER by a wire noose. He came at me with blind wrath. I want to find a way to make him that angry again. So angry that he'll no longer want to scare me. He'll want to kill me."

Yale and Dalton regarded David silently, as though taking in a new person. Carson continued to stitch and pretend he was not listening.

"He's grown more and more aggressive," David said. "You want to intercept that trajectory we talked about? Let's push him to the limit."

"Your getting him enraged did make him more prone to fuck up," Dalton conceded. "He followed you in broad daylight in a vehicle he knows we're on the lookout for. And he attacked you in front of witnesses—that's a first too."

Yale asked, "How do you get him in that state again?"

David guided Carson's hand to help him get a better angle at the wound. "I'm a hot target. The Pearson Home is a hot location. The combination today did the trick. I say we combine the two again. I think it'll be too much for him to resist."

Yale studied the gash in David's side. "I'd rather use undercover cops. Dress some females up as nurses like we talked about, then have them exit the Pearson Home and walk through the deserted streets."

"In that neighborhood? They'll be more likely to get propositioned than attacked. I'm more believable. He knows I'm familiar with the neighborhood. He knows I've gone poking around after him. I'm your perfect lure. If I go near that house, he'll sniff me out."

The only sound was of Carson working on David—the pickups pinching flesh, the needles pushing through skin.

"He's stranded in Westwood without a car," Yale said. "What's to say he'll head back to Venice?"

"He's been persistently drawn back near that house for much of his adult life. He'll find a way. Unless he comes after me at home, someone at the hospital, or the people we red-flagged, in which case we'll catch him anyway."

Yale brushed something off the sleeve of his suit jacket. "We won't hesitate to use necessary force."

"Will you kill him?"

"If we have to," Yale said. He held up his hand when both David and Dalton started to speak, stopping them. "You'll just have to trust me on this one."

David chewed his lip, trying to bring his thoughts back into focus. Out in the hall, an orderly pushed an empty gurney. "I guess we don't have a choice," he said.

For the first time, David couldn't read Dalton's eyes. David stared at the detectives positioned at the foot of his gurney. The room seemed charged, a triangle of intensity moving between the three men.

"Well?" David said. "What do you say?"

Dalton looked over at Yale, clearly waiting for him to make the call. Carson finished the last suture, pulling the excess through until the last segment of the wound was brought to a close.

"All right," Yale said. "I'll run it by the Captain, and we'll flesh out a plan once you're . . . intact."

David offered a weak hand and, at last, Yale stepped forward and took it.

CHAPTER 68

LYING on the gurney in the empty room, floating on a post-morphine mist, David surveyed the tools and equipment around him. A wall suction unit, lead aprons, otoscope and ophthalmoscope hanging on the walls. Casting his mind back over the past seventeen years, he tried to think about how many accident victims he'd seen wheeled in this very room, how many family members he'd consoled, how many he'd reassured. People left in wheelchairs and gurneys, they left walking and limping. Sometimes they left in bags.

He tried to figure out why he had been so fortunate. Why the wood hadn't struck half a foot to the left and perfed his intestine, or a foot higher and pierced his heart. He would have liked to think it was because of fate—that he was a divine instrument whose usefulness had not yet been depleted—but he knew that was not the case. He would live for the same reason that a three-millimeter embolus had lodged in Elisabeth's basilar artery and killed her. Brute chance.

David recognized the last couple of years for what they'd been—his period of mourning, his time withdrawn. He'd been letting go of Elisabeth in small, meaningful steps, savoring each part of her before relinquishing it. The soft skin of her nape. Her cold feet pressed against his legs beneath the sheets. The cant of her smile—slightly left. The last memories of his wife, lingering in his half-closed hands like hourglass sand.

A flash of Nancy lying upstairs, her mouth moving in a chant. *I wanna die I wanna die I wanna die*. Clyde's flat, senseless eyes: illness incarnate. They'd all retreated into their respective agonies—why had David been left a road back?

A knock on the open door drew his attention. Diane.

She did not advance. Her face was unbandaged, and her wounds looked raw and healthy. She propped a shoulder against the doorjamb and regarded him for a full minute. A tear swelled at the brink of her left eye, then dropped.

"I wasn't worried about you at all," she said.

"Nor I you," David said.

"I don't think you're fucking insane," she said.

A little boy walking by in the hall stopped to stare at Diane's face until his mother whispered an apology and tugged him along. Diane raised her eyebrows at David, a gesture of mild amusement. "We're like Beauty and the Beast without a Beauty."

"You can be Beauty," David said.

"You're sweet when you're wounded." She crossed her arms, then uncrossed them. "Plastics checked me out. I'm again free to enjoy life, liberty, and the pursuit of the paparazzi." She smiled, but sadness found its way through.

They stared at each other across the distance of the room.

"Are you going to come over here?" David asked.

"No." Diane shook her head, tilting it back slightly so she wouldn't spill more tears. "No."

Snapping her cell phone closed, Sandy turned into the doorway, almost colliding with Diane. She stepped into the procedure room, looked at David, and said, "Christ."

Looking from David's face to Diane's, Sandy took note of the emotional current, and her lips pressed together disapprovingly.

"Sandy," David said by way of greeting. He raised his head from the pillow.

Sandy's eyes traced down the front of his hospital gown. "Your catheter's out. Have you voided?"

He nodded. "Let's just say now I know what it's like to have the clap."

"Antibiotics?"

"Unasyn. Started with two grams."

Sandy slid her cell phone into her white jacket and rubbed her hands together quickly, as if to draw warmth. "Look, I can see this isn't the best time, but, well, tact has never been my long suit." Hesitating, she glanced over at Diane.

"It's fine," David said. "What is it?"

A momentary droop in the firm line of Sandy's shoulders. "You've been asked to step down as chief. By the board. There was a vote."

Diane pushed herself off the wall as if she were going to say something. Sandy kept her eyes trained on David.

David's laugh was a bit giddy from the morphine.

"Goddamn it, David. You've had angry confrontations with police, you've been playing Nancy Drew around the hospital, you assault a colleague—"

"Assault," David repeated with amusement.

"—and don't even bother to appear when summoned to the board. What did you expect?" She shook her head in exasperation, then ran a thumb along the bottom of her painted lip, removing excess lipstick. Walking over, she sat on the gurney beside David. "I'm having Dr. Nelson take over responsibilities temporarily—I'll be fucked if I'll give Don the satisfaction. If you spend your time off quietly and distance yourself from this case, maybe things will settle down. Then I could see about—"

"No," David said.

He shifted on the bed and a dagger of pain shot into

his side. Sandy moistened some gauze padding and dabbed around the edges of David's wound. By the door, Diane watched silently.

"Back off this case," Sandy said. "The press is making you look like an ass."

"To be honest, I don't really care anymore."

Sandy wadded the gauze pad into a ball and shot it at the trash can. It hit dead center. "You don't have your mother's sense, do you know that, David? You'll never be the doctor she was."

"No," David said. "I won't."

Sandy looked at him, reading his face. Evidently, she didn't find what she was looking for. "Goddamn it, David. Goddamn it." She reached out and patted him on the cheek roughly, almost a slap. "Whichever way this lands, I'm going to be unhappy, aren't I?"

Her expression textured, an odd blend of nostalgia and loss, and David knew she was thinking of his mother. When she looked at him, he sensed a glimmer of newfound respect. She spread her arms so he could hug her, which he did, despite the pain.

She squeezed him tightly, as if afraid to let go. Her lips were close to his ear, so he heard her perfectly when she whispered in her smooth, deep voice, "I'd recommend your not coming in for a while."

They broke off the embrace and regarded each other.

"I understand," David said.

He nodded. Sandy rose to leave, still not so much as acknowledging Diane.

"What was the vote?" David asked.

Sandy paused by the door. "Excuse me?"

"You said the board voted for me to step down. I'd like to know what the vote was."

Sandy readjusted the brooch on her suit jacket—a gold scarab. "Fourteen to one."

David pushed himself up to a sitting position, letting his legs dangle over the side of the gurney. He studied his bare feet. "Who was the one?"

"You know I can't disclose that."

"Who was the one?"

Sandy sighed. "You know who the one was." Her hand described an arc in the air and landed back on her hip. "Me." She nodded curtly and walked out, leaving the door open behind her.

David pressed on the flesh around his wound to gauge its redness. His white fingerprint slowly faded. When he looked up, Diane was watching him.

"I cannot believe they'd have you step down as chief. I mean, it's ridiculous. It can be overturned. You'd get staff support, I'm sure."

"Not anymore," David said.

"Aren't you going to protest?"

"It's an appointed position, not a political race."

"Okay," Diane said. "Okay." She drummed her fingernails against the door.

He stood up. The thumping pain in his side alerted him that the morphine was fading. His face still felt loose and blurry, and he knew he probably looked like hell. Unhooking his IV bag from its pole, he carried it with him as he walked over to Diane. He stopped a few feet short of her.

Diane blew a strand of hair off her face. He watched her closely, lovingly.

"I don't adore you," he said. "Not at all."

"Good." Some of the anger left her face. "I don't adore you either."

CHAPTER 69

CLYDE'S breath fogged the window against which he leaned as he gazed down the seven-story drop to the dark square of the UCLA Medical Center quad. The top tier of the PCHS parking structure glowed beneath the lights, crammed with cars and trucks. The security guards moved up and down the rows in their nurse-white shirts. The top floors of the office buildings on Le Conte were also in view, sticking up above the fringe of trees like dominoes, and he could just make out the splintered wreckage of the scaffolding.

Clyde kept his eye on one car in particular—the olive-green Mercedes parked in the choicest spot near the hospital. From this distance, the ASHOLE lettering on its side was visible only as a red smudge.

A few drops of condensation resolved on the foggy glass and trickled to the sill. He'd been watching for some time.

He spotted the white coat first, then recognized David walking tenderly up the concrete stairs to the top level, Diane Trace slightly in front of him. At either side of them were men in suits—one standing tall and lean, the other wide and slumped. The detectives.

After discussing something animatedly, they helped David into his car. Then they headed down to the lower tier, escorting Diane to her Explorer.

The Mercedes pulled out of the parking structure,

Diane's car just behind it. When they passed the parking kiosks, a van pulled out from the curb and followed them both, about a block back.

Clyde pressed both palms against the glass on either side of his face, like a mime, and watched David's car until it disappeared from view.

Don strode up to Sandy's door, white coat flaring. He raised his hand to knock, but before he could, Sandy's voice issued through the solid door. "Come in."

A Bic pen behind her ear, Sandy worked at the conference table under the glow of the green banker's lamp. She flipped through a contract, sighed, tossed it to the side, and glanced at the next document in the pile before her.

"Dr. Evans, I'd like to thank you for your support in this matter, regarding Dr. Spier." Sandy did not look up. Don waited for a response, but finding none, continued. "It was, uh, a wise decision, I believe, for the division."

Still looking down at her paperwork, Sandy mumbled something under her breath.

"I'm sorry?" Don said.

Sandy finally looked up. "I said, 'Go fuck yourself,' Dr. Lambert." She pulled the pen from behind her ear and attacked the next file in her stack.

Don watched her work for a few moments, his mouth slightly ajar. He made sure to close the door quietly behind him when he left.

David was vaguely aware of the carpet cleaning van following him and Diane a few blocks back; Yale had selected it as the undercover vehicle, as it wouldn't be out of place in upscale Brentwood. It parked across the street when David pulled into his garage. Diane left her Explorer at the curb, near the mailbox. She helped David inside, and in a confusion of beeps and codes, he disarmed the security alarms.

She walked him down the long hall to his bedroom, one arm looped across his back, and deposited him on his bed. He lay back on the stark white pillows with a groan, holding her hand. His eyes were swollen, underscored by bags so dark they resembled contusions.

He held her hand and looked up at her. She was scanning the plain, empty room, the white walls, the lonely chair in the corner, and David felt a sudden, intense vulnerability—a concern that his bedroom revealed more of his life than he himself wished to grasp and convey.

"You should go," he said. "The cops will escort you home and keep an eye on you."

"Are you sure you want to be alone?"

He nodded. She backed up to go, but he didn't relinquish her hand. Despite the codeine, his wound was throbbing with his heartbeat, regular intervals of pain. The shock of almost being killed had caught up to him all at once, rushing him like a bad dream recalled. And though he'd been anticipating it, the news from the board didn't lessen the sensation that he was badly navigating rocky waters.

"I could stay," she offered again quietly.

He shook his head, but still held her hand, held it tighter.

"It's okay," she said. "You can need me." She looked at him and gave him the silence for as long as he needed it.

"Five minutes," he finally managed.

She let her hand slide from his, then, crossing her arms and shrugging her shoulders, she lifted off her top. Her hair spilled down across her shoulders, a golden fan spreading.

She slid into bed beside him, her back propped up against the headboard, and then he was lying in blissful silence, clutching her, his face pressed to her bare chest, her flesh moist with the faintest recollection of sweat and scented like lilac and summer.

CHAPTER 70

WHEN the dull ache in his side awakened David the next morning, he was groggy from the morphine and codeine, and profoundly fatigued. Diane had left last night after a few minutes more than his requested five. The carpet cleaning van remained curbside up the street, visible through his bedroom window.

He cracked the window, letting the breeze float into the room, and lay on his back, staring at the ceiling and wincing in time to the pulses of pain. A bottle of Tylenol with codeine sat on his nightstand, but he didn't want to take any. Not yet. He wanted to feel the sting of the wound, perhaps in a self-flagellating way; though he could discern no conscious reason why he'd punish himself, the instinctual motives were many and complex. More likely, he found the pain reassuring because the beating wound matched the movement of his heart and reminded him, continuously, sharply, that he was alive.

The insistent ringing of the phone pulled him from his thoughts. The woman's voice on the other end was exuberant to the point of being hysterical. "Hello, Dr. Spier. Kate Mantera from *Time* magazine. We've received word that you suffered a direct attack from the Westwood Acid Thrower. We're thinking of—"

"Alkali," David said.

"Excuse me?"

"He throws *alkali*." David hung up the telephone and it immediately rang again.

A man's voice, deep and rich. "Dr. David Spier, this is John Cacciotti from KBNE—your ride in the morning—and you're on the air. What we'd like to know is—"

David hung up and unplugged the telephone. After unscrewing and examining the showerhead, he took a long, steamy shower. When he got out, he used his cell phone to call Diane at home.

When she didn't answer, he felt a flutter of panic. He called the ER and asked the clerk if anyone had heard from Diane.

"Yeah," the clerk said. "She's right here."

Diane picked up. "Don't worry. I have two University police officers in here watching over me. Right, guys?" Mumbled background accord.

"But your injuries. You shouldn't be working already."

"Oh please, David. What am I gonna do, sit around and heal?"

"I really don't think you should be up and on your feet yet. At least not for a couple of days."

"That's what he'd want," she said. "To shut us down. I'll be damned if I'm going to be emotionally blackmailed into not doing my job. And besides, you should be on bed rest for several days minimum. Are *you* going to follow doctor's orders?"

David wandered down the hall to the living room, his side giving off a dull ache.

"I didn't think so," she said. "Look, we're on overload this morning. Why did you call?"

Switching emotional tracks, he felt suddenly sluggish. "I wanted to say . . . well, last night . . . I guess it was . . ."

"I know, David. Me too." He heard someone shout in the background on her end of the line. "I have to run," she said. "Let's talk later."

He heard himself agree, then hung up. Whatever he'd wanted to convey remained a nervous ball in his chest. He'd been realizing with increasing conviction that he didn't have the world figured out nearly as well as he'd once assumed.

He opened the front door to get the newspaper, and the crowd of reporters stationed at his curb sprang to life, scurrying up the walk at him. Startled, he snatched the paper and slammed the door. The doorbell rang behind him, three times in rapid succession.

After allowing himself a moment for his heartbeat to slow, David glanced down at the paper in his hand. The headline read WESTWOOD ACID THROWER ATTACKS SO-CALLED DR. DEATH. He considered his new moniker. Dr. Death. He could adjust to that. It had a nice alliterative ring to it. Now that he was no longer division chief, he supposed the new title would have to suffice.

As he dialed Peter, he absentmindedly scanned down the article. The news of the Connolly study had leaked, which, in combination with Clyde's highly visible car attack, had kicked media coverage into even higher gear.

"How are you holding up?" Peter asked when he picked up.

"I'm feeling much better. I finally got a decent night's sleep."

"Almost run down in the street and shot like Rasputin. How ignoble." Peter made a clucking sound.

"What's this about you not accepting police protection?"

"I've protected myself just fine all these years, David. I hardly need the Keystone Kops to tuck me in at night. Besides, moving into the new procedure suite has me seeing double. I'm too busy to be bothered."

David walked over to the window and fingered the closed blind. Outside, a uniformed cop was strong-arming the press crowd back toward the street. "I don't think you're aware—"

"Bad assumption, David. I'm always aware. And I must run. I'm behind schedule. I'll check in later."

David hung up and dialed Yale at West LA. Yale picked up on a half ring. "We're lining things out for tomorrow. Don't let the media get to you. We still have a unit out front keeping an eye on things."

"I know. I saw it. I'm actually calling about something else."

"What's that?"

"I spoke with Peter today. He's still closed to the idea of police coverage. And I'd say he doesn't show any signs of changing his mind."

"We told you as much."

"His being covered is absolutely essential. One: His life is at stake. And two: We need to cover all bases for our trap."

"I understand. But without his consent, there's nothing we can do."

"What if there was some way to bug him so we could keep track of him from afar?"

A hint of humor crept into Yale's voice. "I could never participate in such a matter, of course, as a sworn peace officer. But if one were to make such arrangements without my knowledge, I'd be unable to warn him of the illicit nature of such activities."

"I see." Another van screeched up to the curb and a guy jumped out the back, toting cable. An assistant held up a mirror so a reporter in a starchy red suit could touch up her lipstick. "I need to get out of here for the afternoon," David said. "Alone."

"We need to keep a unit on you. If Clyde gets his

hands on you before tomorrow night, you'll lose your utility as bait."

"Peter needs to be protected or watched in some way," David said. "We have to cover that base. Without it, our trap's going to have a hole."

"How strongly do you feel about this?" Yale sighed. "Never mind. Why do I bother asking?"

"There's something else, too. There's no way I can get my Mercedes out of the garage and through the press crowd without being followed. I'll arrange with Diane to borrow her Explorer—it's parked at the hospital right now. Could you have someone pick it up, then call me? I'll climb my back fence and meet the car on Bristol, near the hideous mock-Tudor." He waited, but got no response. "This is part of our deal, Detective Yale. We work together. I keep you in the loop on everything. You can either help me, or I get this done behind your back."

"I have to say, I'm surprised by your lack of respect for Peter's individual rights," Yale finally said, the same trace of amusement in his voice.

"Well," David said, "we're playing a different game now, aren't we?"

⊕

David stepped from the cover of a patch of elm saplings when the carpet cleaning van pulled up to the curb, Diane's Explorer idling behind it. The van's tinted window rolled slowly down, revealing Jenkins and, across in the passenger seat, Bronner. They were both out of uniform; Jenkins in particular looked odd wearing a casual sweatshirt. The scent of Corn Nuts and Kodiak wintergreen wafted from the van.

David drew back his head in surprise. "Gentlemen. I didn't realize it was you out here."

"There was a bit more overtime to go around, and the

Captain decided he'd rather keep it within the division," Jenkins said in his tough monotone.

Bronner smiled, revealing a dark crescent of dip in his lower lip. "Plus, we waxed the Captain's car for him. That tends to help."

David glanced back at Diane's Explorer and saw Blake in the driver's seat. Neither waved. "Isn't that the guy who helped you bring Clyde in?" David asked.

"Yeah. Blake."

David started toward the Explorer, then stopped and turned back to the van. "Officer Bronner, remind me to send you over some slides of lip- and tongue-cancer victims."

Bronner spit a brown jet of saliva into an empty Coke can. "I'll do that," he said.

David gave Blake a slight nod as Blake climbed out of the Explorer, turning over the vehicle to him. David climbed into the driver's seat. He watched his rearview mirror as he pulled out, to make sure Jenkins and Bronner weren't following him.

CHAPTER 71

ED'S voice was high-pitched and irritated. "You paged me 911. This better be an emergency."

"It is."

"Where are you now?"

"I'm in my car."

"Are you in imminent danger?"

"No."

Ed took a deep breath. "All right. We need to get our signals straight. Cornered in a shootout—that's a 911. Waking up in a bathtub of ice with a missing kidney. That's a 911."

"Look, this is extremely important. The cops are staking me out to catch Clyde. I managed to sneak out, and I only have a brief window." David yanked the Explorer over to the side of the road. "Where are you? I'm coming over."

"How do you know they're not following you?"

"Because I've been driving in loops and circles all over the city for the past hour and a half. I'm not as much of a dumb-ass as when you first met me."

"Jury's still out on that one, Spier."

"Where are you?"

"I don't take meetings at home."

"Where are you?"

Ed paused for a moment, as if debating with himself. "I'm at Five-thirty-four Federal, just south of Wilshire. Apartment Six."

"Thank you," David said. "Thank you. I'll be there in less than—" He stopped, looking up at the street sign ahead. "Where the hell am I?"

Before letting David enter, Ed made him explain himself at the door. The small ground-floor apartment was ransacked. Drawers pulled from the dressers and dumped, mattress sliced open, plates shattered. Holes had been punched into the walls at regular intervals in a search that went even behind the sheetrock. Ed moved through the mess with a practiced gait that showed he'd grown accustomed to it.

On a long folding table in the corner sat five or six computers of different shapes and sizes, screens blinking, monitors humming. About ten Nextel cell phones were lined up, charging. A bank of small televisions showed what appeared to be live shots of several rooms, from presumably hidden cameras. David watched a woman lean forward into what must have been a one-way mirror and attempt to floss an entrenched piece of food from between her teeth.

Sitting in a rolling chair, Ed began to splice a wire that led to a minuscule microphone. "Don't ask questions. Not a one."

David looked around for somewhere to sit. Finally, he picked up a slashed pillow and set it on top of an overturned bookcase, forming a makeshift banquette. He sat cautiously so as not to stretch the stitches in his side.

Ed looked up from his work and pointed at David. "Yes, I trust you, but let me tell you, if you mention one thing about this location to one person, I'll know. And believe me, I'm not someone you want to cross."

David gazed across the bank of screens. A skinny man was fucking what looked to be an obese call girl on a mahogany desk somewhere. "I believe you," he said.

A week ago, he would have been horrified to be threatened; now he found it almost flattering.

"Want something to drink?" Ed asked.

David reached for an unbroken tumbler at his feet.

"No, no. I keep the clean ones over here." Ed pulled a glass from a stack sitting atop a fallen dartboard and filled it with water.

He and David sat in perfect silence, David sipping from the glass nervously, though he wasn't thirsty. "So can you do it?" David asked. "Get me a bug of some kind?"

"Yes, and we call it a digital transmitter these days, Joe Friday." Ed flared his hand like a magician, and a flat metal disk appeared in his palm. About the size of a watch battery, it was dense with tiny components, like a computer's motherboard. "Works off radio frequency." Leaning over, he pulled what looked like a walkie-talkie from a desk drawer that had been left on the floor. "Here's your receiver. I go with the Motorola HT one thousand because it's more compact than a Saber, so you can strap it to your belt without looking like you have a perennial hard-on." He smiled, his grin a white crescent in the white of his face. "It'll get the RF transmission and kick it up to this"—he held up a molded, skin-colored earpiece—"as long as you're within a few blocks."

"I won't be within a few blocks. I'll be in the middle of a stakeout in Venice."

Ed ran his hand across the top of his head. It made a rasping sound on the red stubble. "A challenge. I love challenges. Where's Peter live?"

"Westwood. A few blocks east of the hospital."

"Where's his office?"

"On Le Conte."

"How many stories is the building?"

"Four."

Ed rubbed his temples. David opened his mouth, but Ed raised a silencing finger in warning. More temple rubbing. Clearly, he was enjoying this.

"All right, Spier, here's what we're gonna do. I'm gonna put an expensive-as-shit repeater on the roof of his office building. Think of it as a big antenna. It'll pick up the RF transmission and bounce it to your Motorola across town." He spread his arms wide, as though accepting applause. "I am a trained professional. Do *not* try this at home."

"When can you do it?"

"Tonight. Once it gets dark. But let me ask you a question. What good does this do?"

"I'll know where Peter is at all times. I'll know if he finds himself in trouble. As a worst-case scenario, if he's attacked, I'll be able to direct the police to him quickly."

"He'll need a gun."

"Peter won't carry a gun."

"How do you know?"

David regarded Ed wearily. "Trust me on this one."

"Fine. Well, would our liberal and foolish urologist with the apropos name lower himself to carrying a non-lethal weapon?"

"Perhaps."

Ed dragged a large cardboard box from the coat closet across the room and sat back down. The contents gave off a metallic jingling as he dug through them. Proudly, he displayed a weapon with a spear-gun handle that looked as though it shot out two attached electrodes with dart ends. "A taser," he said. "You have to have decent aim, though, and they're a bitch to get through thick clothes. Fucker's wearing a leather jacket, forget it."

David shook his head. "Too . . . complicated."

Ed threw the taser back into the box and removed a pair of spiked brass knuckles.

"Too savage."

Next, Ed pulled out a silver rod with a knob on the end. When he flicked it, it telescoped to form a baton. "The asp."

Again, David shook his head. "Too easily overcome."

Ed grumbled, tossed the asp back into the cardboard box, and continued to sort through its contents. His face lit up. With a Vanna White gesture, he exhibited a large frying pan. "Old Faithful."

David merely looked at him, and he threw it back.

"I think we have a winner," Ed exclaimed. He removed a stun gun, about the size of a flashlight, complete with finger grooves. The black rectangular stock extended into two prongs. He thumbed a switch forward, and a burst of visible voltage shot between the prongs.

"Can it work through clothes?"

"Again, nothing too thick. But a T-shirt or something, you might as well not be wearing anything at all."

"I'll take it," David said.

Ed tossed him the stun gun. "Congratulations. You are now the proud owner of a fifty-thousand volt, hair-standing, cattle-prod special."

"How should I get the . . . bug-transmitter thing on Peter?"

"I could install it in a watch. Could you give it to him as an early birthday gift?"

"No. That would be suspicious."

"Does he have a special pen or something? I could slip it in there."

"I don't know. Nothing I could be sure he'd always have on him."

"So the question is: What sort of pet object does he keep with him at all times?"

An idea hit David with a sudden, bright clarity. He raised his head with a smile. "I think I've got it," he said.

CHAPTER 72

PETER'S office building, a modern four-story structure of dark glass and concrete, sat near the junction of Westwood and Le Conte, a few blocks from the hospital. David parked at a meter. The construction work next door had left a light fall of dust on the sidewalk before the front doors.

When David arrived at Peter's second-floor office, his side was aching and itching, and he couldn't decide which sensation was worse. Peter's office manager was leaving and putting out the lights. David took a quick step back as she locked the door and turned to him, nearly striking him in the gut with a jumbo purse that swung from her shoulder like a pendulum.

"I'm looking for Dr. Alexander," David said.

She continued down the hall, not bothering to make eye contact. "He might be in the procedure suite," she said.

"Across the street?"

"No, in the new one. It's on the third floor. The move's been a royal pain in the rear end. That's why some of us are still here when we should be home with our husband and two daughters."

"Have a lovely evening," David said.

He found Peter in the suite upstairs, skimming through a folder, standing between two procedure tables amid a scattering of moving boxes and file crates. Peter looked up with a smile and took a few heavy steps toward David, assisting himself with his ortho cane. "David. To what do I owe . . . ?"

David thought about pulling himself up to sit on one of the procedure tables, but didn't want to risk tearing the stitching in his side. "I wanted to see you in person, to convince you to let the cops keep an eye on you. Just for a few days."

"I appreciate the thought, David, but this is ridiculous. First of all, Clyde Slade has no reason to come after me."

David fondled the digital transmitter in his pocket. He'd had Ed adhere a small, powerful magnet to its back. Plan B. Getting police protection was still preferable, so he took a deep breath, preparing himself for his next words. He saw no alternative but to attack the issue head-on, despite Peter's repressive preferences. "To be frank, as a disabled man you make an appealing target."

Indignation cast its pallor across Peter's face, mitigated only by a devilish glint in his eyes. He flipped his ortho cane, caught the end, and let the long rubber-coated handle fall between David's feet. With a sharp tug, he yanked David's feet out from under him. David landed on his back, an explosion of pain screeching through his side.

"I can protect myself better than you might think," Peter said.

A groan escaped David as he reached for his side.

"Oh, Jesus," Peter said. "I forgot about your injury. I'm so thick-headed." He attempted to help David rise. Ignoring the pain, David pulled the minuscule transmitter from his pocket and placed it on the inside of Peter's left leg brace, just where it tapered above the ankle. The deceit helped undercut his anger at Peter.

He let Peter help him back to his feet. "Let me see the cut," Peter said. David raised his shirt obediently. The stitches were all intact. "You're fine." He looked up at David, his gray face tired and drawn. True regret. "I'm terribly sorry."

David did not hesitate. "Then promise me something."

Peter cocked a bushy eyebrow.

From his other pocket, David pulled the stun gun. He offered it to Peter, who regarded it like a used handkerchief.

Peter raised his ortho cane and let it thump to the floor. "You *can't* be serious."

CHAPTER 73

LAST night, David had sneaked into his house through the back door like a teenager come home from a night drinking. He hoped none of the press had snapped a photograph of him pulling himself gingerly over the rear fence.

He slept unevenly and awakened early when Ed called him to let him know the repeater was in place atop Peter's building. David slipped the earpiece into place and fiddled with the Motorola until he heard Peter's snoring.

Making his way through the house, he closed all the blinds so the tabloid photographers couldn't shoot him with telephoto lenses. He listened to Peter awaken, eat breakfast, and spend an unreasonable amount of time gargling. Before David showered, he hung a bedsheet over his bedroom window, as it didn't have a curtain. The perimeter alarm Ed had installed beeped at least once every five minutes. David felt paradoxically jumpy and exhausted. Captive in his own home.

By the time Yale and Dalton arrived in the late afternoon, David had long given up pretending he was patient. He'd dressed his wound twice, cleaned the house top to bottom, showered several times, refolded all his clothing, and spent nearly half an hour eating lunch—an eternity for him. He'd heard Peter drive for a while, greet his office manager, and begin seeing patients. Whenever guilt encroached on David for his eavesdropping, he pushed it away, granting himself a twenty-four-hour reprieve. He didn't have time for guilt until after the stakeout.

He was dressed in a pair of scrubs, the Motorola strapped to his waistband. Wearing his work clothes, he hoped, would strengthen his appearance in Clyde's mind as a representative of the hospital. Every bit might help.

Yale folded his arms across his chest, smiled an implacable smile, and said to David, "You have to wear a baggier scrub top if we're gonna hide all this hardware on you."

Dalton self-consciously touched his tie—a brown-striped JCPenney clip-on—and it tilted revealingly from the knot. His eyes found David's earpiece. "What's the other radio for?" he asked.

"We don't know anything about another radio," Yale said.

Dalton pulled the loose skin of his jowls down into a turkey wattle, nodding solemnly. Yale rested an assuring hand on David's shoulder and steered him back to the bedroom. David indicated his side with a tilt of his hand. "I'm pretty stiff. Do you think you could help me out of this?"

As Yale briefed him about the procedures for the sting in a calm, even voice, he eased David out of his scrub top and wired him up, taping the mike at his fifth intercostal space. After selecting a bigger top from the closet, Yale helped David pull it over his head.

David would drive to Healton's in his Mercedes behind Yale and Dalton's car, being tailed by Jenkins and Bronner in the carpet cleaning van. A sweep car would check the route ahead of Yale and Dalton. Once there, David would walk from the parking lot seemingly unescorted, make his way along a highly visible designated route through the neighborhood, and wind up in the scorched car in the abandoned lot. In reality, undercover police officers and SWAT team members would be watching him every minute. Not surprisingly, Rhonda Decker had refused to grant permission for any part of the stakeout to occur on Pearson Home property. David was disappointed; his presence in the house itself would have been a tempting draw for Clyde.

At all times, an ambulance would be standing by a few blocks away. David did not ask who it was for.

Someone knocked in code on the back door, and Yale swung it open to reveal Jenkins and Bronner. Jenkins walked across the living room, boots creaking, equipment jingling on his belt, and leaned against the far wall. Bronner held a plastic cup. He chewed and spat. "We have the van in position," he said.

Yale rubbed his hands together. "All right, crew," he said. "Stay on point. If we fuck this up, the Captain'll put his foot so far up my ass I'll be able to taste shoe polish."

"A lovely image," David said.

"But an apt one. Let's do our jobs, and hope Clyde's drawn in for the . . ." Yale shifted his weight from one foot to the other in a rare display of discomfort.

David took a deep, halting breath. Jenkins watched the emotions working on David's face. "Our guys are in place," he said, in a tone David imagined was as close to comforting as he could manage. "The area's tighter than the Dodgers infield."

David smiled. "This season?"

Some nervous grins. A cough. Dalton fiddling with his wedding ring. Nerves working.

"I'll meet you in the van," Bronner said. He nodded once, gravely, and backed toward the door cautiously, as though leaving a lion's den.

Yale leveled his stare at David. "Ready to roll?"

The three men faced David, and he detected respect in their faces. He had coiled his stethoscope inside his jacket pocket for good luck, and he patted it through the fabric to feel its weight. He took a deep breath, and held it before exhaling. "As ready as I'm gonna get."

⊕

David stood in the dark of his garage, enjoying his last moment alone. The clamor of the press outside seemed amplified through the garage door. A stream of light fought its way through the crack beneath the door, lending the room a dreamlike cast. David had no choice but to forge through the media outside; his Mercedes was a key prop in the stakeout.

In a touching gesture, Dalton had spray-painted over the ASHOLE lettering so the tabloids would have one less thing to screech about. David got into the car and sat with his hands on the wheel for a minute, then he hit the garage door opener and pulled out.

The press flooded toward him. Mikes tapping the car, hands pressed to the windows, faces and makeup and lenses. Cameras flashed. Film rolled.

His first instinct was to stop, so as not to run anyone over, but he continued to back out slowly, carefully, doing his best to fight off claustrophobia. He finally hit the street and accelerated up the block. A few neighbors were standing out on their porches, watching. An old couple up the street wore matching expressions of confusion. The van pulled out immediately behind him, and just before he reached Sunset, Yale and Dalton's car swung in ahead of him. The media brigade followed a few blocks back, but Jenkins did a good job driving poorly to slow them up. As David's eyes darted to the rearview mirror, he realized he was sweating profusely.

Turning right on Veteran, he headed for the police checkpoint. As planned, the two officers pulled aside the sawhorses, letting him through but blocking the following media traffic. One of them offered David a wink as he passed through, and David took note of the clear plastic tube hooked over his ear.

He followed Yale and Dalton south to Wilshire, completing the loop, and the carpet cleaning van was miraculously waiting at the curb after he made the turn. David was amazed at how well Jenkins tailed him to Venice. The van disappeared several times, and David thought for sure Jenkins had lost him for good, but then traffic would thin and there it was again, behind him.

David thought about turning on the radio to relax himself, but not wanting to be distracted by news updates, he hummed instead. He stopped abruptly when he remembered that the wire conveyed his every noise to countless police officers, and it occurred to him with amusement that they'd overhear if he had to take a leak later. In his right ear, he'd been receiving a good transmission of Peter undertaking a procedure—a prostatectomy, from what David could piece together from Peter's concise commands to the nurse.

The sun began its slow fade beneath the horizon. The air was just tainting gray as David entered the familiar neighborhood. He parked in the designated spot, beneath the cone of light in front of Healton's. The other vehicles had disappeared in the last few blocks, as was planned.

He got out of the car and immediately felt a sense of isolation. The neighborhood was quite still. He moved up the first street, his white coat baggy over the wound on his side. He passed the abandoned lot on his right. The scorched car, his final destination, was empty. A homeless man sat bundled against the fence, the front of his worn jacket stained with what smelled like egg. Face ruddy and textured, a thick mustache bristling. Eyes anomalistically clear. Blake. David stared at him a beat too long. Blake raised his eyebrows in a show of impatience. David had another checkpoint to pass down the block in a minute and a half. "Hey, pal, spare a cigarette?"

His voice spurred David to movement. He continued along the path that Yale had detailed for him, away from the lot, past the front of the Pearson Home. He thought he saw a rifle scope flash in one of the apartment windows across the street, but wasn't sure if he'd imagined it since he knew snipers were stationed up there. The thought that Clyde might be here somewhere, in or near the area, quickened his heart. Maybe Clyde was watching him now.

The next intersection was busy and highly visible. Across the street, Bronner was pretending to make a call in the phone booth, wearing a flannel and a Dodgers cap. He did not look over at David, but he touched his shoulder casually with his fingertips, their agreed-upon signal that everything was clear.

David headed down the sidewalk. His path would loop him around past Clyde's former apartment building before returning him to the empty lot. A boisterous group of men exited a bar. David's eyes blurred momentarily, and he saw the faces as a smeared conglomeration—some coming at him, some moving past on either side—and he knew the situation was now beyond his control. His fate was in the hands of the undercover police officers in the area. The wound in his side began to throb, as if in warning. The group went on. Clyde was not hiding in their midst.

David turned left on Brecken Street. Patches of browning grass broke up the sidewalks; the curbs were lined with battered cars and trucks. The sky darkened a bit, discernibly, which he hoped was not a bad omen. He started down the street, with its many alleys and doorways and dark spaces between vehicles. The fact that someone had scouted the area before his arrival provided little reassurance. A chill tangled around his spine when he heard the clicking of footsteps ahead of him, but then he realized it was merely the echo of his own, amplified off the surrounding buildings. He no longer felt any pain in his side; it had gone numb.

He tried to calm himself by focusing on Peter's familiar voice, transmitted to him from the repeater over five miles away. Peter was sending his office manager home. Then, the ding of the elevator, followed by another, rapid ding. A one-floor ride.

In front of David, a form shifted in a doorway and stumbled down the stairs. David took a quick step back, glancing up the street for backup, but none arrived. The man swept by him, drunk and fat, and staggered up the street, murmuring to himself.

David tried to slow his heart. A flash on the roof across the street as a sniper lowered his rifle and sank again out of view. They were here protecting him, omnipresent and out of sight.

David wasn't getting anything through the earpiece aside from a whistling—the fabric of Peter's pants moving across the transmitter? He'd detected a similar sound earlier when Peter had walked from his car to the office. Then, the noise of a key in a lock. Peter must've gone upstairs, to continue setting things in order in the new procedure suite.

David turned down an alley and ducked through the gap in the fence that led to the abandoned lot. No sign of Clyde. Wrapped in layers of clothes, Blake shifted, a formless mass slumped against the base of the fence.

David walked slowly to the middle of the lot, glass popping beneath his shoes. He opened the door to the scorched car and sat down, resting his hands on the steering wheel.

The loop had been unsuccessful.

David tilted his head down and murmured into his

mike, "Nothing." He raised his shirt and checked his bandage. It had blotted up some fluid from the wound, but was still firmly in place. In his right ear, he heard the clink of equipment. Peter rattling the surgery clamps? Testing the cauterizer? David stared through the cracked windshield at the Pearson Home. Layla's skewed silhouette moved against the curtains of the second-floor window. The same room where Clyde had once dangled boys by their necks to watch them gasp and tremble.

David looked at the apartment buildings rimming the empty lot—crumbling brick, rain-beaten wood, the occasional shattered window. So many places for Clyde to hide, to spy. From the house, David heard the wavering, uneven voices of some of the residents singing "Happy Birthday."

Blake rolled over uneasily when David got out of the car and slammed the door. David walked boldly to the front of the Pearson Home. He spoke down into his mike with minimal movement of his lips. "I'm going to the porch."

He knew that somewhere, hidden within the surrounding few blocks, Yale was growing enraged—he had specifically told David to stay off the Pearson Home grounds, in line with Rhonda Decker's directive. But David's walk hadn't yielded anything, and he wanted to take a position that Clyde, if he was in fact watching, would find more provocative and galling. Sitting on the porch of Clyde's sacred, coveted childhood sanctuary, in a position of power and smug presumption, was the most taunting action David had at his current disposal. It was like throwing darts at Clyde's most vulnerable spot.

A rickety wooden chair with a coarsely woven straw seat stood crooked by the front door. David pulled it across the porch and sat, his white coat hanging to his sides like the hem of a skirt. His Mercedes, toplit like a showcase car in the otherwise empty Healton's lot, was visible for blocks. David's new post was also clearly discernible.

Aware that somewhere the cops were complaining and scrambling and reassessing, David leaned back, rested his feet on the railing, and waited for Clyde to appear.

CHAPTER 74

THE fluorescent lights illuminating the new procedure suite were giving Peter a headache, so he turned them off and worked by the light of a desk lamp. It cast a glow on the desktop and around his hands, a small ball of light in the darkness, which he liked, for it made him feel like a medieval craftsman. The blinds remained closed on the window behind him. The desk itself faced the two procedure tables, and beyond them, the door; Peter sometimes had to sit between lengthy procedures to take the weight off his legs. A firmly anchored metal knob, about the size of a fist, protruded from the desktop to aid Peter in sitting and rising. The stun gun lay next to it, where Peter had tossed it after David had left the room yesterday.

Peter lined the cystoscopes side by side, a series of thin stainless steel snakes trailing across the desk and dangling from the edge. They were expensive tools, running about $18,000 apiece with lenses, and he cared for them as though they were museum artifacts. Each one of the scopes had been used countless times to peer into countless bladders; gazing down at them, Peter was filled with a vague sense of wonder at all they had accomplished in their brief material lives. He jotted a note to his technician that they were to be sterilized again.

His left brace had been digging into his ankle all day, and he paused to pull up his pant leg, remove his shoe, and rub the reddish indentation the metal had left in his skin. A rustle at the door caught his attention, and he squinted up into the darkness.

"Yes, can I help you? Hello? Can I help you?"

The form shifted, breathing heavily. The sound of a large person advancing.

Panic stirred and began to sharpen its claws inside Peter. Given his braces, it would take him nearly a minute to rise and shuffle to the light switch on the wall.

Clyde's sallow face pulled into the small ring of light, seeming to float as his body remained lost in shadows. He drew closer, resolving from the darkness. Held limply at his side was a pistol.

Peter's mouth went dry.

The arm holding the gun raised stiffly and mechanically, like a railroad crossing gate, and Peter was looking directly down the length of the Beretta. "We're gonna have some fun, you and me," Clyde said.

Moths clustered around the porch light, making a soft, leathery sound. David scanned the street, his eyes picking over the windows in the apartments facing him.

He expected Clyde to charge the porch.

He expected Yale to pull up and call off the stakeout.

He expected Rhonda Decker to appear on the porch and reprimand him.

The only thing he did not expect was Clyde's voice to cut in over the hum of the unit in his right ear.

He stood, forgetting to favor his wounded side, and

leapt over the porch stairs, wincing when his feet struck ground. "He's got Peter Alexander!" David yelled down into his mike. "They're at Peter's procedure suite. Corner of Westwood and Le Conte."

Blake rolled over onto his feet, looking ineffective and Falstaffian in his bundle of grimy clothes. David passed him in a sprint, straining to make out what was being transmitted in his right ear. Jenkins spilled out of an alley behind him, shouting something David could not make out.

David reached his car, slid behind the wheel, and peeled out.

⊕

Peter struggled to keep his voice even. "I'm going to—"

Saliva flew from Clyde's lips as he spoke. "Don't you talk! Don't you talk to me. You're weak. You're what weakness is. I'm in charge here. I'm in charge of you."

Clyde took a step forward and swept the desk with his arm. Scopes, pens, and papers fell to the floor. The lamp dangled off the side of the desk from its cord, throwing light erratically around the room as it spun.

Peter felt along the desktop for something to grab—a pen, a letter opener—but there was nothing within reach. His eyes flicked across the desktop. The stun gun had caught beside the metal knob. Peter couldn't reach for it; it would be too obvious.

"What do you want?" Peter asked.

Clyde pulled a phone from the wall-mounted unit and punched in a number. Peter took advantage of Clyde's distraction to rest his hand over the stun gun and slide it slowly off the desktop into his lap.

The cord uncoiling across his chest, Clyde pushed the phone at Peter. "Here. You tell David Spier I'm gonna kill you right now. You tell him I know he's in with the cops to get me, so he better come down here *alone* if he wants to stop me."

Peter took the phone with his left hand, holding the stun gun in his lap with his right. Clyde leaned in close, pistol pointed at Peter's head. If Peter raised the stun gun from its hiding place, Clyde could shoot him instantly. Peter wouldn't even have a chance to aim.

Peter offered the phone back to Clyde. "It's the answering machine."

"We're gonna leave him a special message, then," Clyde said, pushing the phone back in Peter's face.

Peter felt the cold barrel pressed hard against his forehead.

"Make some noise," Clyde said. "Into the phone."

Peter's lips started to tremble, but he pressed them together, not wanting to show Clyde his fright.

Clyde cocked the pistol.

"All right," Peter said. His tone was hard, colored with more anger than fear. "Let me stand up. I'm not going to die sitting down."

"I'm gonna hurt you hard. And David Spier's gonna hear it all when he gets home."

Peter held the phone away from his head. "I'll leave your . . . *noises* in a minute." He turned his head and looked up past the pistol into Clyde's dead eyes, tightening his grip on the stun gun. He spoke slowly and adamantly. *"But you let me stand up first."*

Clyde studied him, then his chin dipped slightly. "You make one bad move, you won't have time to leave your farewell message." Clyde stepped closer, standing almost on top of him.

Peter pushed his chair out from the desk, but Clyde kept the pistol planted on his forehead. Still no opportunity to wield the stun gun. He couldn't move it much past his crotch without Clyde noticing and probably shooting him.

Pulling a lever beneath the seat cushion, Peter locked the wheels so the chair wouldn't roll out from under him. He leaned over and locked first his left brace, then his right, so they would support his weight. With a slight groan, he fisted the metal knob on the desktop and pulled himself up out of the chair and onto his reinforced legs. His left pant leg was still hiked up high over the knee from when he'd rubbed his ankle.

He released the knob, standing on his own. The gun barrel slid a bit on his sweat-moist forehead. He felt breathless, as though he'd had the wind knocked out of him. He leaned slightly to his left, bringing the metal of his ankle into contact with Clyde's thin scrub bottoms. He eased his calf over until he felt the press of Clyde's leg. Clyde did not pull away.

Peter turned into the pistol, looking past it again into the slick, depthless eyes. With excruciating slowness, he moved the stun gun over and touched it to the inside of the metal thigh band of his left brace. His thumb hovering over the power switch, he braced himself for the pain and prepared to duck.

"All right," Peter said brusquely. "I'm ready now."

CHAPTER 75

DAVID flew up Lincoln, narrowly missing a collision with a banged-up Pontiac, and floored it, screeching right on Wilshire and heading toward Peter's office. He was shouting into the mike and trying to listen to the earpiece simultaneously, which made both efforts ineffective. A blast of noise erupted through the earpiece, causing him to jerk back his head, then the unit went dead. What could have done that to the digital transmitter?

Concern did him little good, so he tried to think clearly and pragmatically. From what he had overheard, he knew Peter was in trouble, that Clyde had been planning on harming him to frighten David. The cops would arrive at Peter's building soon—maybe they even had by now—but David had to get there as quickly as possible. In the likely event of a standoff, he was certain Clyde would demand to talk to him.

The carpet cleaning van caught up to him after a few blocks but fell back again, and he lost sight of it when he ran the red at Federal. He spoke continuously into his mike, updating the cops on his location.

He careened through Westwood and pulled down an alley into the back lot of Peter's four-story building. Peter's car, a gray BMW with a hand brake sticking up near the wheel, was parked in its usual spot, but there were no police cars.

David got out of his car and glanced up the empty street anxiously. "Where the hell are you guys?" he said, bending his neck so he could speak into the mike. "Why aren't there police cars here already?" He stepped back, glancing up the side of the building at the third floor. No movement or light. Clyde could be there right now, torturing Peter.

David couldn't wait for the police to arrive. "I'm going in," he said to the mike and the empty parking lot.

He searched his trunk for a weapon, but he had nothing, not even a tire jack. An old-style otoscope was tucked into his father's doctor's bag in the trunk, the weighty metal handle protruding. He grabbed it, and snapped off the plastic head used for ear exams. It would have to do.

Tossing the Motorola and the dead earpiece into the trunk, he sidestepped a Dumpster and reached the building's back door, made of glass. The glass, evidently shatterproof, had been dented near the handle, but had remained intact. The lock had been gouged and scratched up with a tool of some sort. The door was slightly ajar, a Carl's Jr. Superstar wrapper wedged between it and the frame to prevent it from closing.

David knew he should wait for the police to arrive, but the possibility that Clyde was torturing Peter was too much for him to bear. He pushed the door, and it drifted open easily, the wrapper falling to the floor. Stepping into the dark interior, he closed the door slowly behind him, leaving it unlocked.

Not wanting to draw attention by using the elevator, David entered the dark stairwell and crept upstairs. He pushed the third-floor door open, peering up the hall, and immediately saw the triangular fall of light from the open door of Peter's procedure suite. He eased his way down the corridor, the thin carpet padding his footsteps. A deep wailing became audible. Mournful sobbing interspersed with violent breathing.

David drew near to the open door, inching his way forward, his hand curling around the metal shaft of the otoscope. The crying continued, broken by fragmented mumbling and a slapping noise. Reaching the door frame, David pressed his face to the wood and rotated his head slightly so he could see into the room with one eye.

It took a moment for his eyes to adjust to the swinging lamp breaking the dimness. Clyde sat despondently against the far wall, holding a pistol limply between his legs. His face was red, his acne standing out in severe blotches. Sobbing and murmuring, he was rocking himself forward and banging his head back into the wall. He stopped only to rend his face with his hands, clawing at his cheeks, knocking the pistol against his crown.

David's chest tightened when he saw the pair of inert legs protruding from behind the desk, the metal bands of the braces visible at the ankles. The rest of Peter's body was out of view. A stun gun lay on the floor in the corner, near Clyde.

A humming in his ears. A tingling in his mouth. He wanted to run downstairs—either Yale or Jenkins should have arrived by now—but the possibility of Peter's needing immediate medical attention held him in place. David couldn't leave his unconscious body up here with Clyde.

Clyde's face was lined with scratches from his nails, some of them beading with blood. He was facing the door—there was no way David could surprise him.

Clyde directed his words at Peter's body. "You weren't supposed to do that." He scrambled to his feet and regarded Peter, like a problem he did not know how to solve. His face vacillated between agitation and confusion as he rocked back and forth. He scratched his head with the barrel of the pistol, then aimed it at Peter.

David had little choice.

Wedging the otoscope in the back of his pants, he stepped from cover, holding his hands out to his sides. Startled into a little leap, Clyde aimed the pistol at him. David made no sudden movements, and prayed Clyde's hands would stop jerking.

"Don't you move," Clyde bleated. "You stay right there." He wiped his running nose with his sleeve. "I'm in control here. I know what I'm doing." Despite his agitated condition, Clyde was steady on his feet, and his slurring had stopped.

"All right," David said. "You don't need to hurt him. I'm here now. You can scare . . . you can scare me directly. Just let me check on Peter first." Calmly, slowly, he pointed at the two inert legs. "Let me . . ." His throat dried up, and he lost the end of his sentence.

Clyde's face trembled; he was still pulling himself back from the edge of sobbing. Raising the torn leg of his scrub bottoms, he rubbed a red patch on his calf. "He shocked me. Knocked us both down. I hit him on the head. He got still." He slapped his head, and the noise rang around the room. "He hurt me, and I've gotta . . . I've gotta take it out of him." He began mumbling incoherently.

The current of electricity from the stun gun must have shorted out the digital transmitter. Which meant the shock had somehow run through Peter's left leg brace. "Can I step forward and look at his body?" David asked. He spoke slowly and clearly, as if to a child.

The pistol snapped back up at his head. "It's a trick. You're here to trick me and—shit, shit . . ." Clyde began to rock his upper torso, his eyes pressing closed. "Three two one the door back from the . . ."

David's head was humming. "Clyde. I'm going to take another step forward. And I'm going to look at Peter. I'm going to do this now." There was something comforting in the knowledge that all his words were being transmitted through the hidden wire to the police officers. It made him feel less alone. Even so, he wondered what was taking them so long to arrive.

Clyde continued to rock, his lips moving silently, but his eyes were open again. David eased slowly forward, and Peter's body came into view behind the desk.

Rage and sorrow mingled, rising from David's gut. He crouched over Peter and raised one eyelid, then the other. He was relieved to see both pupils dilate. Resting two fingers on Peter's neck, he counted his pulse for ten seconds, then multiplied by six. Slightly elevated, around seventy-five beats per minute. He walked his fingers along the back of Peter's head until he found a boggy spot near the base of his skull. A cursory feel revealed it to be a basic hematoma. Peter was going to be fine.

Clyde's body odor hung in the room. The smell was cut with something else, something bitter and medicinal, though David could not place it.

David's lips parted, trembling. He closed his eyes, not wanting to speak, afraid of what he might say. He needed hours to process the scene before him and find the correct words, but he had barely seconds.

David caught a glimpse of guilt and anguish in Clyde's face. Clyde became aware of David's gaze, and anger intensified in the flat stones of his eyes, the change so sudden it was as if he'd donned a mask. "He hurt me, the cripple." He crouched over Peter's head, leering down at him. "You weakling. You got it good." He rubbed the swollen spot on his leg.

David kept his body angled slightly away from Clyde, as if turning from a live bomb.

Clyde looked up at David, his cheeks glistening with sweat. He was breathing hard. "I promised I'd teach you about fear," he said. "It's deep and dark, like a well. I'm gonna put you in it."

David drew one hand slowly behind his back. He had just grasped the shaft of the otoscope when Clyde's eyes snapped back into focus.

"What are you doing? What are you reaching for? Turn around. *Turn around!* "

As David turned, Clyde shoved him against the window, his hand grazing the wound in David's side. David's forehead banged the glass, and his hands gripped the blinds, bending them. He stifled a cry of pain. Clyde ripped the otoscope from the band of David's pants, and David tensed, waiting for it to be brought down on his head.

But instead, Clyde's voice came, low and amused. "You were gonna hit me with a doctor's toy."

Through the bent blinds, David saw the carpet cleaning van in the alley across the street. Two flashlights dancing on the third floor of the building opposite them. David felt a sinking in his gut when he realized Jenkins, Bronner, and the other units had gone to Peter's old procedure suite—the one that was functional and directory listed. Like Peter's new suite, it was also on the corner of Westwood and Le Conte, so David's directions hadn't helped. If he could mention his true location, the mike would convey it to the cops in the field. Watching the flashlight beams play across the dark rooms across the street, David tried to figure out some way of mentioning his location that Clyde wouldn't find unusual. The cops would never spot his gesturing through the dark window. He only prayed Clyde wouldn't notice the flashlight beams in the other building.

A clicking noise as Clyde played with the otoscope, and then a beam of light on the back of David's head.

Clyde's voice was jumbled in his throat. "I'm talking to you."

David turned his head to the side so the intense light shone across his profile, through the bent blinds, and out the window. He hoped Jenkins and Bronner would spot it. "Yes, Clyde?" He turned his head slightly so the edge of his cheek caught the beam, then moved his head again, creating a flickering light to better catch the cops' attention.

Clyde clicked off the otoscope and tossed it aside. "Were you gonna hurt me with this?"

In case no one had picked up the otoscope light issuing from the dark building, David had to try to convey their location, no matter how awkward it came out. "Why are we here at—?"

"I asked you a question."

David was aware with a sudden certainly that his life hung in the balance of the next few seconds. He knew

Clyde was going to press the pistol to his forehead even before Clyde did it.

Knowing his life could end with a one-inch movement of Clyde's finger sent a ripple of terror through David's body. Clyde studied him curiously. David's scrub top clung to his body with his sweat. He could feel the beats of his heart in the blood rushing through his face.

Clyde's uneven voice drifted from behind the gun. "You didn't help me at all. Not like you promised. You took away everything from me. My room and my car and my lye. I can't . . . I can't get at people anymore. To ruin their faces." He twisted the pistol, digging the barrel into David's cheek. David fought not to withdraw, not to react.

"I have no one left to scare." Clyde grumbled, a noise lost deep in his chest. "Except you."

From the jumble in his head, David pulled a thought and shaped it like a weapon. "What did you think about," he asked, in a calm, smooth voice, "when the nurses locked you up in the dark? When no one would take your hand? What did you think about then?"

Clyde drew back his head, as if he'd been slapped. The Beretta wavered slightly in his grasp, but remained against David's forehead. "I'm not . . . I don't . . ." He blinked hard, then pressed his eyes closed as David had known he would. "Three two one stand back—"

David's hand curled into a fist and, jerking his head clear of the pistol, he swung it sideways into Clyde's ear. He struck Clyde's head with bone-jarring force, and Clyde gasped, the pistol kicking in his hand and blowing out the window where David's head had been a moment ago. Clyde sank to the floor, landing with a hard slap. David crouched over him, pinning his gun arm with a hand, his knee pressing hard into Clyde's trachea. Clyde grunted and struggled against him. David dug his fingers into Clyde's forearm, but still Clyde did not drop the pistol. His hand clutched the weapon, the barrel sweeping back and forth, aiming across the open door.

"Stop fighting me!" David shouted through clenched teeth. "Stop—"

Jenkins and Bronner crashed through the doorway, shouting, their Berettas finding Clyde like compasses pointing north.

"Don't move!"

"Back away from the—"

A shot rang out, spinning Jenkins around. He knocked against the door, a growing spot of blood darkening his sweatshirt at the shoulder, and sank to the ground. His legs stuck out before him like a doll's, his pistol hand rendered useless by the shoulder wound. He tried with his good hand to take the pistol from his limp hand, but could not reach.

Bronner's pistol wavered; David was in his line of fire. Stutter-stepping forward with his pistol aimed, Bronner freed his cuffs from the case on his belt with an adept jerk of his hand.

Clyde's hand felt up David's side beneath his shirt and found his wound. A fat finger pried through the stitches. David felt a hot flash of pain and then his skin giving way. He relaxed his grip on Clyde for a split second, and Clyde hurled him off his throat. Ablaze with pain, David rolled into the far wall and knocked his head. Through a drunken haze, his cheek pressed to the floor, he watched Clyde find his feet and start to stand.

Bronner was already mid-dive across the room. He caught Clyde with a staggering right and fell on top of him. He was fighting to angle the pistol barrel at Clyde's chest, but Clyde bit his gun hand, tearing a mouthful of flesh from the fat muscle at the base of his thumb and spitting the pink plug on the floor. Bronner cried out, dropping his pistol. David tried to crawl to it, but was paralyzed with pain.

Clyde and Bronner struggled and rolled, and Clyde's pistol fired, blowing out a chunk of wall. Bronner managed to land on Clyde's back. Clyde's gun hand was pinned beneath his body, and Bronner grabbed his other arm and twisted it back, snapping a handcuff around the free wrist.

Clyde bucked and spun, whipping the loose handcuff around his wrist. The sharp edge bit into Bronner's temple, splitting the skin. Clyde wormed his other arm free. Tightening his fingers around the pistol, Clyde punched Bronner in the mouth with it, knocking him off. Bronner fell to the floor, unconscious, and Clyde scrambled to his feet and flashed past Jenkins.

Though his wounded arm did not move, Jenkins's hand contracted around the pistol, angling it up at Clyde and firing. By the time the report echoed through the empty room, Clyde was out the door into the hall. There was the sound of a door splintering—maybe being smashed in—and then silence.

David and Jenkins regarded each other from their respective slumped positions. Jenkins's head was tilted forward so his chin rested on his chest, his breath fluttering the tattered fabric at the edge of the gunshot hole in his shoulder. His arm lay limp—the shot to the shoulder must have compromised the brachial plexus.

The floor was icy cold against David's cheek. He willed his lips to move. "Do you have an exit wound?" he asked.

His face stretched in a grimace, Jenkins reached behind his shoulder and patted his back. "Not that I can reach," he said. "How's Bronner? Peter?"

"Peter will be fine." David pushed himself up onto all fours. The pain in his side spread quickly through his abdomen, but he started to crawl toward Bronner anyway. Though it was bleeding heavily, the gash above Bronner's temple was superficial. David grabbed the otoscope off the floor, raised Bronner's eyelids, and shone the beam of light into his pupils. They constricted nicely. "Equal and reactive," he said. The wound on Bronner's hand was fairly deep and would need to be treated for infection, but it was not bleeding badly.

Still slumped against the door, Jenkins grimaced again and spoke. "We responded to the wrong location. Six units across the street. Me and Bronner saw the light and came to check it out."

"It was my fault," David said. "I should've thought to clarify which building." He was just about to speak into his mike when he saw Jenkins fumbling for his portable with his good hand. Jenkins held it close to his lips. "Eight Adam Thirty-two. Officer down. Officer down. Officer down. Shots fired. Ten eight hundred block Le Conte. Third floor. Where the fuck am I?"

David looked up from Bronner's hand. "Ten eight seventy-five Le Conte."

"Be advised it's Ten eight seventy-five Le Conte." Jenkins's words were slowing down. When he spoke again, it was little more than a mumble. "Roll an RA. Suspect possibly still in the building . . . considered armed." He released the button on his portable, and his good hand slapped to the floor. His breath came in jerks.

David pulled himself to his feet. A sticky band of blood ran down his side, pooling at the top line of his pants. For a moment, he thought he might faint, but then his adrenaline kicked in, granting him clarity and a momentary relief from the pain.

He trudged over to Jenkins. Jenkins's eyes flickered to the door. "Go get him," he said.

David crouched over Jenkins and pulled him slightly

forward off the door, causing him to cry out. There was no exit wound. David pulled the stethoscope from his jacket pocket, balled up the jacket, and handed it to Jenkins. "Apply pressure," he said. Using the stethoscope, he checked Jenkins's lung beneath the wound. Good breathing sounds.

David strung his stethoscope across his shoulders and stood. His wound was running. "You're going to be fine," he said. "I'm going to leave you here."

Jenkins nodded. In the distance, the pleasing sound of approaching sirens.

David dropped the otoscope, pried the Beretta from Jenkins's inert fingers, and stepped into the hall. The pistol felt weighty and awkward in his hand. One of the doors across the hall had been kicked in, and he trudged over to it, leaving a thin trail of blood drops on the carpet.

He looked down and noticed another trail of dripping blood preceding his own. Clyde had been hit.

David peered past the splintered door, ready to draw back at the first sign of Clyde. He flipped the switch with a trembling hand and blinked against the light. The window across the empty room had been opened. The pistol lay beneath the sill where Clyde had dropped it.

Heavy footfalls thundered in the stairwells—cops on the way to Peter, Jenkins, and Bronner. David limped across the room to the window. The fire escape outside wound down into the construction site of the building that fronted on Le Conte. The building was a confusion of Sheetrock planes and crisscrossing boards. The crooked scaffolding up front had been repaired.

A wide smudge of blood darkened the painted rail in three distinct lines—finger marks. "Clyde's been hit," David said into the mike. "He dropped his gun. And I think he exited the east side of the building." He ducked through the window, biting his lip against the pain in his side, and stood on the metal structure. The wind blew through the skeletal boards and beams, rattling the plastic wrapping covering the wheelbarrows.

David began the slow, painful climb down the metal ladder, stethoscope swinging from his neck, pistol heavy in his hand. He walked through the dark, hollowed interior of the building. The wheelbarrows and slanted boards threw shadows thick and fearful. The hiding places were countless. He lifted the plastic covering on one of the wheelbarrows, but there was only gravel beneath.

One piece of Sheetrock hung off a 4-by-4 beam from a single nail, swaying slightly in the breeze like a weighty pendulum. Tucking his elbow to his wound and taking in air erratically, David walked to it, trudging through sawdust and nails.

As he drew near, the Sheetrock smashed toward him, going to pieces and scattering at his feet. Behind it, three flashlight beams shot out at his face. The planks and boards around him rustled and creaked, then the whole interior of the building suddenly was alive with loud, booming voices and beams of light.

"Put down the fucking—"

"—hands on your—"

"Drop it! Drop it!"

David dropped the pistol immediately. The chopping approach of a helicopter reached a deafening decibel, then a spotlight laid down over David. He raised his arms, even though it sent a screeching pain through his side.

One of the figures stepped forward from behind the Sheetrock, waving his arms, a pistol in one hand. He entered the spotlight, his face glowing in the wan yellow light. Yale.

Behind him, the other men relaxed. Dalton turned his back, barking orders into a portable.

Yale popped out his earpiece. "Are you injured?" he asked.

David shook his head weakly. "Peter, Bronner, and Jenkins are upstairs. They're all injured, but no one's critical. Jenkins sustained a GSW, but he'll be all right."

"The building's already secured. Medics upstairs. What the fuck are you doing with a weapon?"

"It's Jenkins's."

"Oh," Yale said. "Even better."

The officers who'd been hidden in the building around David cleared the area in groups, their loud, forceful footsteps and jangling equipment belts reminding him of platoons deploying.

The helicopter flew away, spotlight sweeping the street. Police cars were suddenly everywhere, herding people off the sidewalks, setting up sawhorses.

Yale glanced down at David's bloodstained shirt. "How bad?"

David shrugged.

"We need to get you to the hospital."

"So you didn't get him?"

Yale's jaw tightened. "We'll get him. He couldn't have gotten far."

"How long ago did you secure the area?"

"Just as you stepped out onto the fire escape."

"He got out the window at least four minutes before that. Look for blood."

"You said he was hit?"

"I believe so. Jenkins got off a shot. There was blood and Clyde dropped his gun, so I think he might be wounded pretty badly."

"Maybe he went somewhere to curl up and die." Yale slid his pistol into his shoulder holster with a quick, practiced movement. Shaking his head, he crouched and picked up the Beretta that David had flung to the ground.

"Stepping into bad lighting and a tense situation with a loaded weapon. Good thinking."

Yale's portable squawked and emitted an indecipherable burst of staticky voice that Yale seemed to understand. "We've got some drunk frat boys messing with the perimeter at Weyburn and Broxton," he said, starting to jog off. "I assume you can find your way to the ER?"

David nodded. Dalton trudged after Yale, face downturned into his own portable. He patted David on the hip as he passed, ballplayer style.

The building was suddenly deserted again. In the space where the dangling piece of Sheetrock had been loomed the sturdy outline of the hospital against the night sky.

David began the tedious walk across Le Conte toward the ER, pain coursing through his gut with every step. Some people had gathered behind the sawhorses at the sidewalk. A news photographer leaned forward into David's face and shot what must have been an entire roll of film. An officer stopped David with a gloved hand on his chest. "Sorry, buddy, no one gets through."

"I'm going to the ER," David said, turning to show his wound. The officer, evidently impressed, let him pass.

Trying to keep pressure on his wound, David walked up the slope, through the clusters of trees near the PCHS structure where Clyde had been arrested, down the curving sidewalk where he'd assaulted Nancy, into the ambulance bay where he'd attacked Sandra.

Manning the security desk in the lobby, Ralph watched David speechlessly as he limped in and shoved through the swinging doors into Hallway One. David spotted the UCPD cops before he saw Diane. They looked on edge; clearly, they'd been alerted that Clyde was in the area.

David nodded at them and peered into the crowded

CWA. His walk over had opened the wound further, drenching his shirt. Diane handed off an armful of folders, barked a few orders into the phone, and wrote an order against her knee.

The taller of the two officers directed an exasperated expression David's way. "She's like the Energizer bunny on coke. We're having a tough time keeping up." He gestured at David's bloody shirt, then inside the CWA. "You'd better get that looked at."

Diane wiped a patient from the board with an eraser and tapped the slot below. "I'll take Van Canton in Four and I need the—" She froze when she saw David in the doorway.

The room fell silent. The nurses and doctors watched them both.

Diane wore an expression of blind panic.

"I'm all right," David said. "It's not a gunshot wound. Just broken stitches."

She dropped her chart on the ground and crossed the room in four furious strides, embracing him hard around his neck. He held her clumsily with one hand, the other pressed down over his wound. When she came away, her scrub top was stained with his blood.

She flicked her bangs out of her face, the color slowly returning to her cheeks. "Let's get you to a room," she said.

The CWA remained silent behind them as she helped David down the hall. The officers followed Diane a few paces behind like obedient puppies. She brought David into Exam Fourteen, Clyde's old room, and sat him on the table.

"He attacked Peter," David said. "I managed to get there before he killed him. We fought, but he escaped. He's somewhere in Westwood—the cops are sweeping the area now."

Diane hugged David's head, burying his face in her chest. "Enough, okay?" she said. "Okay?" She drew back and crouched, raising his shirt. She tested the edge of the wound with a finger. "You need to be restitched."

David reached down and touched her face. Her wounds were closing over nicely, drying out and resolving themselves into faint scars. He felt himself brimming with emotion and knew it showed in his expression. Diane stood and her face softened, laying the foundation for a smile that had not yet come. Her eyes, cool and emerald, were vulnerable and deadly serious.

"I don't love you," David said, a smile touching his lips.

It took Diane a moment to find her voice and respond. "I don't love you either."

Guiding her face with his hands, he kissed her tenderly on the mouth. She leaned into him, and he inhaled the fragrance of her hair.

A loud knock on the door, then it swung open. Jill leaned into the room. "We have a thirtyish Caucasian male, GSW to the right shoulder, just hit the ambulance bay."

From David's embrace, Diane regarded Jill, who raised her eyebrows expectantly.

"Jenkins," David said. "Go."

Diane turned and headed for the door, grabbing a pair of gloves from a nearby cart. "Don't go anywhere," she said over her shoulder.

David sat on the examination table fighting the pain, which was proving to be an exhausting job. He removed the wire from his chest, wincing as he pulled off the tape, and dropped it on the floor.

A gurney swept past the open door on its way to the trauma room, a cluster of shouting nurses and doctors surrounding it. Diane was hunched over the front of the gurney, backpedaling, adjusting the placement of the bell of her stethoscope and shouting orders. Through the flurry of bodies, David saw Jenkins's face, drawn and unamused, but fully conscious.

David wondered about himself. His career at UCLA was likely over. He would receive plenty of opportunities to work elsewhere, he was sure of that. The chief of staff at Cedars-Sinai had been pressuring him for years to come run their department. Switching hospitals seemed appealing, but David thought he'd take a few months off first, for the first time in his adult life.

Bronner came in next, walking unevenly but under his own power, pressing a bloody bandage to his hand. A uniformed cop escorted him. They walked past the open door of David's exam room without noticing him. Peter's gurney followed shortly afterward, surrounded by ER staff. Peter was stirring, but still seemed groggy. David couldn't get a good look at his face, but he saw the braces against his bare legs. Peter straightened his leg, and a patch of cloth fell from the metal joint at his ankle to the floor. Hospital blue. A torn piece of Clyde's scrub bottoms.

One of the doctors pulled up, letting Peter's gurney continue up the hall, and turned to face David through the doorway. He wore a white coat, outdated eyeglasses, and a Zantac pocket protector. His peppery black hair, collected in tufts, was matted down around his skull. The mousy, red-rimmed eyes were magnified through his thick lenses, and David was stunned to realize that he was looking at Ed's latest persona.

Ed's tongue shot out from his mouth, small and pointy, and moistened his lips. He blinked a few times in rapid succession, a perfect imitation of a facial tick, then flipped something up like a coin and caught it. The digital transmitter from Peter's brace. Ed raised two fingers and tapped them to his forehead in a salute. Before David could react, he turned and vanished.

David leaned back on the exam table and focused on breathing evenly. He found the jarring sounds of the ER oddly soothing—gurney wheels on tile, scalpels clinking on trays, monitors beeping as they traced hills and valleys.

An orderly left a covered body on a gurney across the hall from David's room, and shouted into the CWA, "Someone call morgue for a pickup!" before disappearing back down the hall.

David stared at the dark, lumpy body bag. The cadaver inside was obese and tall, like Clyde. The pain in David's side flared when his feet hit the floor. He shuffled to the gurney and leaned over it, taking a deep breath before unzipping the bag.

The face of an elderly black man peered out at him. David let his breath out in a rush. Though the cadaver was fresh, a bitter, medicinal smell wafted from the fabric of the body bag. Just like the odor he'd noticed emanating from Clyde in Peter's office. He bent over slowly, though it pained him, and picked up the swatch of fabric from Clyde's scrubs. He pressed it to his nose, and inhaled.

The stench of formalin.

At once, David knew with the same gut assurance that came when he pulled a cluster of symptoms together and produced a diagnosis. He trudged slowly down the hall, past the frenzied trauma room, back into the heart of the hospital.

"Hey, Dr. Spier," a lab tech called out. "Get back to the room. Someone'll stitch you up in a sec."

David kept walking, drawing looks from patients and other physicians. Blood dribbled from his wound, leaving a vivid red drop every five or so feet—his spool of thread through the labyrinth. He headed down the quieter halls of the hospital.

Punching a four-digit code into the Omnilock, he stepped through the door into the back corridor. He walked slowly to the freight elevators used for hauling dead bodies up to the crypt. The elevator whirred and creaked on its way up, the bright light overhead assaulting his senses.

It halted with a definitive thud on the seventh floor, and the doors spread. David stepped out into the unlit corridor and walked to the anatomy lab. Another door, another four-digit code. The dissecting-table doors that closed up over the cadavers were all laid open, the units resembling hatched pods. The tables were bare and scrubbed clean. David noticed a ball of wadded cheesecloth at the head of one of the tables. Clyde had used it as a pillow these last days; he'd slept on the dissecting table like a vampire in a coffin. Beside the table was a mound of food that looked to be scavenged from trash cans—sandwich rinds, skins of oranges, bent yogurt cups. Next to that, a scattering of scalpels, scissors, and beakers. And, of course, a container of liquid DrainEze.

The light in the prep room was also off. David stepped through, approaching the mighty wooden door of the crypt. The door clicked loudly when he tugged the handle, then he was standing in the flood of light from the interior, the strong odor of formalin gusting around him. Row upon row of bodies hung from their heads, swaying ever so slightly on creaking chains and forcipiform clamps. Propped against the far wall, at the terminating point of a messy band of blood, was Clyde. A handcuff encircled one hand; the other was pressed to the gunshot wound in his side. He'd been crying.

He reached for David shakily, the loose cuff swaying beneath his wrist. No sensation of fear flickered through

David; he felt only a steady, hardened calm. He propped the crypt door open.

Clyde's voice was jerky from his irregular breathing. "They don't . . . they don't look at me here." He gestured to the hanging bodies. "And they don't leave. They can't up and leave me." His face trembled, his lips down-bending and spreading in a guttural cry. "It hurts . . . it hurts a lot."

"I know," David said.

"I just wanted to be better. That's all I ever wanted." Clyde banged his head against the wall, sending a dull vibration through the room. "I took the pills, so many pills, but they didn't work. Nothing worked."

Still swathed in a blanket of veritable calm, David moved toward him.

"Don't take me to them," Clyde moaned. "Please don't let them have me."

David crouched over him, ignoring the hand Clyde curled in his shirt. Jenkins's bullet had left a neat hole in Clyde's right upper quadrant abdomen. The entry wound was just beneath the ribs, angled upward. The bullet had probably nicked the liver. Clyde gasped, sending a spurt of blood through the wound and across his spread fingers.

"God, don't let them poke and pry at me. I'm scared of them. S-so scared." His legs kicked dumbly against the blood-slick floor. "It hurts oh Jesus it hurts."

The top of Clyde's fist pressed hard into David's cheek. David shoved Clyde's hand away roughly, and Clyde whimpered. Panting and grunting, Clyde tried to slide himself up the wall to a standing position, but collapsed. David watched him with an angry calm. He thought of Nancy's distorted face, and Diane's cringing as he kissed her, and felt his anger intensify until it burned hard and gemlike.

Clyde slid away from the wall, using a hand to move

his legs. He eased himself onto his back, trembling, the stray handcuff chattering against the cold floor. He reached gently for David, but, again, David pushed his hand away.

Clyde's voice was a hoarse, terrified whisper. "It's so awful out there. The cops and people who want to pry at me." He looked at David with a startling clarity. "I don't want to leave this room," he said. "Not ever."

Crouching, David slid his stethoscope from his shoulders and into position. He checked Clyde's heart rate. Tachycardic. His ER instincts flared. Call for a gurney, rush the patient down to the ER, get lines into him. "I need to get you downstairs," he said. "You need help."

Clyde's entire face quivered. "No, no, no. Don't make me. I don't want to anymore. I don't want any of it anymore. Give me a pill to make me end in here."

"I can't do that," David said.

". . . please?"

"No. I will not."

Clyde watched him for a moment, his eyes beady and glinting in his wide head. "W-why?"

"I'm your doctor."

"Then let me . . ." Clyde's breath hitched in his throat, a hiccup of a sob. "Let me stay here." He broke down, weeping pitifully. "Please don't take me to them. Any of them."

David felt emotion welling in his throat, his eyes, his face. His voice was shaking. "If I don't get you downstairs right now, you will die," he said, with a slow vehemence. "Do you understand that?"

"Yes," Clyde said. "Yes."

David's fist tightened on the branch of his stethoscope. He should be irrigating Clyde's wound, paging surgery, pushing morphine. He felt something break inside him.

"I'm sorry," Clyde said. "For everything I've done. I wish I could take it back."

David watched Clyde through his thawing numbness.

Clyde's breath hitched in his chest several times. When he spoke again, his voice took on an eerie calm. "It hurts all the time. Into my head. Sounds and noises and such. Like a train. The only calm is around the edges, where there's quiet dark and no one to look at me." His eyes were watering, steady, silent streams of tears carving down his broad cheeks. He reached and clutched David's leg pitifully. David stood and took a step back, his stethoscope falling from his shoulders. Around him, the yellowed bodies hung and swayed.

David thought of the blood Clyde had lost, and the long and painful surgeries he'd have to endure if he hoped to survive. He thought of the slow, agonizing recovery, the grueling courtroom trial, vicious prison-yard tauntings and cell-block beatings, and he realized that the choice Clyde was making was not much of a choice at all.

"Hold me," Clyde cried. "P-please. Don't leave me . . . don't leave me alone." He gasped and bled, his eyes never leaving David's. He tried to touch David's leg again, but could not reach.

David watched Clyde writhing on the floor. After a few moments, Clyde's face blurred before him. David sat down beside him on the cold, hard floor.

He took Clyde's hand. It was warm and sticky with blood.

Clyde's breaths were growing more shallow. They were the only sounds to break the silent hum of the crypt. "You'll stay with me?"

David nodded.

"You won't . . . you won't leave? Until it's over?"

David shook his head.

Clyde squeezed David's hand, his lips trembling. "Okay," he said. "Okay."

He kept his eyes on David, his breaths jerking his chest. An expression of resignation settled across Clyde's features. His body loosened, then his head rolled up and to the side. The wrinkles smoothed from his forehead. David lowered Clyde's limp hand, bringing it to rest on his chest.

He closed Clyde's eyelids with a thumb and forefinger, and stood.

The freight elevator doors opened loudly down the hall. He heard a cavalry of footsteps, and Diane's worried voice calling out, "David, are you here? Where are you?"

He opened his mouth to speak, but was still too close to weeping, so he took a step back from Clyde's body and studied the floor, gathering the scattered threads of his emotions. His stethoscope lay on the tile, curved like a caduceus snake.

Diane cried out for him again, down the hall but growing nearer. Wincing through the pain, David crouched and picked up his stethoscope. He turned to the door, pulling the stethoscope across his shoulders, and began the painful shuffle down the hall to Diane.

"Here," he called out. "I'm here."

If you enjoyed

DO NO HARM

you'll love the following excerpt from

THE KILL CLAUSE

Available at bookstores now from William Morrow

WHEN Bear came to tell him that Ginny's body had been found raped and dismembered in a creek six miles from his house, that her remains had required three biohazard bags to depart the scene, that they were currently sprawled on a pathologist's slab awaiting further probing, Tim's first reaction was not what he would have expected of himself. He went ice cold. There was no grief—grief, he'd learn, takes perspective, recollection, time to unfurl. There was just the news slapping him, dense and jarring like face pain. And, inexplicably, there was embarrassment, though for whom or what, he was not sure. The heel of his hand lowered, searching out the butt of his Smith & Wesson, which of course he wasn't wearing at home at 6:37 in the evening.

To his right Dray fell to her knees, one hand clutching the door frame, fingers curling between the jamb and hinges as if seeking pain. Beneath the razor edge of blond hair, sweat sparkled on the band of her neck.

For an instant everything was frozen. Rain-heavy February air. The draft guttering the seven candles on the pink-and-white frosted birthday cake that Judy Hartley held poised for revelation in the living room. Bear's boots, distressingly carrying the crime-scene mud, blotting the aggregate porch, the pebbles of which Tim had meticulously smoothed on his hands and knees last fall with a square trowel.

Bear said, "Maybe you want to sit down." His eyes held the same guilt and attempted empathy Tim himself had used in countless situations, and Tim hated him unjustly for it. The anger dissolved quickly, leaving behind a dizzying emptiness.

The small gathering in the living room, mirroring the dread emanating from the hushed doorway conversation, gave off a breath-held tension. One of the little girls resumed recounting Harry Potter Quidditch rules and was hushed violently. A mother leaned over and blew out the candles Dray had lit in eager anticipation after the knock on the front door.

"I thought you were her," Dray said. "I just finished frosting her . . ." Her voice wavered hard.

Hearing her, Tim registered an aching remorse that he'd pressed Bear so hard for details right here at the door. His only way to grasp the information had been to try to contain it in questions and facts, to muscle it into pieces small enough for him to digest. Now that he'd taken it in, he had too much of it. But he'd knocked on enough doors himself—as had Dray—to know that it would have been only a matter of time until they'd known it all anyway. Better to wade in fast and steady and brace against the cold, because the chill wasn't going to leave their bones anytime soon, or maybe ever.

"Andrea," he said. His trembling hand felt the air, searching for her shoulder and not finding it. He couldn't move, couldn't so much as turn his head.

Dray bent her head and started to weep. The sound was one Tim had never heard. Inside, one of Ginny's schoolmates matched her crying—confused, instinctive mimicry.

Bear crouched, both knees cracking, his form broad but huddled on the porch, his nylon raid jacket sweeping low like a cape. The yellow lettering, pale and faded, announced U.S. DEPUTY MARSHAL in case someone cared. "Darlin', hold on there," he said. "Hold on."

His immense hands encircled her biceps—no small feat—and drew her in so her face pressed against his chest. Her hands clawed the air, as if afraid to set down on something for fear of what they might do.

He raised his head sheepishly. "We're gonna need you to . . ."

Tim reached down, stroked his wife's head. "I'll go."

The three-foot tires of Bear's chipped-silver Dodge Ram hiccupped over seams on the roadway, shifting the broken-glass dread in Tim's gut.

Composed of twelve square miles of houses and tree-lined streets about fifty miles northwest of downtown L.A., Moorpark was renowned for little more than the fact that it housed the state's largest concentration of law-enforcement residents. It was a low-rent country club for the straight arrows, a post shift refuge from the streets of the off-kilter city they probed and fought for most of their waking hours. Moorpark radiated an artificial fifties-TV-show feel—no tattoo parlors, no homeless people, no drive-bys. A Secret Service agent, two FBI families, and a postal inspector lived on Tim and Dray's cul-de-sac. Burglary, in Moorpark, was a zero-growth industry.

Bear stared dead ahead at the yellow reflectors lining the center of the road, each one materializing, then floating downward in the darkness. He'd forgone his usual slouch, driving attentively, seeming grateful for something to do.

Tim sifted through the mound of remaining questions and tried to find one to serve as a starting point. "Why did you . . . why were you there? Not exactly a federal case."

"Sheriff's department took prints from her hand. . . ."

From her hand. A separate entity. Not *from her.* Through his sickening horror, Tim wondered which of the three bags had carried away her hand, her arm, her torso. One of Bear's knuckles was smudged with dried mud.

". . . the face was tough, I guess. Jesus, Rack, I'm sorry." Bear heaved a sigh that bounced off the dash and came back at Tim in the passenger seat. "Anyways, Bill Fowler was in the handling unit. He firmed the ID—" He stopped, catching himself, then reworded. "He recognized Ginny. Put in a call to me, since he knows how I am with you and Dray."

"Why didn't *he* do the advise next of kin? He was Dray's first partner out of the academy. He just ate barbecue at our house last month." Tim's voice rose, grew accusatory. In its heightened pitch he recognized his desperate need to lay blame.

"Some people aren't cut out for telling parents that—" Bear laid off the rest of the sentence, evidently finding it as displeasing as Tim did.

The truck exited and hammered over bumps in the off-ramp, making them bounce in their seats.

Tim exhaled hard, trying to rid himself of the blackness that had filled his body, cruelly and methodically, somewhere between the porch and now. "I'm glad it was you that came." His voice sounded far away. It betrayed little of the chaos he was fighting to control, to categorize. "Leads?"

"Distinctive tire imprints heading out of the creek's slope. It was pretty muddy. The deputies are on it. I didn't really . . . that's not really where my head was at." Bear's stubble glimmered with dried sweat. His kind, too-wide features looked hopelessly weary.

Tim flashed on him setting Ginny up on his shoulders at Disneyland last June, hoisting her fifty-three pounds like a bag of feathers. Bear was orphaned young, never married. The Rackleys were, for all intents and purposes, his surrogate family.

Tim had investigated warrants with Bear for three years on the Escape Team out of the district office downtown, ever since Tim's eleven-year stint in the Army Rangers. They also served together on the Arrest Response Team, the Marshals' SWAT-like tactical strike force that kicked doors and hooked and hauled as many of the twenty-five hundred federal fugitives hidden in the sprawling L.A. metropolis as they could get cuffs on.

Though still fifteen years from the mandatory retirement age of fifty-seven, Bear had recently begun referring to the date grudgingly, as if it were imminent. To ensure he'd have some conflict in his life after retirement, Bear had completed night law school at the South West Los Angeles Legal Training Academy and, after failing the bar twice, had finally wrung a pass out of it last July. He'd had Chance Andrews—a judge he used to work court duty for regularly—swear him in at Federal downtown, and he, Dray, and Tim had celebrated in the lobby afterward, drinking Cook's out of Dixie cups. Bear's license sat in the bottom drawer of his office file cabinet, gathering dust, preventive medicine for future tedium. He had nine years on Tim, currently apparent in the lines etching his face. Tim, who'd gone enlisted at the age of nineteen, had had the benefit of opposing stress with youthfulness when learning to operate; he'd emerged from the Rangers seasoned but not weathered.

"Tire tracks," Tim said. "If the guy's that disorganized, something'll break."

"Yeah," Bear said. "Yeah, it will."

He slowed and pulled into a parking lot, easing past the squat sign reading VENTURA COUNTY MORGUE. He parked in a handicap spot up front, threw his marshal's placard on the dash. They sat in silence. Tim pressed his hands together, flat-palmed, and crushed them between his knees.

Bear reached across to the glove box and tugged out a pint of Wild Turkey. He took two gulps, sending air gurgling up through the bottle, then offered it to Tim. Tim took a half mouthful, feeling it wash smoky and burning down his throat before losing itself in the morass of his stomach. He screwed on the lid, then untwisted it and took another pull. He set it down on the dash, kicked open his door a little harder than necessary, and faced Bear across the uninterrupted stretch of the vinyl front seat.

Now—just now—grief was beginning to set in. Bear's eyelids were puffy and red-rimmed, and it occurred to Tim that he may have pulled over on his way to their house, sat in his rig, and cried a bit.

For a moment Tim thought he might come apart altogether, start screaming and never stop. He thought of the task before him—what awaited him behind the double glass doors—and wrestled a piece of strength from a place he didn't know he had inside him. His stomach roiled audibly, and he fought his lips still.

"You ready?" Bear asked.

"No."

Tim got out and Bear followed.

The fluorescent lighting was otherworldly harsh, shining off the polished floor tile and the stainless-steel cadaver drawers set into the walls. A broken lump lay inert beneath a hospital-blue sheet on the center embalming table, awaiting them.

The coroner, a short man with a horseshoe of hair and a stereotype-reinforcing pair of round spectacles, fussed nervously with the mask that dangled around his neck. Tim swayed on his feet, his eyes on the blue sheet. The draped form was distressingly small and unnaturally proportioned. The smell reached him quickly, something rank and earthy beneath the sharp tang of metal and disinfectant. The whiskey leapt and jumped in his stomach, as if trying to get out.

The coroner rubbed his hands like a solicitous and slightly apprehensive waiter. "Timothy Rackley, father of Virginia Rackley?"

"That's right."

"If you'd like, ah, you could go into the adjoining room and I could roll the table over before the window so you could, ah, ID her."

"I'd like to be alone with the body."

"Well, there's still, ah, forensic considerations, so I can't really—"

Tim flipped open his wallet and let his five-point marshal's star dangle. The coroner nodded weightily and left the room. Mourning, like most things, gets more deference with a little authority behind it.

Tim turned to Bear. "Okay, pal."

Bear studied Tim a few moments, eyes darting back and forth across his face. He must have trusted something he saw, because he backed up and exited, easing the door closed discreetly so the latch bolt made only the slightest click.

Tim studied the form on the embalming table before drawing near. He wasn't sure which end of the sheet to peel back; he was accustomed to body bags. He didn't want to turn aside the wrong edge and see more than he absolutely had to. In his line of work he'd learned that some memories were impossible to purge.

He ventured that the coroner would have left Ginny with her head facing the door, and he pressed gently on the edge of the lump, discerning the bump of her nose, the sockets of her eyes. He wasn't sure if they'd cleaned up her face, nor was he sure he would prefer that, or whether he'd rather see it as it was left so he could feel closer to the horror she'd lived in her final moments.

He flipped back the sheet. His breath left him in a gut-punch gasp, but he didn't bend over, didn't flinch, didn't turn away. Anguish raged inside him, sharp-edged and bent on destruction; he watched her bloodless, broken face until it died down.

With a trembling hand he removed a pen from his pocket and used it to pull a wisp of Ginny's hair—the same straight blond as Dray's—from the corner of her mouth. This one thing he wanted to set straight, despite all the damage and violation stamped on her face. Even if he'd wanted to, he wouldn't have touched her. She was evidence now.

He found a single ray of thankfulness, that Dray wouldn't have to carry the memory of this sight with her.

He pulled the sheet tenderly back over Ginny's face and walked out. Bear sprang up from the row of cheap, puke-green waiting chairs, and the coroner scurried over, sipping from a paper cone filled with water from the cooler.

Tim started to speak but had to stop. When he found his voice, he said, "That's her."